GOTREK & FELIX
ROAD OF SKULLS

A WARHAMMER NOVEL

JOSH REYNOLDS

GOTREK & FELIX

ROAD OF SKULLS

BLACK LIBRARY

For Mike. The best Remembrancer a guy could ask for.

A BLACK LIBRARY PUBLICATION

First published in Great Britain in 2013 by
Black Library,
Games Workshop Ltd.,
Willow Road, Nottingham,
NG7 2WS, UK

10 9 8 7 6 5 4 3 2 1

Cover illustration by Winona Nelson.
Map by Nuala Kinrade.

A CIP record for this book is available from the British Library.

UK ISBN13: 978 1 84970 291 1
US ISBN13: 978 1 84970 292 8

See Black Library on the internet at
www.blacklibrary.com

Find out more about Games Workshop
and the world of Warhammer at
www.games-workshop.com

Printed and bound by CPI Group (UK) Ltd, Croydon, CR0 4YY

This is a dark age, a bloody age, an age of daemons and of sorcery. It is an age of battle and death, and of the world's ending. Amidst all of the fire, flame and fury it is a time, too, of mighty heroes, of bold deeds and great courage.

At the heart of the Old World sprawls the Empire, the largest and most powerful of the human realms. Known for its engineers, sorcerers, traders and soldiers, it is a land of great mountains, mighty rivers, dark forests and vast cities. And from his throne in Altdorf reigns the Emperor Karl Franz, sacred descendant of the founder of these lands, Sigmar, and wielder of his magical warhammer.

But these are far from civilised times. Across the length and breadth of the Old World, from the knightly palaces of Bretonnia to ice-bound Kislev in the far north, come rumblings of war. In the towering Worlds Edge Mountains, the orc tribes are gathering for another assault. Bandits and renegades harry the wild southern lands of the Border Princes. There are rumours of rat-things, the skaven, emerging from the sewers and swamps across the land. And from the northern wildernesses there is the ever-present threat of Chaos, of daemons and beastmen corrupted by the foul powers of the Dark Gods. As the time of battle draws ever near, the Empire needs heroes like never before.

Norsca
Sea of Chaos...
L'Anguille.
Couronne.
The Wasteland.
Marienburg.
Arden forest.
Gisoreux.
Bordeleaux.
Bretonnia
Brionne.
Quenelles.
Loren forest

PROLOGUE

Worlds Edge Mountains,
The Peak Pass

The sun was an ugly knot in the sky, its harsh light catching at armour and movement in the distance as the enemy approached the throng of Karak Kadrin's position through the winding, crooked crags of the Peak Pass. Borri Ranulfsson, thane and commander of the throng, blinked and squinted, a thin wisp of smoke rising from the bowl of his pipe. 'There are more of them than we thought,' he said gruffly, tugging at one of his beard's plaits. He stood on a heavy, embossed shield that had been braced across two upright stones, worn smooth by time and tide.

'How many d'you think?' a quiet voice asked.

Ranulfsson glanced over at his nephew. The two dwarfs were mirror images of one another, for all that Borri's ginger hair and beard were streaked with white and Kimril's were still dark with youth. Both had the wide, keg-shaped build of their people, and their armour was without the frippery or fancy that adorned the war-panoply of some of the clans of Karak Kadrin. There were better places for wealth to sit than on a shield or an axe's haft or cuirass.

'A thousand, at least,' Borri said, sucking meditatively on his pipe. The contours of the pass made it hard to judge distance properly. It widened and thinned at odd points and the avalanches that were not uncommon in the Worlds Edge Mountains had a tendency to wreak drastic changes on the topography. Too, battle was as common as the avalanches in this region and as in the lowlands, and it had a tendency to re-shape the ground even as it was fought over. More than one throng had been buried in a sudden avalanche or the collapse of a cliff-face, entombed alongside their enemies forever. 'Hard to tell at this distance, but I expect we'll be getting a better look soon enough.' He pretended not to see the jerk of his nephew's throat, or hear his soft intake of nervous breath.

Kimril was nervous, and there was no shame in it. Borri had been nervous as well, the first time he'd been called to the killing fields. His armour had had the weight of a mountain that day, and he'd dropped his axe more than once. Nerves were natural.

Then, he'd only been fighting *grobi*. This… this was a whole other cart of ore.

The cool wind of the heights carried the stink of old blood and men and something else, something infinitely more unpleasant than either of the former, through the Peak Pass and Borri grimaced. Only one thing he knew of smelled that way.

He looked back at the approaching horde, and the feeling of worry gave way to disgust. It wasn't the first time something foul had swept down out of the north. The Chaos filth tried to march through the pass at least once a season, sometimes in fewer numbers, sometimes in greater. Granted, this lot were quicker than usual, and it was a bigger group than he'd been prepared for, thanks mostly to the failure of his scouts to report back.

It had been six days since he'd sent Fimbur and his rangers to inspect the enemy. Borri had a grudging respect for the ranger, though he didn't think spending that much time in the open was entirely healthy for a dwarf, and he hoped they hadn't been caught. There were worse things than being captured by enemies such as these, but none he could bring to mind at the moment.

The horde had swarmed out of the eastern mountains in such numbers that the traders who'd brought word of their coming to Karak Kadrin had said that the dust of their passage had darkened the sky above the Skull Road for miles. They'd thought it exaggeration at first, which was why his throng numbered only five hundred stout clansmen. But now, seeing it, and with the failure of Fimbur to report back, he was starting to think that the traders hadn't been exaggerating at all; they'd been underplaying, if anything.

Borri gave his nephew's shoulder a quick pat. 'We'll be fine, boy. They'll catch one look at this throng waiting on them, and they'll run back north, tails between their legs,' he said quietly. He turned, looking at the throng arrayed behind him. A sense of fierce pride swelled in him, a pride he saw reflected in the eyes of those warriors closest to him.

They were the throng of Karak Kadrin, and they had never failed to hold the Peak Pass when it counted. Borri expelled twin trails of smoke from his nostrils and pulled his pipe from his lips, tapping it on the rim of his shield. He refilled it without looking at it, the habit second-nature to him.

The throng stood arrayed for battle across the point where

this part of the Peak Pass grew narrow and began to rise towards the upper reaches which Karak Kadrin occupied. The high ground was always the best place to be in a slugging match such as this was shaping up to be. Representatives from four clans were present, and their standards, as well as those of the sub-clans, rose above the bristling block formations. The light caught on the golden discs carved in the shape of the faces of the ancestor-gods, and Borri turned away, knowing that Grimnir and Grungni looked down on the throng and were proud.

His reverie was interrupted when another dwarf ambled towards them, his beard tied into two plaits with copper wire and iron hair-clasps, pulled tight over his broad shoulders and tied off to hang down the back of his armour. His armour was heavier than that of either of the others, and he carried a long-hafted hammer slung casually across his shoulders. An ornate full-face helm rested in the crook of his other arm. He whistled softly, not looking at them.

'Feel up to a wager, Ranulfsson?' he said, squinting at the approaching enemy.

'With you, Durgrim, no,' Borri said, lighting a taper on the inside of his shield and holding the tiny flame beneath the bowl of his pipe. Durgrim snorted, his eyes flicking towards Kimril.

'What about you, young Kimril? It's your first taste of battle today… How about a wager to spice things up?' he said.

Kimril glanced at his uncle, who shook his head. Durgrim caught the gesture and rolled his eyes. 'Don't be such a *wanaz*, Borri,' he said.

Borri frowned and glared at the other dwarf, irritated by his lack of respect. 'Where are your ironbreakers, Durgrim? Lounging in the back somewhere, gambling away their weapons?'

Durgrim gave no sign that the jibe bothered him. He extended his hammer. 'We're in the centre of the line, as is our right, Borri,' he said. He smirked. 'Where are *your* warriors?'

'Right where they should be, Durgrim,' a harsh voice interrupted, before Borri could reply. 'As you should be,' the speaker went on, joining them. Bare-chested and scar-faced, the dwarf was a terrifying sight. A thick ridge of greased and crimson-dyed hair flared up from his otherwise shorn skull, and thick steel bands covered his massive forearms. He leaned on the haft of an axe, and a necklace of orc tusks hung from his neck.

'Ogun,' Borri said respectfully. Durgrim looked away.

'Thane Borri,' the Slayer rasped. 'It will be a good day, I think.'

'One can hope,' Durgrim muttered.

The Slayer looked at him, face as hard as stone. The ironbeard pretended not to notice. Durgrim was an effective warrior, but he had any number of bad habits, bred in his time in the deep dark, and he was unhappy being in a subordinate position. But then, Ogun was simply a discomfiting presence.

Even more discomfiting, Ogun had brought a number of his mad brethren with him, though Borri had neither requested nor wanted them. For all that Karak Kadrin was ruled by a Slayer King, Borri had the proper amount of wariness regarding the dishonoured and the doomed. They would not hold the line, nor would they obey his commands. Even Ogun could barely control them, and then only because he had knocked heads in a grand *runk* the night before.

Borri examined the Slayer surreptitiously. Ogun was old for a Slayer, and pragmatic. If he was mad, it was in a quiet sort of way, and he felt a brief flicker of sympathy for the warrior. To be without honour was to be set adrift in a world without sense. He could not imagine what it would be like to lack the solidity of hearth and home and his clan ties. To be so mired in shame that only death could erase the stain. Hopefully, he would never find out.

Kimril's armour clattered as he shifted his shield to a more comfortable position. Borri watched his nephew for a moment, and then noticed Ogun doing the same. The Slayer grunted. 'If we fall here, warning will need to be delivered to King Ungrim,' he said.

Borri met Ogun's eyes. 'We won't fall.' They couldn't afford to. If they gave ground, the horde would have a clear path to Karak Kadrin, though it would take them many days to reach the hold. The Peak Pass was a major trade route and had been since the Golden Age of the dwarf empire. Here and there, hidden now by time and fallen rocks, were the ancient stones of a long-vanished road, which had been ripped and shattered by some forgotten cataclysm. It was claimed that the Peak Pass only existed thanks to Grungni's ingenuity, that the ancient ancestor-god had carved the pass with some long-lost mechanism of masterful artifice.

Ogun grunted and turned away. Borri knew what the Slayer's look had meant and he looked back at Kimril, who nervously shifted his grip on his axe. He had been considering much the same himself, but the lad had to be blooded sooner or later. To deny Kimril the right to stand or fall with his clan was not something that Borri was prepared to do.

From above, a brass-bellied ram's horn gave an eerie moan. The enemy were drawing close. Borri raised his axe, and war-horns sounded from within the body of the throng. The block formations dissolved into heavy overlapping lines. The pass was wide enough to accommodate a half-sized throng such as this one, but their foes would be squeezed tight, with nowhere to go but forwards and upwards, into quarrel and shot. And those that survived would meet the axes of the clan-warriors, Durgrim's ironbreakers and Ogun's motley lot.

Borri puffed on his pipe in contentment. Ogun was right. It was looking to be a good day.

'This will be a good day,' Hrolf growled, hunching low over his horse as it trotted forwards, scaly hide rippling with colour. 'The wind stinks of slaughter.' Hrolf was built large, and as he shifted in his saddle, muscles swelled beneath his scarred flesh. As if to emphasize his point, he took a deep sniff of the air. His lips peeled back, revealing yellowing fangs that jutted from his gums and jockeyed for space with more normal, human teeth.

'You say that every day,' his companion said, his voice echoing oddly from within the black helm he wore. Unlike Hrolf, every inch of the man was shrouded in black iron. The armour was bulky and imposing, but shorn of ornamentation save for the yellowing skulls with strange marks carved into them that had been hung from his pauldrons and cuirass by small, wickedly curved hooks. The armour creaked as he leaned back in his saddle. 'Sometimes I think your nose is clogged with the effluvium of the butcher's block.'

'Efflu-what?' Hrolf growled, his eyes narrowing.

'He's mocking you, Hrolf,' a soft, rasping voice said. 'Aren't you, Canto?'

'That *is* what I'm here for, Ekaterina, as you never fail to remind me,' Canto Unsworn said hollowly, craning his head to look at the woman who rode on the other side of Hrolf. She was a lithe creature, clad in the ragged ruin of a Kislevite boyar's brass-buttoned coat, with the scalps of dead men dangling from her shoulders like hideous epaulettes. Heavy gauntlets hid her hands, one of those resting on the pommel of the sword sheathed on one hip. A sleeve of chainmail covered one arm, stretching to the gauntlet from a light pauldron that had been decorated with a leering face.

She had been beautiful once, Canto mused. She was beautiful still, in the same way that a tiger was beautiful. The icy poise of a well-bred woman of Kislev was still there, despite the hair bound in wormy dreadlocks and slathered with blood and fat, and the slit corners of her mouth that gaped to reveal deep-set fangs when she smiled her terrible, too-wide smile. Her eyes were carmine slits that bored into his own dark ones, challenging him, daring him to draw his own sword.

He looked away.

Ekaterina laughed, and the sound scratched his eardrums like razors. 'You are still so cautious, Unsworn, and so afraid. You should be more like Hrolf.'

Canto glanced over at Hrolf, whose chest swelled as he preened, flashing his ragged teeth at the woman. Canto shook his head. 'I prefer to be what I am, woman. I remain true to myself.'

'A coward, beloved by no gods,' she said.

He ignored her and turned in his saddle. Behind them, the army of Garmr Hrodvitnir, called the Gorewolf by some, spilled through the pass in a cloud of dust and noise. Horns torn from the hairy skulls of beasts wailed and drums made from human skin were beaten, pressing an erratic and discordant rhythm into the very stuff of the air.

Armoured Chaos knights mingled with half-naked Chaos marauders on the shaggy horses of the eastern steppes, and worse things came behind them. A sea of altars and shrines, their brass and iron wheels chewing the rocky ground as monstrous beasts strained against heavy chains, pulling the shrines in their wake. Far behind, men – Norscans and marauders and dark-armoured Chaos warriors – marched, loped or ran in whatever formations made sense to them, and ahead of them all, the Exalted Champions – lords and lady alike – whose combined will worked to hold the natural instincts of their followers in check.

Canto grimaced and looked at the creatures he'd fallen in with. Hrolf was a brute and a lunatic; every dawn shrank the gap between him and the blood-mad beast things that served as his vanguard. The Chaos marauders riding just behind their twitching, muttering leader were nervous of the Chaos hounds that lurched and loped around Hrolf's horse. Even their horses were nervous of them, snorting and bucking every so often, trying to ward off the monstrous canines.

Past Hrolf's warriors were those who followed Ekaterina. Like their mistress, they had been Kislevite, once. There was a rumour, a whisper of a ghost of a story, that those men were all that remained of those who had ridden in pursuit of the remnants of Asavar Kul's once-mighty horde as it retreated north, a captive boyar's daughter in their clutches. Some had been suitors, they said, brothers, cousins, lovers, and now... what?

Ekaterina caught him looking and opened her mouth, the slit edges of her smile gaping to reveal the inwards-curved maw of threshing fangs that hid behind her human lips and teeth. Canto turned away. His own followers, a bevy of horsemen riding powerful, foul-tempered steeds, trotted in his wake, at a respectful distance. Like him, they wore heavy armour, though theirs lacked the protections woven into his during its forging. He noted that several of his men were already showing signs of bending beneath the weight of the gods. Blood-daubed sigils and massive studded collars marked out those whom he might have to cull sooner rather than later.

There were other lieutenants of course, other chosen or Exalted warriors; dozens if not hundreds, whose individual retinues and ranks made up the army, though only eight were of any importance. And of those eight, only four were of importance to him, and of those four, only one was truly important.

He sought out the Gorewolf. He was easy enough to find. Garmr liked to be at the front, where Khorne could see him clearly. Canto fought to restrain a smirk. No one would be able to see it, not with the helm he wore, but lowering your guard, even in private – *especially* in private – was a sure-fire way to wind up with your skull added to one of the shrines. Or worse... Canto shifted uncomfortably in his saddle.

Garmr rode some way ahead of his lieutenants, his night-black horse a handbreadth larger than any other in the army. His armour was the colour of clotted blood and the stink of him was enough to choke even a follower of Grandfather Nurgle on a hot day; or so Canto thought, though only in private. Indeed, Hrolf and Ekaterina seemed to quite like the Gorewolf's stench. Then, he'd once seen Hrolf burrow into the carcass of a daemon-beast and fall asleep; there was little sense in what the worshippers of the Blood God found pleasurable.

Garmr, like his mount, was large, bigger than any man, with arms and legs like bunches of thick rope crammed into baroque armour. He rode almost dejectedly, his great head bowed and his gauntlets limp on the pommel of his saddle. Hundreds of hooks dangled from the edges of the plates that made up his armour, swinging from braids made of hair, flesh and metal. His helm was a snarling brass daemon's head, surmounted by a mane of matted animal hair. A number of chin-scalps – blood-matted beards taken from the mauled bodies of the dwarf scouts they'd run across a few days prior – hung from his saddle.

Canto had never seen Garmr's face. For all he knew, that silently growling visage was the Gorewolf's true face. He touched his own helm, featureless save for the ragged gash of his visor. He had personally herded over a hundred screaming men, women and children into the great black iron wagons that would take them to smouldering citadels in the Dark Lands in payment for his armour. He wondered what Garmr had traded for his. He wondered whether Garmr, like Canto himself, ever wondered if the deal had been worth the making.

Garmr twitched in his saddle. His horse came to a halt, savage hooves digging into the rock as it screamed in impatience and hunger. Garmr straightened, the brass muzzle of his helm rising, as if scenting the air. A long arm rose. The army ground to a halt like an avalanche. Somewhere, someone stumbled against someone else. A horse squealed and swords bit the light of the sun. Canto turned in his saddle, about to order someone to break it up, but the command died on his lips. He shrugged and turned back. It would sort itself out soon enough.

It always did.

'Ahhhhh,' Garmr groaned. And it was a groan. There was pleasure in that sound, and longing, and it carried through the ranks like a plague. His arm fell, and as one his lieutenants rode forwards to join him as the dust of the army's passage enfolded them like a morning fog.

'They have come to meet us,' Garmr said. The dwarf army had occupied the other end of the section of pass the horde was moving through, and awaited them, arrayed in gleaming ranks of sturdy warriors. So disciplined were they that they resembled nothing so much as small, broad statues, paying no heed to weather, time or tide. Even so, there were not many of them.

Hrolf let loose a rippling snarl and his horse stirred uneasily. Canto did as well. When the brute had his blood up, he was dangerous, even to those who nominally shared the same standard.

'How many?' Ekaterina asked, leaning forwards.

Canto stood slightly in his stirrups. 'That's a small throng, even by the standards of the stunted ones. I wonder if we should be insulted...' he said.

'Quiet,' Garmr said. His voice was like the warning growl of a predator. He urged his horse into motion. 'Canto, Ekaterina, Hrolf... follow me. I would see their faces before I peel the meat from their skulls.'

'What?' Hrolf grunted.

'We're parleying,' Canto said.

'We do not parley,' Ekaterina said.

'Well, what would you call riding alone towards the enemy?'

'Fun,' Ekaterina purred.

Canto fell silent. She was right. It wasn't a parley. A parley implied diplomacy. There was no diplomacy, no politesse in Garmr, simply purpose. All of them had purpose, except for him. He jerked his horse's reins, urging the beast forwards, and it snapped its fangs in anger. He joined Garmr ahead of the others. 'This is foolish, Lord Garmr.'

'It is what Khorne wills,' Garmr said. 'We will take the skulls of all who stand in our path. Would you have me add you to the tally, Canto?' Garmr's voice was harsh.

Canto shook his head. 'Of course not,' he said quickly. 'But why not simply smash them?'

Garmr's only reply was to stroke the haft of the great axe that was slung across his saddle and bring his horse to a halt. The weapon was a crude, hateful thing. It was sharp in a way that seemed the apotheosis of the word. It could slice the wind in two, that axe, and Canto had seen it spill what passed for the brains of daemons in the madness of the far north.

He knew the answer to his question, despite Garmr's silence. There were proprieties to be observed, even among the worshippers of the Blood God. Enemies must know each other's faces, for the sacrifice to be a proper one. It lent crude meaning to otherwise meaningless butchery.

Canto shook his head again, and examined the arrayed ranks of the dwarfs. He had faced them once or twice, in other hordes, under other banners. They were fierce, and hard and stubborn in a way that men, even men like him, could not understand. They stood in disciplined ranks, shields held up and weapons low, like stones ready to weather the storm. He calculated less than six hundred, which was no small force, despite his earlier comments to the contrary. Disciplined, holding the high ground, they might be more of an obstacle than Garmr would have liked to admit.

Four squat figures trotted to meet them, their pace unhurried and deliberate. One was red-bearded and clad in dusty, ornate armour; he was followed by a younger, similarly attired dwarf, and a bare-chested, broadly muscled one with an impressive ridge of crimson hair jutting from his skull; the last was more heavily armoured than the first two, and had a hammer slung across his shoulders. The dwarfs were big on formality as well, Canto remembered.

'Turn around,' the red-bearded dwarf grated. 'Go back where you came from. The Peak Pass is property of Ungrim Ironfist and the folk of Karak Kadrin and you will find no passage here, unless it is bought in blood. So swears Borri Ranulfsson.'

Ekaterina chuckled. Garmr raised a hand, silencing her. 'We will grind you into the dust,' he said. He said it as if he were talking of the weather. For Garmr, victory was inevitable and his due.

'Then there's no need to talk, is there now?' the dwarf with the ridge of jutting crimson hair growled. Canto eyed him warily, smelling the rage that boiled off him.

'No,' Garmr said. 'Your souls are already harvested, and your skulls spoken for.'

'Borri–' the fourth dwarf, clad in heavy armour, began. The thane made a sharp gesture.

'Then why bother with a parley?' he said. 'We aren't planning to move.'

'Proprieties,' Garmr grunted. He reached towards his saddle and plucked loose the bloody lot of beards. 'These were yours. This is what awaits you.' He tossed the beards at the thane's feet, and Ranulfsson's face became as still and as cold as ice. Garmr gestured. 'Send me a champion. We must sanctify this ground before battle.'

'What?' Ranulfsson said through gritted teeth.

'Maybe him,' Ekaterina said, leering at the younger dwarf, whose features paled noticeably.

'I'll do it,' the third snarled, stepping past the young warrior. 'I am Ogun Olafsson and I will kill any daemon-lover you send against me, Northman.'

Garmr nodded. 'You have until the fight ends. Retreat or stand, it makes no difference. We will add your skulls to the road regardless.' Without waiting for a reply he turned his horse's head and galloped back towards the waiting horde. Canto and the others followed. As they rejoined their men, Garmr looked at Canto and the others. 'One of you will bring me his skull. Decide amongst yourselves.'

Canto shook his head and stepped back immediately. 'Leave me out of this,' he said.

'Coward,' Ekaterina said, but mildly. 'The honour is mine, Hrolf Dogsson.' She pointed her blade at Hrolf, who gave a bark of laughter.

He looked around, at his men, smirking. They growled and nodded and the Chaos hounds echoed them, displaying maws full of crooked fangs and tearing the ground with malformed talons. 'I think not. No soft southerner is worthy to spill blood for Khorne, least of all a woman.'

'Khorne cares not from whence the blood flows, nor whose hand sheds it,' Ekaterina said. Then, more loudly, 'I am Ekaterina Maria Anastasia Olgchek, Sword-Maiden of Praag. I danced before the balefires of the Beast-Queen and took the heads of the Chattering Legion. I bathed in the Rivers of Red Dust and spat in the eye of the Sleeping God. I have slain a hundred-hundred men and offered up their skulls to the Blood God and I will offer up a hundred-hundred more.' She gestured with her blade, and said, 'Including yours, Dogsson, if you cross me.'

Her followers set up a chant, calling out her name and shaking their weapons. Men among the army, marauders as well as Norscans, took up the chant as well and the rattling hiss of hundreds of weapons clashing against shields filled the air.

Hrolf laughed and spread his long arms. 'Fierce words from a pampered child. I am Hrolf Wyrdulf, Prince of the Vargs. I am the Promised Son of the Witch-Moon and I slew the sea-worm Ship-Crusher after a battle of thirty days and thirty nights. I can lie on the ice and not freeze and I can drink an ocean of blood and not burst. I stalked Hrunting Iron-Axe from pole to pole and placed his smoking heart on Khorne's board. I took the star-skulls of the Women-With-Skull-Faces and flung them into the Sea of Chaos!' His hounds howled and his men roared, shaking their blades at their rivals.

Canto watched them, as they went back and forth. It was a ritual as old as yesterday, or perhaps longer. Every Exalted Champion had a litany attached to their name, mighty deeds and sagas that spoke to their prowess and skill. If there was one thing servants of the Blood God liked almost as much as spilling blood, it was talking about blood they had already spilled. Duelling with stories, however, was only a prelude to the more physical sort. In many ways, the battle had already been settled. Ekaterina's supporters outnumbered Hrolf's and no wonder – no one loved a berserker, even in an army of indiscriminate killers.

Frustrated, pushed beyond the bounds of propriety by Ekaterina's mockery, Hrolf swept his blade out, slicing the air where his tormenter had been. Ekaterina laughed and whirled around him. Hrolf spun, but not quickly enough. Ekaterina's boot caught him in the belly, sending him sprawling. The cheers redoubled in volume and she preened, drinking in the adulation.

Hrolf howled and sprang to his feet. Ekaterina's sword flashed out and the pommel crunched against Hrolf's skull, sending him to his knees. She wouldn't kill him, Canto knew. Garmr still needed bloody berserkers. Too, this wasn't a duel so much as a temper tantrum.

Hrolf collapsed, wheezing, clutching his skull. Ekaterina kicked him in the side for good measure and then extended her sword at the dwarf, Ogun, in a traditional fencing style that had been popular in the Empire decades ago. She wasn't even breathing hard. She looked back at Garmr, who raised his hand as if in benediction, and she smiled, pleased.

The dwarf had watched the fight with studied indifference. At some point during the duel, the other three had walked back towards their lines, leaving the fourth to face Ekaterina, his axe in his hands. It wasn't cowardice, Canto knew, but pragmatism. However long their champion could buy them was time well spent; every moment counted when preparing to receive a charge. The dwarfs would not retreat. They would dig in and stand and the toll they claimed for the horde's inevitable passage would be terrible. 'Well, stunted one?' Ekaterina said, spreading her hands in a gesture of invitation. 'What do you say?'

The dwarf said nothing. Ekaterina laughed and her men chuckled and grinned. Canto climbed into the saddle and walked his horse back a few feet. Hrolf scrambled up and did the same, glaring at Ekaterina as he went. She paid him no heed, her eyes unnaturally wide and her grin nearly splitting her face. She and the dwarf circled each other slowly. From the horde came the thump of drums and the chants of warriors. The dwarfs remained silent.

Then, with a cat-scream, Ekaterina moved. Her blade flickered, and Ogun only brought his axe up just in time. Metal rang on metal, and Canto could tell by the dwarf's grunt that he was surprised by her strength.

His surprise didn't last long. The axe looped out, and Ekaterina flipped backwards, the soles of her boots grazing the blade. She landed and sprang, stabbing. The sword caught the dwarf on one muscular arm, releasing a splash of red. She sprang back and tipped her head, holding the sword aloft. Blood drizzled into her mouth and she licked her lips as the dwarf roared and charged.

They moved back and forth, until the shadows cast by the sun draped the pass in curtains of darkness. Hrolf had already rejoined his howling comrades, bored. Canto couldn't bring himself to leave, so instead he sat on his horse like some black iron statue, watching and waiting and hoping.

After an hour, the moment he'd been hoping to see came. The edge of the dwarf's axe gashed her side and her laughter turned to a snarl of rage. She was spun by the force of the blow, and Ogun pressed his advantage, his weapon spinning in his hands. Canto leaned forwards. The axe rose, the flat catching Ekaterina in the jaw and knocking her sprawling. Ogun bellowed in triumph and the axe swung up in a headsman's blow.

Ekaterina's sword moved so quickly, Canto didn't see it until the blade was exiting the meat of the dwarf's torso. Ogun's eyes bulged, but no sound escaped his lips. Ekaterina rolled to her feet as the axe fell, burying itself in the rock and hard soil. The dwarf leaned forwards, breathing heavily. Blood spilled from his belly, coating his legs and drenching the ground. He hunched over, one wide hand pressed to his belly, looking at nothing.

Ekaterina darted forwards, pinking him. The dwarf tried to hit her, but his movements had become slow and pained. More of his blood joined the first deluge, spattering the rocks as he weaved drunkenly after his tormentor. Finally, she darted behind him and her sword swept through his legs, severing the tendons. The dwarf toppled with a grunt and lay panting in the dust. And still, Ekaterina did not deliver the killing blow. She capered and howled, thrusting her arms up, eliciting roars from the tribesmen and warriors beneath her banner as she danced a gavotte.

Disgusted, Canto drew his sword and urged his horse forwards. Ekaterina's shriek stopped him. 'He's mine, weakling,' she snapped.

'Take his head and stop playing with him,' Canto snapped back.

Ekaterina was in front of him even as the words left his mouth, causing his horse to rear and bugle a challenge. Her blade flashed, slashing through his saddle, pitching him to the ground. He rolled to his feet, clawing for his sword.

'Blood for the Blood God,' Ekaterina hissed, and the words seemed to bounce from peak to peak, carrying to every ear in the pass. 'Blood and souls for my Lord Khorne,' she said, stalking Canto, forcing him to scramble back. She lunged, her carmine eyes burning with slaughter-lust. Canto grabbed her jacket and jerked her aside – even as he instinctively interposed his sword between her back and the dwarf's axe as it bit at her spine.

The tableau held for a moment. Even Hrolf's baying madmen fell quiet. Impossibly, the dwarf had gotten to his feet. Impossibly, he had covered the distance, leaving a red path to mark his trail. Impossibly, at that moment, the dwarf was the most terrifying thing in the pass, his axe creaking against Canto's sword, his muscles bulging and his face set with a grim fatalism that defied even Ekaterina's berserk enthusiasm.

And then she screamed and the horde joined her in that howl as she twisted out of Canto's grip and tackled the dwarf, knocking him flat. Her mouth opened like a flower at the first spring rain, revealing clattering fang-spurs hidden behind her teeth, and she ducked, fastening her too-wide mouth on the dwarf's face, cutting off his last roar. Canto backed away, sword still in his hand, unable to look away as Ekaterina's spine tightened and rippled and her head shot back, gory locks flaring as she tore the meat from the dwarf's skull in one go.

She turned to Canto, shreds of meat dangling from

27

red-stained jaws. Her eyes were wide and staring and he had the sense that she was not looking at him so much as something behind him. And then there was no time to ponder it further.

'He was worthy,' she hissed, her jaw working as she swallowed what she had torn loose from the dwarf. 'Unlike you,' she added, and sprang into the saddle of her horse and screamed again. The horse shot forwards, galloping up the slope towards the dwarf lines.

As one, like some hungry beast that had slipped its chain, Garmr's army surged in her wake, eating distance even as Ekaterina's horse flew over the heads of the front rank of dwarfs and she crashed down among them, her sword flashing in the fading light as she howled out the Blood God's name. Canto, caught between the dwarfs and his side, raced towards the former, cursing with every step.

It was going to be a slaughter.

Canto was not opposed to slaughter; indeed, he had instigated more than one. But since joining Garmr, he'd been glutted on it. Whatever fire it had once stoked in him was now only guttering ashes, and though he could lose himself in the rhythms of battle easily enough, it lacked the comfort it had once provided.

Crossbow bolts struck his armour as he charged up the slope in Ekaterina's wake. He was faster than a man, even in his armour, but even so, the vanguard of the Chaos horde swept him up in its momentum and he crashed into the dwarfs a moment later, using his greater weight and size to bull them aside. He was stronger than any man or dwarf, and a backhand blow from his fist broke necks as surely as his sword cut through them. He lost sight of Ekaterina in the melee as the dwarfs sought to simultaneously pull him down and prepare themselves for the blitzkrieg thundering towards them. Determined not to be caught in the main crush when it came, Canto waded deeper into the dwarf lines, striking out with calculated brutality as, around him, the armoured warriors of Chaos hewed at their enemies with brutal abandon.

The dwarfs held their ground, and hammers and axes sang hollow songs as they struck sparks from his armour. Somewhere, a dirge began, and was taken up by every dwarf with the breath to do so. 'This far,' it seemed to say, 'and no further.'

It was an admirable sentiment.

Canto swept his sword out in a wide arc, bisecting two warriors. An axe crunched into his side and he stumbled, almost knocked from his feet. Blindly, he lashed out. An oath was cut short as warmth spilled down his sword blade. The thunder of hooves was so loud that it shook the slopes, and small avalanches of rock and dust tumbled into the dwarf ranks. Canto, momentarily bereft of enemies, turned.

Hrolf was in the vanguard, of course. His horse was shrieking in reptilian eagerness as he howled wildly and his men howled with him, the dread sound rising above the first clash of weapons, the creak of crossbows firing and the war-horns of the dwarfs. Chaos hounds ran alongside their horses, screaming and snarling.

Canto's blade rose and fell in the red storm that followed, monotonous and unceasing.

It was a slaughter.

And Khorne found it good.

'As any who have met him can attest, my companion, Gotrek Gurnisson, was possessed of an erratic personality on the best of days. While I had grown used to it over the course of our journeys together, his sudden swings of temperament could still surprise me.

In the weeks following our disastrous (at least from Gotrek's perspective) encounter with the creature calling itself Mannfred von Carstein, Gotrek became surlier than ever, as if his near-plunge into the Stir had awakened some long pent-up streak of obnoxious fatalism.

'As anyone who has read the previous volume knows, the Slayer is a seeker of death. And Gotrek's death eluded him with the cunning of a fox fleeing before hounds. If I hadn't been convinced that he was already mad, I would have thought that he was teetering on the precipice of it then. I know better now.

'It wasn't madness that drove Gotrek.

'It was something infinitely more terrible and in its own way, sad.

'So it was that I found myself journeying once more into the dangerous wilds of the Worlds Edge Mountains on the eve of what was to be one of the most peril-fraught experiences in my career as Gotrek's shadow...'

– From *My Travels with Gotrek, Vol. II*
by Herr Felix Jaeger (Altdorf Press, 2505)

1

The Worlds Edge Mountains,
near Karak Kadrin

'Move, manling,' Gotrek Gurnisson rumbled, grabbing a handful of Felix Jaeger's red Sudenland travel cloak and yanking his companion backwards as the sword in the frothing Chaos marauder's hands whipped out, scorpion-quick. The blade missed the tip of Felix's nose only by the smallest of margins as he tumbled backwards onto the hard surface of the path.

The Slayer stepped past Felix, his axe chopping into the marauder's contorted features with a wet crunch. Gotrek pulled the weapon free of the ruin it had made of the dead man's skull without apparent effort and looked darkly at the Chaos marauders who had ambushed them. 'Well, who's next?' he said. *He sounds almost cheerful*, Felix reflected sourly as he scrambled to his feet. He drew his own blade. Karaghul seemed to purr as it slid from his sheath, and it was light in his hand as he gripped it and watched the Slayer toss his challenge into the faces of the men back-lit by the flames rising greedily towards the sky from the ruined structure behind them.

Said structure was a dwarf outpost which clung to the side of the mountain crag like a limpet. It was a blocky thing, and it had been well camouflaged to look like part of the crag it was attached to. Now, however, the outpost belched fire through its entrance and the arrow-slits that lined the craggy, rough walls. The stink of roasting flesh clung to the rocks and Felix had seen the bodies of several dwarfs lying nearby, contorted in death. They had almost killed him then, while he'd been busy staring in stupefied horror.

The path to the outpost was a narrow outcropping that looked out over the River Stir far below as it wound its way into the Worlds Edge Mountains. They'd followed the course of the Stir from the river-town of Wurtbad into the mountains for several days, hunting its origins in the valley near the dwarf-hold of Karak Kadrin. Felix had heard the latter once referred to as 'the spine of the world', and from this height he could see the resemblance. The mountain range extended from horizon to horizon, and spread as far as his eyes could see. The roof of the world, studded with stars, spread overhead, and if one had been prone to vertigo, simply looking up for too long would have been enough to provoke a fit.

Gotrek had insisted on climbing to the outpost when he noticed the light of the fire. 'Dwarfs know better than to light fires by night in these hills, this close to Karak Kadrin or not, unless there's good reason,' he'd growled. How he'd known the outpost was there to begin with, Felix hadn't asked. Slayer or not, Gotrek was still a dwarf with a dwarf's natural taciturnity in regards to the comings and goings of his people.

Why Gotrek should be suspicious was another question he

hadn't asked. There was more than smoke on the night wind, and a rumble way down deep in the ground which Felix had felt before. There were forces on the move in the mountains. He'd expected greenskins... Sigmar knew there were thousands of the beasts infesting these hills.

But instead of orcs, there had been a half-dozen tattooed Northmen clad in ratty furs that exposed bare, scarred chests. Scar-brands and vile-looking tattoos curled across their wind-roughened flesh and they spoke in a coarse tongue. Whether they were Norscans or members of one of the thousands of marauder tribes which infested the Wastes beyond Kislev, he couldn't say. Nor, in truth, did he care. They were here and they wanted to kill him and that was enough.

But while the mountain range held many dangers, including ravening orc tribes and brutish herds of subhuman beastmen, men from the Chaos Wastes were not known for being this far south. The thought sent a queasy shudder through him even as he joined Gotrek, as the Slayer launched himself at their enemies, his axe slicing the air with an audible hiss. *Worry later, Jaeger... Fight now*, he thought, as the Chaos marauders lunged to meet them.

Gotrek moved quickly for a being of his size, and the marauders were taken aback. Two fell in a red rush, and then the rest remembered their weapons. Felix locked swords with a bearded warrior who snapped blackened teeth at him like a dog even as he forced his blade towards Felix's face. Felix was bent nearly backwards by his opponent, but he recovered quickly, driving his heel into the warrior's instep and slashing Karaghul up and across in a classic example of an Altdorf *mittelhau*, by way of Liechtenaur's third law. He had ended a promising academic career with that blow once – two, in fact, if one counted the other student he'd killed in the duel.

The Chaos marauder staggered, vomiting crimson. Felix, the words of his old fencing master beating his instincts into cruel intent, let loose a *schielhau*, parting the warrior's hair permanently. As the man fell, skull cleft, Felix was already moving.

Gotrek's axe had already done most of the work, however. Another marauder was down, looking as if he'd been trampled and gored by a beast. Gotrek pressed the last two hard, uttering the occasional hard bark of grim mirth as a lucky blade touched his flesh or passed close enough to be felt. Felix considered going to his aid, but he'd been the dour Slayer's companion long enough to know that Gotrek wouldn't thank him for such presumption.

Gotrek stamped forwards, never wavering or retreating. Felix thought that he might actually be incapable of even thinking of doing either. One of the Chaos marauders lunged desperately, but Gotrek simply shrugged out of the way, letting the edge of the blade graze his impossibly muscled forearm even as he grabbed the shaggy furs the warrior wore and jerked him forwards into a skull-shattering head-butt. The last warrior, rather than fleeing, flung himself at Gotrek. Gotrek's blow was lazy, and he watched the two halves of the marauder fall with disinterest. He looked at Felix. 'You walked right into that one, manling,' he said. 'If you get your head lopped off, who will record my doom?'

'I hardly walked into it,' Felix protested, cleaning his blade on one of the dead man's furs. He glanced around the burning outpost. It was a small thing, as judged by a man. It wasn't meant to be a home so much as a blind, keeping watch on western passes. There were dozens of similar outposts scattered across dozens of peaks. How they stayed in contact, Felix didn't know. Gotrek had mentioned signal fires once, and mirrors. Felix didn't look too closely at the dead dwarfs. He was too intimate with death as it was.

'They were taken unawares,' Gotrek said, before Felix could broach the question. He dropped to his haunches and yanked a corpse's head up, examining the dead marauder's face with his one eye. The Slayer looked positively simian in that position, all bloated muscle sheathed in weather-hardened flesh, his shorn scalp topped by a towering crest of red-dyed hair. Tattoos and scars clung to his frame. Felix had been present when Gotrek had acquired some of the latter, including the ugly mark that had torn the Slayer's eye from his head. Gotrek hid that one behind a crude leather patch, for which Felix was grateful.

Gotrek thrust a finger beneath the patch, scratching the socket idly. Felix winced and sheathed his sword. 'Why are they even here?' he said. 'I thought they rarely came this far south. And how could they have taken them unawares?'

'Magic, manling,' the Slayer spat as he glared at a dead marauder. There was an area that had been carved to appear as if it were a natural outcropping before the outpost, and Felix strode to the edge of it and looked out over the rim of the world.

The night wind moaned through the crags, and he pulled his cloak tighter about himself as he listened to the crackle of flames. Darkness spread out over the mountains, vast and all-consuming. Felix glanced up at the roof of the sky and saw that the moon was the colour of blood. Flickers caught his attention, drawing his gaze back down. He squinted. 'Gotrek,' he said and pointed.

Gotrek joined him. 'More fires,' he said.

'Those signal fires you mentioned?' Felix said hopefully.

Gotrek didn't reply. His single eye stared off into the

distance. The dwarf's sight was better than Felix's, even with only one eye and in the dark. Then, tersely, he said, 'No.'

In the distance, something boomed. The rock beneath his feet trembled and he hastily stepped back from the edge. 'What–' he began, but a rumble like distant thunder cut him off. A distant light flared; a burp of luminescence that briefly revealed... what?

The crag they stood on looked almost straight down into the valley, and the raging river that curled through it. There had been a forest there once, Felix knew, though the dwarfs had long ago chopped down every tree and uprooted every stump in order to create a killing ground quite unlike any other in the world. The valley was a bowl, and more than one army had funnelled into it, looking to lay siege to what he assumed at first glance must be the infamous Slayer Keep. It looked to Felix's horrified eyes as if that was the case now. He was reminded of ants swarming a dog's carcass. How many men must be down there, hurling themselves against the walls? He swallowed a sudden rush of bile. 'Maybe we should head back west. See if we can–'

Gotrek's axe sank into a jagged fang of rock, shearing the tip off. Felix fell silent, and turned back to the valley below. With the light of the burning outpost behind him it was hard to make out what was going on down in the valley, but the brief bursts of firelight from below and the crimson light of the moon reflecting off the river helped with that. In any event, the citadel would have been hard to miss.

The edifice spoke of brooding power. The fortress had been wrought from the rock of the mountain; the massive outer walls had been built from chunks of lichen-encrusted stone, as had the inner wall, which rose above the wall immediately preceding it to climb the slope of the mountain. To

Felix's untrained eye, it resembled nothing so much as half an onion, with a layer pulled free of the rest, though he did not voice this idle thought to Gotrek. Regardless, the fortress dominated the valley in which it crouched. Felix felt his heart skip a beat as he judged the scale of the walls, calculating their true size. 'Those walls are larger than those of Altdorf,' he said in awe.

Gotrek grunted and spat. 'One of Ungrim's ideas. The true hold is deep in the mountain, as is proper. But Ungrim had a smaller false one constructed, for you humans. They call it Baragor's Watch, after the first Slayer King.' Gotrek's expression twisted into a harsh smile. 'Bait for a trap. Never met a Northman yet who can resist attacking a wall.'

'If it's only bait, why bother to construct them so solidly?' Felix asked.

Gotrek looked at him. Felix raised a hand and said, 'Never mind.'

'Baragor's Watch is nothing, manling. It is a toy, constructed to house merchants and occupy enemies while proper dwarfs go about their business. There – *that* is Karak Kadrin!' Gotrek growled, gesturing with his axe to the structure which rose behind the fortress and easily overshadowed it.

Baragor's Watch had been built on a rising slope, and from its upper levels extended a great stone bridge which was lit by the flames of a hundred braziers mounted on the stone stanchions that lined its length. The bridge spanned a massive chasm and connected the fortress on the slope with an even larger plateau gouged from the very heart of the mountain, where a second structure waited. That one, Felix knew, even if Gotrek hadn't pointed it out, was the true Karak Kadrin. There, on the plateau, a pair of large doors were set into a titanic portcullis which was itself surmounted by the shape of two massive axes, carved into the surface of the mountain.

'Karak Kadrin,' Gotrek said again, his fingers tightening on the haft of his axe. Ancient wood and leather bindings creaked beneath the pressure of that grip. Felix didn't reply. The Slayer had insisted that they travel to Karak Kadrin, though he hadn't said why. Felix had tried to find an outgoing caravan, or even just a group of travellers heading in the same direction, but Gotrek's surly impatience had put paid to that plan before it had even gotten off the ground. Thus, they had wandered into the mountains alone and on foot. Weeks of walking and climbing had worn Gotrek's temper to a nub, easily plucked, and Felix felt little better, though his ailments were physical, rather than mental. Gotrek had shown little sign of wear, setting a punishing pace, as if something were driving him on. Now, staring at the distant fires, Felix wondered whether they were drawing close to that something.

More light splashed across distant stonework, as ancient as the mountains. 'Fire-throwers,' Gotrek muttered. He spat over the side of the outcropping. Felix saw that Baragor's Watch wasn't as sturdy as he'd first thought. The outer wall was already down, or at least no longer in one piece. Breaches had been made and men surged through as another roar of faint sound echoed upwards.

'It sounds almost like cannons,' Felix said. 'But that's impossible, isn't it?' He looked at Gotrek. 'The Chaos worshippers don't use such things, do they?'

Gotrek's face settled into an expression of grim resolution. He didn't answer Felix's question but instead said, 'We need to get in there, manling.'

'And how do you propose that we do that?' Felix said, unable to look away from the battle raging far below. 'I don't fancy our chances trying to wade through *that*.'

Gotrek clutched his axe and for a moment, Felix thought that the Slayer was contemplating doing just that. Then the dwarf shook his head. 'There's more than one way into Karak Kadrin, manling. These mountains are honeycombed with hidden doors and secret gates. If I recollect rightly, there's one close by. We'll find it and then, by Grimnir, we'll find out what's going on down there,' Gotrek snarled, gesturing towards the Chaos forces with his axe.

The Worlds Edge Mountains,
the Valley of Karak Kadrin

Hrolf's skin had taken on a waxy sheen, like something not quite solid. He could feel his hair rasping against the inside of his skin. His horse hissed in unease and he dropped a fist between its leathery ears. The Witch-Moon was high, and his beast stirred uneasily in him.

He and his mount sat a few miles from the keep, in a rough camp that Canto had insisted they set up. Hrolf saw little need for a camp; if men suffered in the weather, then they would take the walls all the quicker. The camp was by the river, 'close to a water source' as Canto said. Why they needed water when blood was readily available, Hrolf didn't know.

Still, it served the plan. He licked his teeth. He looked around him at the men who were moving into the hills, carrying the devices he would use to win victory. He denied himself the joy of battle to oversee them, because of the plan. It was a good plan. Better, it was his plan, not Canto's or Ekaterina's or one of the others'. Something exploded and he jerked in his saddle. The stink of the war-engines of the *dawi zharr* irritated his senses more and more as the siege progressed. The stunted ones had spent millennia perfecting the arts of siegecraft, and their black-iron engines were some of the only things capable of knocking down the fortifications of their southern kin.

They had already done so, in fact. The great outer wall of Karak Kadrin had been cracked open like an eggshell by the cannon that the crooked little daemonsmiths had provided, only to reveal another. Walls, walls, *walls*… Hrolf spat, growing angry as he thought about the walls and those who crouched behind them. Then he grinned. The inner wall wouldn't be a problem for long. A great spurt of fire lit up the night as one of the war-engines – a magma cannon, he thought they called it – vomited out a stream of flame that brushed across the stones.

The fire wasn't hot enough to melt stone, but it drove the defenders back, and his warriors had no fear of climbing into or walking through fire. Hrolf smelled burning pork and saliva washed the inside of his mouth, mingling with the omnipresent tang of blood. His body ached abominably, his bones creaking in their sheaths of muscle like the supports of a dilapidated house caught in a strong wind. Hrolf frowned as crude frameworks of bone and animal gut thumped against the walls, carrying the warriors of Garmr into battle.

They would be driven back soon enough. Hrolf strangled a snarl. They were always driven back and had been for weeks now. Garmr had grown bored after three days and taken the rest of the army back towards the Peak Pass, leaving Hrolf and Canto to take Slayer Keep. There were more enemies than dwarfs to fight in these mountains, and Garmr was intent on killing every last one of them it seemed.

A snarl caught his attention and he shifted his gaze, taking in the war-shrines that stood behind him, overlooking the battle. The beasts that had pulled them had been pressed into service, carrying battering rams and siege equipment into the valley. Now, only their bipedal attendants remained: grunting, slobbering madmen and women, chained to the icons by their thick collars, screeching hoarse praises to Khorne as they tore at each other in a berserk frenzy, driven wild by the scent of a battle they would never be able to participate in. Hrolf grimaced, disturbed by the fanatics. They were being punished, or perhaps rewarded. It was hard to tell sometimes.

Chaos marauders loped past. They wore heavy furs and armour, and their weapons were a motley assortment. Sieges were the one place where Garmr's preference for mounted warfare had to be disregarded. It was rare that those unlucky enough to have a mount got to do more than clean up after the fact. These were chanting the Blood God's name, or the name of their tribe or champion. The words were all one to Hrolf, and he shook his head irritably. He longed to join them. His throat had swollen with an insistent pressure and he gave a grunt as something shifted inside. It was growing harder and harder to control the beast that squatted within him. It was growing larger, and his skin strained to contain it. He touched his flesh, and felt eagerness well up within him. Soon, soon he could shed this worthless skin and rend and slay the way the Witch-Moon wished.

'Hrolf,' Canto said, riding up to join him.

'What?' Hrolf snarled, twisting in his saddle, jaws snapping. He felt his teeth slide in his gums, and blood filled his mouth, calming him. Canto raised a hand in a placatory fashion and Hrolf glared at him. The Unsworn was accompanied by the two other Exalted Champions who had been ordered to attend the siege, Kung of the Long Arm and Yan the Foul. Hrolf was in overall command, but it was a tenuous thing at least where the latter was concerned, and all four Exalted shared such duties as Hrolf did not care to attend to himself.

Canto, as ever, seemed to have no interest in doing anything save hiding and complaining. He was no true warrior – he might as well have been a Slaaneshi for all the good he was in a fight. Canto knew nothing of the joys of battle and blood and slaughter. Hrolf blinked away red-meat images, trying to focus. His armour felt too tight, and he longed to strip it off, but he knew that was impossible.

The armour had long ago set roots into him, merging with his flesh as effectively as the iron collar he wore about his thick neck. The collar too was a part of him. Like the armour, it stretched and spread when his form warped, protecting him even at his most battle-maddened. Khorne's gift to a favoured son, he knew.

He traced the eight-pointed star that graced the much-abused cuirass and felt the warmth of the strange metal. It felt as if it had been just plucked from the forge when he rode into battle, searing his skin and maddening the monster within.

For a moment, he was lost in red memories of those first few days of the siege. He had led his men in taking the first section of wall, striking fast and hard, ignoring the death that rained down on them from above. The dwarfs defended every square of stone as if it were the last, giving ground grudgingly. Hrolf recalled how the boiling tar poured over the crenellations of the parapet and how his men had screamed as the concoction had splashed over them, pulling flesh from bone. He had ignored it then, scrambling up the ladder, blade in hand, head and heart thundering with the rhythm of war. Around his waist he'd worn a kilt of dwarf beards, scalped from the dead in the Peak Pass.

He could still feel that first crunch of blade on bone and taste the first drop of dwarf blood. The wall had fallen quickly, though the dwarfs had not been unprepared. He had had more troops then, and had spent their lives freely, sacrificing dozens to pull down a third that number of dwarfs. The wall had shuddered beneath his feet, pounded by the war-engines of the dawi zharr, and he had laughed as part of it collapsed, nearly sweeping him away.

'Hrolf,' Canto said again, more insistently, his voice a hollow rumble. Hrolf looked at the featureless helm and the dead shark eyes staring at him through the ragged visor.

'What is it, Unsworn?' he rasped.

'They've taken down another section of wall,' Canto said.

'We are ready to press forwards,' Kung rasped, stroking the serpentine length of his horse-gut-cord bound beard. It hung down to his saddle, and the end was capped with a round ball crafted from bone. His hair was loose and whipped around his head like a black halo in the smoke-riddled wind; Kung's status was marked by his unbound hair rather than ornamentation. Only chieftains and war-leaders could leave their hair untied among the diverse tribes of the territories of the eastern reaches of the Chaos Wastes. He wore heavy armour, its blood-stained plates engraved with thousands of gaping, fanged jaws that seemed to snap and bite the air in the light cast by the fires of the war-engines. An axe rested across his saddle; its haft was made from a carved femur and the blade was a beaten crudity which glared at the world with blazing eyes that were set to either side of the jagged edge. Hrolf did not know whether the weapon was alive in the conventional sense; some whispered that it contained the soul of Kung's brother, whom he'd slain to take control of his tribe.

'Your exuberance is matched only by your idiocy, Kung,' the other champion growled. Yan was a Khazag and his armour was covered in the stretched and stitched faces flayed from the skulls of his opponents. Where Kung was big and broad, Yan was lithe and deadly looking, like a needle wrapped in iron. The falchion on his hip had seen use in a thousand battles across a hundred years, and it bore the stamp of the daemon-smiths of Zharr Naggrund. 'There is another wall, Dogsson. And another beyond that like as not... We will grow old and our bones will be dust before we are done with walls.'

'Are you accusing me of building them, Yan?' Hrolf growled. 'Or are you simply yapping to hear the sound of your own voice?'

'I am saying that this is a waste of time,' Yan said. 'We should rejoin Garmr. Let the stunted ones cower in their stone hole.' Yan was a supporter of Ekaterina's, Hrolf recalled, even as Kung was one of his. While every man in Garmr's army was theoretically loyal to the Gorewolf, most were, in reality, loyal only to whatever chieftain or sub-chieftain they had followed before being absorbed into the horde. The Exalted who led the warbands that made up Garmr's horde constantly fought for dominance. Eight warbands, made up of sixty-four smaller bands, and each of those made of still smaller bands with their own pecking orders, for a total of eight thousand men or more. It was only fear of Garmr that kept everything moving in the same direction.

But Garmr wasn't here. Even when he was, it was odds on that a battle would break out between one tribe or group and another. But without him, it was worse. The enemy were unreachable. That meant the warriors of the army now had no one to fight but each other.

'Garmr has commanded that we take this fortress for the glory of Khorne,' Hrolf said.

'Garmr is not here!' Yan said, spitting Hrolf's own thoughts back at him. 'Garmr is off taking skulls and reaping glory for himself, while we sit in the mud and waste ourselves on stone.'

Hrolf felt his hackles rise. This had been a long time coming. Yan had been sniping at Garmr since before they'd crossed the Plain of Zharr, questioning his decisions, taking too many liberties. Yan wanted to be pack leader. But Garmr was pack leader; he would lead the pack to glory whether they wanted it or not, and Hrolf would help him. 'You are impatient, Yan,' Hrolf said. 'We are all impatient, but you take it too far.' Things moved in him, insistent. He forced them down, smashing all of his will down on the wolf, quashing its struggles. He flexed his aching hands, listening to the bones pop and the ligaments quiver. 'Garmr is lord, and we serve him.'

Yan sneered. 'Maybe it is time to have a new lord.'

Hrolf found it hard to think with the smell of blood in his nostrils, but he forced the waking dreams of slaughter out of his head and tried to focus. He needed to remain in control. His time would come, when the plan had been implemented and the damnable walls cracked wide. 'Are you certain that you wish to do this here, Yan?' he said. He spat blood. Some of it speckled Yan's hand. The Khazag's eyes narrowed and he made to draw his falchion. Hrolf urged his horse close and reached out, grabbing Yan's hand, forcing his sword to remain sheathed.

'Release me, dog!' Yan hissed, snapping filed teeth. The others pulled their horses back, watching speculatively. Yan had seized this moment for his own, for good or ill. 'The Blood God demands skulls and I shall give him yours,' Yan continued, his free hand flashing to his hip, where a curved dagger hung. He drew it and slashed out, across Hrolf's face, opening him brow to cheek. Blood-matted hair hung lank from the depths of the wound, and a stink like a dog dead in a ditch for two weeks struck the gathered chieftains.

Hrolf grabbed Yan's throat. Yan's eyes widened as Hrolf

jerked him from his saddle and flung him to the ground. Then, muscles quivering, he prepared to leap on the other champion.

'Hrolf, 'ware!'

His eyes snapped around. Yan's men, his lieutenants, moved forwards with deadly intent. The Khazags took their honour seriously. They wouldn't take the humiliation of their war-chief quietly. Hrolf glanced back and saw Canto moving forwards with his armoured killers in tow. It had been his voice that had shouted the warning. Hrolf snarled. The coward wanted to seize his glory!

He started his horse towards the Khazags, but Canto interposed his own mount. 'No,' he said. Kung followed suit, gesturing lazily with his axe.

'There are enemies aplenty, Yan,' Kung rumbled. 'Do not make new ones before you finish the old.'

'He struck me!' Yan snarled.

'I should have killed you,' Hrolf nearly roared.

'And then your plan would be ruined while we waited for Yan's subordinates to sort themselves out and for a new champion to replace him,' Canto snapped. 'Or, we can follow through with your grand stratagem and end this whole futile affair in one fell swoop.'

Hrolf growled. Canto was right. Canto was always right. Red images blossomed in his head; he longed to kill the man, to prove his superiority over the weakling, but Canto resisted every challenge. Even Ekaterina couldn't draw him into battle, infuriating as she was.

Canto was a coward. Hrolf hated cowards. They refused to walk the Eightfold Path, to set foot on Khorne's stair, and they deserved to die. But Garmr wanted Canto alive. Garmr thought Canto was amusing. Canto was Garmr's pet.

They were all Garmr's pets.

Garmr had beaten him in a duel at the Battle of Ten Thousand Blades, forcing him and his pack into slavery. Khorne only respected strength, and there was glory to be won serving one as strong as Garmr. But even more glory to be won in killing him. Saliva and blood mingled in his mouth and he swallowed, trying to placate the beast. He longed to give in. The dwarfs in the Peak Pass hadn't been enough. He needed more.

He'd sent his Chaos hounds into the peaks to bring him word of any relief force or kill any dwarfs not cowering in their stone hole. The dwarfs had launched a number of counter-attacks in the first week, erupting from hidden gates and holes. The mountains were honeycombed and Hrolf had lost hundreds of men to the trickery of the stunted ones. His army was bleeding soldiers but that didn't matter. There were plenty left.

Besides, he had tricks of his own. His knuckles popped as he gripped his reins. He could taste the flesh of the dwarfs already. He grunted in pleasure. 'Are you coming or will you stay here, safely away from the blood-letting?'

'I'm coming,' Canto said.

'Good.' Hrolf felt his grin threaten to split his face. 'Now, now you will see how wolves hunt.'

2

The Worlds Edge Mountains,
near Karak Kadrin

Gotrek led the way deeper into the crags, eye narrowed. Felix followed, tired and cold. His nose was running and his legs ached. The climb from the outpost had been torturous, and more than once, he'd almost fallen from the narrow ledges and crumbling inclines that the Slayer had crossed with a mountain goat's lack of concern. They'd piled stones over the bodies of the dwarfs before they'd left, and his arms and back were still sore from the effort. And he still had no idea where Gotrek was leading them. Not straight into the melee around the walls of Karak Kadrin, as he'd first feared. Regardless, Gotrek seemed determined to reach *somewhere*.

Then, Gotrek was always determined. But this was different. It had been building for weeks, like a storm on the horizon. A nagging had grown into an obsession, and Felix had watched, afraid. As they had drawn ever closer to Karak Kadrin, Gotrek had spent his nights staring at his axe, as if it were speaking to him. Worse were the times his eye would slide into vagueness and more than once, Felix feared that the Slayer had finally snapped. Maybe he had.

He studied their surroundings as they moved. The Worlds Edge Mountains never changed; or, if they did, it was with such slowness that it was imperceptible to the human eye. Dark, jagged rocks thrust fiercely towards the black, star-studded sky. There was a ragged quilt of green below them. The mountains were threaded with arboreal veins, brief bursts of forest surrounded by broken rocks, full of scraggly trees struggling in the shadows of the mountains. The mountains themselves rose and fell like glacial waves and in places it was easy to forget that there was a world beyond looming walls of lichen encrusted rock. Once or twice, he caught sight of the besieged Baragor's Watch and Karak Kadrin beyond it and he thought perhaps Gotrek was leading him around the circum-ference of the valley, towards the mountain peak which the dwarf hold occupied. The high road was fine with Felix, as long as it meant avoiding the nightmare in the valley below. Better the crags than a Chaos army. But as the days passed, they'd drawn ever closer to the latter.

They were on a path now, a proper one. It had been carved and shaped by dwarf hands, he suspected, given the comfort-ing regularity of it. There were other paths running above and below them, as if this particular peak were ringed about by bands of stone. The dwarfs were meticulous about creating redundancies for the most menial of structures. Men, Felix knew, made do with the barest essentials – rickety bridges and crumbling walls, repaired only when necessary – but dwarfs rarely left such things to the first attempt, or even the second.

Opposite them, across a narrow chasm, more paths rose upwards in a parallel trajectory. The regularity of the chasm was broken at certain points by ancient stone bridges, none wider than two dwarfs and all now mostly split in two, as if whatever great shift had opened the chasm had also cracked the bridges that spanned it in twain. It reminded him of certain cramped back streets in the Luitpolstrasse in Altdorf, where the roots of old bridges reached in vain across the fingers of the Reik that spread throughout the city. Not for the first time, he found himself wondering what the dwarf empire had been like at its height. What secrets did these mountains, once the cradle of that majestic civilization, still hold?

'Where are we going?' Felix said. He kept his voice pitched low. Sound carried surprisingly far in the mountains, as he'd learned to his cost more than once. And with a Chaos force in the immediate area, the slightest shout could draw the veritable wrath of the Dark Gods down on their heads. 'I trust you have a plan of some sort.'

'We're going where we've always been going, manling. Karak Kadrin,' Gotrek said.

'Gotrek, it's back that way,' Felix said, 'and under siege.'

'So?' Gotrek said. He glanced over his shoulder. 'I will go to Karak Kadrin, siege or not.'

'Can we at least wait it out?' Felix said.

'It cannot wait,' Gotrek snarled.

'Why?'

Gotrek spun, the edge of his axe stopping just short of Felix's throat. 'I said, *it cannot wait*,' he rasped. Felix risked a look down. The axe trembled faintly, but Gotrek's hand was steady. Felix swallowed. 'How are we getting in?' he said softly. 'You don't intend to carve a path to the front gates, you said as much.'

Gotrek blinked and shook himself. 'No,' he grunted, turning away. He didn't apologize. Felix hadn't expected him to do so.

Whatever was eating away at Gotrek, the Slayer wasn't likely to share it. Not with a human. Gotrek had his pride.

'I told you, there are other ways in,' Gotrek said.

'And you know of these ways?' Gotrek looked at him. Felix flushed. 'Of course you do. I'm an idiot.'

Gotrek hesitated, and then clapped him on the arm. 'Come on,' he said. 'It's not far.'

'And what is *it* exactly?'

'We'll enter Baragor's Watch through the old Engineers' Entrance,' Gotrek said.

'What's the Engineers' Entrance?'

Gotrek grunted. 'Old King Ironfist doesn't hold with engineers. He ordered them to use a separate entrance, so the guild could move their supplies of black powder and inventions without endangering Baragor's Watch. They recommissioned an ancient trading road, and sank shafts and haulers within the mountain. It's a secret. No one but the engineering guild is supposed to know about it.'

Felix didn't ask the obvious question. He knew little about Gotrek's past, but what he did know included the fact that the Slayer had once been a member of the Engineers' Guild, though for how long and when, he had never said. He wondered if the Slayer had perhaps even had a hand in creating the entrance.

Gotrek abruptly raised a ham-sized hand, waving Felix back. Felix tensed, freezing in place, his fingers brushing against his sword's hilt. The path widened ahead of them, spreading into a dais or plateau of raised stone wide enough for dozens of men. A broken archway, decorated with ornate dwarfish carvings, loomed over them, and beyond it, a number of smaller archways and paths that spread upwards towards a higher, as yet invisible, point.

As they stepped beneath the largest arch, Felix saw that the lichen growing on the ancient stone had been scraped away in places. Gotrek noticed his look and nodded. Felix swallowed. They hadn't been the first to come this way.

The plateau had been sanded flat long ago and the crumbling remains of a curved wall occupied the far edge, rising up as if it and the path as well had once been completely enclosed. On the walls were the remains of weathered carvings that might well have once depicted scenes from the golden age of the Under-Empire. There were more such carvings on the few ragged chunks of the roof that remained. Dwarfs weren't fans of the open air at the best of times, wandering Slayers aside, and Felix wondered what cataclysm had occurred to crack such a structure open. Had that event been the same one that Gotrek had often hinted was responsible for crippling the dwarf civilization?

He opened his mouth to ask Gotrek, and abruptly, he realized that he was alone. While he had been distracted, Gotrek had continued on, unaware of Felix's absence. His heart began to thump in his chest, fear making the rhythm erratic as he hurried on up the closest path, looking around wildly. 'Gotrek,' he hissed. 'Gotrek, where are you?'

Something snuffled. Felix turned. Lupine shadows crossed the surface of the rock wall, prowling parallel to him. He dropped to his haunches, below the line of the broken wall, one hand on his sword and his heart in his throat. Cautiously, he peered through a gap in the wall. The moon rose high and red over the opposite peaks and he saw a hint of hunched, furtive movement.

More shadows, stretching across the rocks, rising and straining away like ink spilling across a page, and more beast-noises, snuffling and growling and panting, echoing weirdly among the rocks. They were going somewhere, but where? Had they caught his scent? Something made a hoarse noise and he rolled into the lee of a fallen stone. Shadows crept across it, cast by the beasts that he felt must surely be stalking him, back along the path he had just ascended. Felix crouched in the shadows, breath straining against his clenched teeth.

The sound of malformed paws striking the ground echoed in his ears, warring with the pounding of his own heart. Eyes like embers peered in his direction from across the chasm, and he heard the sizzle of poisonous saliva dropping from a nearby muzzle to the ground. He eased his sword loose, knowing that if the unseen beast lunged, he'd likely have only seconds.

A howl blistered his eardrums, impossibly close. The eyes vanished and he heard a heavy, awkward shape lope away. Felix let loose a shaky breath.

Something clamped down on his shoulder.

His mouth flew open, and something that smelled of grease and forge smoke clamped tight over it before the cry could escape his lips. 'Quiet,' Gotrek said. 'You'd think even a witless manling would manage better than to get lost in a place like this.'

'W-wolves,' Felix stuttered when Gotrek released him. The Slayer gestured behind him. Felix saw a heavy black shape lying nearby, body cooling on the rocks. Bulging beast-eyes stared at him sightlessly. Gotrek had burst its skull. Felix shivered, realizing that the beast had been creeping up on him. Would he have felt its breath before it closed its jaws about the back of his skull? Nausea rippled through him.

'Not wolves, manling,' Gotrek said. 'They've been stalking us since the outpost.'

'What is it?' Felix said, swallowing the bile that burned at the back of his throat.

'A hound of Chaos,' Gotrek said, and spat. Felix grimaced. Dogs and men were never far from one another, even in the Chaos Wastes. But Chaos hounds were no nobleman's hunting hounds or pampered lady's pets; they were malformed and malevolent beasts, as twisted in body and mind as their human masters. The thought that there were more of them, and close by, caused his stomach to knot in fear. Even worse, such beasts never strayed very far from their masters.

Rocks rattled and fell around them. Felix, against his better judgement, looked up. He saw several shapes scrambling down the rough slope from the path above. Eyes like pinpricks of hellfire gazed down at him and something in him shrivelled. He pushed himself away from Gotrek as the closest of the creatures sprang straight up.

Gotrek whipped around as a wave of beast-stink washed over them. It was a slaughterhouse smell, animalistic. The Slayer's hand snapped out, catching the lead hound's snout and flinging it aside with barely a shiver of effort as it lunged at him. Gristle and wet shreds of tattered meat clung to the beast's stiff red fur. And it scrambled to its feet, panting harshly, ribcage swelling like a bellows. Its talons trailed lazy scratches in the rock and its eyes were empty of even animal intelligence. There was nothing in its hell-spark eyes save the most terrible of hungers. Its muzzle peeled back from dagger-like teeth and it gave out a deep bay. The sound rolled across the peak, and was joined by a cacophony of howls as its pack-mates scrambled towards the duo.

Felix's hand dipped for Karaghul's hilt. More canine shapes loped towards them from the way they'd come, slinking through the archways and over the broken walls. 'Gotrek, they're all around us,' Felix said hurriedly.

'Good,' Gotrek grunted, eyeing the closest Chaos hound

with an almost avaricious gleam in his eye. When the creature sprang towards him, Gotrek was there to meet it, his axe cleaving the air with a savage whistle. Claws scored his flesh, but the Slayer paid little heed. His axe chopped down into the beast's shoulder joint and it screamed, lurching back, pulling the Slayer from his feet as it reared and spun. Gotrek's free hand shot out, grabbing the beast's muzzle in an iron grip.

Felix had no time to see what came next. Claws scraped stone and something heavy and hairy lunged for him out of the darkness, smelling of the butcher's block. He ducked, and claws skittered off his chainmail shirt, leaving ragged holes and bruises beneath. He rolled to his feet, drawing Karaghul just in time. Fangs like kitchen knives snapped at him and he whirled. Karaghul bit deep into a hairy throat, silencing a hungry howl. The body fell, limbs jerking, and then another was coming for him, jaws agape, tongue lolling.

Fear rippled through him as the thing's eyes caught his own. He jerked back, narrowly avoiding the snap of its jaws. His blade sank home, and something hot and foul washed over his arm. As it rolled away, he heard the crackle of snapping vertebrae and looked up. Gotrek, with brutal élan, had hauled his creature backwards by its muzzle, and, with a second sharp blow of his fist, finished breaking its spine. It flopped limply to the stone, the light in its eyes snuffed by a hunger greater than its own. Gotrek jerked his axe free and brought it down, severing the brute's head, and then shook the blood from his axe blade. He gestured to the one Felix had killed.

'Take its head, manling. These beasts are almost as bad as trolls, especially when the moon is high,' Gotrek said. Felix looked down and then hopped back with an oath as the beast he'd thought dead snapped at him. He stumbled back and it slithered, snake-like, after him, jaws champing mindlessly. Gotrek's axe crashed down, splitting its skull. The Slayer jerked his weapon free and then beheaded the beast. He snatched up the mutilated head and hurled it away.

'Cut their heads off, I said,' Gotrek rumbled.

Before Felix could reply, more howls filled the night, shattering what silence there was. Gotrek spun, his eye blazing with maniacal ferocity. By the sound of it, Felix fancied there were hundreds of the beasts surrounding them, more even than Gotrek could handle, though he looked ready to try his luck. Black shapes crawled across the rocks above them or up onto the edge of the plateau, climbing with distinctly un-canine-like agility.

Felix swallowed thickly, and his palms were slick with sweat as he took Karaghul in a two-handed grip and made ready to die. There were too many of them. Gotrek might live through it, but Felix was only a man, and he knew only luck had kept him alive thus far. And luck had a bad habit of deserting him when he needed it the most.

How else to explain how he was even in this predicament in the first place?

Surely he had paid Gotrek back a hundredfold for plucking him from beneath the hooves of the Emperor's household cavalry back during the Window Tax Riots in Altdorf, how many years ago? He had accompanied the Slayer into the dark beneath the world and worse places, fighting mutants, monsters and madmen. Surely, that drunken oath was more than fulfilled.

No. He shook his head free of those thoughts. There was only one way the oath could be fulfilled. There was only one path open to him, and he had come too far not to take it. 'It will be a good story. Several volumes I think; thirteen at least, with perhaps a few more,' he murmured.

'What are you muttering about, manling?' Gotrek grunted.

'I'm composing paragraphs,' Felix said. 'I'll need an accurate accounting, in case you fall here.'

Gotrek gave a bark of harsh laughter, obviously pleased. 'Make them good ones.'

'I hardly see how they could be otherwise,' Felix muttered, stung. He raised Karaghul.

The closest of the Chaos hounds tensed, preparing to leap. Then, from somewhere in the crags above, a howl echoed down. Its effect was immediate. The circling hounds turned as one, their gore-stained muzzles tilting to unleash a communal howl. Gotrek stumped forwards, but not swiftly enough. The hounds turned and with great, bounding leaps, left Slayer and Remembrancer staring after them, the one in rage, the other in quiet relief.

'Get back here!' Gotrek roared, shaking his axe at the departing beasts.

'Stroke of luck, that,' Felix said shakily.

'Luck isn't the word I would use, manling,' Gotrek snapped. 'Where are they going?'

'Same place we are by the looks of them,' Gotrek said. His bad mood evaporated. 'Come on, manling. I don't know how they know about the Engineers' Entrance, but they do, and if those things get into the hold, they'll kill many good dwarfs before they're put down.'

Felix set off after Gotrek as he moved quickly in pursuit of the Chaos hounds. 'What are we going to do?' he said, already knowing the answer.

'We're going to kill them, manling. What else would we do with them?' Gotrek replied.

* * *

The Worlds Edge Mountains,
near Karak Kadrin

'Move, laggards!' Canto bellowed, standing on a rock, sword in hand. Chaos marauders trotted past in a hurry, many with heavy baskets tied to their backs. The latter looked nervous, and they had good reason to be, Canto thought. The explosives they carried were volatile at best, composed of crude fire-pots and thunder-powder, packed into iron spheres; secrets bartered from the Chaos dwarfs who accompanied Garmr's horde.

Canto frowned as he thought of the stunted creatures. Several had accompanied them to Karak Kadrin to oversee the use of their war-engines, and even now, they were with Kung and Yan on the fields before the outer hold, watching and scheming while the two champions led yet another assault. Dark and malformed, with thick tusks and horns protruding from their oily beards and hair, and eyes like guttering embers, the dawi zharr were far too cunning to be trusted, with minds that moved like twisted clockwork.

He'd dealt with the creatures often enough in his time, but he had no love for them. They were as alien in their thinking as any blood-hungry Khornate berserker. He turned and thought, *speaking of which*, as Hrolf clambered down the side of the crag, followed by several of his hounds. The echoes of the other champion's bestial howl still lingered among the rocks. The hounds had been scattered in their packs through the crags as an early warning system, just in case the dwarfs decided to ambush them. Little could escape the noses of the beasts and by their howls, they had found something, though likely it was only an unlucky tribesman or scouting party. The

Chaos hounds were indiscriminate when no one was there to crack the whip on them and they often returned famished and mad, catching and killing dozens every time he summoned them home with one of his bellicose howls. Maybe the appellation of 'Dogsson' was less mockery than the others intended, Canto thought.

'Your hounds are returning?' he called out tersely.

'What?' Hrolf said dully.

'If your beasts are returning, man, you had best keep them under control or they'll tear through our men for lack of better sport!' Canto's voice was a whip-crack.

'Don't tell me that, I know that,' Hrolf growled, shaking his head.

'Then do something about it,' Canto said, one hand on his sword. Hrolf looked at the hand and the sword, and then at the man they belonged to. Canto prayed that he wouldn't choose now to exercise his frustrations. Not when they were close to being done with this whole shambles. Hrolf snarled and trotted away to gather up his brood of filthy killers, leaving Canto feeling at once relieved and nervous.

Hrolf wasn't as stupid as Ekaterina and the others liked to claim. Fools like Yan openly challenged him, thinking he hadn't the wit to notice. But Hrolf knew and remembered every slight and insult, even as a dog remembered every kick. And despite his brutish mien, the champion had come up with a cunning stratagem, as such things went.

While the attentions of the defenders of the outer hold were on the massive army storming their walls, Canto and Hrolf would sneak in through this entrance Hrolf's scouts had found earlier in the week, and they'd blow the unbreakable walls of the fortress down from below. Or at the very least, they'd create havoc and set loose a pack of Chaos hounds and

Chaos marauders into the outer hold to collect what skulls they could before the dwarfs rallied. Khorne cared not from whence the blood flowed, as Ekaterina was fond of reminding him.

Canto, of course, would happily allow Hrolf the honour of leading the assault. He leaned on his sword. The stone portal, wide enough for two men to step through shoulder-to-shoulder and covered in strange engravings, had been well-hidden, but they'd found it after a few weeks. Granted, they never would have even suspected such a thing existed had not the Chaos dwarfs mentioned the possibility of such, in passing.

'They would know about such things, wouldn't they?' Canto muttered. The shaft clung to the rock of the crag at an angle, and once through the stones that had been used to seal it they'd seen that it was a sheer drop into a belly of hidden scaffolding crafted from stone, metal and petrified wood which spread across the steeply slanted shaft like a spider's web. Stone and wood structures and devices of intricate design were set in odd places, and there was a platform which could descend and ascend under the control of a number of levers and pulleys. The whole thing reminded Canto vaguely of the foul mines that dotted the Plain of Zharr like blasphemous molehills, albeit smaller and more claustrophobic. It was a mine-shaft as opposed to a mine.

When it came down to it, he supposed that there wasn't much difference between one group of dwarfs and another. Though the ones in Karak Kadrin didn't seem to have much use for slaves, he thought. Ancient gear-work creaked as levers were pulled and the platform began to descend at an angle into the shaft even as another rose. Hrolf and his beasts would go down next, as the others who had gone ahead set the explosives against the deep portals that the dwarfs had sealed.

They wouldn't have much time, once they blew open the first entrance. Hrolf would lead his beasts into the tunnels that led to the hold, to bite and slay even as Canto and the Chaos marauders sought out the roots of the wall. An entire latticework of ancient roads ran beneath their feet. If they could find the right one, they could set the remaining explosives and crack the hold like a nut.

Or, such was the plan. Canto grunted, shivering in his armour. Something indefinable passed over him, and the feeling of being watched burned itself against his nerves. He cast a surreptitious look around, prepared to see dwarfs popping out of another of their accursed blinds, axes in hand and his death in their crooked little minds. But no enemies revealed themselves.

He looked back at the shaft. It seemed to yawn hungrily, swallowing the tribesmen. Why had the dwarfs left it undefended? True, they had sealed it, but why nothing more? Perhaps they thought that no one would find it.

Canto shook his head. It didn't matter. There was nothing for it. Hrolf's impatience had grown to monumental proportions, and he chafed at being kept from slaughter. Garmr had left them with no warning, up and taking two-thirds of the horde with him to fresher carnage, leaving them the dull, dangerous job of breaking Karak Kadrin open.

The last lot of men had gone down into the pit, leaving only Canto and his bodyguards. Eichmann and Schaever had been with him since the Battle of the Seven Sundowns in the lands of the Mung. Both wore armour similar to his: big and baroque and shorn of sign or sigils. 'We're going to die down there,' Schaever said. Eichmann grunted, saying nothing.

'Possibly,' Canto said. 'Or maybe it will just be you, Schaever.' Schaever had been a philosopher once, in Nuln, or so he claimed. Now he was a gloom-addled berserker. Eichmann was… Eichmann: unpleasant, blessedly quiet and efficient in his work. Neither was a worshipper of the Blood God, or any god for that matter, though Schaever blithely argued with or perhaps prayed to something called Necoho when he thought no one was listening.

'One can only hope,' Schaever said.

Canto shook his head. A wafting odour of spoiled meat heralded the arrival of Hrolf and his pack. The other champion was looking the worse for wear, his face covered in oozing sores. Stiff red hairs extruded through the sores, quivering in the breeze that swept across the crags. Strange shapes squirmed under the nearly translucent skin of his head and neck, and something with hot, hungry eyes and too many teeth stared at Canto through the cloudy barrier of Hrolf's bloated throat. Hrolf made a strangled burping sound and shook his hairy head. He was on foot, and he bore no weapons.

'Issh-is ith-it ready?' he grunted, one eye bulging in its socket as if something pressed taloned fingertips to the back of it. Slobber ran down from the corners of his mouth and his hands flexed in eagerness. His eyes kept straying to the attack on the walls, where men died in their dozens, flung back by the dwarf defenders to fall and be broken on the rocks below.

'It is,' Canto said, stepping down from his perch, his men following. The creeping shapes of the Chaos hounds followed, lean and irritable and savage. They growled at him, and Eichmann made to draw his sword, his flat, empty eyes showing neither fear nor interest. Canto waved him back and gestured to the pit. 'After you,' he said.

Hrolf eyed him for a moment, as if contemplating tearing out his throat. With a grunt he stagger-loped towards the pit and leapt down, his pack following him with a chorus of howls and snarls. The tribesmen manning the levers cringed, holding their weapons close, eyes wide, as the gods-touched beasts descended into the shaft. After what seemed an interminable amount of time, the platform was winched back up.

'Let's go,' Canto said, hesitating only for a moment. There were over a hundred men down there, and it was up to him to see that Hrolf didn't waste them before time. He led the others onto the platform and he marvelled silently at the structure as it swallowed him up, wondering what might remain when Garmr was finished. Would any of this be left or would it all be rendered unto smoke and ruin in the name of a mad god?

'We're going to die down here,' Schaever said again.

Canto turned to reprimand him, only to stumble back in shock as a massive axe-blade sank into Schaever's helm and split the skull within like a melon. A roaring, red-crested nightmare fell upon him, its axe stained with the blood and brains of his bodyguard.

He barely drew his sword in time, narrowly deflecting the axe. And then he was fighting for his life even as the platform sank into the darkness.

'Gotrek, wait!' Felix cried out, even as Gotrek barrelled into the Chaos marauders near the edge of the pit. There were only a few of them, and they acted as if they thought that Gotrek's sudden appearance heralded a dwarf ambush. They attacked wildly, and the Slayer butchered them without hesitation. Gotrek barely paused, flinging himself through the strange stone portal into the darkness of the shaft beyond. Felix followed, cursing himself, the Slayer and dwarfs in general. He'd seen the armoured giants, Chaos warriors, descend somehow, vanishing down into the darkness. Wherever they were going was somewhere he most certainly didn't want to be, but there was nothing for it.

Felix stepped through the portal, tensing as his boot slid across empty air, and then he was plummeting downwards. He screamed wildly as a kaleidoscope of stone, wood and machinery whirled around him and then he struck something hard and rough. Pain shot through his shoulder and he knew it had been dislocated. He choked on a howl of pain and looked for Gotrek.

The platform wasn't very big, large enough for a loaded wagon, perhaps. Gotrek and a dark-armoured Chaos warrior duelled on its edge, neither giving ground, Gotrek's axe dragging fat sparks from the warrior's sword. A second warrior lay nearby, quite obviously dead, given the state of his skull. And there was a third–

Felix rolled aside, moaning as his shoulder was crushed under his weight, even as the sword chopped down into the platform. The armoured giant was a full hand taller than Felix and three times as broad. His armour glistened as if it were covered in pitch and it stank of wet, deep places and foul rites. The warrior jerked the sword free and raised it again. Felix, panicked, lunged to his feet, trying to draw his sword. Instead, he crashed into the warrior, unbalancing him.

The warrior reeled back, dangerously close to the edge of the platform. Felix, head spinning, drove his good shoulder into his opponent's midsection and sent him flying off. The Chaos warrior struck a support beam and vanished from view as the platform began to pick up speed. 'We're going faster,' Felix said mushily. 'Gotrek, why are we going faster?'

Gotrek didn't reply. The air rang with the sound of steel on steel as the Slayer and the Chaos warrior traded blows. Felix realized that Gotrek killing the controllers above meant that they were now in an uncontrolled free-fall. He staggered to his feet, grabbing one of the braziers mounted on the platform for balance. Pain radiated from his arm through his body and he gritted his teeth.

Gotrek leapt, his axe swinging down. His opponent sank to one knee beneath the dwarf's assault, bringing his blade up. It was sheared flat by the force of the blow, and rebounded from his helm. Felix's ears were stung by the crash of metal. The warrior gave a snarl, slashing out blindly. Gotrek wove aside, rolling around the blow, his axe whirling, crashing. The warrior fell onto his back. He began to crab-crawl backwards, sword extended, trying to keep Gotrek at bay.

Gotrek snarled, heedless of anything save the enemy before him. Felix could only cling to the brazier and watch as Gotrek renewed his assault. The warrior squirmed out from under the attack, impossibly quick in his heavy armour. Gotrek's axe carved a canyon in the back of the warrior's cuirass even as the latter leapt, hands stretching into the darkness.

Then, with a crash, he was gone.

'He ran,' Gotrek said, in disbelief. He looked at Felix, his eye wide. 'He ran! They're not supposed to run!'

'Yes, and we're crashing,' Felix yelped.

Gotrek stumped across the rocking, shuddering platform. 'We're not crashing, we're just moving very fast,' he growled, grabbing Felix's dislocated arm. Felix howled as Gotrek idly popped it back into its socket even as he examined the support ropes that kept the platform held level.

'Will we stop?' Felix said, biting back a whimper as he clutched his aching arm.

'No, we'll crash,' Gotrek said. He grabbed hold of one of the ropes and tested its tension. 'Grab hold of the rope, manling.'

'What?'

Gotrek didn't reply, but Felix saw what he intended

immediately. The support ropes weren't tied to the platform, but instead connected to the pulley system that lowered it. The ropes themselves weren't moving, the platform was sliding along them, the ropes slithering through its inset iron rings. 'Gotrek, don't–' he began.

Gotrek grabbed a rope and cocked his axe. Felix leapt to grab the other rope even as the axe flashed, cutting through the support ropes. The platform swung away from his feet, crashing flat against the incline and hurtling into the darkness of the shaft. Felix's shoulder burned with pain as he clung tightly to the rope. Gotrek's bulky form dangled nearby, though Felix could barely make him out.

'I hope you have a plan for getting down,' Felix hissed. The dark seemed to close a tight fist around him, muffling even the thunder of his heart. He could see nothing; he could only make out vague shapes around him.

From below, there was a sudden crash, and Felix realized that the platform had reached the bottom of the shaft. Gotrek grunted and began to lurch back and forth, causing his rope to brush disturbingly close to Felix's. Felix squawked and tightened his grip, his breath whistling in and out between clenched teeth.

'Swing, manling, there's a brace-beam just behind you,' Gotrek said, swinging past him. The Slayer let go of his rope and Felix heard what could only be his axe chopping into the beam. He heard a grunt, then, 'Come on,' Gotrek said.

'Gotrek, I can't see!'

'Jump anyway,' Gotrek said.

'Gotrek, this is no time for jokes,' Felix said, peering into the darkness.

'Manling, I'll catch you. Jump,' Gotrek rumbled.

Felix cursed virulently for a moment, prompting a chuckle

from the Slayer. Taking a breath, Felix began to move back and forth, causing the rope to swing. Then, as it swung towards the sound of Gotrek's voice, he let go, jumping. Vertigo took him in its claws, causing his stomach to flip-flop; the dark seemed to coil around him, cutting off his breath, and he thought, for a moment, that he'd miscalculated.

Then, something grabbed the front of his jerkin and he was dragged out of the void and deposited on a blessedly solid surface. Breathing heavily, he looked around. 'I still can't see anything,' he wheezed.

'I can,' Gotrek said. 'There'll be a ladder here, for repair crews to use. Up,' he added, hauling Felix to his feet. With Gotrek guiding him, Felix found the ladder.

'How far down does this go?' he said.

'Far enough,' Gotrek grunted. 'Hurry up, manling, there's beasts to kill!'

3

The Worlds Edge Mountains,
the Engineers' Entrance of Karak Kadrin

The climb down into the depths of the immense shaft was surreal. Several times, Felix thought he might slip and fall, only to suddenly find the next rung. The ladder was built for dwarfs, but he climbed down it easily enough, despite the ache in his arm. Nonetheless, it took what felt like hours to reach the bottom. When he mentioned such to Gotrek, the Slayer only grunted, 'We could have done it the fast way.' Felix fell silent. After another interminable length, torchlight became visible and he skinned down the remainder of the rungs, sliding the last few without pausing. Felix dropped gratefully, if not gracefully, to the stone floor.

The light hadn't been cast by torches. When the platform had crashed, the braziers mounted to it had been burst and now the wood was being hungrily, if slowly, consumed by flames. Bodies lay scattered around, Norscans, wearing dark leathers and furs. They'd been caught unawares by the platform, and had paid the price. The destruction had been sudden and complete and he counted at least a dozen men or more. They'd obviously been waiting for the three Chaos warriors who'd been on the platform when Gotrek had launched himself upon them. Struck by the thought, Felix looked up, wondering whether or not the third warrior, the one who'd flung himself from the platform rather than face Gotrek, had survived. Was he still up there somewhere, clinging to the structure in the dark? Shivering, Felix turned back to the Slayer.

Gotrek picked his way through the bodies without even glancing at them. Felix followed him silently after hefting a chunk of burning wood to use as a makeshift torch. Distant voices echoed off the stone. Felix wondered whether they'd heard the crash, and whether they cared. Sound travelled oddly in these deep spaces. Gotrek started forwards, towards a stone archway set into the wall. Felix noted a series of tracks set into the rock, much like those he'd seen in dwarf mines. The tracks moved from where the platform would have come to rest and extended into the arch. Gotrek followed the tracks, his pace quickening. Felix hurried to keep up.

Past the arch, the tunnel floor sloped at an angle. Felix had to stoop slightly as they moved down the tunnel. It was one of several, all of them moving out from the bottom of the shaft, and all large and imposing. They had been shaped with the moving of wagons and other heavy loads in mind and the tunnel was wide and solid, made of heavy stacked blocks which seemed easily capable of holding the weight of the mountain.

Despite the openness of the tunnel, there was a strong smell clinging to everything. It wasn't just the stink of unwashed bodies and the beast-stench of the Chaos hounds. It burned his eyes and throat, and he was forced to cover his mouth and nose with his cloak. 'Fire-pots and thunder-powder,' Gotrek muttered.

'I didn't realize that the Northmen had such things,' Felix said softly.

'They don't,' Gotrek said. 'They stole the secrets from my people. Or else…' He trailed off. Felix wanted to prod him to finish, but the look in the Slayer's eye stole his voice.

The tunnel ended, expanding into a vaulted space that took Felix's breath away. It was larger than any cathedral man had built, and more graceful for all that it was built of stone and solid, bulky shapes. The walls of the massive chamber were honeycombed with tunnels, stairs and tracks going in hundreds of directions. Great cracked archways and crumbled statues lined the expanse. Felix caught sight of what must have once been ancient bridges and stairs that curved down into the darkness. 'What is this place?' he murmured.

'*Ungdrin* – the Underway,' Gotrek said, almost reverentially. He touched the wall with a hesitant hand and fell silent. Then, 'Once, these roads led to every Karak and Karaz, manling. Every hold, it was said, was linked one to the next. A dwarf could travel Karak Vlag to Karak Zorn without ever seeing daylight.' Gotrek's voice was wistful. His face fell. 'All lost now. As everything is lost or will be lost,' he said, and Felix felt a chill whisper across his backbone.

'What… what happened?'

Gotrek didn't answer. 'Come,' he grunted. 'I smell Chaos filth.'

Felix did as well, come to that. The foul blood-odour was stronger down one of the tunnels. Gotrek paused. 'This path leads to the fortress. There are only a few ways into the hold proper, and this isn't one of them, but I'd wager that they don't know that. Still, if they get in among the defenders of the fortress, they might just open the gates and get many good dwarfs killed,' the Slayer said. He stepped into the tunnel and Felix followed with one hand on his sword hilt.

There was no question what would happen when they found their prey, only whether or not they would survive the finding. You could move armies down here, he knew, and no one would be the wiser for it. The dwarfs had done so, in their time, but had the Chaos forces now done the same? How many men were they facing down here? Was it dozens or was it hundreds? And that wasn't even taking into account the Chaos hounds. Had they come down here as well? The thought of facing those four legged nightmares down here in the dark wasn't a pleasant one.

Despite his fears, calmness settled on Felix at times like these, a chill resignation. When death lunged suddenly from the darkness, he feared and fought like any man. But when they sought it out, grim necessity washed aside the fear.

From somewhere far above, the noise of the siege drifted down like the occasional curtains of dust that fell upon them from the vaulted roof, the distant sounds carried on the bones of the mountain. What was going on? Were the walls holding? Dark thoughts flapped across the surface of Felix's mind. At first, he'd thought that getting into Baragor's Watch was their best chance for survival. Now he wasn't so sure.

The sound grew louder as they travelled, and Felix hoped that they were getting closer to the fortress. Despite Gotrek's impatience, they stopped for a time in a narrow antechamber, where a thin, pathetic stream of cool, clean water ran through the cracks in an ancient wall carving, splashing out of the open mouth of a carven effigy of some nameless dwarf hero. They consumed the last of the supplies they'd bought in Wurtbad, and assuaged their thirst; though Gotrek drank the water only grudgingly, no ale or beer being to hand. In the dark, Felix rested fitfully, unable to sleep despite his best efforts, and Gotrek, he thought, slept not at all.

When Felix at last gave up on getting any sleep and opened his weary eyes, Gotrek was stepping back into the antechamber. 'We're not as far behind them as I thought, manling,' he said. 'We may just catch up with them in time.'

'Oh joy,' Felix muttered, climbing stiffly to his feet. Sitting on cold stone was something he had grown depressingly used to over the course of his journeys with Gotrek, but his thoughts had been dark and unpleasant. He supposed it was his surroundings. It wasn't so long ago that he and Gotrek had been lost in the tunnels beneath Wurtbad, battling old, dead things. He recalled pale, feral features and the hideous strength of undead claws on his throat. He shook his head, banishing the thoughts. Better to worry about the horrors he had yet to face than ones he had already survived.

Gotrek grinned at his obvious discomfort. 'Hurry up, manling. There are things needing killing.'

They crept out of the antechamber and back onto the path. The tunnel gave way to a wide cavern; indeed, not just a cavern, but something which would have easily contained the dark, ghoul-haunted crypts beneath Wurtbad or the massive chamber they'd just left a hundred times over. Barely visible in the light cast by his torch were what could only be vast supportive arches of carefully placed stone holding up the cavern roof, putting Felix in mind of the roofs of the larger temples he'd had the misfortune to visit during his life.

Things flew through the darkness above, though whether they were large or small, he couldn't say. Too, strange noises echoed, mingling with the sounds from above and what could only be the distant thunder of the Stir as it raced through the underground arteries from which it originated. He'd never thought that such deep places could be so loud, but time and again, he'd been proven wrong.

Ahead of them was a wide stone bridge which crossed a deep gash in the floor of the cavern. The bridge had been a thing of beauty once, but now it was cracked and missing chunks. The statues which had once lined it had all fallen or been shattered to lay across the expanse of the bridge with the other rubble. They were forced to make their way along the far edge, and Felix made the mistake of looking down into the almost solid darkness of the chasm below. For a moment, the world spun and he felt that if he fell, he would not stop until he came out the other side of the world. 'How far down does it go?' he said, half to himself.

'All the way to the guts of the world,' Gotrek said. 'Best not to fall, if you can help it.'

'Duly noted,' Felix said and swallowed nervously. 'How in Sigmar's name did those engineers you mentioned get their mechanisms across this thing?'

'What sort of fool question is that?' Gotrek grunted, 'One piece at a time, of course. It only took them a few weeks at worst. Not long at all.'

Felix shook his head. The sort of patience such an undertaking must have required was incomprehensible to him. Looking sideways at Gotrek, he found himself wondering if the Slayer, impatient and quick to become angered by even the most minor of delays, had ever possessed such qualities. Gotrek boosted himself up onto a statue that lay on its side, its stone eyes glaring accusingly back the way they had come. He crouched and waved a hand at Felix. 'Stay down, manling,' he hissed through the gap in his teeth.

Felix sank to his haunches behind the statue, one hand on

his sword hilt. 'What is it?' he whispered. Gotrek slithered off the statue and dropped down beside him.

'Sentries,' he muttered. 'They're taking no chances on my people catching them unawares.'

'How many of them are there?'

'Three,' Gotrek said dismissively. 'But one has a horn, and sound carries quickly down here. One good blast and we'll have the rest of them down on our heads before the echo fades.' He gnawed on his lip, visibly considering the problem.

At any other time, Felix knew that the Slayer would have simply bulled ahead, shouting for all he was worth and damn the consequences. But Gotrek had other priorities now, for which Felix breathed a silent sigh of relief. Long odds were fine for gambling, but not so much for combat. 'We could sneak past them,' he said.

Gotrek growled wordlessly. Felix shook his head. 'Fine, what do you suggest then?'

'We kill them,' Gotrek said. 'But quietly,' he added.

Felix snorted. 'That'll be a first,' he said.

'What was that?' Gotrek said.

'Nothing,' Felix said hastily. 'Just some dust in my throat.' He peered through a gaping crack in the statue and saw the not-so-distant shapes of the sentries. They were, like all Chaos marauders, big and bulky and one had a large, brass-banded war-horn dangling from a strap across his shoulder. He could not make out their expressions, despite the flickering light of the half-dozen watch-fires they'd lit around them at various spots on the bridge. The latter consisted mostly of overturned shields that had been turned into makeshift braziers, piled high with something flammable and set around at certain points.

'I'll take the one with the horn,' Gotrek said, heading for the other side of the statue.

'Which means I have to take the other two?' Felix said, but Gotrek had already vanished. Felix cursed under his breath and moved carefully through the field of rubble that separated him from the sentries. He left his torch behind. There was no need for it, and he didn't want to attract any undue attention. He moved in quick bursts, scrambling on all fours, his cloak, which was coated in dust from their journey thus far and now less red than brown, draped over him to stop any light from catching on his mail shirt. He stalked the Chaos marauders, keeping his eyes on them at all times and trying not to imagine what sort of horrors might be doing the same to him as he crept through the forest of fallen stones and toppled statues.

The three warriors grunted to each other in their own barbarous tongue. Two stood and the third sat slumped, occupied in running a whetstone across his sword. As he drew close enough to smell the unwashed stench of them, Felix realized that he would have to step into the light to confront them. Unless…

Felix undid the clasp on his cloak and slowly pulled it off. Then he snatched up a heavy stone and tossed it back the way he had come. The sound was loud and its result, sudden. The sentry who had been slumped in apparent indifference sat up immediately, eyes narrowed. He barked a question at one of his companions, and the latter hurried towards Felix's position, a cruel looking axe in his hands. He wore no armour save for fur-covered pauldrons crafted from wolf skulls. Felix pressed himself back against the gloomy brow of a toppled statue, his cloak held in both hands, and his legs and arms tense and trembling as he fought down the queasy anticipation of the next few moments.

Though he had killed, and often, since he'd become Gotrek's Remembrancer, this wasn't the same. It reminded him too much of his last days at the University of Altdorf, Three-Toll Bridge and the Luitpoldstrasse. He remembered the shock of his sword sliding into Wolfgang Krassner's belly, and the way the other student had folded over and expired. He shook his head, clearing the cobwebs of memory.

The Chaos marauder stepped past him and Felix flung his cloak over the bigger man's head. Then, before the warrior could react, Felix twisted the ends of the cloak tight, jerked his captive off-balance and pivoted, dragging the Chaos marauder from his feet and slamming him against the face of the statue. In an eye-blink, Felix had his dagger out and thrust it upwards into his opponent's heart, burying it to the hilt. Foul air whooshed through the weave of his cloak and washed over him as the Chaos marauder sighed and bent forwards, limp. Felix took the weight on his shoulder and pulled the body out of the way, back deeper into the shadows. He extracted his dagger and absently wiped it clean on his cloak as he pulled it free of the corpse.

A grunted question echoed among the stones. Felix crouched and waited, his heart thudding in his chest. When he heard no movement, he crept back to his previous position. The two Chaos marauders were peering in his general direction, and both looked distinctly suspicious. The one with the horn began to raise it.

Out of the darkness behind him, wide hands appeared to either side of his head. The hands snapped shut like the jaws of a trap, catching the sentry's head in a vice-like grip. With a motion so swift that Felix could barely follow it, the sentry's head was twisted all the way around in a corkscrew motion. Bones popped and snapped loudly and the remaining sentry whirled, mouth opening. Felix darted from hiding, dagger in hand. He grabbed a handful of the Chaos marauder's hair and made to cut the man's throat, but brawny hands grabbed his and he found himself suddenly hurtling over the sentry's shoulder. He slammed into the ground and Gotrek vaulted over him.

The Slayer's meaty paws fastened themselves on the sentry's windpipe with ferocious accuracy. Cartilage crunched as the man's eyes bugged out of their sockets. Gotrek hefted the Chaos marauder and wrung his neck as if he were a chicken. After several moments, the Slayer gave a satisfied grunt and let the body flop bonelessly to the ground. 'Where's the other?' he said.

'Back there,' Felix said.

'Dead?' Gotrek said.

'Of course,' Felix said, slightly insulted.

'Good, manling.' Gotrek grinned at him and Felix felt his gorge rise. For the Slayer, this was little more than an exercise in pest control. Gotrek retrieved his axe from where he'd set it aside and took the war-horn from the dead man's body.

'Why are you taking that?' Felix said, swinging his cloak about his shoulders and re-attaching the clasp. 'Surely it will only alert the enemy.'

'Aye, that's the plan,' Gotrek said, starting off towards the entrance to the tunnel that the sentries had been set to guard.

'We have a plan?' Felix said.

'Of course we have a plan, manling,' Gotrek said. 'There's always a plan.'

'Silly me, I didn't think "run at them and chop them off at the knees" was a plan,' Felix muttered.

'Best one there is,' Gotrek chortled. He waved the horn. 'But this is a different one.'

'Oh?'

'Aye, in this plan, they run at us,' Gotrek said. Felix fell silent. The tunnel beyond the bridge was marked by a sturdy portcullis set into the cavern wall, which had long since been blasted to jagged stumps by some fell force. Above it, he could see the squat shapes of blockhouses that projected from the stone like grotesques on a temple wall, such as lined the walls of the frontier forts of the Empire – enclosed boxes that sat atop towers, though these were constructed of stone rather than wood. The tunnel beyond the portcullis was larger than any of the others they had so far traversed, and had all of the appearance of being an ancient entry hall. 'The Engineers' Entrance,' Gotrek hissed. Felix could hear the sound of bestial voices, echoing off the stone.

Gotrek waved Felix back, and they pressed themselves tight to the wall. Normally, Gotrek was without caution. He was taking this more seriously than normal, Felix knew. Just as he knew that the Slayer was not seeking death, for once. For Gotrek, this was more important than his doom.

Gotrek cast a wary eye in the direction the noise was emanating from, and then turned to the wall. He muttered to himself in Khazalid, the dwarf tongue, as he ran his hands across the wall. Felix heard a click and then a square of stone, about the right size for a dwarfish door, swung inwards to reveal slabbed stone stairs. Gotrek nodded in satisfaction. He caught Felix's astonished look and said, 'We build to last, manling. It'll be another six centuries before those hinges even start to rust.'

Felix followed Gotrek up the stairs as the door slid shut behind them. They were plunged into darkness, but only for a moment. A soft glow spread across the stone walls. 'Glowmoss,' Gotrek said softly. 'Watch your step.'

Felix took the stairs slowly and the going was awkward. They weren't made with men in mind, and he had to stoop and contort himself to keep up with the Slayer. 'Where are we going, Gotrek?'

'Up to the old badger-run,' Gotrek said. 'When this entrance was first constructed, back before the Engineers' Guild got their hands on it, it was a strong-point of the Underway. The ironbreakers of Karak Kadrin were stationed here, between delvings. It was built to hold off an army, or contain one, if the worst happened.' At the top of the stairs was what Felix assumed was an enclosed parapet, running between the blockhouses. Gotrek led him to one of the blockhouses that overlooked the bridge. Inside, Felix saw two large bolt throwers, one at each corner of the wide opening that marked the front of the structure; each was stationed on a stone dais that he suspected would rotate. Gotrek had no interest in the bolt throwers, however.

'Manling, come here,' he said. Felix joined him in the centre of the blockhouse, where a heavy wooden lever jutted from the floor. Gotrek gestured to it and said, 'When I tell you to, throw this.'

'What does it do?'

'It evens the odds,' Gotrek said. The Slayer stumped to the opening and lifted the horn. Felix realized what he was about to do a moment before the Slayer planted the horn against his lips and blew a winding note out towards the bridge.

'What does that accomplish?' Felix cried.

'Just do as I tell you, manling,' Gotrek growled. Then he blew the horn again. The horn was a crude instrument, but the power of the dwarf's lungs compensated for it. The note was flung out over the bridge, to echo through the vast cavern. And someone below took note. Felix shuddered as he heard more horns howl and then heard the sound of running feet.

Gotrek flung the horn aside and crouched at the opening,

peering down. His one eye glinted in the dim light. He raised a hand, but didn't look back at Felix. 'Get ready, manling.'

Felix set himself. What was Gotrek up to?

More horns sounded, and the cries of Chaos marauders drifted up towards them. The blockhouse seemed to tremble with the fury of their passage through the entryway below. How many of them were down there? For a moment, Felix thought that Gotrek was counting them, tallying future notches for his axe. It was the sort of thing he thought the Slayer might do.

'Now,' Gotrek barked and chopped the air with his hand.

Felix thrust himself against the lever and it moved grudgingly at first, then, as if some massive weight had shifted, it was ripped from his hands and slammed against the floor in the direction he'd been pushing it. The floor trembled. Gotrek gave a bellow of laughter and shook his axe as the sound of ripping stone filled the air and Felix stumbled back, his hands clapped to his ears. 'What happened?' he shouted. 'What did we do?'

'See for yourself, manling!' Gotrek said. Felix stumbled towards him and peered out over the lip of the opening. Down below, all was chaos. Almost fifty men or more were on the bridge and a cloud of dust had enveloped them. Some were standing while others were lying still, their bodies caught in the explosion of falling rock that had sealed the tunnel beneath his and Gotrek's feet. Gotrek gazed longingly at the bolt throwers, as if weighing the effort it would take to load them and vent his fury on the men trapped below. Instead he shook his head and left the blockhouse. 'Come, we need to see to the rest of them before they do whatever it is they're planning to do.'

'How long will those rocks keep the rest out, you think?' Felix said, hurrying after him.

'Only dwarfs possess the skill to move those rocks, manling,' Gotrek said and then frowned. He muttered something in Khazalid.

'What?' Felix said.

'Nothing,' Gotrek snapped. 'Hurry, manling.' He led Felix across the parapet towards a second set of stairs. These curved downwards and led to a flat landing that looked down into the courtyard below. A further set of stairs led to the latter, but the way out was blocked by what looked to Felix to be a silk screen. He and Gotrek crouched on the landing, the Slayer waving him to silence. 'Quiet, manling. The rock-cloth will mute any sounds from us, but hounds have keener hearing than men.'

Felix looked at the rock-cloth and recalled that Gotrek had once mentioned that it was used by dwarf rangers for camouflage when they camped in the hills. It was darker on one side than the other, allowing them to look through it with effort but thanks to the unguents and coarse weave, it would appear to be a part of the surrounding stone if anyone looked at it from the other side. Of course, that didn't stop the Chaos hounds from sniffing them out, but the beasts were too agitated by the sudden collapse of the tunnel to be curious.

The chamber beyond was the size of a temple, albeit one that was less the size of the Grand Temple of Sigmar than the Plaza of Saints in Nuln. There were close to thirty Chaos marauders remaining, and they were quickly manhandling baskets and crude-looking iron spheres into position against a large sealed archway as their leader, a bulky monstrous-looking man, bellowed orders in a slobbering tone. Behind them, more Chaos hounds prowled, snuffling eagerly, their grotesque limbs jerking and twitching with feral impatience. Counting those they'd trapped outside, Felix knew they'd only brought around a hundred men. It was small for an assault, but then, how many were really required? Once a hole had been made, how hard would it be to ferry more men inside? Karak Kadrin would be under siege on two fronts.

More baskets and spheres were set off to the side, guarded by a half-dozen burly Chaos marauders with faces like carved teak and dark scalplocks. They carried hide shields and curved spears or butcher's blades, with ring-holes punched in the rusty metal to lighten their weight. They were armoured better than the others, and bore themselves like professional killers, albeit nervous ones who seemed ready to face an ambush at any moment. Dust boiled through the chamber, issuing from the tunnel that the rocks had sealed. If the Chaos marauders were wondering at the fate of their comrades, they didn't show it. Felix supposed that they had grown used to the dwarfs' mechanical trickery in battle, and so assumed that any unexplained noise was another trap or ambush.

'If they blow open that door, they'll be into Baragor's Watch,' Gotrek growled softly, his eye narrowing as he gauged the distance from the landing to the aperture. One good leap would carry the dwarf through the rock-cloth and into the chamber.

'And we can't let that happen, can we?' Felix said, knowing the answer. Gotrek gave him a brief, gap-toothed grin. Then, with a roar, the Slayer pushed himself away from the wall and into the chamber beyond, his axe looping out to sweep the cloth aside.

Gotrek caught a surprised hound in its arched spine. It screamed and folded, but the Slayer didn't pause, jerking his axe loose and turning on his heel to send a second blow chopping into a Chaos marauder's belly. The warrior was lifted from his feet, his cry of agony caught in his collapsing lungs. Gotrek was a hurricane of single-minded destruction, not bothering to kill, only to maim or bludgeon. And as all eyes were drawn to the diminutive killer, Felix took his chance and darted towards the tribesmen setting up their explosives at the archway.

He didn't really have a plan, only a vague notion of preventing the explosion for as long as possible. His guts felt like ice as Karaghul hummed through a raised wrist. The blade caught on the bone and Felix was forced to lash out with a boot to dislodge it from the screaming tribesman. He felt a whisper of air on his neck and spun, letting Karaghul slide into the softness of an unarmoured torso.

Felix felt an iron grip fall on his shoulders and then he was flying through the air. He hit the ground and skidded, all of the wind knocked out of him. A man stalked towards him, big, bigger than he had any right to be, and looking as if he were gripped by some degenerative disease. His flesh rippled with blisters and boiled-looking patches and things moved within the waxy opalescence, like maggots in a wound. He bore no weapon, but his mouth was a nest of fangs.

Felix scrambled to his feet and gasped as agony flared in his shoulder. It still ached from before and though adrenaline had let him ignore it, he was paying for it now. He shifted Karaghul to his other hand as he backed away from his opponent.

The man stretched lazily, and Felix felt queasy as bones popped and ligaments squelched. His flesh puckered and thin drizzles of blood dripped from the corners of his mouth. Hooked fingers reached up, grabbing the flesh of his face. Felix saw his belly bulge obscenely beneath his cuirass, followed by his throat, and then his mouth spread impossibly wide as something evil and red was vomited into the torch-light.

The man's flesh slithered down the length of the red-furred form, like the shed skin of a snake. In places, it snagged and tore, leaving gory rags wrapped about the beast's limbs. It was akin to the Chaos hounds, but larger and darker and even more savagely terrifying. Brass-hued horns jutted from its wolfish skull and the crimson hair that covered it was shot through with patches of brass scales. It stared at Felix in hungry anticipation and then rocked back on its haunches and tilted its muzzle up, releasing a howl that curdled the marrow in Felix's bones.

4

The Worlds Edge Mountains,
Karak Kadrin

With a roar, the monster lunged, claws scraping stone even as Felix hurled himself aside. The monster whipped around, yellow eyes opening in its arms and torso, gazing at him with fiery hate. It took a step towards him. Old, half-remembered stories swam to the surface of his mind, scraps of stories told to him by his mother and her maids, of black-souled men that became beasts when the Witch-Moon was high. 'Sigmar help me,' he whispered, the words packed with loathing and fear.

'Just another beast, manling,' Gotrek said.

The monster turned, and looking past it, Felix saw Gotrek, streaked with blood, gesture with his axe. 'Leave the manling alone. He owes me a saga, and I'll not have him eaten before he can pen it.' The monster howled again and leapt, and Gotrek moved to meet it.

Felix thrust himself to his feet as Chaos hounds bounded towards him, slavering jaws wide. The Chaos marauders were staying back, save those setting the explosives, letting the beasts have their fun. Breath burning in his lungs, Felix ran towards the archway.

While he'd been occupied, they'd lit the fuse cord and a spark of flame crawled towards the heap of spheres and jugs. He had to reach it! The moment stretched, impossibly long. He heard Gotrek's bellow of pain, and a beast's howl of triumph. Felix lunged, stretching, Karaghul descending. He groaned as he missed and the spark sped out of his reach. Jaws seized his legs and he was wrenched around and dragged back towards a snarling morass of Chaos hounds even as a grimy foot slammed down on the spark, extinguishing it.

A mace snapped out, crashing into a toothy muzzle, sending a shower of teeth peppering Felix's face. And then, a roar from a dozen or more throats, and bodies surged into the chamber from a hidden opening. Felix was jerked to his feet by strong hands and pitched into the arms of a man, a human, he noted with surprise.

The battle was joined. Slayers, dozens of them, fell on the snarling beasts and shouting tribesmen. Brightly hued crests cut through the ranks of the Chaos horde like the fins of sharks in shallow waters. 'What–' Felix began.

'Koertig,' the man said gruffly. He wore a battered cuirass over clothing that had seen much hard travel, and a dented helm that covered the top half of his face, leaving an unsmiling mouth and square jaw exposed. 'Can you use that sword?' he said. His accent possessed the guttural tones of Nordland and he carried a long-hafted war-axe.

'Yes, but who–'

'I told you. Introductions later; now we fight,' Koertig grunted, lunging at a screaming Chaos marauder. His axe sheared through the warrior's jaw and the force of the blow spun the dying man. Felix parried a thrust spear and spitted its wielder even as he sought out Gotrek.

The Slayer was clinging to one of the monster's brass horns, his axe embedded in the ornate cuirass it still wore. Its claws tore trails in Gotrek's tattooed flesh, but the Slayer hung on with inhuman determination. Around them, the beast's followers battled the newly arrived Slayers, including the one who'd saved Felix.

The latter was bare-chested like most Slayers, though he lacked the shorn skull. Instead, his hair had been greased and twisted into long spikes, as had his beard. A ring had been clipped to each nostril, with a chain attaching it to the appropriate earlobe, and he wielded a mace that looked to have been crafted from a chunk of firewood and an orc skull. The Slayer bellowed with laughter as he swatted a Chaos hound in the head, knocking it sprawling. Koertig grunted unhappily. Felix glanced at him.

'Are you–' he began.

'Yes,' Koertig said, sullenly.

'How–'

'I don't want to talk about it.'

Felix glanced back at the Slayer, who had fastened his teeth in a wolf's ear even as he brought his mace down on another's paw. 'Is he–'

'*I said* I don't want to talk about it,' Koertig growled.

'Fair enough,' Felix said. A Slayer hurtled past him, wreathed in red. The newcomers weren't having it all their own way, despite the element of surprise. The dwarf struck the wall and flopped bonelessly to the floor, his doom found. Felix stared at the body for a moment, wondering whether the Slayer had found satisfaction, or at least relief, in those final, painful moments.

Then, a paw almost took off his head, and he shook himself from his reverie. Karaghul pierced a hairy flank, eliciting a shriek of pain. The Chaos hound was large for its kind, and all the more vicious for that. Claws hooked his cloak and Felix stabbed out. Koertig joined him, bellowing a war-cry and sinking his axe into the creature's back. It shrugged the Nordlander off and, frothing, snapped its jaws at Felix.

An orc-skull mace cracked down on the creature's muzzle. It staggered, shaking its head. It stumbled back, pressed by the Slayer's enthusiasm if nothing else. Felix started forwards, but the orc-skull mace tapped him on the chest, stopping him. The spiky-haired Slayer looked back at him and shook his head. 'Mine, I think,' he said, flashing metal teeth.

Felix nodded curtly. He looked for Gotrek, determined to help at least one Slayer. The chamber was growing quiet. The hounds, blood-hungry and savage, were growing few. The Chaos marauders were all dead, lying in broken heaps, their only-human savagery paling in comparison to that of the Slayers. Only the beast-thing that had led them into the dark remained.

The latter stood amongst the bodies of a half-dozen Slayers, still clawing at Gotrek, who clung limpet-like to its armour. It staggered back and forth, its howls having degenerated to wheezing pants of effort. Gotrek too looked winded. Even so, his shoulder muscles swelled and he pried his axe free from the thing's armour. It tossed its head and Gotrek swung his axe and then he was flying free, a shattered horn in his hand. Gotrek hit the ground and bounced almost immediately to his feet, albeit unsteadily. Breathing heavily, Gotrek eyed the beast. 'Come on,' he hissed.

The creature snarled and lunged. Gotrek met it, axe in one hand and its horn in the other. Felix ran towards them. He heard shouts behind him, but he paid them no heed. Something hairy and strong snaked around his throat and hefted him from the ground, talon-tips digging into his neck. An animal stink washed over him and he stared up into eyes that swam with blood and rage.

Malformed jaws dipped in anticipation, and Felix screamed.

'Ho, beast, he's not yours to kill!' Gotrek's axe thudded into the hairy arm, eliciting a screech. Felix was flung through the air. He hit the ground and lay, breathless. 'Come on then,' Gotrek continued. 'Or did that hit take all of the fight out of you, cur of Chaos?'

The creature's only response was a howl as it ripped through the air towards the Slayer, talons flailing. Claws thudded down and Gotrek only narrowly avoided a messy bisection. His own weapon whipped out, carving a crimson canyon across the thing's malformed shoulder, causing it to reel back with a wail. Gotrek spat in disgust and closed in. A fist backhanded him with bone-bruising force and sent him skidding across the ground.

'Ha! My turn,' the Slayer wielding the orc-skull mace yelped, his weapon thumping against the creature's skull. The Slayer leapt and dived, avoiding blows that should have pulped him and returning them with interest. Nonetheless, the monster barely staggered and a contemptuous kick sent the mace-wielder flying past Felix. It was looking as if the damnable thing was impossible to kill. It lunged and its jaws closed over another dwarf's head. It tossed its head and decapitated its prey, sending a crescent of blood spattering across the other Slayers who pressed close about it. '*S-skulls,*' it snarled as it spat out the mangled head. '*Skulls for the Skull Road!*'

'You want skulls? I see one ripe for the plucking,' Gotrek growled as his axe buried itself into one hairy thigh. The beast screamed and whirled, reaching for him. The Slayer avoided the talon, but only just, and he lost his grip on his precious weapon. The creature wrenched the axe from its leg and flung it aside, hard enough to drive the blade into the rock of the chamber floor. Slavering, it stalked towards Gotrek, who climbed to his feet and waited for it, fists raised.

Felix knew that even the Slayer had little hope of defeating such a beast without his axe. Even with it, it was looking to be impossible. There had to be something he could do. He cast about, mind racing, and then he caught sight of one of the metal spheres the Chaos marauders had brought into the catacombs. It was an ugly thing, made of sharp-edged iron plates welded together, with a fuse that extended like a rat's tail. He snatched a striker up from out of the limp hand of a dead Chaos marauder and sliced the fuse to barely more than a nub with Karaghul. Then, with a shaky prayer to Sigmar on his lips, he lit it and gave it a kick, sending it rolling. The dwarfs who saw it coming scrambled aside with what, in other circumstances, Felix might have considered amusing alacrity.

'Gotrek,' he shouted. 'Get out of the way!'

The Slayer's eye widened as he saw the explosive sphere rolling towards him. Then, to Felix's horror, he snatched the sphere up and, muscles bulging, hurled it straight into the chest of his monstrous opponent. The beast caught it instinctively and grunted in confusion. Felix felt someone grab him. 'We have to get out of here,' the spiky-haired Slayer barked. 'Everyone out, now!'

The explosion, when it came, was sudden and violent. Felix was flung back into blackness as the world fell in on them. Heavy stones fell, and a cloud of smoke and dust rose to meet them. The sound was thunderous and deafening. Felix fell flat, his hands clapped to his ears. He felt as if his skull was about to pop or his bones to vibrate from their envelopes of flesh. When he felt no crushing weight, he cracked open an eye.

He had been pulled back by the spiky-haired Slayer into whatever hidden aperture the Slayers had emerged from. It was yet another tunnel, but this one was more heavily, and more recently by the looks of it, reinforced, with thick stone struts and supports. Even so, it shuddered around them as dust and debris billowed through the opening. Felix flinched as tiny flecks of stone stung his hands and face. He shoved himself to his feet, though the corridor continued to shake. It sounded as if the tunnel section that he and Gotrek had traversed was falling in on itself. 'Gotrek,' he coughed, and then, more loudly, 'Gotrek!'

'I don't think he made it out, human,' the spiky-haired Slayer said. Another explosion shook them, and dust drifted down from the roof of the corridor. More dust and smoke choked the air and the Slayer grabbed Felix. 'Back the way we came,' he rumbled. 'This place is coming down, and we'll be joining your friend if we don't get out of here. This whole section is going to collapse.'

'No,' Felix said, staring at the billowing cloud of debris. 'Gotrek,' he shouted.

A clawed hand erupted from the dust and Felix stumbled back, falling on his rear. The monster coughed blood and its eyes were glazed with agony as it forced itself through the narrow aperture. The collar on its bifurcated neck seemed to pulse and steam. Felix scrambled back, gawping at it.

'Grimnir's guts, that thing just doesn't want to die,' the spiky-haired Slayer shouted.

Its sides heaved like a bellows as the wounded creature shoved itself towards them. It was bleeding from hundreds of shrapnel wounds and the explosion had seared the flesh from its bones in places. Nonetheless, it continued to move, compelled by some hellish will to continue. Felix felt disgust and horror ripple through him. This – this was the end result of Chaos. A man once, and then a beast, and now some brainless, slobbering thing, trapped in a hulk of broken meat. It was hunger given form, and nothing more, the atavistic need to devour with no will or soul to guide it. To kill it would be a mercy.

It bawled out a challenge, even as it choked on its own blood. Then, before it could lunge forwards, an axe buried itself in its back, cleaving its spine and dropping the creature flat to the ground, where it flopped bonelessly. Its fangs chewed the ground.

'Stop running from me,' Gotrek croaked, days of frustration boiling behind the words. His flesh was streaked with blood, ash and dirt, and his crest had been bent and smashed down, but he looked as ready for a fight as ever.

Gotrek dropped off the squirming beast and walked around it. The creature eyed him dumbly, as if unable to comprehend that its doom was approaching. Gotrek stopped and stared down at it, making no move to kill it.

'For pity's sake, Gotrek,' Felix said, unable to stand the sounds the monster was making. 'Kill the thing and be done.' Gotrek didn't acknowledge that he had heard Felix, nor did he deliver the killing blow. Instead, he stood, waiting.

The creature was dying, but not quickly. Whatever fell power had made it had also imbued it with an inhuman vitality that not even such damage as it had already taken could kill it outright. It writhed, jaws snapping. With a convulsive jerk, it flung itself forwards, maw wide. Gotrek made no effort to step aside. For a moment, Felix feared that Gotrek was going to let those maddened jaws close around him. Instead, the

Slayer's axe snapped down with finality, cutting the monster's noise short.

Gotrek turned. 'Slayers have no pity, manling,' he rasped.

'Gotrek, are you all right?' Felix said, in the silence that followed.

'I'm fine, manling,' Gotrek said. 'Had to get my axe.'

'You don't look fine,' Felix said.

'What?' Gotrek growled.

'Nothing,' Felix said quickly. He looked around. They were in a sloping corridor that rose upwards. It was in better condition than the tunnels, and showed signs of regular use. He wondered idly how many redundant passageways the dwarfs had in these holds. Did they simply dig new ones when they became bored with the old ones? Or was it more akin to the fabled lost streets of Altdorf – streets that were forgotten and built over after invasions and fires.

'I've never seen a Chaos beastie go out with quite so big a bang,' the spiky-haired Slayer said cheerfully, his mace resting on his shoulder. 'I've heard the stories, Gurnisson, but I'd have never believed them had I not seen it with my own eyes.'

'You know of me?' Gotrek said.

'Everyone knows you. Gotrek Gurnisson, the Doom-Thief and Jinx-Slayer,' the other said, chuckling. 'Slayers tell stories about you when they want to scare themselves.'

Gotrek's eye narrowed and he spat at the other Slayer's feet before turning away. The Slayer shrugged, unperturbed. He looked at Felix, flashing a metal grin. Every tooth in his head appeared to have been replaced with what Felix thought were gromril replicas. 'They call me Biter,' he said.

'No one calls you Biter,' Koertig said sullenly.

'Everyone calls me Biter,' Biter said, still smiling. 'Except for my Remembrancer here,' he added. He slapped Koertig companionably on the arm, nearly knocking the Nordlander off his feet. Felix looked at the scowling Nordlander and nodded in sympathy. If Koertig saw, he gave no sign.

Biter sniffed at Gotrek's back. 'He's not exactly pleasant company, that one. Then, neither am I.'

'And why should any of us be?' another Slayer grated, rubbing ruefully at a set of slashes in his chest. He wore a harness with a number of strange clay pots attached and there were powder-burns on his cheeks and jaw. 'There are only so many dooms to go around and fewer now. Less, if Gurnisson is here.'

Felix looked around. Of the thirty or so Slayers who had poured into the chamber, only half were left, the others lying tangled in death with the wolf-things and the human tribesmen. He was startled by the number, wondering if Gotrek's determination to find a worthy death was unique to him.

'Quiet, Agni,' Biter said.

'I am merely saying what we're all thinking,' the Slayer protested. He pointed at Gotrek. 'Gurnisson is a jinx! You said so yourself!'

'I said... quiet,' Biter said, not firmly, or harshly. He tapped Agni's bulbous nose with his mace. 'You are being impolite.'

Gotrek stood apart from the others, and they seemed content to leave him be. Whether he had heard Agni's outburst, he gave no sign. Felix joined him as did Biter, unbidden.

'We've been waiting for them to give this entrance the old Guild try since they found it,' Biter said, idly kicking a rock aside. 'I thought Iron-Rear was mad for–'

'Iron*fist*,' Gotrek snapped.

Biter grinned. 'I thought Iron*fist* was mad to station us there, away from the fighting, but he's cannier than he looks, the beardling.'

'Beardling,' Felix said. 'I was under the impression that the Slayer King was older than that.'

Biter snorted. 'Who said anything about the Slayer King? I was talking about–'

Before he could finish, a grinding of stone made the survivors turn to the archway, where the wall of rocks that had seemingly sealed it off revealed itself to be a cleverly designed rotating door. As it shifted aside, a Slayer stepped through. But he was unlike any Slayer Felix had seen before – his beard was woven into five thick plaits and golden discs stamped with the scowling faces of dwarf ancestor-gods dangled from each. His scalp was surmounted by three large crests of orange-dyed hair. In his hands he clutched twin axes, which were connected to thick iron bracers on his equally thick wrists by heavy chains which rattled softly as he walked. He smouldered with a visible resentment and his gaze was hard. Behind him came a number of dwarf warriors, clad in armour and carrying crossbows.

'Garagrim,' Gotrek said. 'The War-Mourner of Karak Kadrin.'

As the words left his mouth, the new arrival's eyes found Gotrek and instantly narrowed to slits. He raised an axe and barked something in Khazalid. The newcomers raised their crossbows and, without hesitation, aimed them all squarely at Gotrek.

'Gotrek Gurnisson,' Garagrim Ironfist said. 'You will lay down your axe and surrender yourself to the justice of Karak Kadrin, or you will die here, unmourned and unabsolved.'

Felix's hand found his sword-hilt, but Gotrek's meaty paw caught it before he could draw Karaghul. 'Gotrek,' Felix said, eyes widening.

Gotrek shook his head.

'I will come,' he said. But it was evident to Felix that he

wasn't happy about it. His shoulders and arms were tense and his grip on his axe was tight. The newcomers must have noticed too, for the guards took Gotrek's axe from the Slayer and Karaghul from Felix as well. Felix, bewildered, allowed the guards to move them through the hidden doorway. Gotrek said nothing, his expression vague as he stumped along. Felix tried to talk to him, but a glare from one of the guards silenced him. In the years he'd known him, Gotrek had proven more than once that he'd rather die than be parted from his axe.

The other Slayers followed at a respectful distance, Biter leading the way, Koertig beside him. Felix didn't bother asking them what was going on. They looked as confused as he did, though one or two, including Agni, looked pleased.

Was Gotrek really so hated? They had met other Slayers on their travels, and it had seemed to Felix that wariness was built into them, as essential to dwarfs as their beards. But what if it was something else? What had Biter called Gotrek – Doom-Thief? Was that what this was about?

He looked at the Slayer. Gotrek looked tired. Not weak or fatigued, not in body, but in soul. His eye held little of its usual intensity, and his hands, normally active with pent-up energy, were balled into tight fists. Felix knew the Slayer was angry as well, but it was a smouldering anger, rather than the more usual volcanic rage. Something was going on. But until someone chose to fill him in, he wasn't going to know what it was.

Felix took the time to examine his surroundings. Baragor's Watch was a forbidding place, even once inside the walls. The keep was a thing of crude design, though whether that was by intent or happenstance, Felix couldn't say. There was none of the sturdy beauty of the dwarf holds here – this was a foundry of war and trade and little else. Dour and effective, it needed no grace, much like its inhabitants.

On the walls, horns sounded and drums beat, the echoes of the noise thrumming with vibrant power through the stones beneath his feet. Warriors were on the wall and the clash of weapons was loud in Felix's ears. Bolt throwers and grudge throwers sent death flying into the as yet unseen foe. They were moving through a covered corridor at the base of the inner wall. Felix heard the tread of feet above as dwarfs moved up steps onto the wall. The stink of fire-pots and blood choked the air. Screams and cries and howls wrestled and mingled overhead.

The corridor trembled around them as something big hit the wall. It was an explosion, perhaps, or something worse. He paused, but a nudge from one of the guards set him to moving again. Dust sifted down into his hair and across his shoulders. Gotrek looked upwards longingly. 'We should be up there, manling,' he said.

'Honour is for those who deserve it,' Garagrim said. They were the first words he'd spoken since he'd ordered them taken into custody. Felix looked at the War-Mourner; he was slimmer than Gotrek, and younger, though by decades or centuries, Felix had no way of telling.

'And you and your father would know all about who deserves what, aye?' Gotrek said, with a hint of his normal quarrelsomeness.

Garagrim stopped and spun, gesturing with one of his axes. 'Better than you, Doom-Thief,' he growled.

'I'm no Doom-Thief, princeling,' Gotrek rasped.

'What you are is yet to be decided, son of Gurni,' Garagrim said, turning away.

Felix watched the exchange in silence. He caught Biter's eye, and the cheerful Slayer shrugged, obviously at just as much of a loss as Felix himself.

They left the corridor behind and Felix felt relieved, just for a moment, to be out in the open air, away from the stifling tunnels. Then, the smell of war hit him, and the yearning to find cover quickly replaced the relief. They were in the inner keep of Baragor's Watch, Felix judged. The sky overhead was black with smoke. The noise, previously somewhat muffled by the rock surrounding him, now gave full vent to its fury and he winced. Dwarfs not on the walls were hard at work, tearing down the by-comparison flimsy houses and businesses of the human population of Baragor's Watch. Felix had been surprised at first when he'd learned that men and dwarfs lived in such close proximity anywhere outside the Empire, but it made more sense now, knowing that the former were confined to this bastion. Karak Kadrin was a centre of trade famed far and wide, and there was a substantial human community in the outer fortress, including businesses of various sorts. That the dwarfs tolerated such bespoke the relatively cosmopolitan nature of the Slayer Keep.

The humans who'd owned those homes and businesses were refugees now and were streaming across their path in a less-than-orderly queue towards the portcullis that allowed passage from the inner keep of Baragor's Watch to Karak Kadrin proper. There were hundreds of them, men and women and children, and Felix felt a stab of pity for them. How many had lived here all their lives, only to now lose the only home they'd known? 'Where are they all going?' he said.

'They're seeking refuge in the hold. There are spaces in the lower levels where they will be put on boats and sent down the Stir back where they came from,' Garagrim said, in what Felix suspected was smug satisfaction. 'For too long, these humans have dirtied our stoop. This invasion was a blessing, according to some.'

'Like you, beardling?' Gotrek said. Garagrim ignored him. He ordered some of his followers forwards and they moved to clear a path through the refugees in a less than kindly manner. Felix's palm itched for the hilt of his sword as he saw men and women shoved aside by the dwarfs and separated heedlessly from their loved ones.

Biter thumped his mace into an open palm. 'War-Mourner, might we trouble you for a bit of relief from guard-duty?' he said.

Garagrim looked at the surviving Slayers and frowned. 'If you would go, go. Or stay, I care not. The Engineers' Entrance has been effectively sealed, thanks to Gurnisson's rashness.' He glared at Gotrek, who matched Garagrim's two eyes with his one.

'It was a pleasure, Gurnisson,' Biter said, saluting Gotrek with his weapon. 'Come, Remembrancer. It's time for you to watch me kill various and sundry things.'

'My joy knows no bounds,' Koertig muttered, hefting his axe. He slumped after his capering Slayer, the image of dejection. Gotrek looked similarly stricken, watching his brethren in madness go to war.

'It was hardly rashness,' Felix said, stung on Gotrek's behalf. 'And better it is sealed than sit inviting attack as it was, I'd have thought.'

'What you think is of no concern to me, human,' Garagrim said haughtily. 'Only my father's wishes matter.'

'Then let us cease yapping and see him,' Gotrek rumbled. 'I grow weary of your company, beardling.'

Garagrim flushed and his axes twitched. Was Gotrek trying to provoke him? But before Garagrim could reply, something arced up over the walls and crashed to the street, hurling flaming potsherds in every direction. One of Garagrim's warriors fell, his armour wreathed in sticky flames. Felix rushed towards the fallen dwarf and whipped off his own cloak, thinking to smother the blaze, but Gotrek grabbed him.

'Leave it, manling, there's no putting out a fire of that sort. You'll just burn with him,' the Slayer rumbled as the dwarf died. Alarm bells were sounding in the city. More flaming pots crashed down and liquid fire crawled between the cobbles of the street. Horns wailed and the relative order of the refugees had dissolved into madness as people ran as fast as they could towards the supposed safety of the next wall. The dwarfs, in contrast, were heading towards the noise, faces set and weapons ready.

'What is it? What's going on?' Felix said.

'They've gotten through what's left of the outer wall,' Garagrim snarled, clashing his axes together in frustration. He looked at Gotrek. 'I have no time to deal with you, Doom-Thief, and it seems you'll get your wish.' At a barked command, his warriors returned his and Gotrek's weapons. 'To the wall,' Garagrim roared, raising an axe high.

'Let's get to the wall before all of the enemy are dead and the beardling changes his mind,' Gotrek said eagerly. He shoved Felix along and they joined Garagrim as the War-Mourner led his followers towards the steps which led to the parapet of the inner wall.

'I don't think there's any danger of that, more's the pity,' Felix muttered. Garagrim and his warriors were already climbing the stone steps leading to the top of the closest section of the inner wall, where great grudge throwers hurled stones and massive bolt throwers fired into the unseen ranks of the enemy. Felix followed Gotrek, his heart thudding in his chest, his hand on his sword hilt.

As they reached the top, he could make out the shape of Baragor's Watch better. From these walls, narrow stone walkways spanned across the keep towards the final wall. The parts of the outer fortress which were above ground were designed like a series of ever-shrinking half-rings within half-rings. Invaders would be forced to breach two great walls and cross the inner killing grounds before they could even attempt to assault the final wall that separated Baragor's Watch from the bridge to Karak Kadrin. Felix passed a number of dwarfs who were pulling back to that wall. Some carried only their weapons while others were manoeuvring war machines off their rotating platforms and dragging them to platforms set further back. When he mentioned it to Gotrek, the Slayer grunted, 'Ironfist is canny. If Baragor's Watch falls, he'll need warriors in place to cover the retreat.' Gotrek said the last as if it were a dirty word.

'And the war machines?' Felix said, watching as a group of dwarfs grunted and cursed as they unhooked a catapult from its stone and metal stabilizers.

'Range, manling,' Gotrek said. 'If they get past the outer wall, they'll need to be able to fire into the keep to destroy any buildings that haven't been torn down that the enemy can use for cover or shelter. Better to see such things destroyed than touched by followers of Chaos.'

Felix frowned. There was a pragmatism to the way Gotrek said it that only served to reinforce the differences between the Slayer's people and the men of the Empire. Felix had known more than a few men who went in for burning fields and homes in order to deny them to the enemy, but they were, by and large, considered extremists. But for the dwarfs, it was a given that destruction was preferable to surrender.

Gotrek had told him more than once of entire holds that had collapsed into darkness and silence and ruin when it looked as if they'd be overrun.

For men, where there was life, there was hope. But for dwarfs, hope was secondary to honour, and seemingly no dwarf sought a better life when a good death was easily available. They were a fatalistic people, but stubborn in that fatalism. Hope was compromise, and for the dwarfs compromise was weakness. Thus, they had no hope and no reason to surrender, even when the odds were stacked so high a giant might not see the uppermost.

Following the Slayer onto the parapet, Felix again contemplated what strange set of circumstances had set him in Gotrek's wake. Did the dwarf fatalism extend to Gotrek's own desire for a grand death? That didn't seem right. Gotrek appeared hopeful, at times.

Maybe that hope was part of his shame. Or maybe it was something he allowed himself now that he was outside of the rules and strictures of orderly dwarf society. Felix shook his head. Or maybe Gotrek was simply suicidal and mad.

At the top of the parapet, a vista of horror unfolded before Felix like something out of a nightmare. He looked out over the serried ranks of the enemy army, and his breath died in his lungs and all thoughts and musings over honour and hope vanished from his mind. 'Sigmar's oath,' he whispered.

It seemed as if a howling sea was crashing against the walls of the inner keep. The ruined shapes of the lower wall thrust up crazily from the depths of that sea, and as Felix watched, a section crumbled, collapsing atop the invaders with a roar of grinding stone. The remaining Chaos troops didn't seem to have noticed, or else didn't care.

They stretched as far as the eye could see: a rolling,

ever-shifting tide of enemies. Chaos marauders and Norscans charged towards the wall that Gotrek and he now stood on, chanting the names of their dark gods. Grisly banner poles jutted from that morass of moving bodies, heavy with skulls, scalps and ruinous icons that stung Felix's eyes, even from a distance. Many warriors carried hideous looking siege-ladders crafted from what could only be giant bones and strange metals and sinews on their shoulders, while others wielded great torches to light the way. Some of the latter were sent whirling into ruined buildings, where the wood quickly caught and blazed high, casting a grotesque light over the invaders. They seemed undeterred by the steep slope between one wall and the next, and chanted as they ran. Chaos hounds threaded through their feet, loping alongside their human masters, and giving voice to terrible bays full of un-canine like ferocity. The heavy, ponderous shapes of mutated trolls and bellicose, monstrous ogres forced their way through the press eagerly. At the head of the horde, the heavy, armoured shapes of the Chaos warriors led the way, silent and inevitable. Some wore black armour, others brass or virulent crimson, all the colours of savage death and brutal violence.

Felix sucked in a breath. They looked unstoppable, inexorable, like an oncoming storm. Part of him wanted to flee, to find a hole and pull the earth in over him and wait for this all to pass. But one look at Gotrek sent his fear fleeing. The Slayer stood on the parapet, legs braced, axe extended before him and he bellowed an extensive litany of curses, in Khazalid as well as several languages that Felix didn't recognize, at the onrushing Chaos troops.

A moment later, the siege-ladders struck the stone and the barbaric shapes of Chaos marauders clambered up them, screaming blasphemous prayers. As soon as they set foot on the parapet, Felix was subsumed into the frenzy of battle. A bellowing Chaos marauder, his face almost featureless amidst the scrawled scars that covered him brow to jowls like a mask, swung a rusty axe at Felix's head as the siege-ladder he rode crashed against the parapet. Karaghul slid easily from its sheath and Felix chopped down. His blade sank between the marauder's neck and shoulder and screeched as it grated against the single rusty pauldron the barbarian wore.

The warrior slumped back, only Karaghul's bite keeping him from toppling backwards into those of his companions who were climbing the siege-ladder. Felix grunted and jerked the sword loose. The marauder disappeared, only to be replaced by another. Then Gotrek was there, shouting in harsh joy as his axe swept out, beheading the next warrior to try his luck on the wall.

More ladders settled on the parapet. Hundreds of marauders surged up the bones, throwing themselves on the defenders with brute abandon, seemingly not caring whether they lived or died. Felix was momentarily adrift, his sword lashing out automatically at foes he barely had time to glimpse before they were gone, the only sign of their presence the blood on his hands and face.

Soon his arms burned and ached as he cut and thrust with mechanical repetition, killing in a dull fog. For every Chaos marauder who fell, another seemed to take his place. Had every attack been like this, Felix wondered? The sheer mindless ferocity to the assault was mind boggling. Surely no army, not even one made up of Chaos-worshipping savages and daemon-worshippers, could sustain this sort of savage pace. But bad as it was for the attackers, it was worse for the defenders.

The dwarfs were doughty enough, but they were not many.

Even the Slayers among them were like rocks in the tide and not entirely stable ones, and as Felix watched, a Slayer screamed wildly and hurled himself over the parapet, into the maw of battle. Instinctively, he sought out Gotrek. He hoped the Slayer wouldn't be tempted to do the same.

Gotrek had climbed atop the parapet and was roaring, 'Come on, scum! Come to Gotrek! My axe thirsts!' Warriors rushed to answer his challenge. Two siege-ladders dropped towards the Slayer, snarling warriors crouched atop them, spears in their hands. Gotrek chopped his axe into the stone of the parapet and reached out. The heads of the ladders slapped into his waiting palms and he gave a grunt of exertion, his muscles straining. For a moment, Felix feared he would lose his balance, and he stretched out a hand. The spears of the warriors on the top of the ladders stabbed out, one skidding over the flesh of Gotrek's shoulder. Felix struck, slicing the weapons in half and leaving their wielders staring in stupefaction at their broken weapons. A moment later, Gotrek gave a great heave, sending the ladders hurtling away from the wall. Those warriors still clinging to them screamed as they were carried away from the wall and disappeared into the successive waves of the horde.

Another ladder slapped against the wall in front of Felix, forcing him to jerk back. He stepped forwards and drove his shoulder into the edge of the siege-ladder, his flesh crawling at the touch of it. Strange runes had been carved into it and he felt an unnatural heat emanating from it. 'Gotrek, help me!' he shouted.

Gotrek reached out with one hand and gave the ladder a shove. It slid sideways, carrying its cargo with it. A fire-pot struck the wall nearby, and Felix twitched as a wash of stinging heat caressed him. 'There must be thousands of them,' he said.

'The more the merrier,' Gotrek said, uprooting his axe. Felix turned, looking for the others. Garagrim and his warriors had moved to the centre of the wall, where the fighting was heaviest. The prince's axe flashed out, sweeping the head from a screaming warrior as Felix watched. Then, from within the guts of the horde, horns sounded. As if in reply, from a high dais on the wall, a dwarf blew a large, curled horn.

As they watched, the seemingly endless horde, improbably, impossibly, began to retreat. Not out of fear, Felix knew, but simply because their momentum had been broken. A dulled edge needed to be re-sharpened. They left their dead heaped where they lay, retreating in grudgingly good order. Champions, marked by the gods, stood and shouted parting imprecations at the defenders before turning and trotting after the rest. Gotrek spat over the side of the wall. 'They'll bring up the siege-weapons,' he growled.

'Aye, but they're done for now,' Garagrim said, marching towards them. 'We have unfinished business, Gurnisson. The king waits, and you shall see him.' Felix stepped back, only to be nudged forwards by one of the dwarf warriors. Garagrim, without waiting for either of them to reply, turned on his heel, leading the way towards the palace of the Slayer King.

5

The Worlds Edge Mountains,
the Valley of Karak Kadrin

Canto cursed for the fifth time in as many minutes as he watched Hrolf's lieutenants battle each other for the honour of taking control of his warband. They were a hairy, uncouth lot, Vargs and Sarls for the most part. Norscans, rather than marauders, like Kung and Yan. The latter stood beside him, watching the ritualized idiocy with apparent glee.

'So the idiot cur finally got what was coming to him, eh?' he cackled, touching a burned patch of flesh on his arm. 'Good, more glory for the rest of us.'

'Why aren't you with Kung, seeing to the assault?' Canto said, not looking at him. A Varg named Gurn roared and stamped, and the pulsing tendril that replaced his left hand shot out, undulating around the scaly throat of another champion, this one a bloated cannibal clad in ragged armour that barely fit his overly muscled and bulky frame, named Harald the Lean. Harald grabbed the tendril and bit down, sinking scissoring wide, shark-like fangs into it. Gurn yelped and jerked his arm back, flinging Harald to the ground.

'Because Kung enjoys scaling walls and I don't. Besides, there are more profitable things to be done,' Yan said, flexing his scorched arm. 'That's why you're here, after all.'

Canto glanced at his fellow Chaos champion. Yan grinned at him. 'I know you, Unsworn. Always seeking the advantage, looking to make allies. You're here to get Hrolf's replacement, whoever it is, on your side.'

'And is that so unheard of?' a deep voice gurgled. Both champions turned as two stunted, broad shapes stumped towards them. The face of the first was obscured by a featureless iron and brass mask; a heavy black beard, curled and bound into worm-like plaits, hung below it, fanning out across a deep chest hidden within a heavy cuirass of blackshard iron. The Chaos dwarf wore the heavy armour of the Infernal Guard, and carried a large axe. The axe's cruel blade was wreathed in runes of torment and death and it steamed and hissed as if it were fresh plucked from the forge.

It was the second who had spoken. Unlike the first, his face was uncovered, revealing cruel features the colour of fire-blackened stone to the world. Thick tusks jutted from his mouth and small horns protruded from his broad brow over eyes that glowed like forge-struck sparks. A wide, spade-shaped beard, divided into oiled and curled ringlets, jutted from his thick chin. More disturbing than the tusks were the thin cracks that ran through the flesh of his face, and the red light that seeped from them. He wore heavy-looking armour covered in strange runes and grotesque gargoyle faces. Khorreg the Hell-Worker, Daemonsmith of Zharr Naggrund, smiled at the two Chaos champions, displaying teeth the colour and shape of obsidian shards. 'Indeed, I had feared that none of you possessed even the slightest modicum of cunning, manling,' the Chaos dwarf sorcerer croaked, nodding to Canto.

Khorreg was the leader of the small party of dawi zharr whom Garmr had hired for use of their war machines. The Hell-Worker had accompanied the bulk of said engines to Karak Kadrin to oversee their proper testing in battle, leaving two of his assistants to oversee the rest with Garmr. The silent, masked dwarf beside him was called Khul, Canto thought, though he'd never heard the Ironsworn speak.

Canto had known Khorreg for longer than was entirely pleasant to consider. The creature was not a friend, never that, but familiarity formed its own bonds. It was Khorreg who had crafted his armour, and Khorreg with whom he'd bartered slaves for weapons and devices. And it was Khorreg whom he'd saved in a moment of black cunning at the Battle of Seven Towers, when the vast fortress-leviathans of the dawi zharr had been swept aside by the daemon-princes of the Arashem Conflagration. Canto had acted as Garmr's envoy to Zharr Naggrund, bargaining with his old acquaintance for use of the war machines that even now pounded the walls of the dwarf fortress.

Canto returned Khorreg's nod. 'You have it?' he asked. Khorreg grinned and extended the cloth-wrapped bundle he held. Canto took it and quickly unwrapped it, exposing a black-bladed sword that glistened with vile runes and sigils. 'Beautiful,' he said.

'A toy,' Khorreg said, mouth twisting in what was supposed to be a smile. 'Barely worth the effort, Unsworn.'

'Nonetheless, you have my thanks, Khorreg,' Canto said gravely, settling the sword in his sheath. It fit perfectly, and he grunted, happy to have a replacement for the sword he'd lost in the shaft.

'It's not your thanks I want, Unsworn,' Khorreg said. 'The second of my debts to you is settled.'

Canto inclined his head, ignoring Yan's look of suspicious curiosity, and turned back to the fight. Gurn was on his back, jerking and choking as Harald gnawed at his throat. The gods had blessed Harald with an unholy resilience and a strength that rivalled Hrolf's own. Harald rose from Gurn's twitching body and raised a bloody fist in triumph. Then he pointed a crooked finger at the next challenger, a thin, slim-muscled creature called Alfven, whose apparent youth was belied by the cold, calculating look in his unnaturally bright eyes. 'Come, stripling,' he hissed, gnashing his teeth. 'Come get in my belly.'

'All the better to have your heart, Lean one,' Alfven purred, stepping forwards lightly. His armour was less bulky than that of his fellows, though equally baroque and, it was said, oiled with the unspoiled blood of virgins, though where he'd found them nobody could say. Long hair, greased with blood and offal, hung down his back, tied into a single serpentine lock. His sword hummed like a wasp as it sliced up across the palm of Harald's too-wide hand as the latter groped for him.

'I'll bet two horses and a hound on the pretty one,' Yan said gleefully, rubbing his scarred hands together. Canto said nothing. He had already calculated Alfven's chances. Harald was a brute, like his late unlamented master, and lacked the finesse and skill of his current opponent, though he did out-match him in raw strength. But strength alone did not make one the strongest, and only the strongest could lead a war-band within Garmr's horde.

But, determining who was the strongest was never a simple thing, nor a quick one. Chaos warbands were disorganized things, little more than ambulatory battles where everyone happened to be moving in the same direction. Scouts had reported that tribesmen had already begun killing each other in the crags around the hold, fighting over territories not yet earned. Such was the way of it, and where one group was annihilated, two more waited to take their place.

Canto shook his head. There was still a wall between them and the object of their siege and their forces were being bled white the longer the dwarfs held out. He needed Hrolf's men, now more than ever; especially considering that the Dogsson had gotten himself buried in his own trap. Canto had barely made it out alive. He touched the mark on his cuirass where the dwarf's axe had gouged him. He felt no shame in his flight from the dwarf, nor any regret. The dwarf had been mad, obviously. Practically foaming at the mouth, and that axe... There had been something about that axe that set his hackles to bristling. It hadn't been a normal weapon, and the dwarf who'd wielded it as if it weighed no more than a feather had been no normal dwarf.

Canto knew about Slayers. He'd even killed one, once. They barked and howled like broken-backed wolves and fought like devils, but they were mortal, and they died easily enough. But that one hadn't. He was something else, something that had terrified Canto to his very core.

He knew enough to listen to his fear and to flee when the fight turned against him, even if flight meant hurling himself into the void. It had only been by sheerest luck that he had slammed into something solid and managed to climb back out into the light.

Khorreg had seen his gesture, and stepped closer. The Chaos dwarf smelled of burning metal and ash. 'Proper blackshard iron, this,' he rasped, running stubby, probing fingers across the mark. 'To mark it thus must have required great strength and magic, or both.'

Canto grunted. 'Yes. He's the one who did for Hrolf, I'd wager. Little one-eyed maniac.'

Khorreg grunted. 'One eye,' he murmured. 'An axe, was it?'

'Yes,' Canto said, stepping away from him. 'Quite a big, unpleasant one.'

'The best ones always are,' Khorreg chuckled, grinning nastily. 'Oh, that's unfortunate.'

Canto looked and saw Harald sink to his knees, his thick arms held tight to his belly in a doomed attempt to hold his guts in. Alfven took his head a moment later and gave the still upright body a contemptuous kick. The handsome champion spread his arms and flashed a smug smile. 'Come, who will challenge me? You, Skrall, or perhaps you, Hrodor?' he asked, gesturing to two of the other champions.

Skrall wore a horned, featureless helm and his body was twisted with overlapping scaly plates the colour of dried blood that seemed to grow through the gaps in his armour. Both of his arms terminated in festering, boil-covered bone spikes that glistened with blood and serum. Hrodor was comparatively normal looking, clad in heavy armour festooned with spikes and ridges, and he wore no helm, exposing a hairless head studded with dozens of iron nails that formed strange, nauseating patterns.

'The gods are watching us,' Alfven said, smiling widely. 'Bow or fight.'

Both of the remaining champions stepped back after sharing a look. It was a wise move, Canto knew. Alfven was an old hand at challenges such as this, and the Blood God doted on him. Alfven laid the flat of his sword across his shoulder and turned, eyes blazing with infernal pride. Yan gave a wordless shout of encouragement.

Canto moved, quicker than any of them could react. He lunged forwards, one hand on his sword hilt. It sprang out of its sheath even as he slid past Alfven. The handsome champion lurched forwards, shocked. He staggered around, mouth working, his hand trembling as he reached up to touch the thin red line that grew around his neck. Then, with a ripping sound, Alfven's head toppled from his shoulders. Canto twitched the blood from his new sword and sheathed it.

Yan stared at him in shock. Khorreg wheezed laughter and clapped his hands. Canto looked at the remaining champions. 'I am Canto the Unsworn. I serve no god save ambition, no master save necessity. Follow me or you will be served thus.' He kicked aside Alfven's head as he turned and rejoined the others. Yan frowned at him.

'You cannot do that! Alfven won his challenges! The Dogsson's warband was his by right.'

'Unless you're planning to challenge my actions, Yan, I'll thank you to shut your mouth and rejoin your men. We have a fortress to take and we have wasted enough time with this spear-shaking ritual nonsense,' Canto grated, not looking at him. 'Garmr has charged us to take this fortress and I will do so, with your help or without it.'

Yan growled wordlessly and strode off, one hand on his falchion, leaving Canto with Khorreg and Khul. Behind them, Canto's new lieutenants fell to squabbling over the armour and weapons of their dead companions. Soon enough, Alfven's fine armour and sword would decorate the frame of another warrior, as would the gear of Gurn and Harald. Canto left them to it.

'Well done, Unsworn,' Khorreg said, his weird eyes glittering with malice and cunning. 'You are cunning indeed. Almost as cunning as my people.'

'High praise indeed,' Canto said in a tone that implied anything but. If Khorreg took offence he gave no sign. Instead he gave another gurgling chuckle and he turned his gaze towards the fortress keep. Horns blew as Kung pulled the horde back. 'One wall left.'

'There will be nothing left, if you let me unleash my pets,' Khorreg said. Canto grunted at the mention of 'pets'. The Chaos dwarf was talking about the siege-giants he'd brought from Zharr Naggrund. The idiot brutes had been the work of the daemonsmiths of Zharr Naggrund; Garmr had traded a thousand captives for each of the beasts, and they were, next to the Hell-Worker's war-engines, some of the Gorewolf's most prized weapons.

'And then you can get your engines in position to attack the hold proper?' Canto asked. Khorreg smiled cruelly.

'If your warriors can hold the bridge, we can knock down our cousins' paltry walls. But we must do so quickly. If they have time to fall back, they will destroy the bridges that lead to the hold, and your army will be trapped on this side, now that the Underway is lost to us.' Khorreg looked at him. Canto nodded. The Chaos dwarf was right, of course. With the explosion that had killed Hrolf, they had lost access to the Underway. Barely a score of men had escaped the subsequent collapse of the caverns, and they were still down there, as far as he knew. There was no way to retrieve them, and he wasn't inclined to waste time doing so in any event.

It would take too much time to burrow through those collapsed caverns, time they didn't have. If Garmr were here, perhaps, but he wasn't and there simply weren't enough men to simultaneously see to clearing the tunnels as well as taking the walls of the outer keep. If they lost the bridge as well, the siege was as good as done. The dwarfs could sit behind their walls forever, and Garmr's forces would tear themselves apart out of boredom.

'Bring your pets up, Hell-Worker,' Canto said. 'That fortress must *fall*.'

Baragor's Watch,
Karak Kadrin

The palace occupied part of the central plaza of the inner keep. Like the rest of Baragor's Watch, it was a thing of hard angles and rough artisanry. It had been built as a fortress within a fortress, rather than a place of opulence and comfort. It reminded everyone who entered that the fortress was the first line of defence from any assault from the north. Gotrek had mentioned once that the king used it for greeting guests away from the sacred confines of the hold proper. Here, Ungrim Ironfist could meet with foreign dignitaries, merchant-princes and the like, without risking the secrets of Karak Kadrin.

The throne room was large, almost grandiose in its sweeping, vaulted ceiling. Pillars lined the entryway and led the eye to the throne of the Slayer King. That the king had chosen to meet them here, rather than someplace more sensible given the circumstances, told Felix that whatever was going on, it had more weight than he'd first thought.

Around the throne was arrayed a small bodyguard; not Slayers these, but elite hammerers, as the dwarfs called them. Heavily armoured and wielding two-handed war-hammers, they looked capable of taking on twice their weight in opponents. Felix was momentarily bemused by the thought of acting in such a capacity for a king who had taken the Slayer's Oath. Were the bodyguards there for his protection, or to keep him from getting himself killed? Was there any difference?

The Slayer King was a brooding, squat figure, seated upon a throne of stone, gnarled fingers tapping out a martial rhythm on the armrests. Like his son, Ungrim Ironfist was a Slayer, though in deference to his title and position, he wore a weighty crown which cast some slight shadow on his heavy features. His nose was thin and hooked, like the beaks of the eagles that inhabited the peaks and crags of the mountains, and his eyes burned with a feverish intelligence. When he spoke, his voice was as deep and as resonant as the Mourning Bells of the Grand Temple of Morr in Altdorf.

'Greetings, Gotrek, son of Gurni. Greetings, Felix Jaeger,' Ironfist said. The words and tone were measured and polite, in contrast to Garagrim's snarling.

Felix was tempted to bow, but when he saw Gotrek remain standing, he resisted the urge. Instead, he stood just behind the Slayer, his hands at his sides. 'I am told that we have you to thank for the defence of the Engineers' Entrance,' Ironfist went on. 'Though in an unorthodox fashion,' he added.

'Good riddance,' one of the hammerers said. He was as broad as he was tall, and had the heavy white length of his beard tucked into his wide leather belt.

'Snorri, Son of Thungrim,' Ironfist said, gesturing. 'He is my hearth-warden and Reckoner. My right hand, even as my son is my left. It is on his counsel that you stand here, Gotrek, son of Gurni. His and that of Oleg Axeson, priest of Grimnir, warden of the temple.'

'Axeson,' Gotrek muttered, his eye flashing. His knuckles popped as his massive hands clenched.

'Aye, you know him, and he knows you, Gurnisson, and neither of you have much liking for the other, of that I am well aware.' Ironfist leaned forwards on his throne. 'But it is because of that dislike that I heeded his words. He asked that we send a messenger to you, before...' He gestured. As if to emphasize his point, another thunderous boom sounded. The hammerers shifted uneasily. 'Well, but it seems that won't be necessary now.' His eyes glittered. 'You are here and they are here and it seems the portents were correct.'

Gotrek blinked and said, 'Portents?'

Felix felt a chill sweep through him at the word. He thought he heard something, just at the limits of his hearing. A throaty, purring laugh that demanded he risk a glance. But he saw nothing save the shadows coiling in the spaces between the great pillars. Nonetheless he could not shake the feeling that his every thought and action was being observed.

'Portents and prophecies, Gurnisson, that concern you and us, and the army that currently sheds its foul blood on our walls,' Ironfist said.

'Where did it come from, if I might be so bold, mighty king? This army, I mean? We heard nothing about it travelling from Stirland,' Felix said. Rumours travelled fast on the rivers, carried by peddlers and merchants and mercenaries. And Chaos armies were notorious for being less organized military undertakings than natural disasters, spilling over into neighbouring lands like a spreading wildfire. Even this far from the Empire, the rumours of its movements should have been flying fast and thick through frontier towns like Wurtbad.

'Why would you have?' Garagrim spat. 'They besiege us, not your precious provinces.'

Ironfist raised his hand and his son fell silent. He looked at Felix with a measuring gaze. 'They keep to the crags, these ones,' he said finally. 'They do not stray far afield, as such forces are normally wont. They are unusually focused, and on Karak Kadrin. We first got word of them some weeks ago, and we sent a throng to deal with them. In vain, as it turned out. They perished, to a dwarf.'

Gotrek was silent. Then he nodded. 'So what's this got to do with me, then?'

'Everything, unfortunately,' a deep voice growled. Felix turned.

The dwarf who'd spoken was as broad as Gotrek and his face looked as if it had been set into storm-clouds, such was the sheer mass of silvery-grey hair that he possessed; though from his features, Felix thought he was too young for it, even for a dwarf. His beard was forked and curved, jutting out like a defensive palisade, and his eyebrows were parapets. He wore thin robes over a heavy, ornate cuirass. From the front of the cuirass, a symbolic representation of Grimnir's scowling features glared at them. From that, Felix knew he was the priest that Ungrim had mentioned.

Oleg Axeson matched Grimnir's scowl when he caught sight of Gotrek. 'Well, I see you're still alive,' he said as he strode past Ungrim's guards, who made no move to stop him, to join them.

'Not for lack of trying,' Gotrek grunted.

'Try harder,' Axeson said.

Gotrek growled and his axe twitched in his hand. Garagrim stepped forwards, before Gotrek could reply. 'I have brought him, Axeson, as you asked.'

'I see that, Garagrim,' Axeson said. Garagrim's cheek twitched. 'And you didn't bring him. He came of his own will, didn't you?' Axeson looked at Gotrek, eyes narrowed speculatively.

Gotrek glowered at Axeson, but said nothing. Uncomfortable, Felix stepped forwards. 'If I might be so bold, why did you ask King Ironfist to send for us?'

Axeson glanced at him, as if surprised he could speak. 'I

didn't ask him to send for you, human. Just Gurnisson,' Axeson said harshly.

Felix flinched at the tone. Axeson seemed to be an equal opportunity insulter, and he wondered whether perhaps he had found a dwarf even more irascible than Gotrek.

Gotrek stepped forwards. 'Talk then, *priest*,' he said. Had Gotrek hesitated before that last word? Felix looked at the Slayer.

Axeson frowned. 'Have you put your name on the pillar in the Temple of Grimnir yet, Gurnisson?'

'What does one have to do with the other?' Gotrek said, knuckling his eye-patch. 'No, I haven't, as you well know.'

'Aye, you haven't. You were never one for tradition, were you?' Axeson said.

'Is that why you brought us here?' Felix asked, before he could stop himself. Gotrek didn't look at him. Axeson smirked.

'Of course it wasn't, human. No, Gurnisson came because he couldn't do otherwise, not when there's doom on the wind.'

Gotrek stared at Axeson. 'What doom, priest? Stop talking in riddles or else–'

'Or else what?' Axeson said. 'Will you smash the life from me, Gurnisson?' He stepped close, his beard bristling, and for a moment, Felix wondered whether Gotrek would. Gotrek's eye widened slightly and he stepped back, shaking his head. Axeson's expression changed then. The sneer faded, and Axeson looked away, almost ashamedly. Something had passed between them, Felix knew, but he couldn't say what, and for a moment, just a moment, a surge of jealousy possessed him.

It wasn't the first time that some hint of Gotrek's past had been teased before him, some moment, frozen in time, that he would never be allowed to examine. Mostly, he didn't think about it. It served no purpose other than idle curiosity. But other times, the need to know was almost overpowering. Did Axeson know Gotrek's shame? Did he know what crime had set Gotrek on his current path? Was that the source of their mutual dislike? Felix knew that if he were foolish enough to ask, he would never receive an answer.

'The Skull Road,' Axeson said. 'What do you know of it?'

'It is the road of retreat,' Gotrek said. 'We walked it when the coming of Chaos drove our people south.' Felix had heard the term before, though only rarely, and only from dwarfs. The path that led into the Worlds Edge Mountains from the Chaos Wastes was a road few travelled and fewer still returned from.

'Some clans call it Grimnir's Road,' Ironfist said, softly.

Axeson nodded. 'Aye and it is at that.' He looked at Felix. 'Do you speak for this manling, son of Gurni?' Gotrek nodded once, brusquely. Axeson grunted and went on. 'The skulls the road is named for are not ours, or those of elves or men. They are the skulls of daemons and those foul things which marched beneath the banners of Chaos. They are the skulls which Grimnir took on his last march north.' Axeson shook his head. 'Grimnir cut through the very stuff of Chaos, and made order from it, in that place. He bathed those lands in the blood of daemons and drove back the Wastes.'

Felix's mouth was dry. As Axeson spoke, he could almost see that which he described. In his mind's eye, he saw one lone dwarf, pitting himself against the entirety of Chaos, and forcing it back, mile by painful mile, through sheer determination and ferocity. He glanced at Gotrek and the others and knew that they were seeing something similar in their heads.

'Grimnir made a road of skulls into the north, and disappeared. And now, something has come south, following the same route and bringing ruin with it.'

A chill mass settled in Felix's gut. He had seen the horrors of Chaos before, far too closely for his liking. He wanted to speak but couldn't. Gotrek didn't have that problem. 'And what has this to do with me?' he said, almost hopefully.

'Nothing,' Axeson said. The word echoed in the silence of the temple. 'In fact, you shouldn't be here at all.'

'What do you mean by that?' Gotrek snarled, a vein pulsing in his head. His own eye bulged and blazed with barely restrained fury. 'Speak, priest, what do you mean?'

Before Axeson could reply, there came the deep, rolling sound of a war-horn. It echoed through the temple, and King Ironfist sat up straight on his throne, cursing. Felix couldn't tell the difference between one horn blast and another, but the dwarfs reacted as if this one was different to the others. 'What is it?' he said. 'What's going on?'

'It's another assault,' Garagrim growled, hefting his axes. 'A big one,' he added, smiling crookedly at Felix. 'Gurnisson's stunt in the Underway must have annoyed them.'

'So?' Gotrek snapped. He glared at Axeson. 'Get back to this doom of yours, priest!'

Ironfist and his son were already heading for the doors, the hammerers marching in formation around them. There was neither discussion nor argument. They simply moved as one, knowing their priorities instinctively. Ironfist paused at the doors and turned back. 'Son of Gurni, if you are interested in a doom, there will be more than one on the walls!' he called out.

'Listen to him, Gurnisson,' Axeson said, locking eyes with Gotrek. It was something few others had ever done, and Felix found himself quietly impressed with the aged priest. 'I will still be here when you are finished.'

'Maybe I will find my doom here,' Gotrek said, not looking away.

'Do you really believe that?' Axeson said.

Gotrek flushed. His teeth surfaced from his beard, flashing in a tiger's grimace. He was working himself up to a killing fury, Felix knew. 'Gotrek,' he said. Gotrek hesitated, and then looked away from Axeson.

'Let's go, manling,' he said, stumping past. 'I want to kill something.'

Felix made to follow him. A hand on his wrist stopped him. He looked down at Axeson.

'Keep him alive, Remembrancer,' Axeson said quietly. It wasn't just a warning, he thought, but almost a plea. Felix blinked, suddenly uncertain. Gotrek was already gone, following the others. Felix nodded jerkily in reply to the grim-faced priest and hurried after the Slayer.

6

Worlds Edge Mountains,
the Peak Pass

'Tell me of the road, Grettir, and you will live another day,' Garmr said to his cousin, as he stood atop the war-shrine and placed another skull. It was the fifth today, and it was still red and raw and wet.

At the foot of the shrine, Grettir gazed hatefully up at his enslaver and said, 'The road is blocked, as it was yesterday and the day before, cousin.'

Garmr grunted, one steel-shod finger tapping the skull. 'Karak Kadrin still stands.'

'Of course it still stands,' Grettir spat, hauling at the chains that held his slim form bound to the altar. He was, or had been, a tall man, as tall as Garmr. Now he was hunched and broken from years of being dragged behind the war-altar he was chained to. More chains criss-crossed his chest and arms like a harness, making it hard for him to move or even breathe. His robes, once fine and the colours of magic itself, were now soiled and stiff with grime. His hands were locked in taloned golden gauntlets and they flexed as if aching to unleash the magics which were his birthright. Instead, the fingers curled into tight fists and he glared at his cousin's back through the hundred and one eyes which blinked on the surface of his crystal mask.

'Of course it still stands,' he said again. 'It stands because you dragged half of your army away to do… What? What are we doing here, cousin?'

Garmr glanced at Grettir. 'So much spite, Many-Eyes,' he murmured. 'What a warrior you would have made.'

Grettir snarled wordlessly and jerked at his chains. Garmr chuckled and turned back to the skull. He ran his fingers over it, tracing sharp patterns in the red. Then, abruptly, he turned and strode down the eight stairs of the altar and jerked his axe free from where he'd embedded it in the ground. With one hand he grabbed Grettir, and with the other, he swung the axe down, severing the chains that held the sorcerer tied to the altar.

The war-altar and shrines sat amidst the ragged camp that the army had created amidst the crevices and crags of the Peak Pass, and the nooks and crannies of the nearby mountains were now stuffed with skulls. Garmr had collected thousands since he'd left the far north, and their placement was the careful work of weeks. Auguries had been cast, and each skull had its place. Some had been set into the ground like paving stones. Others had been hung from the scabrous trees which clung stubbornly to the hills. Still more had been placed in cracks in the stones of the slopes. Eight had been nailed to the walls of a long abandoned dwarf outpost. Three had been hung carefully from the neck of a wild griffon, though it had cost the hanger's life to do so. The creature had gone mad, bucking and screaming, and flown off.

Orcs and worse things occupied these peaks, and his army had spent their time here well. There were enemies aplenty, including the servants of lesser gods. Garmr glanced to the side as he hauled Grettir along. A lithe warrior, hermaphroditic and alluring even now in its agony, dangled from a roughly constructed wooden 'X'. Shreds of black robes and the ragged remnants of pink and cerulean armour hung from its androgynous form as it strained against the brass spikes set into its hands and feet.

The Slaaneshi had attacked soon after they'd begun to travel up the serpentine length of the Peak Pass. They had a fortress here, in a fallen dwarf hold somewhere in the deep mountains, many hundreds of miles to the north. Hundreds of hell-striders, men with coruscating tattoos, riding hideous daemon-things that were more serpent than horse and more woman than serpent, had ridden down on Garmr's army in an orgy of violence, accompanied by scything hellflayers and screaming seeker chariots. Horsemen had clashed in the narrow crags, and Garmr himself had brought this one, a rival champion, down, shearing through the neck of its mount with one blow of his axe.

It had put up a semi-respectable fight, even then, leaping and slashing with its wailing, weeping spear. Garmr had easily silenced the spear's noise and had beaten the champion to the ground. He'd considered killing it then and there, and taking its skull, but the potential for future amusement had stayed his hand. They were fragile, the Slaaneshi, but they recovered quickly enough.

Garmr stopped, looking up at it. It snarled down at him, a long, serpentine tongue extending from its lamprey mouth, the stinger on the tip jabbing uselessly at the air between them. Garmr laughed. 'Look at it, cousin. Look at the weakness that it embraces.'

'One man's weakness is another man's strength, cousin,' Grettir said. Garmr looked at him, his gaze unreadable behind his snarling helm.

'What would you know of strength?' Garmr asked softly. 'You chose the path of weakness, cousin. Our tribe would spit on you.'

'You mean if you hadn't slaughtered them?' Grettir spat. 'You mean if you hadn't butchered every single one of them, including my wife and children, your nieces and nephews – *our kin*!'

'It was an honour. Their skulls are the roots of the road, cousin.' Garmr stared in incomprehension at the cursing sorcerer. 'They would have understood.'

'What would you know about it?' Grettir barked, throwing Garmr's words back into his face. 'I cast my lot with the Changer to find a way to teach you the error of your ways, cousin. I sold my soul for vengeance.'

'You sold it cheaply then,' Garmr said, chuckling. 'The Changer delivered you into my grasp quickly enough. You should be grateful I didn't simply kill you out of hand.'

'I'll make you wish you had,' Grettir snarled.

'Maybe. But until then, you have your uses. Bring a beast,' Garmr roared out, dragging Grettir into the centre of the camp. 'I would speak to my servants.'

Slaves wearing little more than scars and collars hustled to obey; one of the massive gorebeasts, mutated animals fit only for labour, war or slaughter, was jerked forwards on heavy chains by dozens of slaves. It shrilled as it was hauled from the traces of the chariot it had been attached to and thrust out with its horns and talons. Its porcine jaws slammed shut on a slave who got too close and the man's howl of agony was cut short as he was flung into the air and trampled beneath the creature's claw-hooves. It bucked and kicked, crushing bone and pulverizing men with every wild motion.

Nevertheless, the slaves managed to drag it towards Garmr, who shoved Grettir to the ground and raised his axe. The gorebeast shrugged the slaves off with a last burst of frantic strength and gave a deafening grunt as it charged forwards. Garmr didn't move. As the beast drew within an arms-length of him, Garmr's axe crashed down, splitting its brute skull from crown to chin. The beast dropped to the ground, dead on the instant. Its back legs lashed out, once, and then it was still.

Garmr pulled his axe free and gestured. Slaves hurried forwards, grabbing the beast's legs and hauling it over onto its back. Garmr put a foot on its chest and split its sternum with another stroke of his axe, opening its chest wide. Then, at a slight motion, warriors lunged forwards, grabbing several slaves before they could scurry away. A gibbet, heavy with meat-hooks and iron chains, was wheeled forwards and the struggling slaves had their arms lashed to their sides and their ankles tied together as they wailed and howled. Then, one by one, they were hung upside down on the gibbet, their heads dangling over the gaping cavity of the dead beast's torso.

'Ekaterina,' Garmr said. 'Fill the bowl.'

The sharp-toothed woman slid forwards through the crowd, holding a curved blade in one hand. With practised efficiency, she slit the throat of each slave in turn, cooing and gently scolding the next in line as she did so. Blood spilled into the dead beast, overflowing its split ribcage. When each slave was silent and draining, Ekaterina stepped back, her tongue caressing the dagger's blade.

'Work your witchery, cousin,' Garmr said, looking at Grettir. 'Show me what I wish to see.'

Grettir leaned over the blood-soaked carcass, grunting in distaste. His clawed fingers cut the air above the blood, swirling it. Garmr watched intently, hungry for something he couldn't quite put his finger on.

The hunger, the *need*, had been with him for centuries as mortals judged such things. He had spent what seemed like millennia wreathed in the comforting savagery of the eternal battle which raged across the northern pole. Garmr had fought his way there from the lands of the Kvelligs, butchering hundreds in the process. He led armies and warbands and marched alone when no one else was left. He had clawed his way ever northwards, drawn by the scent of the Blood God's breath.

Farther and farther north he went until he entered the mad cacophony of the Eternal Battle, where immortal armies waged unceasing war. Brazen fortresses rose over blistered veldts of hairy flesh and plague-clouds spurted from brightly-hued rocks. It was everything he could have wished.

There, amid the cosmic blood-letting, Garmr had earned the title 'Gorewolf', bathing in seas and messes of blood, piling skulls to Khorne. And it seemed to him, in those heady days of war, that Khorne's fiery gaze fell upon him and found his efforts good. As Garmr's strength waxed, so too did his prestige. Chieftains and captains and heroes flocked to his banner, killing each other just for the chance to serve him. He roamed the Wastes, spreading the Gospel of Murder.

But it had not been enough. It was never enough.

'I can drink an ocean of blood, and my belly will not burst,' Garmr murmured. It was something Hrolf was fond of saying, and for Garmr it was the truth. He looked away from Grettir's display. It would take time for his cousin to shape his auguries. Every minute not spent in pursuit of Khorne's will felt wasted and the urge to kill rose in him. It was a sign that he was favoured. And why would he not be favoured? Was he not the Gorewolf? Had he not taken the skulls of the mightiest champions? Was he not the one who had defeated the King of Skin and the Howling Queen? Had he not taken the spine-ring of the Gynander? Had he not bound the Slaughter-Hound?

At that thought, he shifted slightly, feeling the red haze of the Slaughter-Hound as it prowled the crags nearby. Brute-thoughts, mere bursts of desire and frustration, sizzled up and down their mental link, enhancing his hunger for battle. The Slaughter-Hound was always hungry. It was always angry. It existed in a state of constant *berserkgang*, never calming, never sleeping, but only killing, even as he once had.

It was not a thing of Khorne, not really. And yet Khorne had gifted it to him. Khorne had led him to it, had delivered Grettir into his hands, giving him the tools necessary to bind it. It was as much a part of Garmr as Hrolf's beast was of him.

Ulfrgandr, the Slaughter-Hound, the Great Beast of the Tenth Peak, whose jaws had cracked the scales of Scaljagmir the toad-dragon, and whose claws had shredded the Storm-Pillars of the Mountainous Hierophant. The beast whose heart now beat in time to his and whose bloodlust he could feel. It was unstoppable and immortal and as a consequence, so too was Garmr. Bound to the beast as he was, he was unkillable as long as it lived. And there was nothing short of Khorne himself that could slay the Slaughter-Hound. His fury fed the beast and calmed the red tides that washed his soul. It took the war-madness from his eyes and let him see the world clearly.

It had let him see that the world was not enough. There was

more to be had. There were greater battles, wars undreamt of by mortal man, waged on worlds far from this, against enemies unseen. An eternity of slaughter beneath the stars was what he wanted.

The Eternal Battle was what he desired, not just to participate, but to spread it. He would banish the barriers that kept the Chaos Wastes confined and the Eternal Battle, the war without end, would spread with the Wastes, engulfing the wide world in a conflagration of cosmic proportions. Khorne would teach men new ways to revel and rejoice and kill and the world would become a cinder, burned clean by unceasing slaughter. A battlefield as wide as the horizon, and enemies everywhere, that was what Garmr wanted. That was what all of this was for.

Warriors murmured. Garmr's eyes snapped open. Grettir's ritual was reaching its crescendo.

A pillar of blood had risen from the dead beast's carcass, coruscating reds and browns that shimmered with buried images. Grettir dragged his talons through the shimmering column, painting the air with great sweeps of blood that did not splatter or fall. At his gesture, the bones of the carcass punctured the flesh and rose with splintering cracks and crunches, forming a floating ring that spun about the column of blood like a halo, and intestines draped over the broken bones like decorations. The creature's hide ripped and spread like a carpet and faces that hissed and babbled in a hundred different tongues rose on the mangled hide like blisters. The bones cracked and shed layers, unravelling like scrolls as strange writing was scratched into them by unseen talons.

Grettir stepped onto the carpet of faces and tapped the bone-scrolls with the tips of his fingers, and then sank his arms into the column of blood. His hands moved and worked at something unseen and faces and words formed in the viscous liquid, showing distant events.

He saw his army crash like a wave against the high walls of the outer fortress that barred their path, surging and retreating as the dwarfs met them and forced them back. He saw cramped tunnels. He saw a one-eyed dwarf, and an axe cutting contrails of fire in the dark. He saw it all and he let loose an anticipatory breath.

'Is he the one?' he said. 'The Doom-Seeker?'

Grettir dropped his hands and the blood slopped downwards, splashing over everything. Bones fell and the faces diminished with soft, lingering sighs. 'Who can say, cousin?' he said. He looked at Garmr. 'Why not ask your god yourself, cousin, since you two are so close–'

Garmr's hand slashed out and Grettir toppled backwards, falling into the mess of the dead beast. 'Even my tolerance has limits, Grettir. There are sorcerers aplenty, should I require one.' Before Grettir could reply, Garmr turned away and stalked towards his tent, his mind occupied by the image of the one-eyed Slayer.

Was he the one?

Yes. Yes, he had to be. Why else would he have seen him in the augury? Yes. He was the one. Garmr would take his skull. And then the road would be complete and the world would drown in War Everlasting.

'Skulls for the Skull Throne,' he said.

Karak Kadrin,
the Walls of Baragor's Watch

Outside the palace, the air had darkened. More smoke, augmented by the crackle of flames. As he stepped away from the doors, Felix saw more dwarfs heading for the walls. The tide of refugees seemed undiminished, and he feared what would happen if the wall fell before they were through the last portcullis. It would be a slaughter of monumental proportions. 'How are they going to get them all across in time?' he said.

'We will buy them the time in blood,' King Ironfist said, almost cheerfully. 'That is what dwarfs do best, Felix Jaeger. We sell lives to hold back the inevitable.' His hammerers had formed up around him in a phalanx and they started towards the stairs that would take them to the parapet. 'It will be glorious, manling, glorious!'

'I haven't seen Ungrim that happy in a long time,' Gotrek said grimly.

'Well, he is a Slayer,' Felix said.

'Aye,' Gotrek said, after a moment. 'Let's go, manling, there's no sense in letting him have all of the fun.'

'You say that like it's a bad thing,' Felix said, as he followed the Slayer. The parapet was crowded with dwarfs, most of whom were sitting down, resting after the stresses of the last attack. Grudge throwers and bolt throwers sat silent and ready, and keen-eyed crossbowmen picked off Chaos marauders who got too close to the wall. On the wide landings set below the parapet at regular intervals, dwarfs gathered around cooking fires and drank ale and beer and gambled, even as warning horns sounded and others struggled to get back to their posts.

Biter was the centre of attention in one of the latter groups, flinging bone dice with more energy than skill and crowing over every roll whether it was successful or not. Felix watched the Slayer for a moment, wondering what shame crouched in him, driving him. Had he always been so boisterous, or was it, like Gotrek's reticence, a facet of the life he had chosen?

'They retreated into the cover of the lower wall after that last sortie, but they're ready for another go, by the look of them,' Biter called out as Gotrek and Felix climbed past him.

'Good,' Gotrek said loudly. 'So am I.'

Garagrim and his warriors were already atop the parapet, when they reached it, looking down at the heaving mass of Chaos marauders, who seemed less concerned with the enemy before them than each other. As Felix reached the top, he looked down. The Chaos forces had, for all intents and purposes, carved a canyon through the lower wall of Baragor's Watch, steadily knocking holes in each section of wall and spilling through those gaps into the next ring of the fortress. They had paid for their methodical advance in oceans of blood, but such losses seemed only to have inflamed them, rather than sapping their courage.

'What in Sigmar's name are they doing?' he said as he looked down. Below, Chaos marauders fought each other with as much fury as they'd shown the dwarfs. A closer look showed him that not all of them were involved, but only select groups. Champions, he supposed. 'They'll finish each other off at that rate,' he muttered.

'They're followers of the Blood God, manling,' Gotrek said, leaning over the parapet to watch. 'When no enemy is at hand, they'll tear their own guts out just to see some blood.' The Slayer spat and turned away. 'Like as not, they're simply deciding who'll lead the assault,' he said.

Felix didn't reply. His attention had been caught by a heavily armoured man who stood on a collapsed section of the fourth wall and watched the sprawling combat playing out below him, his posture one of attentive satisfaction. Felix studied him. He was a big man, with a serpentine length of beard that hung down to his waist, the end capped with a round ball. His hair was loose and whipped around his head like a black halo in the breeze. His armour was crafted of thick, stained plates and his gauntlets rested on the haft of the large axe planted head-first on the wall between his feet.

'Offhand, I'd say it's him,' he said, gesturing. Gotrek snorted.

'Aye, likely you're right.' He peered at the distant champion and pursed his lips. 'He'd make a fight, by the look of him.'

'He's mine, Gurnisson,' Garagrim said, striding over to join them. He puffed out his chest. 'I am War-Mourner of Karak Kadrin and it is only fitting that the leader of the enemy be my doom.'

'If you get to him first, beardling, be my guest,' Gotrek said, grinning insolently. The grin slid from his face as he looked back towards the fallen wall. As Gotrek spat a curse, Felix followed his gaze. A duo of heavy machines was being pulled through the gaps in the wall by a number of ogres. The brutes were heavily scarred and their limbs were chained together, and there were cruel-looking collars about their thick necks.

Suddenly, the air was filled with a particular sort of tension. Every dwarf on the parapet, Slayer and clansman alike, had a look of intense loathing on their faces. Mutters and curses slipped quietly into the air. Felix looked from the dwarfs back to the devices, which he thought must be the war machines of the enemy. The engines were harsh-looking things, heavy with what he thought were unnecessary scalloped blades and scything edges. One was recognizably a cannon of some sort, while the second machine appeared to be some form of bolt thrower. The ogres pulling them had the dull look Felix associated with broken farm animals, beasts used to the lash and the chain. Regardless, they still looked fully capable of ripping a man's head off with one twist of a meaty paw.

Felix wondered what it was about the machines that had

set the dwarfs off, but before he could even attempt to frame the question, the reason became obvious. Two squat figures stumped into view through the ruined section of third wall to join the machines. They wore coats of dark, burnished mail and cuirasses of complex design. Heavy helms sat on their squat heads, and great beards flared out from their jutting chins. One carried a heavy glaive, while the other rested his palms on the butts of the two pistols holstered around his waist. Their faces were twisted into expressions of brutish malice and cold-blooded glee as they surveyed the obstacle before them.

Felix felt a rush of horror fill him as he stared at the twisted mockeries of dwarf-kind. His mouth felt dry and he looked at Gotrek. The Slayer's teeth were exposed in a snarl that conveyed the millennia-old grudge of the dwarfs for their corrupted kin. Felix had heard dark legends of such Chaos dwarfs, though he'd never attempted to broach the subject with Gotrek, thinking the former merely a slanderous myth and not wanting to antagonize the latter.

'Gotrek,' he said softly. 'Are they–?'

'The dawi zharr,' Gotrek spat.

As Felix watched in horrified fascination, the Chaos dwarfs saw to the placement of their war machines. A whip was uncoiled and snapped, directing the ogres. The cannon was a massive construct of iron and brass that seemed to growl and shake in its traces like a beast of prey as the ogres shifted it into position behind a bulwark of toppled stone. The great chains used to move it were then attached securely to the ground by iron stakes and the furnace attached to the rear was wrenched open by an ogre. A burst of predatory heat escaped from it, washing over the ogre and sending the poor beast into paroxysms of agony. It fell to the ground, its body cracked and blistered. The Chaos dwarf with the pistols stomped towards the groaning ogre and drew one of his weapons, an expression of annoyance flashing across his barbaric features even as he shot the brute in the head. At a barked command from the Chaos dwarf, the dead ogre was swiftly torn apart by his fellows, whose gleaming, sweat-streaked muscles bunched as they each grabbed a limb and twisted. Then each chunk was tossed into the waiting furnace. Felix looked away as more bodies, Chaos marauder and dwarf alike, followed.

That there were masses of Chaos marauders between the cannon and the wall did not seem to concern the Chaos dwarfs. Steaming liquid dripped from the end of the cannon's barrel and it melted the stone of the ground where it fell.

The second device was smaller than the other, but Gotrek's grunt of concern caught Felix's attention. 'Rockets,' the Slayer said, scratching his beard. 'No wonder they got through the walls so quickly.'

'Aye, Gurnisson,' Garagrim said. 'They can clear a parapet with one of those.'

'You should have led a sortie to destroy them when you had the chance,' Gotrek spat. Garagrim flushed and half raised his axes.

'We did,' Ungrim said, bustling towards them, his axe balanced on his shoulder and the thumb of his free hand tucked into his belt. A cloak of dragon scales hung from his shoulders and his crown gleamed in the weak, smoky light of day. 'But the dawi zharr can repair those devices of theirs as quickly as we can spike 'em. Not to mention that they've never brought them this close to our lines before today.' The King of Karak Kadrin hawked up a gobbet of spit and sent it sailing over the parapet. 'No, they want to be in at the kill now, the bastards.'

'How long have you known that they were out there?'

Gotrek said, almost accusingly. Ungrim frowned.

'Does it matter?' he said, looking towards the machines.

Gotrek's scowl spoke volumes. But before he could reply, the air was split by a whistling shriek that had everyone groping to cover their ears. A moment later, a thunderous boom cracked the sky and then, farther down the parapet, a huge chunk of stone was blasted free, carrying dwarfs with it to their doom. The whole wall shuddered from the impact and Felix nearly lost his balance. 'What in Sigmar's name was that?' he shouted.

'Mortar,' Gotrek roared. 'There's a Grimnir-be-damned mortar out there somewhere!'

As if that had been the signal he had been waiting for, the Chaos leader lifted his huge axe in one hand and flung out his other towards the fifth wall. He roared out a single word that Felix needed no one to translate for him. With a communal roar that shook him down to his bones, the Chaos forces launched themselves to the attack.

The dwarfs responded swiftly. Signal horns wailed and crossbows and handguns spoke, dropping the first ranks of the attackers as they sought to clear the distance to the wall. The withering hail of fire did little to diminish the Chaos marauders' enthusiasm. Fallen banners and siege-ladders were scooped up from the hands of the dead and dying by those who trampled over them, and the armoured shapes of Chaos warriors chivvied the mortals along, urging them to greater speed with hoarse, hollow bellows.

More dwarfs joined those already on the parapet. Ungrim marched up and down, shouting out encouragement and orders in a booming voice. The dour being that they had met in the palace had been replaced by an eager berserker, Felix realized with a chill. Garagrim took up position amongst his men and clashed his axes over his head in an eagerness that rivalled his father's. He began to sing a war-song, his voice carrying with more strength than rhythm.

For his part, Gotrek waited silently, his eye locked on the enemy commander. As Felix watched, the Chaos champion stalked down towards a waiting bodyguard of malformed, armoured shapes. A moment later, they joined the flow of bloodthirsty bodies sweeping towards the wall, their banners lost amongst the sea of such that rose and shook over the army. Gotrek grunted and shook himself. He gave Felix a grin. 'Prophecies be damned, eh, manling? Give me a battle any day.'

Felix didn't reply. His blood had frozen in his veins. With a shaking voice, he said, 'Gotrek, look. What are those things?'

Titanic shapes loomed over the warriors scrambling ahead of them towards the walls. They shoved their way through the ruins, scattering rubble in their wake. They were immense, far larger than any living thing had a right to be, and when they roared, the sky itself seemed to shiver in fright. The lumpy, awkward figures strode forwards, heedlessly crushing men with every step. They were clad in piecemeal armour, and great plates were seemingly riveted to their gangly limbs. Faces that were yards across squirmed and grimaced in berserk pain within cruel helmets.

As he watched in growing horror, a bolt thrower on the wall fired, sending an arrow the size of a man towards one of the giants. The bolt struck the overlapping armour plates and shattered, the force of the blow barely staggering the monstrosity. Indeed, it only seemed to spur the beast and it roared and stumbled forwards, raising its arms to reveal that its hands had been cruelly amputated and replaced with massive steel hook-blades that looked as if they could pull apart stone.

Another beast had a set of flails attached to its forearm stumps, each length of chain tipped by a weighted iron sphere. It jerked its arms and the flails swung ponderously. The third had wide-bladed pick-axes, each as large as an ore-cart, chained to its gauntleted hands and it clashed them together in a discordant cacophony as it stomped forwards.

In addition to their weapons, each of the monsters wore a heavy harness of chains and ropes that swung about their legs. As Felix watched, the boldest among the men who ran around the giants' feet clambered up the ropes and chains with wild shouts. The walls trembled beneath Felix's feet with every step the creatures took.

'Siege-giants,' Gotrek said, and spat. 'Prepare yourself, manling. They intend to tear this wall apart and us with it.'

The giants stomped forwards, their cries of mingled anger and agony washing over the defenders. Felix wanted nothing more than to run, to jump down from the wall and to go elsewhere. Anywhere was better than here. Gotrek, in contrast, seemed to be right where he wanted to be.

'Grungni, they're huge,' a dwarf said in a horrified voice.

Felix turned to see the dwarf stepping back from the wall, his eyes wide. He held his axe loosely, as if he'd forgotten he had it. He saw Felix looking at him and he said, 'How do we beat them?'

'You fight,' Garagrim snarled, hooking the dwarf's arm with the curve of his axe. Blood ran in thin rivulets where blade met flesh, and Felix felt a stab of pity.

'Leave him,' Gotrek rumbled.

Garagrim glared at the other Slayer. 'Who are you to give me orders, Gurnisson?'

'No one,' Gotrek said, stepping past Felix. Garagrim stepped back, pulling his axe away from the dwarf, and Gotrek took the latter by the bicep. His eye narrowed. 'When we were crafted, fear was not part of our forging,' he said, so softly that Felix almost didn't catch it.

The dwarf looked at him, mouth open as if he wanted to reply. Gotrek met his questioning look squarely and said, simply, 'Turn around.'

The dwarf stiffened and turned back to the wall, his jaw and throat working, his eyes wide. Garagrim met Gotrek's gaze and nodded sharply. Gotrek grunted and turned back to the wall, his eye on the giants. Felix noted, however, that the taciturn Slayer stayed within grabbing distance of the dwarf. Whether perhaps to prevent another outburst, or simply to provide some form of comfort, Felix couldn't say.

Then, there was no more time to think of anything save survival. The fastest of the siege-giants had reached the walls, its flails lashing out in wide, wild blows. Vast swathes of ancient rock were scoured from the wall as the weapons connected and the parapet was cracked and shattered in that first explosive stroke. Dwarfs were sent hurtling from the wall, their bodies bent and twisted by the force of the blow. Shrapnel filled the air as the giant set about methodically smashing the wall and those who stood upon it to flinders.

Felix ducked beneath a flying chunk of stone and ran to join Gotrek as he charged heedlessly towards the monster, his lips peeled back in a wild grin. A length of chain cut the air with a whistle and Felix felt it pass just over his head as he hunched low. This close, the giant stank of decay and he felt sickened as he saw that its armour had been riveted to its very flesh. Blood and pus wept from the joins and seams of its armour as it struck about it with its flails. No wonder the brute was in pain.

The massive sphere topping one of the flails struck the parapet in front of Gotrek, splintering the stonework. The Slayer didn't stop. Instead, he propelled himself into the air, through the cloud of dust and stone shards. His axe licked out, chopping into rust-riddled armour plating. And then he was in the air, hooked to the giant's arm as it brought its flails back for another blow. Felix didn't stop to watch. He leapt straight up as a second set of flails skidded across the parapet just beneath his feet, and landed awkwardly, pain shooting up his leg. The chains rasped as the giant pulled them back, but Felix was already moving. Crossbows thrummed as dwarf quarrellers fired at the beast.

The second giant had moved off, and the great hooked blades it had in place of hands chopped straight through the wall before becoming lodged in the stone somewhere in the middle. As the beast struggled to free itself, the men who'd caught a ride on its chain and rope-bedecked harness swarmed up and across it onto the damaged wall.

Felix moved towards them, leaving the giant to Gotrek. Once again, he thought of Axeson's words, but he brushed the thought aside. There was little he could do to help Gotrek in any event. Karaghul vibrated in his hands as he brought it down on a hastily interposed shield made of crudely beaten metal, with strange glyphs and markings scattered across its surface. The warrior who bore it shoved Felix back with a growl and struck at him with an axe. Felix gave a frantic shout and grabbed the man's matted beard, and jerked his head down against the stone of the parapet. His head cracked like an egg.

Behind them, the siege-giant howled. Felix turned and saw that Gotrek had reached the rounded shoulder-guard and that his axe was buried in the giant's cheek-guard. As he watched, Gotrek wrenched his blade free and chopped it in again. He was hacking at the armour, trying to get at the creature within.

Marauders were climbing up towards him, intent on stopping him from killing their living war machine, or perhaps just intent on killing Gotrek.

Something grabbed him and jerked him aside even as a sword looped towards him. 'Watch yourself, Jaeger. If you lose your head, Gurnisson will be inconsolable, I have no doubt.' Felix turned and saw the gleam of metal teeth. The Slayer called Biter smiled up at him and then whirled him out of the way so that he could lunge past him with his mace. A Chaos marauder slumped, head burst like a melon. 'Glad you could join us,' Biter continued, flicking blood from his weapon.

'Wouldn't have missed it,' Felix grunted.

'That's the spirit!' Biter said cheerfully. 'Oh look. More toys!'

Felix looked. Behind the siege-giants, siege-towers had been mobilized. They were, like everything else the enemy had constructed, brutal-looking things, built heavy and impossibly vile looking. They were pulled by teams of mutant spawn and mutated trolls, who roared and gibbered as they dragged the towers towards the wall. There weren't many of them, but with most of the defenders concentrating on the trio of giants, they were unopposed as they drew close to the walls.

The third giant drove its shoulder into the wall further down, close to where King Ironfist had made his stand. The massive pick-axe in its hand slashed out, not at the rock, but at the dwarfs who stood on it. The armoured body of a hammerer flew backwards from the wall. Ungrim roared out a dour chant as his axe flashed, chopping through the haft of the giant's weapon, shattering it. The giant screamed in rage and its second pick-axe sank into the parapet with a crash. With a jerk of its deceptively gangly limb, it tore a section of the wall away and flung it heedlessly behind it. A siege-tower exploded, caught in the wrong place at the wrong time.

Ungrim didn't seem perturbed by this display of monstrous strength. He tossed his axe to his opposite hand and snatched up the hammer of one of his fallen guards. With a snarl worthy of the beast he faced, he crushed the skull of a marauder who'd dared to try the parapet.

Garagrim howled as he flung himself at the second giant. His twin axes clashed against the giant's blades, causing it to jerk away from the wall. Felix heard the screams of the warriors it crushed beneath its heels. Then his view was obscured as a siege-tower smashed into the cracked and shattered parapet. Biter gave a pleased bark as the ramp dropped and marauders leapt out, almost as eager as the Slayer who went to meet them.

Felix saw Koertig wade into the warriors from the side. Biter's Remembrancer fought without his charge's glee. Felix could sympathise. He knew what it was to be pulled in the wake of a Slayer. It required a certain flexibility that he thought the Nordlander struggled with. Dwarfs hurried to join the duo in repelling the enemy. Felix left them to it, even as another tower joined the first. As the ramp fell, he set a foot on it and charged in. Biter followed him with a whoop.

In the sweltering darkness, Felix sliced Karaghul across the line of snarling faces. He had no thought save preventing any more of the enemy from getting onto the wall. A giant roared and there was a crash that shook the tower. *What's left of the wall*, Felix thought grimly. Biter was screaming curses as he thrashed and battered at the marauders. Felix tried to protect the wild-haired Slayer as best he could.

A serrated spear-blade dug at him, opening a line along his face. One more scar for the collection. Warmth spilled down his neck and he stumbled, falling back against the wall. The spear came for him again, stabbing into the wood and bone of the tower.

With a stupefying crash, the top of the tower was ripped free by a tornado of slithering chains. The spearman was gone, ripped into the sky by the giant's flail. Felix sank down, watching as the flail slashed down again, taking half of the siege-tower with it in a cascade of splintered wood and bone. The giant had staggered into the tower and was jerking and lashing out wildly, screaming in agony.

Gotrek clung to its head, one hand gripping the cheek-flap of its helm. The flap was attached to the flesh of its jowl, and every flex of Gotrek's muscles pulled it painfully taut. The Slayer wielded his axe one-handed, slashing at the marauders who crawled like fleas across the giant's shoulders and chest. A Chaos marauder was struck and he screamed as he was catapulted off the giant, trailing red.

'That's the way, Gurnisson! Ha-ha!' Biter howled, shaking his mace. The siege-tower shuddered, already beginning to come apart thanks to the giant's blow. Felix and Biter made it off just as the tower gave a groan and slumped, crashing down to the ground in stages. Another tower burned merrily, but there were more Chaos-worshippers on the parapet than off. The wall shuddered again as the hook-claw-armed giant tore single-mindedly at the stonework, despite the wounds Garagrim's axes had made in its arms and shoulders. The War-Mourner himself was occupied by marauders, who swarmed around him, stabbing and hacking, trying to bring the princely Slayer down. Garagrim cleaved through ragged furs and primitive armour, but he was steadily pushed away from the giant despite his best efforts.

Biter caught Felix's eye. 'You handle yourself, Jaeger?'

Felix nodded brusquely. 'Go help him,' he said. Biter grinned and charged wildly towards the struggling knot centred on Garagrim. Felix swatted aside a heavy blade, nearly numbing his wrist in the process, as a marauder frothed at him. Karaghul spun up and across and the marauder staggered back, clutching at his face. Felix moved past him, pushing the wounded warrior over the parapet with his elbow as he went. It wasn't strictly honourable, but as far as Felix was concerned, honour went out the window when it was life or death.

Gotrek had surmounted the siege-giant's head. His axe drew sparks as he hammered at the helmet, seeking to crack it. The giant was no longer concerned with the wall; instead it pawed vainly at its head with its wrist stumps, its flails clattering as they struck its armour. It staggered away from the wall, and for a moment Felix feared that it would carry Gotrek out amidst the enemy. Then, the helmet split in two with a screech, tumbling from the giant's head, tearing flaps of skin and scalp as it did so. The giant stiffened and gave an agonized shriek. Gotrek had one hand dug into the raw morass of the giant's head, holding on for dear life. His axe came up and slammed down, right at the central point of the crown of the giant's skull. Its shrieks became slurred and it staggered forwards, straight towards the section of wall Felix was occupying.

Felix threw himself out of the way as the monster collided with the wall, dislodging stone and shaking the edifice down to its roots. It collapsed, head and shoulders over the parapet, its flails striking ineffectually against the stone. Gotrek, still perched on its head, jerked his axe free and struck home again. The giant thrashed but it seemed unable to pull itself up. Gotrek roared out an oath and struck a third time. The giant gave a wheezing whine and went limp. A death-stink billowed from its massive carcass, washing over Felix, causing him to gag. Gotrek dropped off it onto the parapet. He was breathing heavily, and his entire frame was streaked with blood and sweat and grime. He grinned at Felix. 'That one took a good bit of killing,' he said. 'Too stupid to know when they're dead, these big ones.'

'Sounds familiar,' Felix said.

'What was that, manling?'

'I said things look bad,' Felix said. The wall was swamped; organized defence had given way to chaotic melee. Despite the dwarfs' best efforts, the siege-giants had done their work and done it well. Whole sections of the wall were shattered and split by the war machines of the Chaos dwarfs, and Chaos marauders poured through the gaps on horseback or on foot, howling as they entered the inner keep.

The final wall had fallen.

7

The Worlds Edge Mountains,
the Peak Pass

Ekaterina spun, her curved blade licking out like the tongue of a serpent. The Norscan howled as she opened his guts to daylight. His companions backed away, nervous. The dying man sank to his knees and she used him as a springboard, lunging for the next. He narrowly blocked her blade, his eyes wide with fear. She could smell the stink of his weakness and it infuriated her. She hissed and bent back, hooking his ankle with her foot. As he fell, she split his skull. The third man screamed and charged. His axe lopped off a lock of her hair as she jerked her head out of the weapon's path. Her sword caught him in the belly and with a cruel smile she dragged it upwards, angling to avoid the heart.

He gasped and slid off the blade. She watched him writhe dispassionately. His next few moments would determine his final fate. In satisfaction, she watched him flop forwards and try to lift his axe.

She walked around him, tracing the circumference of his scalp with the tip of her sword. 'You are as brave as you boasted, Artok. Maybe you are worthy at that.'

He gave a wordless roar and swiped clumsily at her. She stepped on the flat of the axe and drove it down, and pierced his eyeball with the tip of her blade. With a casual shove, she perforated his brain and then retracted her sword smoothly. Artok toppled, dead.

Around her, the horde set up a roar. Weapons rattled and men shouted until they were hoarse. The madmen harnessed to the war-altars shrieked and snarled, pawing at the air. Ekaterina traced her fingers through the blood on her blade and stuck them in her mouth as she stepped over the bodies and sauntered towards her master.

The thought set a snarl rumbling in her belly. No man was her master. Not even a man like the Gorewolf. Once, maybe, he might have been, but she knew better now. There was only one master, and her oaths of loyalty to him were of sterner stuff than any foresworn words to a mortal warlord.

Garmr sat slumped in his throne-altar, watching her, his eyes as unreadable as ever. The lupine features of his helm resembled those of the leering face she saw sometimes in her dreams, but Garmr was only a pale imitation of the god he professed to serve.

'Well?' he said.

'Two skulls for the road, my lord; the third stank of fear.'

Garmr grunted. She licked her fangs. 'I have tested them, as they wished, and found two more step-stones for our Lord Khorne to march upon.'

Garmr nodded. At a lazy gesture, men scrambled forwards, skinning knives in their hands. Swiftly they set to work, freeing the skulls from their casings of flesh. The third body was dragged away, to be fed to the beasts. Ekaterina glanced at Grettir, who squatted, as always, beside Garmr's throne like a malevolent toad. The eyes on his helm blinked in strange patterns and made her queasy if she looked at them for too long.

That Garmr had not yet killed the creature was incredible. They needed no sorcerers for their task, and she could feel Khorne's displeasure thrumming through her every time Garmr sought his cousin's auguries. But Garmr insisted on keeping the maggot alive. It was a folly on his part, one of many.

Garmr jerked on Grettir's chain, pulling the sorcerer off his feet and into the dust. 'Tell me of the road, cousin. Tell me what I wish to hear,' he rumbled.

'It is not yet complete. The skulls of barbarians, brave or not, you have aplenty. You lack keystones, cousin,' Grettir spat. 'I have told you that.'

'Have you?' Garmr snarled. 'It grows harder to pierce the veil of your mewling and glean meaning.'

Something howled, as if to echo his snarl. Horses and gore-beasts screamed and squealed as the reverberations of the cry slithered over the rocks and sent daggers of ice into the nape of every warrior's neck. Even Ekaterina shivered. The Slaughter-Hound bayed again, high in the wild crags. Something shrieked, the sound caught and buffeted by the deep, thunderous bay. A troll perhaps, or some devolved Chaos-beast following in the army's wake. Regardless, the Slaughter-Hound had it now and it would soon be nothing at all.

On his throne, Garmr shuddered, and Ekaterina knew that he was seeing what the creature saw, and tasting the blood it tasted. She remembered Garmr before he had bound himself to the beast; he had been a warrior then, all blood and fire and ferocity. But something had changed. Spilling blood for

Khorne was no longer enough for the Gorewolf. Something, some desire, ate at him. It had grown worse when he'd forced Grettir to bind the Slaughter-Hound, Ulfrgandr. In binding the beast, Garmr had lost something. His ferocity had dimmed and his love of battle had passed into the beast that loped on the far flanks, venting its fury on the world, rather than their enemies.

Garmr was no longer beloved of Khorne. She knew it, though she could not say how. She heard whispers sometimes, and the rattle of cloven hooves just out of sight. She felt hands on her shoulders, guiding her, stirring her rage to a fine white heat. Eyes like twin stars, red and dying, met hers and a soft voice, like the rasp of a cat's claws on flesh, spoke in her head and she felt powerful.

'Mistress,' a voice said.

She turned. 'Boris,' she said. Her man was bulky, his face hidden behind a leather mask. He had followed her from the dark, distant times before she had taken her destiny and throttled it, and his composure now belied his rage in battle. 'Well?'

'He sent them, as you said,' Boris growled. 'Two riders, with news of the siege.'

'What news?' she said, feeling not hot now, but an icy calm.

'They've taken the outer keep. The men said that Hrolf is dead'

She grunted and said, 'And what of Canto and the others?'

'They said nothing of Kung or Yan, but Canto demands that Garmr return,' Boris said, his disdain evident. Ekaterina's lips curled.

'Coward,' she muttered, but her contempt was tempered with thoughtfulness. The army at Karak Kadrin would fail. Garmr was counting on it, she knew. Another of Grettir's blasted prophecies. But Canto was resourceful. Cunning, even, and more so than Hrolf, especially, and he would retreat, rather than die fighting. The question was, would he return, or would he flee west or further south?

'What about the Hell-Worker?' She would not weep if the stunted ones were killed; she had little love for their clanking contraptions, and could not imagine that Khorne favoured those who used them. Two of Khorreg's assistants – daemon-smiths, they called themselves – still remained with the horde, overseeing the growling, shuddering hellcannon that the dawi zharr had brought at Garmr's request. As much as she despised the stunted creatures, she liked their war-engines even less. Something about the cannon put her in mind of the Slaughter-Hound; it was all crouching menace and bloody promise. It ached to break its chains and destroy all that lay in its path. While she could well understand its feelings in that regard, she had no wish to be in its path should it ever gain its freedom.

'He still lives,' Boris grunted. She nodded. If Khorreg fell, it was likely that the remaining dawi zharr would leave the horde. Garmr's bargain had been with the Hell-Worker alone, after all. She had intimated to Yan that if something were to happen to the Hell-Worker, it would be all to the good.

'What of the messengers?' she said.

'We did as asked,' Boris said and mimed slitting his throat.

Ekaterina nodded, satisfied. Garmr grew more impatient by the hour and every day without news drove him to use Grettir to see what was going on. The horde could sense their lord's impatience and were growing restive. The battle with the Slaaneshi had not been enough. More and more fights broke out by the day, as the warriors' bloodlust sought an outlet among their closest companions. The army would be drowning in blood within days or else be on the move, as Khorne willed.

Someone laughed. She turned and saw Grettir watching her. Garmr was preoccupied, watching the images the sorcerer had conjured in the puddles of blood spilled by her opponents. She lifted her blade and raised the sorcerer's chin with the tip. 'What amuses you so, Many-Eyes?'

'A great number of things, woman,' Grettir said, shuffling forwards, his chains rattling. He let her blade drift across his windpipe and past his jaw. 'Do you plot treachery, or aid?' he hissed. 'What thread do you pluck?'

'I serve the Blood God,' she said, stepping back. Grettir smelled of thunderstorms and sugar and her stomach lurched.

'Of course you do,' he said. 'We all do.'

'Not you.'

'Don't I?' Grettir said. 'Not willingly, I admit.'

Ekaterina chuckled and sheathed her sword. 'What do you care what I do, sorcerer?' she said.

'I don't. I am merely curious.'

'A lie,' she said.

Grettir shrugged. 'You intend to challenge him. He will kill you.'

Ekaterina's smile faded. She longed to split his skull and spill his crooked mind in the dirt. 'You have seen this?' she demanded. She immediately regretted it. That was Garmr's weakness, not hers.

Grettir chuckled. It was a wet sound. 'I see many things. This, I simply know. You are not strong enough to challenge him. That is why you are still alive,' he said.

Grettir stepped back and shuffled away, leaving her standing staring after him. Ekaterina looked at Garmr, slouched on his throne, his great helm nodding, though whether in sleep or boredom she could not say. For a moment, it seemed as if he were cloaked in the shadows of great wings. And then the moment passed and Ekaterina's hand slipped to the hilt of her sword, her fingers playing across the pommel.

She gnawed on her lip with a fang and then turned away. In the depths of the camp, she found Bolgatz the Bone-Hammer and Vasa the Lion. As she came upon them, Vasa sank curved fangs into the neck of a horse that had been strung up on chains from a tree. As the creature kicked and shrieked, he tore out its throat and chewed hungrily. He was a big man, bigger than any who followed him; almost a giant, with rolling muscles covered in fur the hue of rust, and he had the head of the beast he was named for. Feline jaws worked methodically as he chewed the meat, his eyes tracking her warily. Claws slid from his fingers as he reached for the heavy broadsword sheathed on his hip.

Bolgatz sat nearby sharpening the bone spurs that jutted from his hands with a whetstone. The Bone-Hammer had been named such for good reason; his fists could shatter armour and he had ripped beasts and men alike apart with his bare hands. Bolgatz's fame had been assured when he had crushed and eaten the contents of the skull of the great Shaggoth Hurgrim Peakgouger.

Their warbands, along with hers, comprised more than half of the remaining warriors of the horde. Like she and Canto and the rest, they had given oaths of servitude to the Gorewolf, and they chafed beneath them, now more than ever. It was easy to follow another into battle, but this sitting had frayed their tempers and weakened whatever bonds of loyalty they felt for Garmr.

'Hail, Ekaterina of Kislev,' Bolgatz rumbled. 'The Bone-Hammer greets his sister-warrior.'

'And I greet you, Bone-Hammer,' she said, inclining her head. 'And you, Vasa.'

'Woman,' Vasa said, licking his bloody jowls. 'Come to challenge me at last?'

'Not today,' she said, smirking. 'Though it is challenges I wish to speak of...'

Karak Kadrin, Baragor's Watch

Gotrek cursed, and Felix knew he was contemplating hurling himself onto the sea of enemy troops pouring into the hold. The sound of horns filled the air and Felix turned to see Garagrim hurrying towards them, his remaining men following him. 'Fall back across the bridge, Gurnisson, unless you'd like to find your doom out here,' Garagrim said stomping past Gotrek.

'Fall back? We've got them right where we want them!' Gotrek blustered.

'You mean in control of Baragor's Watch, running riot?' Felix said, hurrying after Garagrim.

Gotrek said nothing, but Felix took his silence for assent, and the Slayer followed them. Dwarfs still struggled with knots of Chaos marauders on the crumbling wall, even as most of the surviving defenders made a fighting retreat across the stone walkways that connected the two walls. War-engines rained death on the Chaos marauders pouring into the space between the walls even as lines of dwarf quarrellers and thunderers blasted those on the parapets to cover the withdrawal of their comrades. But the Chaos forces had war-engines of their own; screaming rockets spiralled into the remaining wall, opening great craters in its surface.

Felix knew with sickening certainty that the last wall would not hold for long. Not against a concentrated assault. As they joined the withdrawal, Gotrek stared longingly at the remaining two giants. 'Stay, if you wish,' Felix said, disregarding Axeson's warning to him. Gotrek shook his head and grunted.

'There is a grander doom awaiting me than this,' Gotrek said.

'Besides, it's not like you'd die anyway,' Biter said, flashing his metal teeth at the other Slayer. He and two other Slayers were standing beside the great stone bridge that connected the outer keep to the plateau of Karak Kadrin, waiting for the other dwarfs to pass them. 'Care to help us hold the last path, Gurnisson?' Biter asked. 'The engineers will need time to break the keystones and collapse the pathways, and we thought it might be a nice gesture on our part to give them that time, eh?'

'No! Let him hold some other path,' another Slayer snapped. Felix recognized him as the same one who'd first called Gotrek a 'doom-thief' in the Underway. He wore a thin harness from which a dozen metal flasks hung. Felix had a feeling that whatever was in those flasks would make someone, somewhere, unhappy.

'I go where I want to go,' Gotrek said. He raised his axe for emphasis. 'Feel free to try and stop me, Agni Firetongue.'

Agni blanched and gripped his own axe more tightly. Biter laughed. He nudged Koertig. 'Gurnisson knows the secret to making friends and influencing people, eh?' he said, chuckling. Koertig didn't laugh. The Nordlander looked exhausted, and his armour was as stained and battered as the man wearing it. Like Felix, the other Remembrancer had been in the thick of the fighting.

Felix looked at the parapet. The two remaining siege-giants

had pulled back, their job done. The last he'd seen, they were crouching some distance from the wall, eating their dead companion. Felix felt a surge of disgust, but pushed it aside. Even with the giants gone, the Chaos marauders were climbing the wall. More and more ladders and at least one siege-tower were in place and there weren't enough dwarfs remaining on the wall to dislodge them. Too, the war machines of the Chaos dwarfs were belching fire and flame. The wall separating the inner keep of Baragor's Watch from the bridge to Karak Kadrin, thick and sturdy as it was, would not last long.

Ungrim and his remaining guards were the last across, and the Slayer King looked disappointed that his advisor Thungrimsson wasn't going to let him help hold the bridge. 'You are needed elsewhere, my king,' Thungrimsson said firmly. 'Orders must be given and hearts bolstered, and that is the King of Karak Kadrin's duty.'

'Do not worry, father, I will fight for the both of us,' Garagrim said, almost gently. He placed his hand on his father's arm and Ungrim laid his own over his son's. 'And if the time is right, I will gladly die for the both of us as well,' he added. Ungrim scowled, but said nothing in reply. He didn't seem particularly happy with his son's assertion.

'And what's that about then?' Felix murmured to Gotrek.

'Ask them if you wish to know, manling,' Gotrek said sourly. He didn't seem pleased at the prospect of fighting alongside the War-Mourner. Going by Garagrim's idle glare in Gotrek's direction, Felix thought that the feeling was mutual.

'Are you planning on telling me what you did to make the prince of Karak Kadrin hate you?' he asked quietly.

Gotrek didn't reply. Felix snorted. He should have known better than to have asked the question. Dwarfs were close-mouthed by nature, but Gotrek's taciturnity was almost a weapon. He parried inquiry as easily as he did the swords of the enemy.

When Ungrim was across the path, the Slayers arranged themselves across the width of the bridge. Garagrim and Agni took one side and Gotrek, Biter and a Slayer called Varg took the other. Koertig and Felix stood behind their respective Slayers on the bridge.

The air was thick with smoke and the hum of crossbows. The Chaos marauders on the parapet were trying to regroup, but the remaining dwarfs were giving them no leeway. More of the northern warriors were climbing the interior stairs to reach the top of the outside wall, chanting as they ran. There was no strategy that Felix could see, only a blind hunger to get to grips with the enemy. The Chaos marauders didn't seem to care that the bridge was a vital strategic objective, they only wanted to wet their blades in dwarf blood.

On the whole, Felix preferred opponents who wanted to live as much as he did. It meant he stood a better than even chance of survival. He tensed, holding Karaghul in both hands. Koertig leaned on his axe, his shield hanging loosely from his arm. 'Nervous,' the Nordlander said. Felix didn't know whether it was a question, but he nodded.

'Always,' he said.

'I meant me,' Koertig said.

'Oh,' Felix said, glancing at him.

'I hope he dies this time,' Koertig muttered. He had the slightly glazed look of a man pushing the boundaries of exhaustion. Felix knew the feeling, and thought he might have the same look on his own face.

'You mean Biter?'

'Who else would I mean?' Koertig grunted. 'He's been promising me that he's going to die soon. Swears by all his little stunted gods that today is the day, but he never does.'

'Slayers can't simply *die*,' Felix said, recognizing the frustration in Koertig's tone.

'I know that,' the Nordlander spat, rapping the head of his axe against the bridge rail. 'He's making a mockery of me.'

Felix didn't know how to respond. He looked back at the plateau, where the last of the refugees were being ushered through the great doors of Karak Kadrin. Cannons, organ guns and grudge throwers lined the edge of the plateau and were unleashing a storm of death on those Chaos marauders who had managed to get over the final wall and down to the courtyard before the bridge. Dozens died, ripped apart by the war machines. Nonetheless, the followers of Chaos came on remorselessly. Sickened, Felix looked away. His gaze was drawn down, over the edge of the bridge into the chasm below. He was reminded of the bridge he and Gotrek had traversed in the Underway, and wondered if the chasm now yawning beneath his feet was part of the same great gap.

He was surprised to see a second bridge – no, less a bridge than a simple walkway – extending far, far below the edge of the plateau and slightly off to the side of the one he stood on. Indeed, such was the cleverness of its construction, Felix doubted he would have noticed it, save that he was staring straight down at it. He knew that it must extend into the Underway from the depths of Karak Kadrin, and he wondered whether it was part of the now destroyed Engineers' Entrance, or some other route into the depths of the mountains.

A shout dragged him from his reverie. The Chaos marauders had reached the Slayers. Gotrek, of course, was the first to react, leaping to the attack. His axe caught the firelight as it slashed out in a wide arc, opening the guts of a quartet of marauders. Those behind stumbled on the bodies, and Gotrek shoved himself into the momentary gap like a hound at the kill.

Biter gave a high-pitched yell and shook his mace. He seemed to be enjoying himself, which only made Koertig glower darkly. Varg started forwards to aid Gotrek, but Biter grabbed his arm and shook his head. 'Best give Gurnisson room to work, friend. We'll get the run-off.'

'I'll not have my doom filched by that jinx,' Varg growled. 'You might be content to live with your shame, but some of us have more honour.'

'Who was talking about honour? I just meant that we can't trust the manlings to hold the bridge alone,' Biter said. He glanced back at the two men and added, 'No offence.'

'None taken,' Felix said. Koertig grunted. By the same token, Varg seemed mollified. He gripped his axe in two hands and swung it experimentally.

Gotrek's attack had blunted the assault, but only momentarily. Warriors clad in the stiff hide armour of the eastern steppes and carrying short, serrated blades bounded forwards like wolves alongside the bulkier tribesmen from the north, both groups screaming. Felix tensed, readying himself to meet any that got past the two Slayers. The haft of Biter's mace slid through his hand and swung out, smashing aside the first Northman to reach him. Varg jerked forwards and cut the legs out from under a screaming nomad.

Then the first marauder squeezed past the occupied Slayers. The man was big, but whipcord-thin, with scars that created patterns in the shape of screaming faces across his bare flesh.

'Valkia, see me!' the warrior screamed, lunging for them, his blade licking out with more enthusiasm than skill. 'Collect their skulls for the road!'

'Collect your own skull, savage,' Koertig growled, catching

the lunatic's sword blow on his shield. Felix seized the opening, driving Karaghul between two of the man's ribs. The marauder's eyes locked with Felix's own.

'Valkia,' the Chaos marauder hissed, reaching bloody fingers towards Felix. Felix jerked back and ripped Karaghul free. The abrupt motion sent the warrior tumbling from the bridge and down into the chasm below. Felix shuddered. He felt as if he had swallowed something hot and unpleasant. He looked around. Garagrim and Agni fought grimly nearby; both Slayers looked as if they had waded through a river of blood and gore, and the War-Mourner's flashing axes were taking almost as terrible a toll as Gotrek's. Biter laughed and swung his mace, crushing skulls and breaking weapons with every wild blow.

Felix's attention snapped back to Gotrek as the Slayer roared and backhanded a bearded giant of a man who had stooped to stab him. The Slayer seemed to spin in place, his axe levying a brutal toll. However, there were simply too many of the Chaos marauders. They poured towards the path with undimmed ferocity, cheered on by their companions. Their chants hammered at the air, and Felix's skin crawled at the sound of Khorne's name as it echoed all around him. The name felt like a slow acid, etching his bones with its darkness.

The marauders seemed to gather strength from the noise. Varg shouted in pain as a hook-bladed spear sank into his belly. The Slayer's axe took off the top of the spearman's head, but his moment of weakness drew more blades, spears and axes. Felix felt a sinking sensation in his gut as a dozen marauders fell on the staggering Slayer, hacking and stabbing.

'Lucky wanaz,' Biter laughed as his fellow dwarf died. 'Hey, Gurnisson, looks like someone else beat us across the finish line!'

Gotrek's bellow was equal parts frustration and anger. He barrelled into the marauders gathered around Varg's mutilated corpse, his axe slapping the life out of them one after another. Blades dug for Gotrek's squat form, and a spear grazed his calf, nearly hamstringing him. Felix felt his heart seize and Axeson's plea echoed in his head.

He started forwards, ignoring Koertig's cry of protest. But before he could reach Gotrek, a familiar shape hove into view, armoured fists beating aside Chaos marauders, and a crude axe blade surmounted by cunning, daemonic eyes slashed out in a wide arc, lopping off heads and arms with contemptuous ease.

'Away, dogs,' a growling voice roared. 'Away! Kung of the Long Arm comes for his due!' The armoured champion Felix had seen earlier tore through his own men in his determination to reach Gotrek. The Chaos marauders pulled back, opening a space for Chaos champion and Slayer to face one another. Kung gesticulated with his strange axe. 'You shed blood like a hero, dwarf,' the champion rumbled, displaying yellowed fangs in a grin of exultation. 'But I have killed many heroes. Kung of the Long Arm has built a mountain of corpses to take the sweet kisses of daemon-women and has fed the crows of a thousand battlefields!' His armour was composed of baroque blood-stained plates engraved with thousands of gaping, fanged jaws that seemed to snap and bite the air as he moved.

'You'll feed them here as well,' Gotrek said. He leapt forwards, and the two axes crashed together with a shivering noise that caused Felix's ears and eyes to sting. The eyes on the Chaos champion's axe rolled frightfully as the crude weapon connected again with Gotrek's. Runes flared on the champion's blade and Gotrek's own weapon seemed to glow with an inner light.

They traded two more blows and then broke apart. Kung's eyes narrowed. 'You fight well, dwarf. But the bridge is ours. We will pull down your hold, stone by stone, and perform the Blood Eagle on your men and give your women to the dawi zharr as their due.'

Gotrek's eye blazed at the mention of the Chaos dwarfs and he roared in fury. He sprang at Kung and his axe spun so fast that Felix could not follow the path of the blade. Sparks flew as daemon-weapon met rune-axe and Kung held his ground for a moment, but only a moment. Inexorably, the Chaos champion was forced back, step by step, off the bridge. By the way his eyes bulged Felix could tell that he was surprised by the sudden onslaught. He stumbled back into his warriors, but found no respite. Gotrek tore into them as if they were nothing more than chaff, his axe releasing a swathe of crimson and screams from the Chaos marauders who got in his way in a gory display.

Kung swung his axe up in a desperate blow, his mouth working in a silent snarl of battle-fury. The daemon-weapon shrieked as it descended. The shriek became something altogether more horrible as Gotrek's axe rose to meet it and the edges met in a shuddery display of sparks and tearing metal; and then, with a howl, the daemon-weapon exploded, showering the crowd of Chaos marauders with shards of steaming iron.

Kung reeled, gaping at the decapitated weapon in his hands. Gotrek gave him no time to recover and darted in for the kill. His axe sank into the point where the Chaos champion's neck met his shoulder, dragging the big man to his knees with brutal speed. Gotrek wrenched his blade free in a splatter of blood and buried it into Kung's skull with a loud, wet sound. The Slayer's foot shot out, catching the twitching champion in the chest, and kicked the corpse free of the blade. Chest heaving, Gotrek glared about him, as if daring the Chaos marauders to seek vengeance on their champion's behalf.

For a moment, Felix thought that Gotrek's look alone would be enough to hold the enemy at bay, but all too quickly, the marauders began to close in on the Slayer. Gotrek readied himself as they closed in around him.

Then, suddenly, a burst of heat and light sent the marauders fleeing in screaming disorder. Felix turned and saw Agni Firetongue stomp forwards, holding a flask in one hand and his axe in the other. As Felix watched, Agni tipped the flask back, gargled and then spat a plume of fire onto the closest of his enemies. He had cleared much of the bridge in the same manner, and his path was littered by burning bodies.

A crash followed moments later, and Felix flinched as part of the remaining wall crumbled, showering the enemy below with fragments of rock that caused almost as much damage as the Slayers themselves. Garagrim followed Agni, dispatching any marauders who had survived the other Slayer's fire-breath. Felix knew that when the sixth wall finally came down, there would be nothing standing between the enemy and the bridge.

Smoke coiling from his char-stained lips, Agni glared at Gotrek. The Chaos marauders' momentum had been broken, but they were regrouping. Agni hiked a thumb over his shoulder. 'Get across the pathway before they blow it, Gurnisson. I'll not risk this.'

Gotrek growled. 'Who are you to tell me where to go, fire-eater?'

'I'm a Slayer who's owed a doom,' Agni snarled, nearly bumping against Gotrek. 'You've had your taste of glory. It's my turn now!'

'Gurnisson, get across the path,' Garagrim said. The War-Mourner glared Felix and Koertig into motion. 'The rest of you as well. The Firetongue has claimed this doom for his own, and as War-Mourner I declare it his.'

Gotrek opened his mouth to argue, but said nothing. He glared at Agni, who smirked, and then stumped across the bridge without a backwards glance. Biter followed him, whistling tunelessly. At the other end of the bridge, dwarf engineers worked furiously, dislodging the last few stones. The pathway trembled beneath Felix's feet and he picked up his pace.

'I wasn't aware that the War-Mourner could do that,' he said to Gotrek as they crossed.

Gotrek sneered. 'It's an old custom. If he wasn't Ungrim's boy, I'd–'

'You'd what, Gurnisson?' Garagrim said, close behind.

Gotrek flushed. 'I'd show you what happens to arrogant beardlings who stand between me and my doom.'

'Any time, Doom-Thief,' Garagrim spat.

'Garagrim,' Ungrim roared. Garagrim blanched. Felix saw the Slayer King coming towards them. 'Now is not the time,' Ironfist grated, staring his son down.

The path collapsed with a groan. A massive cloud of dust washed upwards as the bridge collapsed into pieces and those pieces fell down into the chasm below, gouging the sides and tumbling past the smaller pathway below. Felix turned with the others to watch Agni. The Slayer, true to his word, had remained behind, calmly barring the path to the Chaos marauders. Now that the chance of reaching the bridge was gone, the tribesmen seemed intent on revenge. Agni seemed content with this and he used the tip of his axe to nick each flask, weakening the seal on each in turn. He waved his axe in a 'come hither' gesture. 'What's in those things?' Felix murmured.

'Fire water,' Gotrek grunted. 'It burns until there's nothing left to burn, when it touches the open air.' The Slayers watched almost reverentially as their brother stalked towards the enemy. Felix thought that with the War-Mourner's declaration, Agni's doom had become less a personal moment than a public rite. Here, in the city of the Slayers, beneath the eyes of Grimnir, one of their own was carrying out his oath. It was almost a religious affair. Dwarfs up and down the edge of the plateau began to sing a dirge and their voices met and matched the bloodthirsty cries of the horde with inexorable strength.

Felix felt a chill as the dirge grew in volume. Agni seemed to swell as the sound swept around him. Gotrek hunched forwards, nostrils flaring, his eye burning jealously. He had remained silent as the others joined the song. Then, as if against his will, he added his own voice to the dirge.

Agni drained his flask. Smoke curled from his nostrils. He spread his arms.

The Chaos marauders charged as one. Agni spewed fire. Then, with a hoarse cry, he slammed into the charred wreckage of his attackers. As he fought he tore open flasks and drained them, spitting fire. Felix had a momentary premonition, guessing what would happen when a lucky blow struck one of the flasks.

That premonition was fulfilled a moment later. A sword chopped into Agni's chest and a flask exploded, spreading fire around. Agni was silent as flames crawled across his body, turning his beard black. He fought on, wreathed in flame. Other flasks, touched by the fire, popped like handguns going off, spreading more fire. Agni staggered forwards, a dwarf-sized torch, his burning axe smashing out without pause.

Silently, remorselessly, the burning shape of Agni Firetongue fought the invaders. Those that faced him burned or were chopped down. The rest staggered back, their chants to Khorne turning to ashes in their mouths. The horde had fallen silent, their eyes on the Slayer as he began to stalk towards them, his enemies retreating before him, their eyes wide with what might have been fear. One step, then two steps and Agni stumbled. He was completely engulfed in flame now. His eyes were gone, burst by the heat. His beard, his crest, all singed to scrapes of greasy smoke. Several of the flasks hadn't yet exploded. Dwarf workmanship was sturdy. His axe fell from his hands, trailing bits of his fingers. Felix wanted to close his eyes but he couldn't look away. The dwarf dirge rose, cresting high.

Agni leapt towards the closest knot of Chaos marauders.

The explosion sent tendrils of fire coursing through the packed keep. Stone and flame flattened the marauders in their dozens. Men and horses ran screaming and burning. The ground behind the sixth wall became an inferno as the fire spread, clinging to greasy furs and oily flesh.

Felix turned away, his cloak held over his nose and mouth as the smell drifted across the chasm. He met Gotrek's eye. 'It burns until there's nothing left to burn,' Gotrek repeated. He chuckled bitterly and the fire was reflected in his single eye.

8

Karak Kadrin,
the Slayer Keep

The great doors to Karak Kadrin had swung shut hours earlier, but Felix could still feel the reverberations in his bones. Huge and ancient, their motion had set the mountain shaking and he thought that even now the echoes of their closing probably sent ripples across the surface of any underground lakes and streams below Karak Kadrin. He and Gotrek had not moved past the entry hall, and the Slayer's eye had not left the doors since they'd closed. All of the war-engines had been pulled back into the hall, to save them from being bombarded to bits by the siege-engines of the Chaos dwarfs, which had arranged themselves in the ruins of the outer keep and were even now firing at the mountainside in which Karak Kadrin nestled in what Felix considered to be sadistic petulance.

Faint trickles of dust occasionally drifted down from the far upper reaches of the hall. Other than the dull reverberations of the shrieking rockets and belching cannons, that was the only sign that an attack was even under way. He couldn't bring himself to feel more than faintly concerned; Gotrek had assured him more than once, vociferously, that dwarf holds were nigh impregnable from without.

There were hundreds of humans in the hall, and about that number of dwarfs. The humans were being taken in groups deeper into the mountains, to the far distant underground docks, where boats waited to go by the underground waterways – long ago constructed by the first dwarf inhabitants of the hold – to the safer reaches of the Stir. Karak Kadrin's docks were no patch on those of Zhufbar, according to Gotrek, but Felix thought the very idea of underground docks was impressive enough.

In fact, everything about the Slayer Keep was impressive. The entry hall was a huge space, with vast fluted galleries that swept up into smooth balconies that looked as if they had been coaxed from the stone by the hands of a sculptor rather than a stonemason. Ancient tiles, worn smooth by generations of traffic, lined the floors, each one a work of art in and of itself, depicting a moment from the history of the hold. Large ancestor statues, representing past generations of kings, thanes, and lords of Karak Kadrin, lined the walls, each ensconced in its own nook or cranny.

Globes containing luminescent liquid hung from stone half-arches spaced evenly along the length of the hall, casting a soft glow across everything below, and the light carried far better than any torch or lantern Felix had seen. At the other end of the hall was a second set of great doors. These were another defence measure, sealing off the next section of the hold from invasion. Felix knew that dwarf holds had many entrances – not just the ones you could see. There were doors everywhere on every level, some hidden, some not.

Regardless of the size of the attackers' force, there was simply no way to lay siege to a dwarf hold. Not in the sense of the common understanding of the word. A mountain could no more be surrounded than it could be levelled by conventional means, Chaos dwarf ingenuity aside. With the destruction of the bridge connecting the outer keep to the plateau on which Karak Kadrin's doors sat, the Chaos forces were stymied. Or so Felix hoped.

'They can't really build another bridge, can they?' he said. 'Not just like that.' Gotrek didn't reply. Felix looked at him. 'And even if they did,' he went on, 'it's not like they could burrow into the mountain.' He peered at the Slayer and said, 'Gotrek?'

Gotrek glanced at him and knuckled his eye-patch irritably. 'That death was mine, manling,' he said. 'It would have been legendary.'

Felix shook his head. He'd known it was going to come back up. 'It would have been stupid,' he said.

Gotrek flushed. 'What?' he snarled.

'I said it would have been stupid, going up like a powder-keg, like that. Is that really how you want people to remember Gotrek Gurnisson dying?' Felix knew he shouldn't be challenging Gotrek this way, but he'd grown tired of the Slayer's more-than-normal surliness over the past few hours.

'Careful, manling,' Gotrek rumbled warningly.

'I am tired of being careful, Gotrek. If I am doomed to write about your doom, it had best be a doom worth being doomed to write about!' He fought to calm himself. 'Besides, you weren't planning to stay anyway, were you? You said so yourself. You're meant for a grander doom.'

Gotrek snorted. Then, not unkindly, 'Perhaps you're right, at that.' Then, he blinked. 'What did you say, manling?'

'What?' Felix said.

'Just now, about powder-kegs,' Gotrek said. He stroked his beard. He looked at the doors again. 'Ha,' he said, darkly amused.

'What is it?' Felix said.

'Come, manling. I must speak with the king,' Gotrek said, moving towards a set of stone stairs set into the walls beside the doors of the hold. Felix shoved himself to his feet and followed. He hurried after Gotrek, squirming through groups of dwarfs to keep up with the Slayer.

They found Ungrim in one of the stone blockhouses which lined the cliff-face above the doors of Karak Kadrin. The section of the blockhouse that faced out over the chasm was solid stone, reinforced by iron bands. Where the roof met the wall were a number of thin slits. Thunderers stood on a ledge that allowed them to aim their weapons out. A circular stairwell rose up at an angle into a reinforced cupola. A dwarf sat within the cupola, which rotated with a hiss of steam and a whine of gears, startling Felix. Every so often, the dwarf would shout down to a companion, who scribbled something into a heavy notebook.

Gotrek saw Felix's questioning look and grinned. 'Have to keep accurate records, manling. They'll identify the tribes and such afterwards and record the grudge appropriately. Can't let scum like that out there get away with knocking down a keep like that.'

'Future generations must know of such perfidy,' Ungrim said. The king stood at a circular stone table, leaning forwards on his knuckles. Before him, flat on the table, was a disc of hammered gold upon which what Felix took to be a map of the hold had been engraved. Snorri Thungrimsson and Garagrim stood nearby, as well as three other dwarfs that Felix thought must be the other prominent clan leaders.

'If we survive,' Snorri grunted.

'Karak Kadrin will weather this, as it has weathered every other affront to our sovereignty,' Ungrim said confidently. He looked at Gotrek warily. 'What do you want, Gurnisson?'

'To help,' Gotrek said bluntly.

'Go man the interior defences,' Ungrim said.

'The enemy aren't inside,' Gotrek said, his axe resting on his shoulder. 'Not yet anyway. I want to lead a sortie.'

Snorri goggled at him, as did the other clan-leaders. 'Are you mad?' Thungrimsson said. The hammerer caught himself. 'Never mind, of course you are. No,' he said.

'What sort of sortie, Gurnisson?' Ungrim said.

'A quiet one, right up until it gets very, very loud,' Gotrek said, flashing a gap-toothed smile. 'They tried to blow their way in before. I simply want to return the favour, with interest.'

Ungrim stared at him for a moment. Felix could almost hear the gears turning in the king's head. Then the Slayer King slapped the table and gave a loud bark of laughter. 'Ha! That's the best idea I've heard all day!'

'Indeed. One might almost suspect that Gurnisson had ulterior motives,' a familiar voice said.

Gotrek swung around as the priest, Axeson, stepped into the blockhouse. The priest of Grimnir was clad for war, but he raised a hand in a peaceful gesture as Gotrek glared at him. 'I intended no insult.'

'You gave one anyway,' Gotrek said.

'When I heard that a mighty doom had been achieved, I thought it might have been yours,' Axeson said.

'It wasn't,' Gotrek said.

'No,' Axeson said, nodding agreeably. 'We have business, you and I.'

'None that I can see,' Gotrek snapped.

'No, but then you only have one eye.'

Gotrek's mouth thinned to a razor-line of disapproval. It didn't take much to set him off, and Axeson seemed to be trying to make him angry, though there was no gain in doing so, to Felix's mind. For some reason, the priest's waspishness put Felix in mind of his own, back when he'd argued regularly with his father over his intent to become a poet, rather than a merchant. The insults had flown fast and thick and personal between them. 'I did not come to Karak Kadrin to be insulted by you,' Gotrek growled.

'Then why did you come?' Axeson said.

Gotrek's mouth opened and then closed with a snap. Felix, who had been leaning forwards in interest, felt a surge of disappointment. 'That's none of your concern,' Gotrek said after a moment.

'It is my concern, Gurnisson,' Axeson said softly. His eyes fell to the axe in Gotrek's grip, and then up, meeting Felix's gaze. The look in the priest's eyes was sad, as sad as Felix had ever seen a dwarf look, but also bitter, as if he bore Gotrek a personal grudge, just like everyone else in this fortress of madmen. 'Your doom is the concern of all who dwell within Karak Kadrin.'

Gotrek grunted. 'What do you mean?'

'I have seen you fall, Gurnisson. I have seen your doom, and writ in that doom was the end of all dawi. Karak Kadrin will be but the first,' Axeson said. His tone was portentous, but Gotrek gave no mockery. Instead he shook his head.

'Speak plainly, priest. What do you mean?'

'I mean what I say, son of Gurni. If you meet your doom, Karak Kadrin falls.'

Gotrek was visibly dumbstruck. Felix said, 'How do you know this?'

Axeson looked at him. 'I have seen it, as I said. More is not for you to know.'

'It damn well is,' Gotrek snarled suddenly, lunging forwards, his hand knotting in the priest's beard. He shoved him back against the wall. 'How do you know this? Who denies me my doom?'

'Release him, Gurnisson! Release him, I say,' Ungrim bellowed. Dwarfs leapt to grab Gotrek, but none could break his hold on the priest. The Slayer was immovable.

'Grimnir,' Axeson said simply, answering Gotrek's question. 'There is a mighty doom coming from the north, Gurnisson. Something that will eat an army of Slayers and still not be filled, and if you face it, if you meet it in battle, you will find the death you seek, but the world will die with you.'

Gotrek released the priest and stepped back as if he'd been struck. 'No,' he said hoarsely.

'Is my word not good enough?' Axeson said.

'No. Not yours. Never,' Gotrek hissed. His eye glinted. 'Prove it, priest, or I shall march through those gates tonight.'

'You will not,' Ungrim said. He looked at Axeson. 'You are certain?'

'As stone, my king,' Axeson said.

'No,' Gotrek said, shaking his head. His hand clenched and unclenched and his axe trembled. 'No, you lie,' he burst out.

The blockhouse fell silent. Gotrek flushed. Felix's hand crept towards his sword-hilt. Every eye in the structure was turned towards the Slayer and every face was set like the stones that made up the walls. Gotrek hunched into himself, jaw jutting as if he were, for once, feeling the weight of his people's disapproval. He took a breath and straightened.

'I do not lie,' Axeson said.

'I do not care,' Gotrek retorted, but calmly. He looked at

Ungrim. 'I will lead my sortie now, before the Chaos filth figure out that they're sitting ducks.'

'The sortie will go ahead, aye, but you will not be the one leading it, Gurnisson,' Ungrim said harshly. 'No, you will stay here, where someone can keep an eye on you.'

'And how will you make me, oh king?' Gotrek said.

Ungrim flushed. Despite being a Slayer himself, Felix could tell that King Ironfist was unused to having his authority challenged so blatantly. Felix tensed, knowing that the next words out of the king's mouth would be something to the effect of 'chains,' 'imprisonment' or 'arrest them'. Would Gotrek insist on fighting his way out? He hoped not.

'There is no reason for Gurnisson not to go,' Axeson said, piercing the growing tension. Felix glanced at the priest. 'The doom I foresaw is not here. Indeed, I'd say that without him, this sortie he proposes is likely to fail.' He looked at Gotrek. 'I will prove my words when we return, Gurnisson, if you are brave enough to heed them.'

Ungrim stared hard at the priest. Gotrek did as well. Neither seemed quite able to believe the words that had just come out of Axeson's mouth. Ungrim's hard gaze swivelled to Gotrek. 'My son will lead the sortie, Gurnisson. You will accompany him, but in an advisory capacity. I well know of your skills in such matters, and so the priest may be right.'

Gotrek stood still and silent for a moment, but then he nodded brusquely. 'I will go with them as well,' Axeson said, with his thumbs hooked in his belt. Ungrim gaped at him, but recovered quickly.

'Yes, fine, go,' Ungrim said, twitching a hand in assent.

'No,' Gotrek growled, shaking his head.

'Now who's denying whom?' Axeson said, eliciting another glare from Gotrek. 'You hold no sway over me, Gurnisson.

Not now and not here. It is the will of Grimnir that I go, so…
I go.'

Gotrek turned away, mouth working. Felix thought he
looked as if he were choking on whatever it was he wanted to
say, but in the end he swallowed the words and stomped out
of the blockhouse. Felix made to follow, and Axeson fell in
beside him, keeping pace easily.

'You seem to get some pleasure in pricking him, master
priest,' Felix said. It was obvious that Gotrek knew Axeson
from a previous encounter. He had never mentioned the
priest before, but that wasn't unusual. Gotrek was as frustrat-
ing a subject as any biographer had ever had the bad luck to
be pledged to. He refused to speak of his past or even of his
present. To Gotrek, only one thing mattered, and that was
how his story would end.

'So it must seem to a manling. I assure you, I get no pleasure
from it,' Axeson said, not looking at him. 'Very little about
this pleases me, in fact.'

'How long have you known Gotrek?'

'Longer than is healthy,' Axeson said. Felix was surprised. He
hadn't truly expected an answer. Despite Felix's first impres-
sions, the priest seemed not to hold him in the same casual
contempt that most dwarfs held for men. It was no coinci-
dence that the Khazalid words for 'badly made' and 'man'
were very similar.

'So longer than a week then,' Felix said.

Axeson surprised him again by chuckling. 'Oh yes. The last
time I saw him, he did not have a Remembrancer, nor, it
seemed, a desire for one. Even then, he was selfish.' He caught
Felix's look. 'All Slayers are selfish, Jaeger. Grimnir marched
north against the advice of his fellows and deprived our people of his might in our darkest hour. Thus do Slayers emulate

him, separating themselves from our society and spending their remaining years seeking their own way,' he continued.

'I have always assumed that it was by mutual consent that Slayers leave,' Felix said, glancing at Gotrek moving ahead of them, pushing his way through the dwarfs in the blockhouse with single-minded heedlessness. Most got out of his way quickly enough and more than one dwarf turned away from Gotrek's belligerent gaze. Everyone knew who Gotrek was, it seemed, and no one seemed happy to see him.

'Does that make it any less selfish, that we let them go?' Before Felix could reply, Axeson made what might have been a frustrated noise. 'But it is a facet of our people to be selfish. Just as it is a facet for us to be generous, or dour or boisterous. The gods crafted us as artificers craft gems, and we are complex and varied.'

'You have a way with words,' Felix said.

'A good priest must know how to talk. And we dwarfs appreciate words in ways that your people do not. To speak is to chisel the air, which is why it must be done sparingly and with precision. Careless talk causes as much damage as a rock fall. And to write... Well, to write is to carve the very stuff of history, Jaeger.' He looked at Felix. 'He did not choose wrong in you, I think.' He looked back at Gotrek, his expression considering. 'He is prideful. *Ufdi*, as my people say. Vain, as you manlings might call it. He is too proud to submit to death's whim, too proud to seek an appropriate end. For him, it must be the greatest doom, the final doom, because nothing else will extirpate his shame.'

'Was it so bad then, what he did?' Felix said, hesitantly.

Axeson was silent. Then, 'He thinks so. And that is enough.'

'If you're finished talking about me, I would have you with me when I speak to the beardling, priest,' Gotrek grumbled, without turning around. Felix felt a stab of shame. How long had Gotrek been listening? Axeson seemed unperturbed.

'A sensible plan. The War-Mourner finds you offensive, Gurnisson,' he said.

'The War-Mourner finds much to be offensive. Let him stew, I care not,' Gotrek said. They had arrived at a second blockhouse. This one was much the same as the other, though the noise-level was louder and more raucous. Inside, a dozen Slayers surrounded Garagrim, arguing over one another in a display of obstinate determination that was awe-inspiring to behold. The War-Mourner was trying to keep the peace, but his voice was only one among many.

Biter and Koertig stood off to the side, the madcap Slayer leaning on his mace, the orc skull easily taking his weight. He caught sight of them and waved them over. 'What is this madness?' Gotrek demanded.

'It's madness all right,' Koertig muttered. Biter swatted him in the belly with a casual thump of his hand.

'They want a sortie. The story of Agni's doom has spread and now the others are getting all hot in the trousers to get their own. The largest Chaos horde in years is camped on their doorstep, and they want to have some fun,' Biter said.

'You're not with them?' Felix asked.

'My doom is written, what good is it to seek it out or run from it? It'll happen when it happens,' Biter said shrugging.

'Not soon enough,' Koertig said.

'Does your Remembrancer have as much faith in you as mine in me?' Biter said, grinning cheerfully at Gotrek. But Gotrek had already moved away, towards the crowd of bawling, bellowing Slayers. Felix felt a knot in his gut. Axeson smiled thinly.

'This should be interesting,' the priest said.

'If old Ogun were here, none of this would be happening,' Biter said. 'He was the beardling's second-in-command. Kept the rest of us in line, old Ogun did.'

'What happened to him?' Felix said.

'He died,' Biter said cheerfully.

Gotrek had climbed up on the table, a second axe gripped in his free hand. As he stood, he brought the axes together with a crash. All eyes turned towards him. 'You want a sortie?' Gotrek rasped, facing the expectant Slayers. 'I've got a sortie for you.'

'Gurnisson–' Garagrim began, face twisting in anger.

'King Ironfist has already agreed, Prince Garagrim,' Axeson said, loudly. Garagrim transferred his glare, but Axeson met his gaze blithely.

Gotrek nodded brusquely to Axeson and then raised his axe. 'I go to rip the guts out of the Chaos army with their own weapons. Who will come with me?'

'And how will you do this, death-jinx?' a Slayer called out. 'Will you walk amongst them and let them kill each other rather than you?' His laughter faded as Gotrek pinned him in place with a one-eyed stare.

'Come with me and see, Dorin Borrisson. Unless you fear to do so,' Gotrek said. The Slayer called Dorin bristled, one hand reaching for the fat-bladed dwarf sword sheathed on his hip. Another Slayer grabbed his arm and shook his head. The latter spoke up.

'Come where and do what, Gurnisson?' he said. Other Slayers spoke up in support of the question. Gotrek looked at him.

'We will go into the Underway, and take the fight to that cowardly filth outside,' Gotrek said. His gap-teeth flashed. 'We're going to blow up the ground beneath them and by Grimnir we'll cut the heart of their army out in one blow!'

In the end, twenty Slayers were selected. Felix felt relief when it was over, and without the violence he'd feared. Garagrim joined Gotrek on the table and chose Slayers seemingly at random, among them Biter and Dorin. The others dispersed with much grumbling, but no violence. 'That went better than I thought,' he muttered to Axeson, who nodded.

'Such is the War-Mourner's responsibility. It is he who chooses those whose turn it is to be slain, when the great throng of Karak Kadrin marches forth. Once, it was the responsibility of the temple. I am glad that it has passed on.'

'Were you ever–?'

'How old do you think me, Jaeger?' Axeson said, cocking an eye at Felix. Felix spluttered, trying to take back what he perceived to have been an insult. Axeson's chuckle alerted him to the contrary. He smacked Felix on the arm, in much the same way as Gotrek. 'Easy, manling,' he said.

'I'm not used to dwarf humour, I fear,' Felix said, rubbing his arm.

'No, I don't suppose you would be,' Axeson said, looking at Gotrek.

Gotrek conferred with Garagrim for a moment and then joined them, looking inordinately pleased. 'Well, manling, ready to go back underground?' he said, grinning at Felix.

'If we must,' Felix said.

The chosen Slayers were a loud bunch, excited by the prospect of battle. One of them started a song, and another broke out a cask of ale, one of many stored in the blockhouse.

'I still don't understand what you're planning,' Felix complained as Gotrek joined him, a foam-capped mug in his hand. 'What good can come of creating a crater in the middle of their army, save giving them another avenue of attack? We nearly died keeping them *out* of the Underway once, now we're inviting them in?' He swept a hand out. 'They care nothing for losses, Gotrek, nothing for odds or strategy.'

Gotrek nodded agreeably. 'True enough, manling. But even the bravest man will be crushed when he is caught between two forces.'

Felix blinked. 'The explosion–'

'Gets us amidst them,' Gotrek said, running his thumb along the edge of his axe. He watched blood bead on the ball of the digit and then flicked it to the floor. His eye caught Felix. 'Twenty Slayers will set the blood to flowing, manling, but five times that of stout clan warriors will march out of that pit while we keep them occupied; more than could attack from any hidden tunnel or disguised door set into the mountains. And when they turn, and they will turn, Ungrim will lead a sortie of his own through those hidden doors and tunnels. We can move hundreds from a dozen different directions while they're occupied.' Gotrek made a fist. 'They will learn what it means to attack us, manling. They will learn that we are not men, to cower behind walls until the last gate falls. These are our mountains and we will not suffer northern beasts to desecrate them.' He smiled a hard, wild, cruel smile. The smile faded as abruptly as it had come, and Gotrek went quiet.

Felix looked askance at him. 'Why did we come here, Gotrek?' he said, quietly.

'What was that, manling?'

'Why did we come? Axeson said that you couldn't not come… What did he mean by that?'

Gotrek frowned. 'You shouldn't listen to that stripling,' he said sourly.

'You've been acting oddly for weeks now,' Felix said, over-riding his fear of Gotrek's temper and plunging ahead. 'You're moodier than normal, though that's hard to tell sometimes.'

'Moody?' Gotrek said, raising his eyebrow.

'You know what I mean,' Felix said hastily.

'No, manling, I don't. Enlighten me,' Gotrek growled.

'Something is bothering you.'

Gotrek didn't reply. Felix sighed. 'We didn't know that Karak Kadrin was under attack, so it couldn't have been that,' he said. He looked at Gotrek. 'Could it?'

Gotrek was as stiff and still as a statue. Only his eye moved, his gaze dropping to the axe in his hand. His thumb caressed the runes carved into the width of the blade. 'I had a dream,' he said, after a long silence. Felix waited for him to continue, but he didn't.

They stood in silence after that, Gotrek likely imagining the sea of enemies awaiting him, and Felix looking inwards, thinking of what awaited them below. As plans went, he could see little fault in it. It was direct and to the point. There was no subtlety to it, but then, there was little enough to Gotrek. If it worked, the army laying siege to Karak Kadrin would be broken. What little Felix knew of military matters assured him of that, as did his experience with the followers of Chaos. Like orcs, they were brave in numbers, but as individuals they were as easy to spook as any provincial peasant. Some would fight, but those would die. The rest would run. Or so he hoped.

Karak Kadrin was not quiet, as the evening deepened. Fires burned in the entry hall, and dwarfs spoke and sang and boasted. A grim sort of mirth pervaded the hold, Felix thought. Not quite amusement, but almost a fatalistic joy, akin to the cynic's pleasure at being proven right. For the dwarfs, this was the way of things. Every stand was the last, and every dwarf knew that it was not a question of if, but when.

For men, every dawn brought new hope. For dwarfs, it brought new grudges. Felix looked at Gotrek, examining his bloated musculature, so different to that of even the other

Slayers. Gotrek was a dwarf's dwarf and the epitome of his people to Felix's eye, taciturn, brutal and dour. Perhaps that was why he seemed to offend them so... In Gotrek was every failing and strength of the dwarf race made manifest, and to look at him was to see those qualities with dreadful clarity.

'Gurnisson, come,' Garagrim said, stepping out of the blockhouse. Felix jerked out of his reverie, realizing that the cheerful noise from the blockhouse had died. While the others had celebrated, Gotrek had stood with him, staring into the darkness for who knew how long. The Slayer met his eyes and nodded sharply. Felix followed him as they joined the others.

Garagrim marched purposefully down the stairs from the blockhouse, Gotrek just behind him. Felix fell in beside Axeson. Behind them came Biter and Koertig and the other Slayers chosen for the sortie. At the bottom of the stairs, Snorri Thungrimsson was waiting for them, a number of his hammerers in tow. Past them, Felix saw a small throng of dwarfs, each carrying a crossbow and an axe. They had a rough look to them, and their armour bespoke hard use. Two from among them stepped forwards to join Snorri. One was tall, the other short, but both were muscular and stout.

'Lunn and Steki Svengeln,' Thungrimsson said. 'They are cousins to Fimbur Svengeln, who fell at the Peak Pass, and rangers, like him. Good ones, if the truth be told.'

'The best,' Lunn said.

'Better than any of the rest,' Steki added.

An armoured dwarf stepped forwards at Snorri's curt gesture. 'Bael Grimbold, ironbreaker.'

He was slim, by dwarf standards, but his armour added bulk to him. Young as well, Felix judged. He tapped his brow with the back of his axe. 'We are ready to go into the dark,

War-Mourner,' Grimbold said, his voice surprisingly deep.

'Who isn't?' another dwarf spoke up, pushing past Grimbold, who grimaced. He was ancient, judging by the pure white of his beard, and he wore a dented and wax-splotched helm and his armour was stained with dust and ash. 'Always up for a stroll, me,' he said, tapping the ironbreaker on one gleaming pauldron with a wicked looking pick-axe. 'Gurnisson, I hear this was your idea, you great *wattock*.'

'Aye, Copperback,' Gotrek said, his eye alight with amusement. 'Is that a problem?'

'Bah,' Copperback waved his pick, forcing Grimbold to step back to avoid its keen bite. 'I've lived long enough, I expect.'

'Are your kin still trying to find your hoard, you old *boki*?' Gotrek said. 'If they hear you're going with us, they'll probably throw us a leaving party.'

'It'll be a poor one,' Copperback said, yellow teeth surfacing from the white spray of beard in a crooked grin. 'Not a nugget between them, the *wazzoks*.'

'If you're done socializing,' Garagrim growled between gritted teeth, 'we have a sortie to get under way.'

'Impatient as always, these beardlings,' Copperback said, letting his pick rest on his shoulder. 'Don't worry, Prince Ironfist. My miners and I will lead you straight and true.'

'And then, we'll show the daemon-lovers what Slayers can do,' Gotrek said. He raised his axe, and the other Slayers followed suit. 'Their god wants blood and skulls? Well, we'll choke him with equal measures of both!'

Canto cursed as he looked down at Kung's body. The latter still clutched the shattered remains of his axe, and his eyes stared up blindly on either side of the cleft in his skull. That was why he had ever evaded the eyes of the gods. Only so many ascended into their graces, the rest fell and became food for worms.

Once on that path, those were the only two fates allowed you, victory or death. It was so limiting, that path, and yet so many gleefully trod it, hoping, anticipating that they would be the ones to please the fickle gods and become as the daemons which whispered on the northern wind, that they would be as those whose names were inscribed on the ancient monoliths which jutted like signposts in the bleaker regions, names like Valkia or Lothar Bubonicus.

Canto hated them. He hated them and respected them in the way that a jackal respects a wolf. They had had the courage of their convictions and had reached a dark pinnacle only dreamt of by many. It was hard not to admire that. But he hated them none the less.

He was tempted to go south. To take what forces he could gather and head into the bleak wilderness to burn and pillage and sate the ache in him for another century. When he'd been only a man, he'd dreamed of owning a villa in the south of Tilea, on the golden shores. A stupid dream for a down-at-heels nobleman, but one he'd never been able to shake. Comfort, not carnage, was what he desired.

But if he did that, Garmr would have no choice but to hunt him down. Rebellion and betrayal the Gorewolf could tolerate and even encourage, but desertion – never. No, Canto was bound to the horde now, by ligaments of fate.

At the time, it had seemed the lesser of two evils. He recalled the battle – multi-coloured dust coating the air as thick as paint, a million men crashing against one another like waves made of flesh. There had been a hundred sides present, all striving against one another. There had been a hundred champions, leading their followers in battle beneath the frosty gaze of the northern sun, bellowing out bellicose cries to their gods. Banners crafted from stretched human flesh, gemstone feathers and motes of light dancing like fireflies around brass poles swung high above the fray, heralding identities and allegiances.

Canto had been in the thick of it, not by choice, but his bargain with Tzerpichore the Unwritten had been binding. The squawking bird-brain had ridden a tortoise of iron and crystal into battle, and he had hurled witch-fire from a golden palanquin mounted on the golem's shell. His acolytes had joined him, their heads bobbing like a harmony of song-birds as they lent their petty centuries' worth of accumulated arcane knowledge to their master's design.

Tzerpichore had been collecting daemons, the weaker kind, those unaligned, amorphous entities which clung to the undersides of magical storms and mighty rituals. The sorcerer had been plucking them from the aether that collected above such battles, where they circled like carrion birds. Canto had been there to protect him from the madness of battle.

In retrospect, he hadn't done a very good job.

Garmr had bulled through the chaos of battle, hacking his way towards Tzerpichore, who by his very nature, was offensive to the Gorewolf. Canto had tried his best to delay the killing-mad warlord, but he'd been swatted aside again and again, only the enchantments woven into his armour saving him from death. Garmr had leapt up on the tortoise and for a moment, it appeared as if Tzerpichore's magics had undone him. Fire had wreathed Garmr, consuming him. Then he stepped through it, his axe singing out, and Canto watched as Tzerpichore's head had bounced across the ground towards him, a vaguely accusing look in the fast-dimming eyes.

After that, the tortoise had plodded on, uncontrolled and abandoned as Garmr had lifted Canto's chin with his axe and given him an ultimatum. Canto had agreed quickly enough.

Sometimes, though, he wondered what had happened to the tortoise.

'Well,' Canto said, thinking of the tortoise, 'that's that.' He looked at the shattered bridge in frustration. He'd been counting on Kung to take it. Without it, Karak Kadrin was effectively inviolable.

Khorreg the Hell-Worker frowned and turned to watch as the ogres dragged the third of the war-engines into position. The Dreadquake mortar had done its work well, hammering most of the outer fortress flat. Now the weapon was being reloaded in preparation for bombarding the mountain that threw its shadow over them. Privately, Canto had doubts that the war machines, effective as they were, would do any good given the current situation.

'It's not,' Khorreg said, eyeing him with smug assumption. Behind the Hell-Worker, Khul stood silently, axe gripped horizontally in his hands, his featureless helm fixed on the enemy bastion.

'What?' Canto said, irritated.

Khorreg gave a rasping laugh. 'It can be brought down.'

'By your devices,' Canto said.

'Possibly, or others,' Khorreg said, his cracked and unpleasant features twisting into an expression of cunning. 'More deals could be struck, more engines brought from the east, with such a prize to be gained.' He gestured towards the massive double doors across the chasm.

'Unfortunately, Garmr is not here to make those deals or bargain for those engines, Hell-Worker,' Canto said. He clasped the hilt of his sword and shook his head. 'Besides, I doubt the dwarfs will sit around and wait for us to knock down yet more of their walls.'

Khorreg snorted. 'They are weak, and content to sit and wait where braver folk attack.' The Chaos dwarf chuckled, and the glowing cracks on his face widened disturbingly. 'They will not come. We have time.'

'Maybe,' Canto said. He turned and saw Yan approaching, a number of other champions behind him, including Skrall and Hrodor. The latter duo looked wary, but Yan was grinning insolently, his fingers dancing across the pommel of his falchion. His armour was covered in dried blood and soot, but he looked as fresh as if he'd newly arrived to the field of battle. 'Then, maybe not,' Canto said. 'What news, Yan?'

'There's little to pillage here,' Yan said, shrugging. 'Nothing useful, at any rate, and the men are getting restless. With the bridge gone, there's no reason to stay.'

'Except that Garmr ordered us to take Karak Kadrin,' Canto said.

'Except that,' Yan said. His eyes drifted down to Kung's broken form then back up to Canto. 'I have accepted the sworn oaths of Kung of the Long Arm's warriors. They are grateful to join a warband whose leader is not so great a fool, they assure me.'

'Do they?' Canto said. Yan nodded.

'Your men, meanwhile, asked me to speak with you,' he continued.

'Did they?'

'There is nothing to be gained by staying here, Canto,' Yan said, loudly. Canto could feel the eyes of Chaos marauders and Chaos warriors alike drawn towards them. It was less an ambush than a long-delayed thrust from an expected quarter. With Kung dead, that left only they two in control of the army. It didn't matter who the other champion was – it could have been Kung or Hrolf, for all that Yan cared. He would have chosen his moment regardless.

He chose his next words carefully. 'Is that cowardice I hear? I should have expected such from one called the Foul.' His voice was deeper than Yan's, and louder. It echoed from shattered pillar to cracked post and more men joined the rest in watching the confrontation. More softly, Canto said, 'These aren't your words, Yan. They're Ekaterina's or I'm a Slaaneshi concubine. Is that why she insisted that you be sent, rather than Vasa or the Bone-Hammer? You've been trotting in her shadow since we crossed the Howling Chasm.'

Yan snorted. 'She is strong, Unsworn. She is blessed and beloved. My folk know of the deadliness of queens.'

'And Garmr is not?'

Yan made a face. 'Garmr is not here. Ekaterina is not here. We are here and there is nothing for us.' He swept out his falchion, gesturing across the chasm. 'They hide from us. We cannot reach them and we cannot pluck their skulls, so why do we stay? Let us find battle, Unsworn, unless your heart is too craven to do so!'

Canto looked around. Two accusations of cowardice; if he and Yan had been different sorts of men, they would have already come to blows. But Yan hadn't become a Horselord of the Khazags by being rash to action. Even the most war-like nomad favoured the surgical thrust over the bull-headed frontal assault. So where–

Skrall made a sound halfway between a squawk and a cough and raised the boil-covered bone spikes that had long ago replaced his hands. His horned, featureless helm bobbed, and he gurgled something and clashed his spikes over his head.

Canto nodded. So that was it. Yan intended to let Skrall do the dirty work. The red-scaled champion wasn't quite the ber-serker Hrolf had been, but he was dangerous nonetheless. His spikes could rip through stone and puncture iron as easily as they did flesh. Canto knew that he couldn't simply kill Skrall, not as he had Alfven. Once was a lesson, twice a blasphemy. So it was to be a fight, but that didn't mean it had to be a long one.

'We don't have these problems among my people,' Khorreg said helpfully.

'Yes, assassination and enslavement is so much easier,' Canto muttered. Khorreg nodded agreeably.

'You manlings are inefficient as well as stupid. Frankly, you need overseers,' the Chaos dwarf said and laughed, clapping his hands to his belly.

Canto ignored the horrible chortling of the stunted Daemonsmith and drew his blade. Skrall gurgled again and gesticulated with his spikes. Canto had never bothered to learn how to translate the champion's speech, so couldn't say whether he was being cursed at or whether Skrall was simply reciting his pedigree. Nevertheless, he didn't wait for him to finish. His sword licked out, carving a scar across the cheek-piece of Skrall's helmet, startling him. A spike punched towards him, driven by a muscular, scaly arm. The overlapping scaly plates that covered Skrall's body were as effective as any dwarf-forged armour and Canto's riposte crashed harmlessly off the champion's upper chest.

Men were cheering now and stamping their feet. Yan watched with a wide smile. Hrodor was circling around the fight, armoured fingers tapping at the dagger sheathed on his belt. Canto took it all in at a glance, his well-honed sense of self-preservation screaming a warning at him. Nomads always went for the hidden thrust and, truth to tell, if the situation had been reversed, he might have tried something similar. Skrall came in again, bisecting the air with his spikes, throwing his arms out in a wide, sweeping gesture and forcing Canto to step back. Hrodor, the nails in his skull glistening weirdly, drew his blade and lunged, seeking to plant the dagger in the small of Canto's back.

Except that Canto wasn't there. The blade plunged into Skrall's throat, lodging itself in the reptilian scales there and causing the champion to reel and gag. He staggered back, pawing ineffectually at the blade's hilt with his spikes. Hrodor gawped in confusion, but his hand was already dipping for his sword hilt instinctively as he turned to see Canto beside him, the edge of the latter's sword pressed tight to Hrodor's throat. Skrall sank to his knees, still pawing at the blade. It wasn't a fatal wound, but it would make it hard to concentrate on anything else. Canto lifted a boot and kicked the hilt of the dagger, lodging it further into Skrall's larynx and knocking the champion onto his back. Then he looked at Yan, whose grin was stretched tight and becoming a rictus snarl.

'They call me the Unsworn, Yan, not the Unobservant,' he said.

'They'll call you nothing at all, soon enough,' Yan snarled, slicing the air with his falchion. 'I'll take your skull for my banner and lead this army to war–'

Khorreg said something in his own language. There was a spurt of heat as the magma cannon belched and strained in its chains, spattering onlookers with burning dollops of liquid fire. At some point during the confrontation, Khorreg had signalled that the cannon be turned about to face the gathered Chaos forces. The ogres were already dragging the Deathshrieker launcher around as well. Khorreg's two assistants had joined him, and they chuckled and laughed harshly at the dumbfounded expression on Yan's face as he took in the steaming, dripping barrel of the magma cannon.

The champion lurched towards Khorreg, blade out, but the armoured bulk of Khul interposed itself.

The Ironsworn was only half the height of the champion, but thrice the width. Yan stopped dead. Khul raised his axe slowly, letting the fading light of the day catch on the runes of death and pain that had been wrought into the blade.

Yan licked his lips. 'You only get one chance, dwarf,' he said. 'There are more of us than you can kill quickly enough with those weapons. We'll take your beards as surely as we took those of these others,' he added, gesturing around at the fallen keep.

'Either way, you'll lead an army without our help, manling,' Khorreg rumbled. His eyes glinted with ageless malevolence and cunning. 'And you do need us, if you want to reap the skulls and spill the blood your puny god has demanded.'

'We need no cowardly weapons such as these,' Yan protested.

'I wasn't talking about weapons, manling,' Khorreg said. He hiked a thumb over his shoulder at the chasm separating the Chaos army from their chosen prey. 'I was talking about a bridge.'

'What do you need?' Canto said quickly, not taking his eyes from Yan.

'Slaves, raw materials,' Khorreg said, stroking his beard. 'One will serve as the other, in a pinch.'

'Take these two and what remains of their warband,' Canto said, nodding to Hrodor and Skrall. 'They'll be useful one way or another. Unless you'd like to disagree,' he added, looking at Yan.

Yan opened his mouth, but then closed it with a snap. His eyes were on the hold across the chasm, and his mind was on the glory to be reaped and the skulls to be collected. Canto nodded in satisfaction. 'How long?' he said to Khorreg.

'A few days,' the Chaos dwarf said. 'Depends on the strength of the materials,' he added wickedly, leering at Hrodor.

'Good enough,' Canto said. Then more loudly, to the cheers of the surrounding warriors, 'And then we pull Karak Kadrin apart stone by stone!'

9

Karak Kadrin,
the Slayer Keep

'They've gone below,' Thungrimsson said as he entered the blockhouse.

Ungrim Ironfist looked up from the map. He had not left the blockhouse since the great doors had closed, needing to be as close to the battle as possible, Thungrimsson knew. 'How long will it take for them to reach their goal?'

'A matter of hours, if Copperback can be trusted,' Thungrimsson said.

'Are your warriors ready?' Thungrimsson and his hammerers would be at the forefront of the second sortie, the edge of Karak Kadrin's axe as it cut into the army at their gates. It was an honour to be the first to battle, and his chest swelled slightly as he thought about it. He had fought in dozens of campaigns over his lifetime, battling grobi and ratkin and worse things, and he had never failed in his duty.

'Are you?' Thungrimsson said. They were alone in the

blockhouse, by the king's command, so there was little need for formality. Outside, weapons rattled and the stone vibrated with the tread of booted feet as the defenders of Karak Kadrin readied themselves for battle anew. Past the walls, horns wailed and beasts howled as the Chaos army was brought under control and aimed once more at their enemies. Something was going on out there, over the chasm, but no one had figured out what yet.

Ungrim snorted. 'Need you ask? I ache for battle, old friend.' He stepped away from the table, hefting his double-headed axe. 'My axe is thirsty.'

'Speaking of thirsty,' Thungrimsson muttered, striding to the keg set upright near the table. He filled a mug and threw it back. Wiping foam from his mouth, he looked at his king. 'Gurnisson is quite charismatic, when he wants to be.'

Ungrim grunted, watching the lantern light play across his axe. He said, 'And what of my son?' Thungrimsson fell silent. Ungrim grunted again, and sighed. 'I know,' he said.

'He will learn,' Thungrimsson said, setting his mug aside. 'You have taught him much.'

'I have little left to teach him,' Ungrim said. 'And what I have taught him, I fear, has made him less than he should be.' He looked at Thungrimsson. 'I should not have let him take the vow.'

'That is not for me to say, my king.'

'You are my hearth-warden, and my Reckoner, and come to it, my Remembrancer, Thungrimsson. Of all those who serve me, you alone have leave to say what you wish, when you will,' Ungrim said. 'I should not have let him take the oath.'

'No, you should not have,' Thungrimsson said.

Ungrim looked up, eyes blazing. He bit off a retort and then released an unsteady breath. 'He insisted,' he said. It was less an excuse than a simple statement of fact. Garagrim had insisted, and Ungrim could deny his only son nothing. Not even the decision to take on an oath that would doom him. Thungrimsson nodded.

'He had his reasons,' he said.

Ungrim's face twisted. 'Oh aye, he had reasons, and foolish ones at that. The king of Karak Kadrin carries the burden of our shame, not the prince. He thinks to buy my freedom with his death, and I'll not pay that price, not for all the gold in these mountains.'

'Have you told him that?'

Ungrim slumped. 'What good would it do, Snorri? Would he listen? Has he *ever* listened?'

Thungrimsson had no answer for his king. Ungrim stumped back to the table. 'If Gurnisson makes good his vow, we will know it. Nonetheless, we need to keep them occupied and looking at us.' He stroked his beard, losing himself in the sway and flow of future battle. Thungrimsson couldn't help but admire his king. Ungrim Ironfist possessed the finest battle-sense of any dwarf king yet ruling a hold, and Karak Kadrin had been shaped over the centuries by that sense. It was as much a war machine as any catapult or bolt thrower, when Ungrim saw to its defences.

'There are paths from the inner keep to the outer,' Ungrim said, referring to the hidden, sloped tunnels that acted simultaneously as drainage as well as strong-points for the defenders of the hold to launch blistering guerrilla attacks. The paths weren't large, and once revealed, would have to be sealed after the dwarfs had retreated. If they had to retreat, if any of them were left to retreat.

'Thunderers,' Thungrimsson said.

'Mm,' Ungrim said noncommittally. 'No, axes, I think. We'll

wait for those blasted *gronti* to get close,' he said, referring to the siege-giants.

'That'll be a suicide mission,' Thungrimsson said softly.

Ungrim nodded grimly. 'There are over a hundred Slayers left in the hold, maybe more. Gather as many as you can find. They'll be happy enough to do it.' There was no way to keep an accurate count of Slayers at the best of times, let alone in a siege. They came and went as it pleased them, and there were always more hanging around than was entirely healthy to Thungrimsson's thinking. Not without reason was Karak Kadrin called Slayer Keep. Nonetheless, the way Ungrim spent them like quarrels from a crossbow did not sit well with him, even in circumstances such as this.

Ungrim saw his expression and sighed. 'I know your feelings, old friend. But you are not a Slayer, and Grungni willing, you never will be. They – we – are already dead and we have been since our names were inscribed on the pillar in the temple of Grimnir. Some, like Gurnisson, are simply more stubborn about it than others. Bringing down one of those thrice-cursed walking siege-engines will be a doom equal to Agni Firetongue's.' Ungrim's eyes glinted. 'I'd go myself, if I thought you'd let me.'

Thungrimsson tensed, but Ungrim waved a hand. 'I know. My oath as king supersedes my personal shame. I will lead the second sortie, and, Grimnir willing, you will crown Garagrim as king and strip the dye from his hair and perhaps Karak Kadrin will have a proper king again.'

'It has a proper king now,' Thungrimsson said. Ungrim didn't reply, his eyes on the map. His king was no longer listening. He rarely listened. At times, Thungrimsson thought that there was very little left of the beardling who'd taken the throne, his jowls and pate stained with dye. He'd been much like his son, devoted and determined. Now, he was obsessed. Under his unflagging leadership Karak Kadrin had grown in prestige and power. For many in the city, the hold was the fulcrum about which the world revolved, and it was at Karak Kadrin that the last battle before the end of the world would come. When war was on the wind, the Slayers came, hungrily hunting doom in defence of the bar that kept the cursed north at bay. But even as he'd made an impregnable fastness of the hold, he'd become more and more doom-hungry himself.

Ungrim wanted to die so badly that he invited war to his people's doorstep. Expeditions to the north left from Karak Kadrin, bearing his seal. They were challenges, tossed into the teeth of Chaos. Trapped here by duty, he tried to draw enemies to him, without regard for the consequences.

Somewhere, somewhen, Ungrim Ironfist had joined his Slayer brethren in madness, Thungrimsson knew. And it was a madness that could very well spell the doom of not just Ungrim, but his people as well.

Karak Kadrin, *the Underway*

The dwarfs called the bridge the Deep Span. It was a narrow thing, barely wide enough for two dwarfs to cross side-by-side. Besides the massive main bridge that had extended from Baragor's Watch to the entryway to Karak Kadrin proper, it was the only way into the section of the Underway directly beneath the ravaged outer keep that didn't involve an arduous week-long trip through the mountains. Felix eyed it with trepidation as he squatted in the lee of the great portcullis that marked the beginning of the bridge. A similar portcullis occupied the other end.

The bridge didn't look as big as he'd have liked, or as wide. The sheer enormity of the chasm wasn't helping matters. It was a vast, yawning silence that seemed to swallow up all noise and light. Even worse, they were travelling across it in the dark in small groups, so as not to attract any undue attention from the forces perched on the lip of the chasm above.

Felix started as Gotrek slapped his back. 'Just keep your hand on my shoulder, manling. We can't have you slipping off, not so close to what may be my hour of doom.'

'No,' Felix said through gritted teeth. 'What will we face up there, Gotrek?' he said, changing the subject as they waited for their turn to cross.

'The enemy, manling,' Gotrek said.

'I meant from the – ah – the dawi zharr.' He said it hesitantly, half expecting Gotrek to explode with fury. Instead the Slayer became quiet.

'There won't be many of them,' he said at last. 'No more than a handful. They never come this far south in numbers more than a handful.' He grunted. 'Watch their hands, manling. They are dwarfs, and though they are debased and twisted, they still have cunning. They make terrible weapons and they use them at the least provocation. Don't let them get close, don't let them see you or catch you unawares.'

'What about their weapons?'

'We will destroy their corrupt machines. That shall be the task of the Slayers,' Garagrim said, joining them, Biter following behind him. 'When we emerge, we shall make for their guns, to destroy them and their masters. The dawi zharr cannot be allowed to escape.'

'No,' Gotrek said, in agreement, 'They cannot.' Garagrim looked almost surprised at Gotrek's statement, but he refrained from commenting. Gotrek smiled sourly. 'That is more important than any doom, War-Mourner. The safety of the hold comes first.'

Garagrim gave a curt nod. A moment later, it was their turn to cross. Felix thought about closing his eyes, reckoning that sight would do him little good in any event, but decided against it and instead kept his eyes firmly on the back of Gotrek's head. The trip across the bridge did not go quickly, but Gotrek's sure-footed movements kept Felix to the path without a misstep, and his hand on the Slayer's shoulder kept him from wandering too close to the edge. He looked up only once as they moved across the span, but could see nothing save a distant slash of starry sky. The sounds of industry rattled down periodically from above, and dim sounds that might have been screams.

As they reached the other side, he said, 'What are they building up there?' For he knew that was what those sounds had been, and he had a dark premonition of the stunted shapes of the Chaos dwarfs crafting some new hellish engine in the ruined belly of the captured keep.

'It doesn't matter,' Gotrek muttered. 'They'll never finish it, whatever it is.'

The darkness of the Underway was even more claustrophobic the second time around, Felix felt. One hand clenched achingly tight on Karaghul's hilt, he moved through the vast silence, one shape amongst many. Dwarf engineers carried explosives in heavily reinforced kegs. They were surrounded by ironbreakers and rangers, protected from any threat that might choose to try its luck on the small army moving through the depths.

As improbable as it sounded, Felix had been assured that there were such things. Brooding horrors unleashed into the depths by an ancient cataclysm and by more recent incursions by goblins and skaven and worse things. 'There are worse things than grobi in the depths,' the miner Copperback had said, with far too much enthusiasm for Felix's taste.

After hearing that, Felix couldn't help but see monstrous shapes in every shadow and nightmares crouching in every forgotten archway. Even worse, from above, he could hear the sounds of cannon-fire picking up once more where it had left off. Every boom from above echoed and re-echoed until it was a thunderclap below.

'The ground is weak,' Gotrek said as dust drifted down in a choking cloud.

'It'll be weaker after we blow a chunk of it into the sky,' one of the Slayers murmured, his voice echoing oddly in the suffocating quiet.

'If you have a problem with it, you should have stayed behind,' another rasped. 'It's not like we'd miss your axe, Berengar.'

The Slayer called Berengar let loose a punch that connected audibly with the other Slayer's shoulder. Garagrim, not far ahead, turned. 'Quiet, the pair of you,' he growled.

'Quiet yourself, beardling,' an older Slayer, with one milky white eye and a short, stiff crest that looked like a white stripe painted across the top of his sun-browned scalp, said, glaring at the War-Mourner. Garagrim blustered, unused to his authority being questioned. Gotrek grinned mirthlessly, watching the exchange.

Felix let himself fall back from the main bulk of the Slayers. He dropped into a trot beside Biter. The latter was the most open-mouthed dwarf he'd ever met. Biter was watching one of the younger Slayers, who walked beside Garagrim. 'Why does Garagrim keep him so close?' Felix asked.

'That's the War-Mourner's duty,' Biter said, the head of his mace bouncing on his shoulder. 'He chooses who's to die. Then he makes sure that it happens.' He chuckled. 'Most of us don't need his help, which annoys the beardling no end. Princes are worse than kings for royal commands.'

'You could probably use his help,' Koertig said.

Biter laughed. Felix looked from the sour-faced Nordlander to the Slayer.

'Forgive me for asking, but–' he began.

'I don't want to talk about it,' Koertig growled.

'I got him drunk,' Biter said, leering suggestively. 'You man-lings swear your strongest oaths with a bit of ale in your belly.'

'Why?' Felix said.

Biter shrugged. 'I needed a new Remembrancer.'

'What happened to your old one?' Felix said, though he didn't think he really wanted to know the answer.

Biter's smile faded. 'He got old,' he said. He looked at Felix. 'You humans grow old so quickly. One day he was by my side and then, he was gone. He went in his sleep.'

'That doesn't sound so bad–'

'A giant stepped on him while he was sleeping. We prob-ably shouldn't have drunk so much,' Biter said mournfully. 'My fault, I suppose.' He grinned. 'Still, I feel lucky this time.'

'You said that the last two times,' Koertig said. 'And the dozen times before that.' He looked at Felix. 'At least yours tries. Mine thinks it's a joke.'

'It *is* a joke,' Biter said. He looked at Felix. 'Grimnir had no sense of humour, they say. Not a smile to be had when he was around. So we do the same. We cut it out, the way we cut our beards. Not me, though. If I'm already dead, I intend to enjoy the afterlife. Wine, women and song, isn't that what you humans say?'

Felix couldn't help smiling. 'Yes, something like that.'

'I can do what I want now, Jaeger,' Biter said. His eyes were bright with a peculiar sort of madness. 'For the first time in my life, I can do what I want. No clan, no king, no rules. That's the joke, that's why Grimnir went north, you know. Not for shame or duty or honour, but because he was just so damned tired of being told what to do by his peers, by his king, of being crushed by the mountains we dwarfs carry on our backs,' he continued. Then, 'That's the joke,' he said, more softly.

Felix looked away, feeling faintly ashamed though he couldn't say why. Koertig merely grunted. The Nordlander was used to his Slayer's mercurial shifts of mood, obviously. Biter fell silent, his eyes locked on that middle distance that Felix knew well enough.

The dwarfs moved mostly in silence. If they felt any nervousness, no bearded face showed it. The ironbreakers walked on the outskirts of the throng, alert gazes sweeping the darkness. The rangers stayed close to the engineers, and most of the miners moved far ahead, the lights of their candle-helmets piercing the gloom. The rest walked with the throng, holding long poles topped by enclosed lanterns that enveloped the other dwarfs in a warm, protective glow. The Slayers, of course, strode through the darkness, their voices loud. Some shouted challenges into collapsed tunnels, while others occasionally wandered off, only to return looking disappointed. Only Gotrek, Garagrim and Biter stayed with the throng the entire trek. Was it a sign of patience, Felix wondered, or was it simply that once they had a doom in their sights, they were determined not to waver from it?

Axeson walked amongst the throng, whispering softly to the younger warriors at times. In other instances, he walked out into the darkness and returned with a shamefaced Slayer trotting dejectedly in his wake. Felix joined him. Axeson gripped a heavy axe, its blade dripping with strange runes.

'Why did you come with us?' Felix said. Axeson glanced at him, but didn't reply. Felix frowned, irritated by the priest's sudden taciturnity. 'What does it have to do with Gotrek?'

'Who says it has anything to do with Gurnisson?'

'You told me to keep him alive. Then, later, you said that if he died, Karak Kadrin would fall. What did you mean?'

'I merely passed on what the ancestor-gods told me,' Axeson said.

'I was given to understand that Grimnir was not the most talkative of gods,' Felix said.

'He's not. Which is why dwarfs listen when he chooses to speak,' Axeson said. They walked in silence for a while. Then, 'The ghost of civilization,' the priest murmured. 'What do you think of it, Jaeger?' He waved a hand at the arching, vaulted roof of the Underway, stretching high into the shadowed recesses above them.

'Gotrek said it once stretched the length of the Worlds Edge Mountains,' Felix said. Immense archways lined this section of the ancient road. Without exception, all of them had been sealed with massive blocks of cut stone. Felix shivered, briefly imagining what might be scratching at the other side.

'Farther,' Axeson said. 'My–' He hesitated. 'My father used to tell me that it was the spine of the world, connecting the far northern holds to those in the distant south. Thousands of dwarfs – merchants, peddlers, adventurers – would travel these deep roads, spreading out in a vast wave, taking our artisanry, our civilization, to every corner of this world. Some say that we even had roads that travelled beneath the sea,' he said wistfully. He coughed in embarrassment.

'What happened?'

'What always happens, manling,' Gotrek said, appearing suddenly at Felix's elbow, causing him to jump. 'Chaos came, and brought the Golden Age to an end. Then the elves turned on us.'

'And your people superseded both of ours in the aftermath,' Axeson said.

'That's a matter of opinion,' Gotrek said. 'And it's a debate for another time.' He pointed. 'We're here.' The road had widened into what resembled a large antechamber, and great statues stood silent sentry over shadowed corners. Grime-shrouded mosaics covered the circular walls and despite the detritus of years, the sheer artisanry of the edifices that lined the space was impossible to deny. Ancient aqueducts stretched along the ceiling, and, impossibly, water still sloshed softly through them.

'It was a marketplace once,' Axeson said. 'We're beneath the section of the keep where Ungrim's outer palace was built. This was once the central hub of the Karak Kadrin markets.'

Felix could believe it. He imagined that stalls had once filled the shadowy berths that lined the chamber and the corridors that spread out from it. What had it been like, in those long-gone days? How many dwarfs had packed into this place to dicker and bargain over goods?

'The markets were famed throughout the Empire,' Garagrim said, picking up where Axeson had left off. The War-Mourner's hand stroked the stone wall reverentially. 'We were the centre of the world then: Karak Kadrin, where all roads met and gold from a thousand holds traded hands.' He turned and gestured. 'That road led to Barak Varr, and far below, at the bottom of the Hundred Thousand Steps sits the Market-Dock, where the traders who once plied the deep rivers and oceans upon which the good stone of the earth rests would set sail for the sea-fortress and Zhufbar on the Black Water. And there, the pathway into the Badlands that once led to the Silver Pinnacle, aye and long lost Karak Eight Peaks. We were the centre of the empire; not its heart, perhaps, but mighty in our own way. Mighty...'

Garagrim trailed off and shook his head. The dwarfs had paused in reverential silence, even the Slayers. For them, this was their history, rendered in stone and inviolate despite all that their people had undergone. It was as much a part of them as their beards or their songs. And now, they had come to destroy it, in order to destroy an enemy, and Felix was struck by the sad necessity of what was to come.

Gotrek seemed to know what he was thinking, and he grunted. 'It has always been thus, manling. We sacrifice of ourselves to kill our foe. Stone or flesh, it makes little difference. When the time comes to pay the price, we pay it gladly.'

'Some of us more gladly than others,' Garagrim said. He slapped the rock wall and the sound echoed throughout the chamber. 'We were mighty once. We could be mighty again!'

'Those days are gone,' Gotrek said, and his words settled like a shroud over them all. 'These caverns are tombs now, fit only for memory and death.'

No one spoke for a time. After a long silence, the engineers set to work. While half began to oversee the construction of bulwarks against the force of the explosion from tumbled stone and debris, the others set about placing the explosives. They placed their explosives more carefully than the Chaos marauders had. Felix thought that they were perhaps almost hesitant, and that this might almost be a taboo of some sort. Would the dwarf gods look kindly on their people unmaking that which they had made aeons past? For that matter, would their fellow dwarfs? Or would there be a particular sort of unacknowledged shame attached to the names of those who had taken part in this mission, that they had committed some crime; a necessary one, but inescapably wrong for all of that?

Gotrek alone seemed unbothered by that fact, though Felix thought that he simply hid it better than the rest. 'The roof was made with escape in mind,' Gotrek said approvingly, turning in a short circle. 'Flat braces of rock that will tip and crash if the supports are blown. It was supposed to give our people a way to get above-ground in the event of a collapse. Blowing down just one is enough for our purposes.' He rubbed his patch with the heel of his palm. 'Which is good, because the rest of them will shatter, if I judge their condition right,' he added. 'Time cripples even our work.'

Puzzled, Felix watched them work. There was an art to it, it seemed, and it was one that Gotrek seemed proficient in. He oversaw the placement, ordering changes with brusque directness when something didn't match up to the calculations in his head. The other Slayers, and not a few of the other dwarfs besides, watched him with a mixture of wariness, hostility and admiration.

When they had finished, Felix felt a sudden nervousness. There was no guarantee that the dwarfs' explosives would serve them any better than theirs had the Chaos marauders. He'd heard tell of accidents at the Nuln Gunnery School that had resulted in even experienced gunners and sappers being blown sky high by their own weapons, and he didn't want to experience that first hand. The dwarfs, on the other hand, seemed eager for the fireworks to begin as they moved back into the tunnels and behind the makeshift bulwarks. An engineer poured a trail of black, sulphur-smelling powder from and to each keg and then away, towards the group. When he'd finished, Garagrim lit a torch and held it aloft. 'Well, who wants it?'

A dozen Slayers raised their hands. Garagrim snorted and handed the torch to the Slayer Berengar, who looked at it as if it were an adder about to bite him.

'Time to stand back, manling,' Gotrek said, laying one ham-sized hand against Felix's chest as Berengar stepped towards the trail of powder and let the torch dip. Around them, dwarfs crouched and placed their hands over their ears and let their mouths open the way Imperial gunners did before a cannon fired. 'It's about to get very, very loud in here.'

And then, very abruptly, it did.

Karak Kadrin,
Baragor's Watch

Standing before the broken remains of the bridge leading to Karak Kadrin, Canto watched the Chaos dwarfs work with a mixture of disgust and admiration. The stunted ones had set up a makeshift workshop in the lee of the final wall of the outer fortress and were busy at work.

On the precipice, the siege-giant howled in agony as it was forced to kneel, its abused ligaments popping like cannon-fire. Even stretched out, the beast wouldn't reach across the chasm, but that wasn't Khorreg's intent. Instead, he and his assistants had overseen their ogre-slaves in extracting certain materials from the gutted ruins of the keep. Iron struts and ironwood supports from the fallen walls were dragged towards the chasm by the ogres as well as the remnants of Hrolf's warband, now pressed into service by Canto's order. The lengths of solid wood and stone were held by the giant as the ogres, under the cold gaze of one of the Chaos dwarfs, began to drive immense lengths of twisted metal through the wood and into the stone below, anchoring it in place.

'The giants are no use in cracking the hold,' Khorreg said, stroking his beard and watching the construction. 'The brutes wouldn't live long enough to get through the doors let alone into the upper levels of the hold – they'd be dead the minute they assaulted the gates. But, he who wastes not wants not,' Khorreg continued gleefully. 'My kin have used breathing bridges to great effect elsewhere. We'll just need to see that they're properly supported, but once that's done, we'll have them lay down and then we'll make sure they don't get any ideas about moving. And we'll need to be quick about securing a hold on the plateau. We'll take the magma cannon over first and get it chained to the ground before the doors. Your savages can see to keeping it protected, just in case our weakling cousins decide to try a sortie through the main gates.'

'How long will this… breathing bridge hold out?'

'As long as the beasts do,' Khorreg said. 'They'll last long enough to get most of your troops over and into the hold through whatever cracks we carve into it. After that, well, your troops are in need of supplies, aren't they?'

Canto grimaced at the thought of eating one of the smelly beasts. 'Once we're in, how long will it take you to build something more permanent?'

'A few weeks, more or less,' Khorreg said confidently. 'I have no doubt our cousins have the materials within their pathetic hold somewhere.'

The Dreadquake mortar gave a rumbling roar that shook the ground beneath Canto's feet and fired a moment later, belching destruction towards Karak Kadrin. Part of the mountain face crumbled, showering the plateau with rocks. It was followed by a number of rockets, which streaked towards the doors, leaving behind immense craters to mark the points of impact. The doors held firm, though Khorreg didn't seem disappointed. When Canto mentioned it, the Chaos dwarf gave a cackle.

'Doors won't matter when we rip the front of that mountain off, manling,' he said.

Canto was about to reply when the world was suddenly ripped asunder, as if by the hands of the gods. Stone was wrenched from the ground and hurled skywards, along with men and animals, in a vast volcanic gout of hot air and destruction as the ground was ruptured from below. The wall behind them disintegrated into a hurricane of stone flinders and death. Men were reduced to pulp by flying stone and debris. The Deathshrieker rocket launcher was knocked over and the remaining rockets exploded, ripping apart both the ogres responsible for loading them as well as the Chaos marauders and Chaos warriors nearby. The magma cannon broke its traces and the massive engine rolled through the destruction with a booming snarl of triumph as the daemon animating it suddenly found itself free to hunt its own prey.

Canto, knocked flat on his back, saw the daemon-engine lurch towards him through the shower of rock and flaming debris. As it lunged past one of Khorreg's assistants, its great iron and brass wheels pulped the Chaos dwarf, reducing him to a dark red smear on the cracked stone of the ground. He clawed for the hilt of his sword, knowing even as he drew it that it would be of little use. The cannon would devour him, sword and all. Then Khorreg was there, and he flung out his hands and something round and hissing flew towards the engine – a small explosive, Canto belatedly realized. The cannon's wheels exploded and the engine toppled over with a roar.

Khorreg glanced over his shoulder at Canto. 'The third debt, Unsworn, is settled. Two left, by my reckoning,' the Chaos dwarf said.

Canto rose to his feet. The ground trembled as tremors rippled outwards from an immense column of smoke that now dominated the sky above them. 'What was that?' he snarled.

Khorreg grinned. 'Big explosion, manling... Looks like our cousins are coming out to play after all,' he said. The Hell-Worker turned and began to bellow orders to his surviving assistant. He turned back to Canto. 'Best get your troops facing the right direction, before you find yourself cut off at the knees.'

Canto grunted and grabbed the first Chaos marauder to stagger out of the smoke and dust. 'Sound the rally,' he roared. 'We're under attack!'

10

Karak Kadrin,
Baragor's Watch

The explosion rocked the chamber and though he'd been prepared for it, Felix was sent flying. He struck an outcropping and slumped, dazed by the sudden rush of sound and fury. For a moment, the air was filled with an almost solid bombardment of noise and destruction and Felix scrambled about on his knees, his hands clapped to his ears as a flood of stone dust billowed through the chamber. The echoes of the explosion faded, and Felix caught the groan of collapsing stone as he cautiously removed his hands.

The antechamber was large, almost the length of the outer wall of Karak Kadrin. The explosion had been like a precise blow, tipping the first in a row of pegs. Bodies tumbled into the gash opened in the roof even as that gash split and spread like cracks running across ice. Gotrek had been correct, the ground above was weak; what age and disuse alone had failed to do, the explosion had accomplished. Vast flat stones, formerly part of the roof of the Underway, slammed down against the road, creating rough ramps, even as Gotrek had predicted. Even as Felix staggered to his feet, dwarfs covered in dust and grime shook themselves free of the devastation and the Slayers charged up the makeshift ramp, scrambling part of the way then running with their weapons swinging.

Dazed Chaos marauders who had somehow not fallen were slapped aside, and dead ones were trampled. The bodies of the latter littered the floor of the chamber three-deep, and Felix was forced to clamber over them, his stomach rebelling at the sight of what the force of the blast had done to them. Even the hardy men of the Chaos Wastes were as nothing before the power of the explosion that had ripped open the ground beneath them.

The dwarfs moved surprisingly quickly, following the Slayers. The miners had given a number of the latter sturdy metal ladders that could be carried rolled up and then unrolled when needed. The Slayers had done so as they reached the top, and the rangers followed them, climbing swiftly. Felix went up with Koertig and Axeson. Both men had been abandoned by their Slayers.

The climb was arduous, despite the relative shallowness of the slope. The dwarfs managed it easily, but both Felix and Koertig were sweating and shaking by the time they reached the top. At some point during their travels, the sun had begun to rise, and thin daylight pierced the heavy cloud of dust and smoke that the explosion had thrown into the air. He emerged from the oppressive silence that followed an explosion into the clangour of battle. His eardrums ached and Karaghul was in his hand, though he didn't recall drawing it.

The devastation was breathtaking. The explosion hadn't simply opened a hole in the battlefield. It had gouged titanic talon marks through the already ruined outer keep, ripping the bastion open like a savaged lamb. Felix could not even begin to comprehend what the reverberations had done to those distant portions of the Underway. How much ancient history had been lost, buried forever by one lit trail of powder? The fortress looked as if it had been raised up and then tossed down, some places sunken lower than others as buried supports collapsed in a slow domino-tilt of destruction. Smoke and dust obscured the sky, issuing in ominous clouds from the ruptured soil. It was as if the very ground had decided to reject the Chaos horde's presence.

The rangers had arrayed themselves around the circumference of the newly made crater and their crossbows were pointed outwards, firing into the melee that surrounded them. Felix hastily moved away from the crater as ironbreakers and miners clambered to the surface. He looked for Gotrek, but couldn't spot him in the chaos of battle.

The Slayers had seized the initiative, and their assault rippled outwards in a spreading circle of destruction as twenty doomseekers pitted themselves against ten times their number in an orgy of violent redemption. The explosion had shattered whatever cohesion the marauders had possessed, erupting beneath the largest mass of men. Now they fought not as a horde, but as individuals or small groups, and in that, they were little match for the ravening Slayers.

Felix caught sight of Dorin, wide sword in hand, as he lopped off a leg at the knee and bounced over the falling warrior to launch himself at the man's wide-eyed fellows. A milky-eyed old Slayer spun his axe in a crooked figure-eight and tattooed tribesmen shrieked and fell. But where was Gotrek?

He heard a shout, and found himself thrust aside by the metal-plated arm of the ironbreaker, Grimbold, whose axe looped out, shearing off the jaw of a howling Northman. 'Step aside, manling, and let us do our job,' the ironbreaker snarled. Behind him, another ironbreaker raised a curling war-horn to his lips and let loose with a low, loud sound that rose up over the fading noise of the explosion and bounced through the ruins. Grimbold and his warriors moved outwards in two rings past the line of rangers, dispatching those men the Slayers hadn't. Unlike the latter, however, the ironbreakers did not spread so far as to weaken their own lines. Felix felt a bit in awe of the dwarfs' martial precision. Each of the dwarfs seemed to know by instinct where his companions were and move accordingly, shield held aloft and axe flashing. As with everything else, the dwarf approach to war was that of craftsmen, organized, precise and effective.

He looked around, sighting the shattered, gaping outer walls of the fortress. Men poured out, abandoning the siege for battle. Horns screamed and tribal chieftains tried to maintain order, but just as with the earlier internecine blood-letting the war-hunger of the Blood God's worshippers could not, would not be denied. They had been forced to wait for too long; now that their opponents had come to them, they would neither slow nor retreat.

'I should never have accepted that drink,' Koertig muttered. He raised his shield and slammed the flat of his axe against it. 'Come on then!' The first Chaos marauders reached them a moment later. Koertig caught a blow on his shield and let his axe drop, taking his opponent in the head. The Nordlander knew these men of old, for his people had fought them since before Sigmar had first raised his hammer, and he met their savagery with cold hatred centuries in the making.

Axeson, in contrast, fought with an almost Slayer-like ferocity. His axe in one hand and a short-hafted hammer in the other, he used the latter to break a charging marauder's leg before cleaving his head with the former. He fought in silence, unlike the warrior-priests of the Empire who went into battle belting out hymns.

Karaghul shot up, narrowly deflecting a clumsily hurled spear. Weaponless, the frothing warrior leapt at Felix, arms outstretched. Felix ducked beneath those arms and his blade sank home. As the Chaos marauder fell, dragging him around, Felix jerked the blade free and turned to meet his next opponent. A crossbow bolt took that one in the head, pitching him backwards. Felix strode past him without pausing.

He searched for Gotrek. It was instinct by now, a compulsion to make sure that he didn't miss any moment of what might be the Slayer's final battle. The battle spun around him, and there were more orange crests to catch his eye than normal.

There! Gotrek's arm swung out, his massive fist connecting with a helmeted head, denting baroque metal and breaking bone, sending the Chaos warrior tumbling down like a sack of broken sticks. His axe swung out as if independent of him, a predatory curve of steel seeking its morning meal. Like Axeson, he fought quietly, without his usual excitement. It was unnerving, as if the Gotrek he had known had become something else – a mechanism of destruction, feeling nothing, not even anticipation. The Slayer fought steadily, his every step littered with human wreckage.

In contrast, Garagrim fought almost joyously. The War-Mourner seemed to have left behind the weight of responsibility, and his axes licked out as if they weighed no more than feathers. But despite his abandon, Felix noted that he stayed close to the equally wild younger Slayer he had noticed with the older dwarf in the tunnels. The War-Mourner guided the young Slayer into the thick of the battle, almost herding him into combat.

The sound of galloping hooves shook the air. Felix turned and saw a wave of marauder horsemen crushing their own ground-bound allies to reach the dwarf line. The riders whooped and howled as they came on and Felix threw himself to the side, narrowly avoiding being trampled. A Slayer wasn't so lucky, and the orange crest was flattened ignobly into the mud of the battlefield. Felix couldn't tell who it was.

He brought Karaghul up in time to block a spear-thrust and then the horseman was past him. Crossbows fired, picking riders from the saddle. Then, it was axe-work. Horses shrieked as pick-axes swept their hooves out from under them and sent them rolling. The dwarfs, while possessing no cavalry of their own, had long ago learned the art of dealing with a charge, especially one as ragged as this.

More riders came on, however. The dwarfs would be overwhelmed, unless–

More horns, but not the brute things of the enemy. No, these were the brass-banded dragon-horns of Karak Kadrin, sounding from somewhere nearby. The second sortie had begun.

So distracted by this was Felix that he only caught sight of the looming rider at the last second, and a falchion sliced through the edge of his cape and across his cheek as he twisted aside.

The Chaos marauder was lithe and deadly looking, like a needle wrapped in iron, and his armour was covered in stretched and stitched faces that looked as if they were screaming. He whooped and jerked on his mount's reins, his eyes alight with battle-lust. He stank of the stuff of slaughter and Felix gagged as he brought Karaghul up to block another sweeping blow from the falchion. His opponent was stronger than he anticipated, and Karaghul bent back, nearly gashing his shoulder. Felix fell and the hooves of the horse rose over him. He closed his eyes.

A shout thundered in his ears. The young Slayer who'd been beside Garagrim flung himself at the rider, axe licking out to cut through the straps on the man's saddle, spilling him to the ground in a heap. But as quickly as he'd fallen, he was on his feet, falchion sweeping upwards in a brutal arc that split the Slayer's skull jaw to crest and sent his body pin-wheeling into the air.

The Chaos warrior gave a bone-rattling guffaw as the body hit the ground. 'That's for you, you stunted monkeys. Yan the Foul is no dog to be beaten by apes with hatchets!'

Felix scrambled to his feet and lunged, hoping to bury his sword in the warrior's back before the latter remembered that he was there. The Chaos warrior turned as Felix's boot-soles scraped on the stone and caught Karaghul in one gauntlet. Sparks spat from between his fingers as he wrenched the blade down, nearly knocking Felix from his feet. With barely a sneer of effort, the Chaos warrior jerked the sword from Felix's grip and sent him scrambling back with a cursory swipe of his own blade. He examined Karaghul and gave an appreciative grunt, his weather-seamed face splitting in a vulpine grin. 'I'll have this, I think. And your skull to go with it,' he said, pointing both swords at Felix, who felt his heart drop into his belly.

'Only if you get past me,' Garagrim rumbled, clashing his axes together. 'That manling is a guest of Karak Kadrin and he is under my protection.'

'Another shaved monkey,' the Chaos warrior said, turning to face the War-Mourner. 'Tell me your name, monkey, so that I might have it to remember you by after I knock your stone lair down.'

'Garagrim Ironfist, Prince of Karak Kadrin and War-Mourner of the Slayer Keep,' Garagrim growled, stalking towards his opponent.

'And I am Yan the Foul, Yan of the Khazags, Beast of the Steppes, Wolf of the Plains, Master of–' Yan began.

'I don't care,' Garagrim said, lunging.

His axes skidded off Yan's hastily interposed blades. Yan grunted and shoved the Slayer back. 'Master of the Red Lodge and Servant of the Eightfold Path,' Yan continued, eyes flashing. 'There. Now we're properly introduced. Time to die, little monkey.'

Karaghul hummed like a wasp as it slashed out, shaving the top inch off Garagrim's crest. The falchion snapped down, nearly catching his leg. The War-Mourner turned and brought both axes around in a sharp arc that caught Yan on his cuirass, shearing away the flayed skin and staggering the Chaos warrior. Yan swept Karaghul up in an awkward slice and Garagrim parried the blade with one axe and then brought his other down on the Chaos warrior's extended wrist, severing it completely. Karaghul, still clenched in Yan's fist, tumbled across the stone towards Felix, who leapt for it.

Yan gave a howl and jabbed his gushing stump at Garagrim, blinding the War-Mourner with a spray of brackish blood. The falchion gashed the dwarf's shoulder and sent him tumbling. The Chaos warrior lunged, trying to capitalize on his foe's plight. But Garagrim was quicker. One axe snapped out, chopping into Yan's foot and pinning the warrior in place even as the other sank into his opposite knee. The Chaos warrior screamed and crumpled to his knees.

He slashed ineffectually at Garagrim, and the War-Mourner took his other hand with an almost lazy swipe of an axe. 'Karak Kadrin still stands,' Garagrim said calmly. Then he buried the blades of both axes into either side of the Chaos warrior's neck until the blades met and Yan the Foul's head toppled free to bounce along the stones, its expression one of bewildered frustration.

'Up, human,' Garagrim said, shaking blood from his axes with a rotation of his wrists. 'There are still enemies to be killed and Slayers seeking doom.' He looked at Felix. 'You are a Remembrancer. You should be with your Slayer, so that his doom does not go unseen.'

'One would think that you wouldn't mind that,' Felix said, prying his sword free from the Chaos warrior's clutching hand. Garagrim's expression turned sour.

'Whatever else I may think of Gurnisson, Jaeger, I am War-Mourner and he is a Slayer. My oath is to see that his... that all of their oaths are fulfilled.' He strode off and Felix followed warily after him. Gotrek and the other Slayers had left a trail of carnage from the crater up to the ragged gap in the sixth wall where the Chaos army had brought their war-engines.

As the Chaos marauders moved to meet the organized dwarf attackers in their midst, the Slayers had been given a relatively clear path to the war-engines. They had chopped and bashed their way through anything and anyone that tried to stand in their way, losing individual Slayers along the way. Now only eight remained, but Gotrek was among them, as was Biter, Berengar and a few others that Felix dimly recognized. Garagrim slapped a Chaos marauder aside and he and Felix joined the group as it made its way towards the engines of the Chaos dwarfs.

'Not dead then, manling?' Gotrek said. 'I thought I'd lost you there, for a moment.'

'Almost, but not quite,' Felix said. 'Garagrim came to my aid,' he added, somewhat acidly. It rankled a bit whenever

Gotrek abandoned him in the middle of a fight to go haring off on his own. The Slayer had saved his life on numerous occasions, but even so, that sum was outnumbered by the times that he'd led or left Felix to situations where he could have easily perished. Gotrek grunted and nodded, as if he'd expected the War-Mourner to do no less. Felix gritted his teeth and turned his attentions to what awaited them.

Someone had been busy organizing a defence of the war machines. Chaos marauders were arrayed in defensive groups around the mammoth devices, as were the ogre crew. The latter brutes, scarred and beaten, clutched tools rather than weapons, but they looked no less imposing for all of that. Those that weren't readying themselves to fight were lugging the cannon around to face the gap in the wall. Behind them, a large mortar set into a brutal-looking wheeled chassis gave a rumbling bellow that set Felix's ears to ringing and nearly knocked him off his feet. Somewhere behind them, more of the fortress was flattened in an explosion of dust and fire.

'Take them,' Garagrim said, quietly. The Slayers charged and the Chaos marauders came to meet them. The battle was as short as it was brutal. All around them, horns sounded as the dwarf forces in the outer keep swept the disorganized and dis-arrayed enemy before them. Somewhere along the way, chain of command had broken down in the enemy army, and now individuals and small bands fought not as an army fights, but for survival.

Felix blocked a sword-blow and gutted his opponent, look-ing past him towards the cannon as it was finally turned about, its maw dripping with fiery liquid. Gotrek saw it as well and as the cannon belched a stream of liquid fire, the Slayer turned and grabbed Felix, jerking him out of the way. One of the Slayers wasn't so lucky and his form was consumed in moments by the deadly blast.

'We have to take that blasted thing out,' Gotrek growled, releasing Felix. With that, the Slayer launched himself towards the cannon and its ogre crew. The two beasts stomped forwards to meet the Slayer, one swinging a hammer, the other reaching out with blistered and blackened hands.

Felix's attention was pulled from the fight as he heard the crack of a pistol and felt something tug at his cloak, nearly spinning him around. As he spun, he saw a grinning Chaos dwarf lower the smoking wheel-lock pistol he held and raise a second, this one aimed unerringly at Felix's breastbone. The Chaos dwarf shouted something in what sounded like a debased form of the dwarf tongue and fired. Felix lunged forwards and felt what he thought was the bullet burn across his back and tug at his cloak and his mail shirt. The Chaos dwarf's piggy eyes widened and he tossed aside the pistols and reached for the hammer hanging from his belt.

Felix stabbed at him with Karaghul and the dwarf roared as the blade danced across a bare bicep, creasing the soot-stained flesh with a line of red. The hammer caught Felix a glancing blow on the side, which was enough to knock him from his feet. He rolled aside as the hammer slammed down, cracking stone. He drove his sword up, piercing the brass-hued scale mail that the Chaos dwarf wore. The dwarf grunted and his weight nearly drove Felix to the ground.

The dwarf cursed and scrabbled at Felix's throat with his thick fingers. Even with a sword sawing up through his guts, he was determined to throttle Felix. Then, a bloody hand reached down and fixed itself in the Chaos dwarf's beard and the weight was hauled up off Felix. Gotrek, covered in ogre blood, dragged the Chaos dwarf up and back, tossing the wounded dwarf back onto the stones.

Gotrek glared down at the wounded creature as the Chaos dwarf tried to staunch the blood pumping from his belly. The latter returned the Slayer's glare and spat a curse. Gotrek raised his axe, but hesitated. Felix knew that dwarfs were reluctant to take the lives of other dwarfs, but did it extend even to these twisted mockeries? 'Gotrek,' he began.

The axe fell and a bearded head rolled away across the stones.

The Slayer said nothing, merely turned and glared at the cannon, where it sat untended. 'It needs to be destroyed, manling. The dawi zharr forge daemons into their engines. It can kill even without the help of a crew.'

'So it can, and so it will, weakling,' a raspy voice rumbled. 'My pretty engines will go forth and maim and slay until this ruin stinks of the dead.'

Gotrek turned, and Felix with him. Behind them, stepping from around the mortar, were two shapes, one big and the other not. The latter was a Chaos dwarf, though broader and more corrupt looking than the one Gotrek had just killed. But the other figure... Felix felt his jaw sag in recognition as he saw the Chaos warrior looming behind the Chaos dwarf who'd spoken. 'Gotrek, that's–'

'Aye, the one who got away,' Gotrek snarled, raising his axe. 'I see you, coward! Come and taste my axe!'

'I tasted it well enough earlier,' the Chaos warrior rumbled. 'Kill them, Khorreg!'

'Don't rush me, Unsworn,' the Chaos dwarf, Khorreg, said, licking his blackened lips with a tongue the colour of soot. 'I want to enjoy this. Khul! See to this dishonoured wretch while I bring that mountain down, eh?'

Gotrek started for Khorreg, a menacing glint in his eye, when a third form interposed itself. It was another Chaos dwarf, but this one was clad in black plate and a featureless helm. The Chaos dwarf held an axe almost as malevolent-looking as Gotrek's own and the eagerness of the newcomer's movement mirrored Gotrek's. 'Khul Ironsworn, Captain of the Infernal Guard, dishonoured and disgraced, you will win the right to remove your mask if you bring me this dwarf's skull,' Khorreg bellowed. 'Kill him! Kill them! Kill all of them!'

Khul lunged and Gotrek met him, their axes striking sparks off one another. Felix could only stare in awe as, for the first time, the Slayer seemed to have found an opponent who matched Gotrek's incandescent rage and lust for battle. Khul made no sound as he swung and hacked at the Slayer, and neither did Gotrek. For long moments, there was only the sound of the axes screeching against one another and the slap of the duellists' feet against the stone.

Then Gotrek roared, 'Manling, stop them! They're going to fire the mortar again!' and Felix was shaken from his reverie. He plunged into motion, diving towards the great war machine. But even as he did so, the Chaos warrior stepped into his path, black-bladed sword shrieking out in an over-handed blow aimed at Felix's head. Felix stepped aside, but only just and his opponent's elbow caught him in the jaw, knocking him back against a sagging buttress of stone. The Chaos warrior whirled, lashing out, and Felix ducked. The black blade carved through the stone, showering Felix with debris.

'I intend to see that hold pulled down, stone by stone, and no one is going to stop me,' the Chaos warrior boomed hollowly. 'I'll have something for my trouble, one way or another.'

'Death is something,' a voice said as an orc-skull mace impacted with the small of the Chaos warrior's back, knocking him sprawling. 'Hello Jaeger, I see you and Gurnisson are hoarding all the best dooms again,' Biter said, waving cheerfully at Felix as he stepped quickly towards the Chaos warrior. Biter let his mace rise and fall, but the Chaos warrior's sword was there to meet it. The mace crashed against the black blade and it shattered, the orc bone no match for the mystically-wrought iron. Biter stumbled back, gaping at his ruined weapon.

The Chaos warrior surged to his feet and his next blow caught Biter across the face, bursting his eye like a grape. Biter roared and staggered and Felix rose to his feet, intending to help the Slayer. The Chaos warrior wheeled, whipping the bloody Slayer into Felix by his beard like a cannonball, and they both went down in a tangle. 'Khorreg, fire that damn thing,' the Chaos warrior shouted.

The Chaos dwarf had climbed up onto the mortar, but so had Garagrim and several other Slayers. One of the Slayers died as an axe appeared in Khorreg's hands and took off his head, but the others closed in on the debased dwarf. Khorreg disarmed a second by chopping through his weapon. The disarmed Slayer had no time to contemplate the destruction of his axe, for Khorreg's hand closed on the front of his head, crushing his face and skull into an unrecognizable mass in a display of prodigious strength. 'Bah, soft,' he said. 'All soft. Are there no real dwarfs left in these mountains?'

'Is a prince of Karak Kadrin real enough for you, Cursed One?' Garagrim said, attacking. His axes carved gouges in the metal of Khorreg's armour as the War-Mourner's furious assault drove the Chaos dwarf back until Khorreg toppled from the mortar with a strangled squawk of outrage. He clanged as he hit the ground, and he was slow to rise and strange noises escaped from his armour. Dwarfs – not Slayers, but clansmen – approached cautiously, and as Felix struggled to extricate himself from Biter's groaning form, he realized that the battle was for all intents and purposes over. The sounds of conflict had faded, leaving only the screams of the dying and the crackle of flames. He saw Axeson among them, and he noted that the priest's eyes were locked on Gotrek's struggle with Khul, rather than Khorreg.

'On your feet, Hell-Worker,' the Chaos warrior snapped, lashing out at Garagrim and driving the Slayer back before he could leap on Khorreg. 'The situation has become untenable.'

'My – *ha* – my thoughts exactly, Unsworn,' the Chaos dwarf rasped, glaring about him hatefully. He turned and reached into his robes and drew forth two heavy flasks. With a snarl, he flung them and they exploded when they hit the ground, driving Garagrim and the other approaching dwarfs back with a rush of flames. In the glare of the fire, Felix lost sight of both man and dwarf. From the shouts and curses, Felix thought the dwarfs had as well.

As he got to his feet, he turned and saw that Gotrek was still locked in combat with Khul. The dwarfs strained against one another, their axes locked between them, neither one budging or giving an inch. Then, impossibly, Gotrek's foot slipped and Khul shoved him back. Gotrek fell and Khul's axe hissed as it clove the air on a collision course with Gotrek's skull. Gotrek's hand shot up, catching the axe just below the blade, halting its descent inches from his face.

Khul rolled his shoulders, trying to bring more strength to bear, to force the blade down into Gotrek's face, but the Slayer's muscles bunched and he forced the blade up and to the side, where it sank into the stone. Gotrek's own axe chopped up into the tangled mass of Khul's beard, and a gush of blood suddenly spurted from within the hair. The Ironsworn staggered back, groping blindly. He sank to his knees and seemed to stare at Gotrek for a long moment, and then he toppled over, unmoving.

Gotrek looked down at him. 'Good fight,' he said. He looked around. 'What did I miss?'

'I think we won,' Felix said wonderingly.

'You had doubts?' Gotrek said.

'Perhaps a few,' Felix said, stooping to help Koertig haul Biter to his feet. The Slayer had one hand pressed to his ravaged eye-socket. Nevertheless, he still grinned.

'It was quite a fight, eh, Gurnisson?' he called out. Gotrek ignored him. Biter took his hand away and chuckled weakly. 'That was my favourite eye, too.'

'Not to mention your mace,' Felix said.

'Easy enough to get a new one,' Biter said, 'or an axe, even. I don't think Berengar will mind me using his, considering that he got ground into mince. I always fancied it, I must admit.' He gestured to the body of the Slayer that Khorreg had crushed.

'Using another dwarf's weapon? Have you no shame?' Garagrim said, stomping towards them. The War-Mourner looked as if he had bathed in blood, and his axes still dripped.

'I'm a Slayer,' Biter replied.

'Here,' Axeson said, handing Biter his own rune-writ axe as he joined them. 'I shall take Berengar's weapon and return it to his clan. They shall welcome it, now that his shame has been expunged.' Biter's remaining eye blinked.

Then, he nodded. 'My thanks, priest. I'll shed much blood with this,' he said, turning the axe over admiringly in his hands. Garagrim grunted, apparently mollified, and looked at Gotrek.

'I saw your fight with that... thing, Gurnisson. It was a

mighty battle.' He nodded towards the Chaos dwarf's crumpled body. The dwarfs were giving it a wide berth, the way Felix had seen men avoid getting too close to the body of a dead mutant or a mad dog, as if even in death, the taint was still dangerous.

'It was a good fight,' Gotrek said.

Garagrim scowled. 'We were not here for your satisfaction, Gurnisson. We were here to break the siege, and we did. We have won a great victory for Karak Kadrin!' He raised his axes.

'Don't confuse this victory with winning the war, my prince,' Axeson said. 'This was but the merest tendril of the evil we face.' He swept his hand out. 'And we have already suffered much.'

Felix followed the gesture, and had to admit that the priest had a point, however depressing it might be to contemplate it. The dwarfs might have killed their weight in Chaos marauders, but the latter could replace their losses far more easily and far more swiftly than the former.

Garagrim frowned again. He didn't like being reminded of the cost of his glorious victory. That was one point where men and dwarfs were far too alike at times, Felix thought. He looked back at the flames where he'd last seen Khorreg and his hulking companion. 'Where do you think that Chaos warrior and his friend went?'

'Wherever they go, we will follow them,' Garagrim said, shaking his axe at the enemy. 'We will harry them back to the Chaos Wastes, if that's what it takes!'

'Got to find them first, beardling,' Gotrek muttered. 'Them and the ones who sent them.'

Felix glanced at Axeson. The priest's face was grim, but he was looking at Gotrek, not Garagrim. Felix felt a chill as he recalled the priest's words. The chill intensified and he heard a snatch of sound; something that might have been laughter, had the wind and distance not muffled it. He turned and his palm was sweaty on the hilt of his sword as he tried to find the source of the sound. A shadow seemed to sweep across the ground, as if something large swooped overhead, but before he could spot whatever had created it, it was gone.

11

The Worlds Edge Mountains,
the Peak Pass

Garmr watched as Grettir's ritual ended and the blood and meat of the sacrifice tumbled down in a cascade. Karak Kadrin still stood, thanks to the Doom-Seeker, but that did not matter. 'They are coming,' he said.

'Good,' Ekaterina said. Garmr caught the look she shared with several of his other lieutenants and smiled within the protective envelope of his snarling helmet.

'The road will soon be completed,' he said. 'Khorne will smile favourably upon us, and the world will drown in fire and blood.' The thought filled Garmr with a thrill of satisfaction. He felt as he assumed an artisan must, approaching the end of his greatest work. Half-fearful that it was coming to an end and half-frustrated that it wasn't over yet.

Idly, he stroked the baroque surface of his cuirass. It had started off unadorned and featureless. As he had walked the Eightfold Path, and taken his first steps on the Eight Stairs, the armour had changed, becoming something other. Faces and worse things grew on the iron, like burrs on a razor. The armour itself set hooks in him, flaying him inside and out, repairing the metal as it became damaged with blood and scabby flesh. The armour was as much a part of him now as his hands or his voice. It enclosed him and was him.

It was that thing, that voice that was his, and yet not, that had first whispered to him of the Road of Skulls. It had echoed up out of the depths of his armour and bones, showing him what must be done. It was that voice that had set him on Grettir's trail, hunting the hunter and binding his sorcerous cousin with chains forged by the daemon-smiths of the East. That voice that had led him deep into the Northern Wastes, where he'd found the God Lights and the vast, uneven slabs of glossy stone rising high into the heavens.

She had descended from them, wings spread, the shadows of them smothering him even as the tip of her spear caressed his shoulder and laid upon him the burden of Khorne's gaze. He saw her eyes still, in the darkness that passed for sleep. Her voice was still with him, and her shadow guided his steps as he gathered his army. She led him to his rivals – Hrolf, Ekaterina, the others – and applauded as he defeated them one after the other and made them serve him. Many hands made quick work... His father had said that, he thought, though he could not remember for certain.

And his work was the road. The last great undertaking that would see the world drowned in eternal war, in oceans of blood. Even now, the bitter tang of the visions that Khorne's Consort had given him still clung to his lips.

He had seen the dwarf, mad-eyed and bloated with muscle and hatred, stalk north. Tattoos that burned like blue fire had etched those swollen muscles, and his scalp was bare save for a bristling crest the colour of a dying sun. Daemons had died the true death in his wake, ripped from the bosom of the gods by the cruel curve of his axe. He could not tell whether it had been happening in the past or in the future, for all times were the present in the Wastes. A man could meet his long-dead grandfather and his unborn grandson on the same day and kill them both, leaving no ripple in his memory to mark their passing.

Regardless of the when, what the dwarf had accomplished was undeniable. Even Khorne shrank from the raw unfettered fury, for too much nourishment is as bad as too little where gods and men are concerned. A hundred thousand daemons died at the dwarf's hands and their shattered essences marked his road into eternity, even as their blood washed away the Wastes, forcing them to contract.

The dwarf had not been alone, of course. There had been others… A confluence of coincidences that had sealed the world forever on the edge of midnight. But only the dwarf concerned him. The illusion of stability pleased the gods, hungry though they were. But the insult given by the dwarf could and should be rectified.

A Skull Road had been carved into the north, into Khorne's domain. And now, a Road of Skulls would be carved south in Khorne's name. It was only just, only right. And it fell to him, Blessed of Khorne, to do so. He would carve a trail of fire across these mountains and write his name on the Worlds Edge. And when he had placed the last skull, when he had taken the skull of the Doom-Seeker and placed it on the road, when the debt the dwarfs owed the Blood God had been paid… then would Garmr have what he desired – a world of war, of battle unending. It was a beautiful dream, full of raw red things and music that sounded like steel on steel and unending screams.

He stepped down off of his throne-altar, a net woven of human hair in his hand. The net was full to splitting with skulls, each having been engraved with one of the eighty-eight thousand names of Khorne. The camp was not quiet. It was never quiet. Champions battled throughout the sea of tents and yurts, testing their might and trying to draw the eyes of the gods. More skulls would be added to the net before the light turned sour with evening. His army died in stages, every eighth man, then eight in ten, singly or in groups, even as it swelled, distant warbands reaching his camp, begging to be allowed to join, begging to serve Khorne's cause.

He would never run out of warriors, no matter how many he sacrificed on blood-stained altars or killed with axe and fang. That too was Khorne's gift to him, his favoured son. Men would come and continue to come until the road was finished. Until Khorne's path was cleared. The more they killed, the more skulls were collected, the more word of his glory spread and the more who would come seeking to join him.

Garmr moved among his men, trusting in their fear and awe to protect him. Assassinations were not unheard of, especially in an army as long-denied as this. All skulls were equal in Khorne's eyes, as well his men knew. Even his own – especially his own, for if he was not fit to lead, he must be struck down. That too was Khorne's gift, the chance to test his abilities against those of the strongest opponents. Garmr strode towards the war-shrine where Grettir crouched. He dropped the net of skulls in front of the sorcerer. 'Tell me of the road, cousin.'

'I think you know enough,' Grettir said, not looking at him.

Garmr kicked him, hard, in the side. Grettir fell and curled into a ball, covering his face with his hands. 'Up, cousin, tell me what I wish to hear.'

Grettir snapped to his feet, far more quickly than Garmr had anticipated. His many eyes glared, but Garmr knew better than to look into them. One hand snapped out, fastening tight around the sorcerer's throat. He jerked Grettir into the air and shook him. 'Tell me of the road,' he snarled. 'Is the one-eyed Slayer coming? Is the Doom-Seeker marching to meet his fate? Has Canto done as I hoped?'

'Y-yes,' Grettir gasped, clawing at Garmr's fingers. 'He comes! He comes!'

'Good,' Garmr sighed, flinging his cousin into the dust. 'And his is the keystone skull?'

'You know this,' Grettir rasped, rubbing his throat.

'Yes,' Garmr said. He gestured to the skulls. 'Tell me where to place these, cousin. Khorne grows impatient with my tardiness, and I must finish the road to open his path.'

'Maybe you should have thought of that before deciding to wait here and let others do your fighting,' Ekaterina said. Garmr turned slowly. Men stopped what they were doing to watch.

She stood lazily behind him with the other champions arrayed around her, their eyes fever-bright with eagerness. The horde might soon have a new lord – or lady, as it were. Garmr had no weapon, but they were all armed. He felt no fear, nor even anxiety. If they did not challenge him, they were not worthy of serving.

He spread his hands. 'Battle is a gift, and an honour, Ekaterina, not a chore. Or perhaps you are simply angry that you were not chosen?'

Her eyes narrowed. She was not challenging him, not quite. Not yet. Not until the gods could see her. He took a step forwards. She hesitated, not willing to retreat. One of the others – Bolgatz, the Bone-Hammer – growled and stepped forwards.

He was big, with club-like fists and only the barest traces of the Marienburg dock-rough he had been centuries earlier visible in his monstrous face. Tusk-like fangs grated against one another as he said, 'I am, Gorewolf. The Bone-Hammer is angry. We have squatted in these rocks for weeks, with precious little blood to spill! I care nothing for your road or your bargains! I would have battle!'

Garmr met his hot gaze unflinchingly. Bolgatz was almost as much of a beast as Hrolf, in his way. Bone-plated knuckles scraped together as he thrust his head forwards petulantly. 'Is it a challenge, then?' Garmr said, softly.

The gathered Exalted Champions traded looks. They were all, in their own ways, blessed of the Blood God, like Vasa with his leonine features or Ekaterina with her murderer's grin. But to lead a horde such as this, well, it would prove that the eyes of Khorne were upon them especially and that they were marked for victory.

Bolgatz nodded. 'The Bone-Hammer challenges you, Gorewolf! The Bone-Hammer will break you! And then he will lead the horde to glory in the Blood God's name!' Bolgatz punctuated this cry with a roundhouse blow that would have taken off a normal man's head. Garmr avoided the blow easily.

He stepped back, avoiding another and another, drawing Bolgatz towards him, forcing the bigger man to get closer. That had not always been Garmr's way, but now such ways of doing things came to him as easily as killing. Once, he would have flung himself on his challenger and buried his teeth in Bolgatz's guts. But now, the red mist did not clog his mind and he could see that the true path to victory was not in mindless violence, but in drawing your opponents into an ever constricting web of their own making, to poke and prod and bleed them until their skulls were ripe for the plucking. There was a weapon for every battle; you simply had to find the right one.

He batted aside a thunderous blow with inhuman ease and lunged forwards. Iron-shrouded talons dug into Bolgatz's throat and he brought their heads together with a crack and then pivoted, tossing the dazed champion over his hip.

Bolgatz scrambled to his feet, blood dribbling from his mouth into his matted beard. He roared and reached out with his bestial paws. He was so incensed that he failed to notice the other champions falling back, stumbling away, eyes wide, their limbs trembling. He failed to notice the vibrations rippling through the ground beneath his feet. He failed to notice the screams and howls of the Chaos marauders, as something monstrous and massive tore through their ranks, heedless of the damage it caused, heedless of anything save Bolgatz. It stank of blood and thunder and its flanks rippled with scars centuries old. It moved with feline swiftness, crushing the men who were too slow to escape its charge.

Bolgatz failed to notice it all, until the shadow coalesced over him. He staggered to a halt, his charge ending before it had begun. He turned, eyes widening. Bolgatz screamed.

'Take him,' Garmr breathed.

And the Slaughter-Hound did.

Karak Kadrin,
the Slayer Keep

It was quiet when Garagrim led them through the outer keep towards one of the secret routes into Karak Kadrin. Dwarfs were not ones for the wild jubilation of men, even after a great victory. Instead, they simply returned to work.

In the ruins of Baragor's Watch, masked dwarfs hurled bodies onto immense pyres, burning the Chaos dead even as others separated the dwarf dead from their enemies, to be taken in ceremonial silence into the depths of Karak Kadrin, where they would be interred in honoured silence for eternity.

Felix followed Gotrek and the others as they moved through the great rent in the outer walls. One of the remaining giants had fallen there, its mammoth carcass draping the inner wall like a fleshy flag. The smell of it was abominable, and Felix covered his nose and mouth with the edge of his cloak. It didn't help much, his cloak being stained with the leavings of the battlefield as it was.

The last giant sat slumped against the archway of the portcullis of the sixth wall, head bowed, seeming somehow shrunken in death, its ungainly armoured body twisted awkwardly. Hundreds of crossbow bolts sprouted from its head and torso, obscuring its features, for which Felix was grateful. Dwarfs had attached ropes and chains to its armour and were attempting to pull it down onto a heavy, flat, wheeled sled that was meant for transporting timbers.

As the enormous corpse slumped and toppled with an earth-shaking crash onto the sled, Garagrim led Gotrek, Felix and Axeson through the open gates, bellowing for dwarfs to step aside. Most did so quickly enough, though Felix noted that some glared at the War-Mourner. Garagrim was a brave warrior and regal, but he was lacking in social graces, to say the least.

Felix looked at Gotrek, who had been lost in his own head since he had killed the Chaos dwarf. He had considered trying to convince Gotrek to leave then, but the Slayer had been insistent that Axeson fulfil his promise and prove his assertions. Thus, they were now on their way into the depths of

Karak Kadrin where the Temple of Grimnir sat. Felix had been surprised by the number of secret pathways that had been revealed in the final sortie. Gotrek's earlier statement that Baragor's Watch was nothing more than a trap for the unwary had been proven, and well. The dwarfs had managed to attack their enemy from multiple directions with almost perfect precision, and the Chaos army had simply disintegrated in the fighting that followed.

A squad of ironbreakers trotted past, weapons hefted and shields held ready, heading towards the lower sections of Baragor's Watch. There were still small, isolated bands of Chaos marauders holed up here and there, and the dwarfs were flushing them out slowly and methodically. Cannons and grudge throwers had been brought out and their crews were studiously hammering portions of the Watch flat. For the dwarfs, there was no reason to fight vermin; especially when they might as well be entombed, so deeply were they dug in. Thus, for the most part, they simply buried their erstwhile enemies and moved on with mechanical regularity. Those they couldn't, the ironbreakers and rangers and even a few lone Slayers dealt with.

Throughout it all, dwarfs had been hunting doggedly for the Chaos dwarf, Khorreg, and the Chaos warrior, who had made their escape in the fire and din of battle. Several rangers insisted that they had escaped into the Underway, while others said that they had seen the Chaos warrior flee the outer keep on horseback, accompanied by a rag-tag band of Chaos knights and marauder horsemen, all galloping north. Personally, Felix thought that both Khorreg and his compatriot were long gone. The latter, in particular, had seemed to display none of the stubborn, mindless propensity for fighting to the last that his followers possessed. A fact for which Felix was enormously, if privately, grateful, despite the fact that it seemed as if the escapee was likely, in fact, the leader of the army in question. Or at least one of them, as the various reports of dwarf observers were collected and compared. The dwarfs had a mania for knowing exactly who was behind such an attack, so that his name could be properly inscribed into the Book of Grudges for future generations to curse.

They left Baragor's Watch behind, moving through the secret routes into the mountains to either side of Karak Kadrin. It took long hours, but Felix was glad enough to be heading into safety, rather than battle. He felt tired, drained of all energy, and though dwarf healers had seen to his wounds, they itched and ached unmercifully. He couldn't help but probe them, wondering how many new scars he'd acquired. Unlike Gotrek, Felix fancied that he'd been handsome, once. Perhaps he still was, albeit in a rougher sort of way, but there was too much scar tissue on him now for him to ever be called classically handsome again.

Then, that wasn't much of an issue, was it? Looks mattered little to the sort of folk he now associated with regularly and the circles he now travelled in. Indeed, looking like six leagues of bad road could only be helpful on the frontiers of the Empire, or in the Border Princes.

Gotrek grew surlier and more withdrawn the closer to Karak Kadrin they drew. He soon refused to speak even to Felix, instead merely gazing at the runes on his axe as if they held some answers to whatever was plaguing him. Felix caught Axeson watching the Slayer, and the expression on the priest's face put him in mind of a man trying to gauge the intentions of a dangerous animal.

The hold was quiet when they entered it through a small, undecorated portal that was nonetheless guarded by several stout clansmen, all of whom made gestures of wary respect in Garagrim's direction as the War-Mourner brushed past them, leading them towards their destination.

The only dwarf hold Felix had been in prior to this was Karak Eight Peaks, and Karak Kadrin was as different from that dead ruin as a living man was from a corpse. Even now, after enduring a siege, it hummed with activity as clansmen put aside their weapons and returned to their work. But it was not only that. The Eight Peaks had been empty of human or dwarf life, being home only to beasts and monsters; the air had been foul and the waters tainted and the streets and passages befouled.

But in Karak Kadrin, life and order yet reigned. Vast slanted walls and columns double the size of the great Pillar of Sigmar in the Koenigspark in Altdorf thrust upwards from the flat stones paving the floor, into the upper darkness. Angled shafts lined with polished sheets of metal mounted on movable frames carried daylight from outside the mountain down into its depths and immense squares of migratory light lined their way, moving with the pilgrimage of the sun across the sky. Everywhere was a vast sense of age, weight and space. Far more of the latter in fact than Felix had expected. He felt no more cramped within Karak Kadrin than he did in any city of the Empire. Indeed, a good deal less so than he had in Nuln. Truly, the hold of Karak Kadrin made the cities of men seem like rat warrens, though he kept that opinion to himself.

The Temple of Grimnir occupied one of the great halls, a towering edifice which dominated all others, crouching amidst smaller temples to other gods like a tiger amongst lambs. It was a thing of sharp angles and heavy domes and before the doors was a mighty pillar which rose high into the upper reaches of the hall. The pillar was as wide as any Felix had seen, but its purpose was not structural. Instead, every inch of its surface was covered in runes.

'Names,' Gotrek murmured. 'The names of those who have found their doom.' He gazed at the pillar wistfully. Felix said nothing, struck by the sight of what must have been the names of hundreds of thousands of Slayers. Centuries of the dishonoured dead, remembered in stone for eternity.

The king's hammerers guarded the doors. They stepped aside, allowing the quartet to enter the temple. The Temple of Grimnir was a shrine to a particular sort of dwarf madness, Felix thought. He would never say so out loud, of course, but it was impossible not to think it, standing beneath the great domed roof in the main chamber of the temple.

The silence was the first thing he'd noticed. In those temples dedicated to the more martial of the human gods, there was always noise, even if it was merely the omnipresent murmur of priests or penitents. But here there was only an implacable emptiness. Dwarfs did not pray as men, he knew. Words were flimsy things; dwarfs measured things in deeds, and it was only for men or elves to mouth words of promise to their gods.

There was no statue to Grimnir, not as Felix was used to them. Instead, two massive stone axes, both as tall as five men, one atop the shoulders of the other, stood beneath the dome, blades crossed, creating a fierce archway over a heavy dais, the centre of which was occupied by a great stone bowl. It was only when he drew closer that he noticed the resemblance between the idealized weapons and the brutally existent one once more clutched in Gotrek's hand.

King Ironfist turned from gazing up at the great stone axes as they entered and said, 'It took you long enough. I should have sent my hammerers to collect you as soon as the battle was done.'

'Did you think the priest needed protection?' Gotrek said, meeting the king's gaze. 'Did you think I would kill him in a petulant fit?'

'I long ago gave up on predicting your whims, Gurnisson,' Ungrim said. 'You do what you want, without regard to anyone else.'

'Some would say that that is the very essence of a Slayer,' Felix said quietly.

'Who gave you leave to speak, manling?' Garagrim snapped, joining his father.

'He is right,' Axeson said, his deep voice silencing the War-Mourner as effectively as a slap. He looked sternly at Garagrim. 'He is a dwarf-friend and a Remembrancer, War-Mourner. To deny him is to deny Gurnisson, and no Slayer can be denied in the house of Grimnir.'

'Except that you *are* denying me,' Gotrek said, glaring accusingly at Axeson.

Axeson sighed. 'Aye, we are.'

'Show him, priest,' Ungrim said. 'Toss the stones. I would waste no more time on Gurnisson's stubbornness.'

Axeson stepped up onto the dais from which the two stone axes rose and leaned over the great bowl that sat there. He reached into his robes and pulled out a small bag. He emptied the bag into the bowl, freeing a cascade of small, flat stones. 'We taught men the art of the stones, in times long past. The words of the gods are sealed in the rock and the dark and it is from within them that we wring glimpses of what must be and what has been.'

The dwarfs gathered around, silent and grim. 'Grimnir carved a road of skulls north, and the blood he shed hardened the world, making what was fluid and foul hard and unchanging. But now, something moves south, following Grimnir's road and making what was solid fluid again,' Axeson said. 'We have seen the signs, in the deeps and in the high places.' He glanced at Felix. 'Your folk sense it too, though they confuse it for one more storm among many. But it is not. It is the same storm that swept the world aeons ago and sent our people into the dark and set us on our path, and with every step it takes, more of the world is lost.'

The stones rattled in the bowl. 'It sweeps towards us, and Karak Kadrin will bar its way, as we have done ever. But, this time, the stones whisper that we will join those who have fallen before. For was not mighty Karak Vlag lost to this storm?'

'The Lost Hold,' Gotrek murmured, his grip tightening on his axe. He stared into the bowl.

'We will be as the Lost Ones, ripped from the bosom of the world and drowned in the river of nightmare,' Axeson continued, his voice taking on the pitch and rhythm of a trained storyteller. 'Unless a Son of Grimnir once more treads the Road of Skulls and puts right that which is wrong.'

'A Slayer, you mean,' Gotrek growled, deep in his throat.

'Aye,' Axeson said without looking at him, his eyes on the stones in the bowl. 'That is what I saw. The truest Slayer must go north and do what has been undone, and find his doom in the process.'

'I will go north,' Gotrek said.

'No, you will *not*,' Ungrim said commandingly. Gotrek wheeled about, a protest on his lips. 'Have you not heard enough? Do you not *see*?'

'Aye, and so,' Gotrek said pugnaciously.

'I told you,' Garagrim said. 'I told you that he could not be reasoned with!'

'Quiet!' Axeson roared. The others fell silent as the echo of that cry faded. He looked at Gotrek; again, that peculiar sadness was in his eyes. 'If you go, Gurnisson, you will find your doom, as I said. But so too we will be doomed with you.'

Gotrek turned away from the bowl. He gripped his axe tightly, almost hugging it to him. Felix made to put his hand on the Slayer's shoulder, but he stopped short. Gotrek would not appreciate the gesture; indeed, it might even offend him. Making a fist and pounding his thigh, Felix turned. 'Then who will go? It's obvious someone must, but if not Gotrek–'

'I will go,' Garagrim said, causing Gotrek to whirl. The War-Mourner met Gotrek's gaze triumphantly. 'I will go,' he said again, thumping a fist against his chest. 'Who better than a prince among Slayers to do this thing?' he continued, looking at Ungrim and Axeson.

'A king,' Ungrim said.

It was Garagrim's turn to spin. He gaped at his father. 'But–' he began.

'I will go,' Ungrim said, not looking at his son. 'It is my right and my duty as the king of Karak Kadrin to do this thing. I will prevent this doom, and accept mine at the same time. I have waited long enough.' As he said the last, his eyes strayed to Gotrek. 'I will not have this doom stolen from me, like so many others.'

Gotrek's jaw clenched. He took a step forwards, one hand tightening around the haft of his axe, the other gripping the rim of the bowl. 'I stole nothing from you, Ungrim Ironfist. Our debt has long been settled. And this doom should be mine!' He glared at each of them in turn, as if daring them to naysay him.

'I am king, Gurnisson, and I will decide when debts are settled,' Ungrim snarled. His voice echoed throughout the temple like the crack of a whip. He pointed a thick finger at

Gotrek. 'You have heard the words of Grimnir, and mine as well. Would you go against the both of us? Are you truly that mad, Gurnisson?'

'I–' Gotrek started, and then he shook his head. His axe dropped, the blade gouging the floor. His eye closed. 'No. No, Ungrim, I will not go north.'

'Swear it,' Ungrim said. 'Give me your oath, Gurnisson.'

Gotrek's eye popped open. 'I have said that I will not. Is that not enough?' he said hoarsely.

Ungrim said nothing, but his face made the truth of Gotrek's words clear. Felix felt as if he were standing in the eye of a storm, and his skin prickled uncomfortably. Every stone in the temple seemed to be listening, waiting for Gotrek's reaction.

When it came, it was loud. Gotrek's axe crashed down, shattering the stone bowl and causing the others to stagger back. Felix flinched as chunks of stone rattled around him, and he felt one nick his chin. Gotrek kicked half of the bowl down the dais and followed after it, his entire frame trembling with barely repressed rage.

'Come, manling,' he growled. 'I would leave this place.'

Felix spared a final glance for the other three dwarfs. Garagrim and his father both appeared enraged, their faces mottled with anger and their mouths open. But Axeson merely looked... What, satisfied?

'Manling,' Gotrek roared, without turning around or stopping. Felix hurried after him, one hand tight on his sword hilt, wondering where Gotrek was planning to go. As soon as they stepped out of the temple, Felix realized that he had an answer, though it wasn't the one he would have preferred.

A semi-circle of crossbows were levelled, the tips of their quarrels gleaming in the soft light of the distant sun. More than even Gotrek could avoid. The Slayer's snarl caused more than one quarreller to blanch. Felix swallowed, knowing that more than a dozen fingers had simultaneously tightened on triggers at that sound.

'Gotrek,' he said. 'Maybe we should–'

'Quiet, manling,' Gotrek said. More than just crossbowmen surrounded them. Thungrimsson's hammerers were there as well, their double-handed hammers held ready. The king was taking no chances it seemed. He turned as Ungrim and the others stepped out of the temple. The king didn't look pleased. That he wasn't enjoying this somehow made it worse, Felix thought.

'I would have your oath, Gurnisson,' Ungrim said.

'An oath forced is no oath at all, Ironfist,' Gotrek said, looking at him.

'You know better than that,' Ungrim said. 'An oath forced binds most tightly of all.'

Gotrek swung around, facing the crossbows, as if gauging the distance. Would he chance it, Felix wondered? Gotrek had been unpredictable lately. Felix looked up. Dwarfs were watching the confrontation from the walls. The sounds of celebration in the immediate area had faded.

'You are honourable, Gurnisson,' Ungrim said. 'You will make the oath, and then you may leave.'

'I will not make that oath,' Gotrek said. 'I... cannot make that oath.' He sounded lost in that moment and uncertain, as uncertain as Felix had ever heard.

'Gotrek, be smart,' he murmured. 'The world is full of dooms. What does one more or less matter?'

'Because this one is *mine*,' Gotrek roared, causing Felix to stumble back. He shook his axe at the temple, as if his rage were directed not at the other dwarfs but at Grimnir himself, and his voice echoed from the stones. For a moment, the tableau held. The other dwarfs appeared shocked at Gotrek's outburst. Felix knew how they felt.

Then, slowly, Gotrek's arms fell to his sides. Chest heaving, he looked at Ungrim. 'I will not make that oath, King of Karak Kadrin. But neither will I resist your authority. Do as you must.'

Ungrim stood like a stone, eyes unreadable. Then, curtly, he gestured. Thungrimsson's men moved forwards, surrounding Gotrek like a phalanx. Felix hesitated and then moved through the group to stand at Gotrek's side. Or, he tried to at least. The dwarfs wouldn't let him until Ungrim made another gesture.

'Would you join him then, Remembrancer?' the king said.

'Can I do otherwise?' Felix said. He unbelted his sword and proffered it to one of the hammerers. 'I made an oath, after all.'

'Aye, you did,' Ungrim said, nodding in approval. 'I am glad to see that some men have not forgotten the weight of oaths.' He barked an order, and the hammerers began to move, taking Gotrek and Felix with them. The quarrellers stayed behind. Despite not trusting Gotrek not to head north, Ungrim seemed to have little doubt that the Slayer would go quietly, having said as much. Gotrek had given him no reason to believe otherwise. Once more, he had allowed someone to separate him from his axe, though in this case it was Axeson who had stepped forwards to accept the massive weapon. The way he grasped it put Felix in mind of a man taking hold of a poisonous snake.

'Where are they taking us?' Felix muttered.

'You should have stayed behind, manling,' Gotrek said, not looking at him. 'There is no reason for you to share my imprisonment.'

'Prison,' Felix said, feeling a sinking sensation in his gut.

'Where did you think we were going?' Gotrek said.

'I didn't, truthfully.'

Gotrek chuckled bitterly. 'That's the problem with you humans.'

Felix felt affronted. 'Thank you, Felix,' he said. 'No no, my pleasure, Gotrek, after all, after all of our adventures, how could I do less?'

Gotrek glanced at him. 'Are you finished?'

'No, but feel free to jump in.' Felix shook his head. 'No wonder you seem to have no friends.'

'What was that?'

'Nothing, Gotrek,' Felix said, looking away. He could feel Gotrek's eye on him and he wondered if he had gone too far. Then, the Slayer sighed.

'Aye,' he said. That was it. Felix snorted. That was as close to an apology as the taciturn Slayer was ever going to come.

'You have something to say, priest?' Ungrim said, watching the hammerers escort Gurnisson and Jaeger away. Axeson shook his head.

'Nothing you'd like to hear, my king.'

'You were the one who said that Gurnisson could not be allowed to go north,' Ungrim said, turning to face the priest. 'That was what Grimnir said, was it not?'

'I did not say that he should be arrested,' Axeson said. His eyes flashed.

'And he hasn't been. He is no criminal, no matter how much I might wish that he were.' Ungrim stroked his beard and looked at the walls. 'No, he has honour, though it's a rougher sort than I like.'

'You call that honour?' Garagrim said, emerging from the temple behind them. He glared hotly at his father. 'He

251

desecrated the temple and spat at your feet. He is an outlaw and you should treat him as such!'

'Do you even know what it was that he did, boy?' Ungrim said, looking at his son. Before Garagrim could answer, Ungrim stabbed at him with a stubby finger. 'No, you don't. You know that he wronged me, so you condemn him. You take my burdens on yourself without heed, making them yours with neither the right nor the warrant to do so. Gurnisson and I have our grudge, and it is ours. Not yours, not anyone's. Even as the Slayer oath our forefathers took is mine and no one else's.'

This last struck Garagrim like a blow. Ungrim felt no pity for his son. He could not afford to. Instead, he marched on, relentless. 'You are brave, boy, but stupid in the way of all beardlings. You think to defy the proper order and for what, to win glory?' Ungrim spat a wad of phlegm onto the street. 'Glory is for warriors, not kings. If you would be king, you must learn that only necessity matters.'

Garagrim had no reply. Ungrim grunted, satisfied that he had been understood. 'I go to meet with the clan-thanes. The throng-of-throngs will be assembled beneath the Ironfist banner and we will march north and harry the Chaos horde until they lead us to their kennel.' He made a fist. 'And then I will free our clan from our shame and save Karak Kadrin.'

He left his son and the priest where they stood and stumped away, followed by Thungrimsson. The hearth-warden said nothing, but Ungrim could sense his disapproval. Then, Thungrimsson was always disapproving. That was his duty. 'What?' Ungrim said, already knowing the answer.

'You have hurt him.'

'He has been hurt before,' Ungrim said. 'He will make a good king.'

'Maybe,' Thungrimsson said. 'But why rush it?'

'You heard the priest even as I did,' Ungrim said. 'Or do you doubt the words of Grimnir?'

'I doubt everything, Axeson especially. He's too smart by half, that one.'

'Are you accusing a priest of Grimnir of playing false?' Ungrim said. Thungrimsson frowned.

'No,' he said shortly. 'But I am saying that he might be interpreting things in a creative fashion.'

'And why would he do that?' Ungrim asked shrewdly. He knew the answer to that as well. That was the secret to being king, or one of them at any rate… Always know the answers before you ask the questions.

Thungrimsson hesitated. He looked uncomfortable. Ungrim had pity on his friend. 'You and I both know he's made of sterner stuff than that. And we both know that if he said Grimnir said something, then it's the plain, bald truth of it. Our gods do not speak in riddles, Snorri. They are not the gods of the elves, calling tunes to some decadent cosmic dance. Our gods speak plain, because to do otherwise is to waste time. No, Axeson's word can be trusted.'

'He has no clan, no ties to hearth or honour,' Thungrimsson said carefully.

'And we do not trust clanless dwarfs, yes,' Ungrim said. 'But every priest of Grimnir is a foundling. It has always been thus. Their only loyalty is to the god and to the hold where their temple sits. So it is with Axeson. And that is enough for me.' He clapped his old friend on the shoulder. 'Now, come. It is time to bargain with my esteemed council of thanes and wrest a mighty throng from their greedy fingers.'

They would howl and tug their beards, as they always did. The cost, the cost, he could hear them say. But in the end, they would do as he asked, because he was not alone in wanting to punish the Northmen for their temerity. Some dwarfs liked to savour grudges, nursing them and feeding them until they had a life of their own, but Ungrim was not one of them. Grudges were burdens, weighing him down, crushing him.

He thought of Gurnisson and then, of his wife, Garagrim's mother. He frowned.

Yes. Some grudges were too heavy to carry alone.

12

The Worlds Edge Mountains,
north-east of Karak Kadrin

Canto rode slumped in his saddle, leading what remained of the army sent to besiege Karak Kadrin towards the Peak Pass. It was only a kernel of the remnant, for most of the surviving Chaos marauder tribes that had left the valley with him had peeled off. Defeat did not breed much in the way of loyalty. What was left was barely an army, more a mob. Men on foot had been left behind; only marauder horsemen moved with Canto and his Chaos knights, and Khorreg, of course.

He glanced down at the wheezing, chuffing form of the Chaos dwarf, who kept pace with his horsemen with barely any effort. Khorreg did not look disappointed, despite the fact they were fleeing in ignominy. Indeed, he looked positively cheerful.

'Life is the greatest victory, manling,' the Hell-Worker said, noting his gaze. 'While we live, we triumph.' A hiss of foul-smelling steam escaped from his armour's joints.

'It's the living bit that I'm worried about,' Canto muttered. They would be pursued. Canto had put it together bit by bit, during the helter-skelter of the retreat. They had never been meant to break the hold, not really. They had been meant to anger the dwarfs. He and Hrolf and Kung and Yan had been bait on Garmr's hook, lowered into the badger's den, and now the beast would be hurrying in pursuit, teeth snapping. He didn't resent that fact – indeed, he admired it. He just wished that he hadn't been part of the bait.

He had abandoned those who couldn't keep up, shedding men like droplets of water. If he were lucky, the dwarfs would take the time to ferret out the laggards. If he weren't, well…

If he weren't, he'd be dead soon enough. He jabbed his horse in the ribs with his heels, trying to urge it to go faster. If he'd had a few of Khorreg's explosives left, he might have been able to cover his trail. But he didn't, so his only option was to move quickly if he had any hope of saving any part of what remained of the army.

Not that Garmr would thank him. The skin on his neck itched as he contemplated the fate that likely awaited him. No, he was as much a sacrificial lamb as Hrolf. Garmr was going to kill him, to show his displeasure. Canto ground his teeth. He didn't deserve to be sacrificed on the altar of Garmr's ambition; Hrolf maybe, or the others, certainly, but not him. He pounded a fist on his horse's neck, causing it to squeal in complaint. 'Quiet,' he snarled.

There had to be some way out. Some wriggle room somewhere. Nothing presented itself, however. He was going to die, and his only choice in the matter was the timing, and whose hands held the axe.

Unless… He looked back at Khorreg. 'What are your plans? Your war machines, save the hellcannon with Garmr, are gone.'

Khorreg chuckled. 'Weapons can be rebuilt, manling. New assistants trained and new slaves gathered. I will return to Zharr Naggrund and rebuild. Perhaps I will come south again and pay the Weak Ones back for their temerity, eh? Would you like that, Unsworn?'

'What I would like is to survive the next week,' Canto said bluntly.

'So survive,' Khorreg said with a shrug.

'You owe me one more debt, Hell-Worker and I would collect on it,' Canto said.

Khorreg looked at him, eyes narrowed. 'I helped you escape,' he said cautiously.

'And I helped you. No, you still owe me a debt and I will collect it,' Canto said harshly.

'You try my patience, manling,' Khorreg said disgustedly. 'You play hard with our friendship.'

'Friendship is for the weak, Khorreg, isn't that what your folk say?'

Khorreg grinned in a ghastly fashion. 'Aye that we do. Well, what do you want?' His expression became cunning. 'Protection from the Gorewolf perhaps... Would you like me to kill him for you?'

'I want you to leave,' Canto said.

Khorreg blinked. Then, slowly, he smiled. 'Oh, I was right, Unsworn. You are a cunning one...'

Karak Kadrin,
the Slayer Keep

Gotrek and Felix walked in silence for some time, surrounded by their armoured escort. The hammerers took them deep into the hold. The sheer scale of the mountain pressed down on Felix with a physical weight the farther into it they went. Stone bastions passed over him, linking the different levels of the hold, and he noted that they were going up, rather than down, as he had expected.

They passed through the great gate that marked the separation of this level. The gate was open, and guarded by parallel lines of scowling statues, clasping axes and shields tight to their bodies. From the heights, Felix thought that they must resemble pieces for some large game. Dwarfs came in and out of the gate, moving about their business. There were a few thousand dwarfs in Karak Kadrin, Felix estimated, though likely fewer now. The Slayer Keep was one of the largest of the northernmost holds, and Ungrim and his forebears had worked assiduously to create a web of alliances and trade agreements to further lengthen the hold's reach.

Past the gate, braziers had been lit, and the dim light allowed Felix to see the massive friezes which dominated the mighty walls of the outer chamber. Scenes from the golden age of dwarf history were depicted with intricate skill on a canvas that was staggering in its size and Felix fought to drink it all in. The poet in him hungered to stay and learn, but he did not think their escort would look kindly on a request to gawp at the walls.

Nonetheless, he could not keep a single, 'Beautiful,' from slipping from his lips.

'Yes,' someone said. Felix turned, and saw a dwarf woman striding towards them, her golden hair bound around her head like a crown, her hands folded beneath her bosom. She was too alien to be attractive, but Felix reckoned that she was a great beauty nonetheless. Warriors stood to either side of her, dressed simply and in utilitarian gear, but they looked as deadly as the hammerers. 'It is beautiful, Felix Jaeger. And you have our thanks for seeing that it stayed such.' She swept a hard gaze across the hammerers. 'We will see Gurnisson to his accommodations.' The tone brooked no argument.

'*Rinn*, we cannot–' one of the hammerers began.

'You have my oath that no harm will befall her,' Gotrek said. His big hands had knotted into fists at his side.

The hammerers exchanged looks, and then one handed Felix's sword to one of the dwarf woman's guards. The hammerers turned and marched away. A sad, small smile crept across the dwarf woman's plump features. 'Hello, Gotrek,' she said.

'My lady,' Gotrek said, inclining his head. There was a gleam in his eye Felix had never seen before.

'I am given to understand that we have you to thank for turning the tide and breaking our enemy's back.'

Gotrek shrugged and looked away, as if the conversation bored him. The woman snorted, as if she had expected such rudeness. She turned to Felix. 'I regret that it has come to this. If you would both follow me?'

'Perhaps it's none of my business,' Felix began.

'It's not,' Gotrek interjected.

'But who are you, if I might ask?' Felix said, ignoring the Slayer.

'You can't,' Gotrek snapped.

'I am Kemma Ironfist, man of the Empire – queen of this hold and wife to Ungrim, mother to Garagrim and friend to Gotrek Gurnisson. Or at least I was.' She looked at Gotrek inquiringly. Gotrek nodded abruptly, after a lengthy hesitation.

'Aye, you are at that.'

'Follow, please,' she said, turning. Her men followed, but not closely. Felix studied them covertly, noting the way they carried themselves. They were clan warriors, grim-faced and hardy-looking. Felix looked from the warriors to their charge. Why had the queen come to meet them? A sudden thought occurred to him – could this, whatever it was, have to do with the mysterious grudge that Ungrim seemed to bear Gotrek? He looked at Gotrek, trying to see something, anything, in the Slayer's scowling, battered features. But nothing revealed itself.

They did not go down, as he expected, but instead, up. 'Don't dwarfs use dungeons?' he said, after a time.

'Aye, but what sense would there be in putting them below?' Gotrek said. 'It never ceases to amaze me how you manlings can take a sensible proposition and invert it.'

'They are not dungeons,' Kemma said, not looking back. 'We do not take prisoners.'

'Surely there must be,' Felix said. 'You have to have a place to put criminals... enemies?'

'The clans take care of their own, in whatever way they see fit. Offences against Karak Kadrin are punished swiftly. It is the way of our hold. But there are... places, where we can put those whose fate has yet to be decided.'

'That sounds entirely too ominous to be healthy,' Felix said, the levity feeling out of place in the silence of the corridors they walked. It never failed to intimidate him, that silence. Dead or alive, dwarf holds were quiet. Human cities and fortresses were filled with noise. This was too much like being in a tomb.

They came to a set of circular stairs, rising upwards in a gentle curve. The work seemed too delicate to be dwarfish, and Felix said so. Gotrek grunted, but Kemma said, 'It is, now. But once our artisans could make the very stones dance with a grace and beauty that would make you weep, human. We have lost much.' She stopped with her hand on the curve of the wall. 'We stand to lose much more.'

'So the priest said,' Gotrek muttered.

'Then you understand why Ungrim does as he must,' Kemma said.

Gotrek looked at her. 'I understand. I do not like it, but I understand.'

She pressed a hand against his arm and Gotrek shrugged it off. The queen pulled her hand back. 'I never thanked you, Gotrek Gurnisson.'

'There was never a need to do so,' Gotrek said stiffly. 'I made an oath, Lady of Karak Kadrin.'

The queen frowned, though whether at his words or at his tone, Felix couldn't say. He shivered as a gust of wind crawled through the stairs. A moment later he saw where it came from. The stairs led to a small balcony, built high on the mountain peak. It wasn't large, but there was room for four or five people. There was a stone fire-pit, long cold, and a large, wide outcropping sheltered that and most of the balcony from the weather. Ancient curtains made from thick wool and furs did the rest. Fresh water, carried from hidden aqueducts and pipe-work, bubbled in a stone bowl set into the floor and there was another hole that Felix assumed was some form of primitive privy. Two pallets, stuffed with straw and covered in fur blankets, had been prepared for them.

The balcony was in a place where three peaks leaned close to one another. Felix could see more balconies studding the distant peaks at various points, and, even more impressive, great faces carved into the very stuff of the mountains, rendered visible by moonlight and watch-fires. They were glowering edifices whose construction must have taken generations. He wondered why he had never noticed them before and then realized that they were hidden by the folds of the mountains, visible only when one looked at them directly, as he was doing now. He felt a sense of age, and unworthiness, as if all of the contempt and obstinacy of dwarf-kind had been chiselled into those haughty, proud faces.

'Who are they?' he said softly.

'The first kings of Karak Kadrin,' the queen said. She gestured upwards. 'There are others above us, and on the opposite peaks. Our ancestors put their stamp here for all time, marking these mountains as ours for eternity. When Karak Kadrin finally falls, her kings shall gaze down upon her ruin and keep watch unto the end of all things.'

'And you think that will happen?' Felix said.

'Everything dies, human,' she said. 'Everything cracks, crumbles and collapses. We cannot weather eternity, no matter how much we might wish otherwise.'

'That doesn't stop some of us from trying,' Gotrek said, suddenly, harshly. 'Fate is for men and elves. Dwarfs make their own way.' He looked at her steadily. After a moment, she looked away. Gotrek stumped past her and out onto the balcony, fists swinging. Felix followed him but turned.

'What–' he began, even as the heavy door crashed shut, shutting them out of the hold. 'Oh,' he said, pulling his cloak tighter about him. 'I see what you meant,' he continued, looking at Gotrek.

The Slayer didn't answer him. Instead, Gotrek's single eye was fixed north, and he stalked to the edge of the balcony and stood, staring out. Felix sighed and sat with his back against the rocks. 'Still, compared to some of the holes we've been confined in, this is fairly pleasant.'

'We used to hold elves here, during the War of Vengeance,' Gotrek said, still looking out.

'Why did she come to greet us, do you think?' Felix said, carefully.

Gotrek, true to form, didn't answer.

'What did you do to Ungrim? Or he to you?'

Still no answer. The Slayer's shape was a blotch in the dim light. He might as well have been a part of the balcony. Felix sighed again and settled back, wrapped in his cloak. *At least we're not going north*, he thought, with some relief. Sometime between that thought and the next, he fell asleep.

As ever after a battle, his dreams were unpleasant things, the colour of rust and smelling of spoiled meat. In them, he strode across an uneven, mist-shrouded landscape, sword in hand. He was hunting something, but he knew not what. And as he hunted, something kept pace with him, leathery wings flapping. Hands traced the contours of his shoulders and a voice like honey poured over an open wound whispered into his ear, guiding his hands as he swung his sword – not Kara-ghul, a different blade, red and weeping – out, spilling the blood of hairy, grasping things which came for him out of the mist. As he fought, the mist cleared, letting him glimpse the ground he walked on and what it was made of and he awoke suddenly, his breath strangled in his lungs.

As he sat bolt upright, every muscle in his body seemed to cry out at once and then fall to muttering steadily as he tried to work some limberness back into his stiff limbs. Felix clambered awkwardly to his feet, his cloak falling away. He stretched, listening with dismay to the symphony of pops and cracks that were his only reward for a life hard lived. A twinge of pain shot through his shoulder, reminding him that it had been flopping loose from its socket only a day or so before. The balcony was swept with a thin light, dripping through the clouds overhead.

Grunting, he rubbed the sore joint and blinked blearily. 'Gotrek,' he called.

'Here, manling, where else would I be?' Gotrek said. The Slayer still stood in the same place where Felix had last seen him before he dropped off into an uneasy slumber.

Felix yawned and shook his head, trying to dislodge the dangling rags of disturbing dreams. He had been exhausted, and for good reason. 'How long will they keep us here, do you think?' Felix said, joining Gotrek at the balcony. One glance over the edge was enough to set off his vertigo, and he turned away, stomach heaving, and set his back to the stern faces carved into the slopes opposite.

'Until the day is won or lost,' Gotrek said. He spat over the edge. 'Until Ungrim meets his doom or returns in victory.'

Felix grunted and ran his hands through his ratty blond mane. 'Why didn't you make the oath, Gotrek?' he asked, not looking at the Slayer.

'I could not. Leave it alone, manling.'

'Right, well, what can we expect, then?' Felix said, heeding the warning in Gotrek's voice. 'Random beatings or will they just leave us to starve?'

Gotrek peered at him. 'Dwarfs do not starve prisoners.'

'No? Glad to hear it. Did I mention that I'm hungry? They do remember that men need to eat more often than dwarfs, I hope.'

As if in answer to his question, the door to the balcony opened with a screech. Felix jerked to his feet, half-formed plans of diving through the aperture fading as he took in the squat shapes of the king of Karak Kadrin and his bodyguards. Gotrek turned more slowly.

'Well, Gurnisson? Ready to make your oath, I trust. It'll be your last chance before I leave,' Ungrim said, his thumbs hooked in his belt, his chest puffed out.

'You're wearing armour,' Gotrek said.

Ungrim's eyes narrowed. He wore a light shirt of gromril mail, and his helm-crown, with its curving horns. 'And what if I am?'

'You have never understood what it means to be a Slayer,' Gotrek said, disapprovingly. Felix looked askance at him, wondering if he had heard Gotrek correctly. Even Ungrim looked surprised. Then, that surprise became anger.

'I know more than you think, Gurnisson,' he said. But before he could say more, Felix said, 'Please pass my compliments on to your queen, mighty Ungrim.' It wasn't a smart thing to say, but Felix knew enough of Slayers to know that both Gotrek and the king were positioning themselves to figuratively charge one another. And if that happened, even if Gotrek won, the results wouldn't be pleasant for either him or, most importantly, Felix.

Ungrim's jaw clamped shut and he transferred his glare to Felix, who tried to hold tight to his nonchalant poise as the Slayer King looked at him. It was hard, especially when Gotrek added his own glare to the equation. 'Mind your own business, manling,' Gotrek growled.

'Enough of this,' Ungrim snapped. 'If you will not swear the oath, here you will stay. I will order your release upon my return and not before.' Felix wanted to ask what would happen should Ungrim not return, something the king seemed intent on, but he held his tongue.

Ungrim hesitated then, despite his bluster. 'Gurnisson, is it so heavy an oath?' he said, half turned away. 'For old times' sake, can you not make it?'

'Would the debt between us be settled then, Ungrim Iron-fist?' Gotrek asked, arms crossed, his one eye baleful.

Ungrim's hands clenched. 'Yes,' he said, between gritted teeth. The bodyguards shifted, clearly uncomfortable with the discussion.

'Then no,' Gotrek said, turning away. 'Go find the doom that should be mine, Ungrim.'

Ungrim growled and turned, half reaching out. Then, his hands dropped and he left the balcony, back stiff, chin jutting. The guards closed the door behind them and Felix heard the lock click shut. He let loose a frustrated breath. 'What did you do to him?' Felix said.

'I saved his life.'

Ungrim stalked from the clan-hall, satisfaction etched onto his face. Thungrimsson followed at a more sedate trot. 'At least *someone* is doing what I ask of them!' the Slayer King growled. He had demanded a meeting with the thanes of the more reluctant clans after visiting Gurnisson, and the anger fanned by the latter had helped him with the former. Ungrim had been in fine form, browbeating the thanes into providing him with the warriors and treasure needed to organize the grandest of Grand Throngs.

'Did you truly expect Gurnisson to change his mind?' Thungrimsson said.

'Yes,' Ungrim said.

'May I speak frankly?'

'No,' Ungrim said.

Thungrimsson ignored him. 'More fool you.'

Ungrim stopped and turned, glaring at his hearth-warden. He pointed a finger, shook it, and then dropped his hand without replying. He turned back and continued walking. Thungrimsson followed. 'Besides, it's not like you require the blessings of an outlaw like Gurnisson, is it?'

'Leave it, Snorri.'

'Not unless you're having doubts about Axeson's prophecy,' Thungrimsson pressed.

'I said leave it, hearth-warden,' Ungrim grated. 'There is no doubt in my mind, no cracks in my conscience.'

'I wish I could say the same, father,' Garagrim said, stepping out of an adjoining corridor and falling in beside them. Ungrim stopped and looked at his son.

'What do you require, Garagrim?'

'The Slayers wished me to petition you. They wish to muster with the throng, and as War-Mourner, it is my duty to pass on their desire.' Garagrim gave his father a gimlet stare, and added, 'Unless, of course, you're worried that they too might steal your glory.'

Ungrim glanced at Thungrimsson. 'See to the preparations, hearth-warden. The prince and I must speak.' Ungrim waited until Thungrimsson had vanished down the corridor before jerking his head towards a set of stairs. Garagrim followed him as Ungrim started down the stairs.

'You are upset,' Ungrim said, tracing the flow of the wall with his hand.

'Not upset, confused,' Garagrim said.

'And you think I should explain myself?'

'I think you owe me that much, yes,' Garagrim said.

The stairs wound around and down and the silence gave way to the echo of hammers ringing against metal. A wash of heat ambushed them in the bend and Ungrim led his son out onto a viewing balcony. Below was one of the great clan-forges. Red fires were stoked in the dim light as water-wheels creaked and anvils sang with the sounds of artifice. Once war was done, most dwarfs returned to work, mining, crafting or, as below, forging new tools and weapons and essentials to replace those lost in the siege. Indeed, a dwarf hold was never more productive than in the days following a great battle.

'Does a king then owe a prince?' Ungrim said.

'A king owes all of his people, regardless of rank,' Garagrim said firmly, arms crossed, jaw thrust out. Ungrim looked at him.

'I've heard those words before, from another,' he said. 'Gurnisson, in fact.' He grinned as a look of discomfort passed across his son's face. 'He was a big believer in what a king owes. Even before he took his oath, if the stories are true.' The grin faded. 'I am paying my debt to you, Garagrim, though you do not see it that way.'

'I took the oath—'

'Against my wishes,' Ungrim said. 'Against your mother's wishes. In one rash action, you deprived her of a son and me of an heir.'

'I did it for you, and mother. I did it to remove the stain of our shame. To free you,' Garagrim said, not looking at his father.

'Do you understand why we still have our shame, boy?' Ungrim said. 'There have been plenty of opportunities over the centuries for one of us to die gloriously, but glory is not for kings.'

'You said that,' Garagrim said sourly.

Ungrim's hand snapped out, catching his son on the back of the head. Garagrim jerked forwards and then spun, eyes blazing. Ungrim jabbed him in the nose with a finger. 'And I shall continue to say it until I am dead or you understand. You were right before, boy. Kings owe their people, and it is a debt that can never be paid, not in full. It renews itself each day, and I will pay it until I fall, and then you will pay it, and your children and your children's children, until the world cracks and burns. We have responsibilities, and those responsibilities outweigh our own desires.'

'Yet you intend to lead a throng into the north,' Garagrim said, stepping back.

Ungrim shook his head. 'I must.'

'But not for glory,' Garagrim said. 'Not to shed our burden.' His tone was one of disbelief. His face fell. 'You deny me one burden only to pass me another?'

Ungrim's eyes narrowed. 'Watch your tone. I am still king. I am still your father, and what I do is for the good of all of us.'

'So you say,' Garagrim growled. There was no petulance in his tone, only anger.

Ungrim turned away. 'Tell the Slayers that all who wish may accompany the throng.'

'Does that include me?'

'It does not.'

Garagrim fell silent, staring out over the forges. Then, 'What is the grudge which binds us to Gurnisson?'

Ungrim grunted. 'That is none of your concern.'

'It seems nothing is,' Garagrim said, turning and starting up the stairs. Ungrim let him go. He looked out at the forges, trying to find some comfort in the dance of the distant flames and the heat and the smell of metal and ash.

Karak Kadrin,
the Temple of Grimnir

Axeson stared at the axe as it sat on the dais. If he didn't know better, he would have sworn that it was staring balefully at him, or perhaps accusingly. It was a mighty weapon, there was no denying it. Even lying there, separated from its master, it looked deadly. Like a leashed beast, readying itself to spring on the unwary if they drew too close. His gaze drifted to the split bowl. The two halves still lay where they had rolled, as did his rune stones. He bent and began to pick the stones up, one at a time, trying to read meaning in how they had fallen.

He heard footsteps behind him, but did not stop what he was doing. 'Is that his axe?' Kemma Ironfist said softly. Axeson straightened and turned, bowing shallowly to the queen of Karak Kadrin.

'It is,' he said.

She stepped past him, her eyes as cold as dampened forges as she looked at the weapon. 'It is a beautiful thing, but ugly as well.'

'I see no beauty in it,' Axeson said, after a moment, 'only cruel necessity.'

'Nonetheless, there is a beauty in necessity.' Kemma was silent for a moment. 'Ungrim intends to march out tomorrow morning. What does Grimnir say?'

'I have not asked. I doubt he would answer. He has told us all he intended to, I think.'

'And is this my husband's doom, then?' Kemma said, turning to face the priest. 'At long last, is the shame of our clan to be stricken from the record of years?'

Axeson was silent. Kemma frowned. 'You have a distressing habit of falling silent just when your voice is most necessary, priest.' She smiled slightly. 'It must be a family trait.'

Axeson looked sharply at her. 'I have no family.'

'No. I misspoke. Forgive me, priest.' She had not misspoken, she knew it and Axeson knew that she knew it. Queen Kemma knew entirely too much for him to play wise priest with her. Dwarf women were often seen but rarely heard, at least in Karak Kadrin, but Axeson knew that it required a woman of unusual strength and patience to live as wife to a Slayer, even if he was a king. That her son had also taken that vow meant that her burden, already weighty, was doubled and doubled again.

There were stories about Kemma that passed through the quiet corridors of Karak Kadrin. She had been a daughter of the Donarkhun clan, as royal as any dwarf not named Grungni or Grimnir, and proud of that, but never haughty. Some said that she had wielded a hammer and borne a warrior's shield in battle against grobi on her journey north to meet her intended for the first time. Her chaperones slain, Kemma had continued on with a determination that made even the most stubborn of longbeards mutter into their beers with shame. She had announced herself at the great gates, a dozen grobi heads tied to her sash and a sack full of gold over one shoulder. Kemma had paid her dowry in skulls and precious metals and Ungrim had had no choice but to accept, for where would he have found a queen more fitting than she?

She had become adept, in the intervening decades, at the subtleties involved in being queen. Dwarf men practised the art of boldness, of bluff and bluster, and many of the women as well, but Kemma had ever been a woman for the quiet word and truth wielded like a blade, rather than a bludgeon. It was Kemma who greeted the envoys of the elves and men, Kemma who dealt with the wizards of the Colleges of Magic who sought rare metals and deep herbs for their spells, Kemma who had discovered the red foulness of the Lady Khemalla and led her own bodyguards in the expulsion of the *zanguzaz* – the blood-drinker – and her shrieking handmaidens from the human quarter of Karak Kadrin. Snorri Thungrimsson was Ungrim's hearth-warden, but Kemma's was the mind that directed Thungrimsson in his tasks.

She was not more intelligent than her husband, for Ungrim

had a keen mind, but she saw the world through clearer eyes. Too clear sometimes, Axeson thought. Ungrim was predictable, if in an erratic fashion, and Garagrim as well. But Kemma was not.

'There is nothing to forgive, lady.' Axeson inclined his head. 'I don't know,' he added. She looked at him, her gaze questioning. He sighed. 'I do not know if the doom I saw is the king's. A Slayer must die, but as to which Slayer...' He shrugged helplessly.

'You only know that it is not Gurnisson,' she said. The way she said his name provoked a thread of memory, of old gossip, well-chewed by the time Axeson had heard it, of an oath given, and an oath fulfilled and a friendship forever fractured because of it.

Axeson nodded jerkily. 'That much Grimnir made plain. Gurnisson's doom is writ in the *Book of Ages* and has been since the first words were set onto the first page.'

'But if he goes, he dies,' Kemma said.

'If he goes with the throng, he dies, yes,' Axeson said.

Kemma's round features crinkled in a sudden smile. 'Ah.' Axeson shifted uncomfortably. She stepped down from the dais. 'Guard that axe well, Axeson. It yearns to be reunited with its wielder.'

'As I'm sure he yearns to be reunited with it,' Axeson said.

13

Karak Kadrin,
the Slayer Keep

'I want my axe,' Gotrek rumbled, staring up at the carved face of an ancient king. Felix thought that there was a resemblance there, however faint. Perhaps it was simply the similarity of the expression on both, the one stone and the one as good as.

'I for one am enjoying our enforced period of relaxation,' Felix said, stirring the fire-pit with an iron prod. 'Seems like ages since we've had a moment just to sit.'

'Slayers don't sit,' Gotrek said.

'What do you suggest then, Gotrek? Overpowering the guards?'

Gotrek looked at him as if he had suggested shaving his beard. Felix shrugged and made to change the subject. 'I hope they bring us food soon.' Guards had appeared early in the evening, bringing flint and tinder to light the fire-pit, but nothing else. Gotrek grunted. Felix heard a distant sound and rose to his feet. 'What is it?'

The Slayer made no reply. Felix joined him at the edge of the balcony. From down below, more sound rose and Felix felt a moment of weakness as he recognized for the first time just how high up they were. Drums and horns sounded from below, and Felix saw a great army of dwarfs marching through the ruins of the outer keep; they issued from the hidden sortie gates and deep paths almost eagerly. Squares and columns of doughty clan warriors, bearing the standards of every clan of Karak Kadrin, marched in perfect unison. It was a magnificent sight, even from the heights.

'The Grand Throng of Karak Kadrin,' Gotrek murmured. 'Ungrim is marching out.' His hands rested on the balcony and the stone cracked in his grip. Felix frowned.

'He's moving quickly,' he said.

'Aye,' Gotrek said. 'I expected the clans to argue more, but...' He shook his head.

'The words of the gods can sway even the most stubborn of men,' Felix said. He raised his hands before Gotrek could reply. 'I know, I know, dwarfs aren't men.'

Disgruntled, Gotrek looked away. 'Never thought I'd be here again,' he muttered, examining the balcony. 'Ungrim has a sense of humour.'

'What do you mean?'

Gotrek smiled bitterly. 'This is the same place he stuck me the last time I disobeyed him.'

'What happened?' Felix said. He was eager to hear the story, rare as it was that Gotrek shared anything relating to his past.

'Nothing worth speaking of,' Gotrek said, waving a hand dismissively. He turned back to watching the throng march out.

'Did it have to do with Queen Kemma?'

Gotrek stiffened. Felix pressed on. 'You said you saved

Ungrim's life, that that is why he dislikes you. She asked you to do it, didn't she?'

'Aye,' Gotrek said, in a quiet voice. 'I made an oath, in the heat of the moment.'

Felix didn't dare inquire as to the particulars of that. It couldn't be what it sounded like. From a man, he would have happily assumed the obvious, but dwarfs, as Gotrek took every opportunity to remind him, were not men. 'That was all.'

'Tell me about it,' Felix said, settling back, arms over his knees.

'Eh?'

'Gotrek, we have nothing but time,' Felix said. It was a blatant attempt to get Gotrek's mind off the marching army below, but Felix had little other way of doing so. 'Tell me how you saved Ungrim's life. If I'm to give a full recounting of your deeds upon your death–'

'If I die,' Gotrek muttered.

'–upon your death,' Felix continued, as if Gotrek hadn't interrupted, 'then I must know them all. *Ipso facto*, as the Tileans say.'

'What do Tileans have to do with anything?'

'I was accrediting the phrase to its proper source. It's a very important skill for a Remembrancer, accreditation,' Felix said primly.

Gotrek shook his head. 'Don't make things up.'

'That's the point of accreditation,' Felix said. 'So people know that I haven't. We wouldn't want anyone questioning the veracity of your saga, would we?'

'Who would dare?' Gotrek growled.

'Plenty of people,' Felix said. 'You'll be dead, remember. And let's be fair, I'm not all that intimidating, Gotrek.' He thrust a finger up for emphasis and continued, 'Hence, *accreditation*, and footnotes, lots of footnotes.'

'Footnotes,' Gotrek said dubiously.

'Lots of them,' Felix said, rubbing his hands together in mock-glee. 'I'll choke every critic between here and Marien-burg with footnotes.'

Gotrek eyed him for a long moment. Then he chuckled and slapped his belly with both hands. 'It's about time you displayed the proper enthusiasm for my death, manling! Fine, I'll tell you. It'll be a grand – eh – footnote.' He leaned forwards. 'It was years before I met you. Not long after I had taken the Slayer oath. We were clearing out a nest of grobi in the northern peaks, where the river runs beneath the last of the ancient skybridges. We were too close to Karak Ungor, but that didn't bother old Ungrim. Nor me, come to that.' Gotrek grinned. 'You should have seen it, manling. The orcs boiled across that bridge like ants, most falling, being pushed off by the ones behind, and only me and Ungrim and a few other lads to bar the way.'

His eye went glassy with memory. 'There was a red rain in the valley below, that day. We held the ancient toll road from sunset to sunrise, killing hard and taking whatever the grobi could throw at us. Old Grimscour fell at dawn, dragged from his perch by a squig with its teeth in his beard. Then young Kromsson, pulled apart like a wishbone by bad old Bashrak himself.' Gotrek grunted. 'The grobi called Bashrak "the Gitsnippa". As big as any three orcs and as mean as a wyvern.' The grin had faded now, leaving a more melancholy expression in its place. 'He killed Falnirsson after that, and Stonechewer. Then it was just Ungrim and I, and the stones were slick beneath our feet and the clouds were the colour of deep ore and full of lightning.'

Gotrek fell silent. Felix knew that the Slayer was watching

the memory unfold inside his head. When he began to speak again, his voice had lost its bluster. 'Only one of us was needed. Reinforcements were coming – the other could have stepped back. But neither of us could give way. Neither of us was willing. So we fought, and I fought not to meet my doom, but to keep Ungrim alive.' He looked at his hands. 'I dragged Ungrim from beneath a pile of grobi and threw him to safety, and chopped through the ancient stone of the bridge. I sent Bashrak and all of his green-skinned court hurtling into the void and Ungrim cursed me for it.' He closed his eye and clenched his fists. 'I swore to keep Ungrim alive and I did, and our grudge stands.'

'Does he know?' Felix said softly. 'About Kemma, I mean. Does he know that it wasn't your idea?'

'Of course he knows, manling. Why else would I have saved him, unless I had made an oath to do so?' Gotrek looked at him as if he were an idiot. 'It doesn't matter. What's done is done.'

'And you all just pretend that nothing happened,' Felix said.

'There is no pretence. She is queen and he is king and I am what I am,' Gotrek said nastily. 'I've changed my mind. This doesn't go in my saga, manling.'

'Perish the thought,' Felix said.

'I mean it, manling,' Gotrek growled, grabbing the front of his cloak and yanking him down to eye-level. 'Such things have no bearing on my doom, footnotes be damned.'

'What about dreams, then? Do those have some bearing?' Felix said, stung. He blinked, surprised at himself. He hadn't meant to say that. Gotrek seemed surprised as well. He released Felix and stepped back. Felix straightened his cloak and said, 'I think it's time you told me why we came here, Gotrek. I have followed you into many dangers and never once have I felt that you have had ulterior motives. But this time...'

'Are you accusing me of lying, manling?' Gotrek rasped, glaring at him. His knuckles popped as his fingers curled into big fists.

'No, no,' Felix said, stepping back quickly, palms out. 'But you aren't telling me everything, are you?'

'I owe you then? Is that what you're saying?' Gotrek said, taking a menacing step forwards. Felix had rarely seen the Slayer so angry, save in the heat of battle. He felt a ripple of fear, not for the first time, that the Slayer might turn his frustrations on his Remembrancer for lack of a better target.

'No, I'm not saying that either,' Felix said. 'I'm merely curious as to how and why we've ended up in this place.'

'Because I would not make an oath,' Gotrek said stubbornly.

'That is not why we came here,' Felix said, feeling fear give way to frustration. 'Why did we come to Karak Kadrin?'

Gotrek's glare redoubled in its intensity. Felix felt sweat bead on his face, despite the chill of the crags. Then, Gotrek looked away. 'I dreamt of my doom,' he said, finally. He seemed to stagger slightly, as if his strength had left him. He leaned against the balustrade of stone. 'I stood in the shadow of mighty mountains, and I could hear the tread of a thousand enemies,' Gotrek intoned, looking out at nothing. 'A dwarf, an ancient ancestor, his beard the colour of the snows of the high far peaks, came to me, cloaked and hooded, and pointed north.'

Felix didn't know what to say. He stood silently, waiting. Gotrek shook himself. 'I looked north and saw a great light, like the fires that burn deep and forever in some lost mines. And I knew that my death was calling to me, manling. My doom was beckoning to me at last.'

Felix cleared his throat after several minutes of long silence. 'Gotrek, did you refuse to swear an oath to Ungrim because of your earlier oath to the queen... or because of your dream?' he said carefully.

Gotrek's muscles bulged abruptly. The balustrade shuddered in his grip and stone cracked. Felix spun as the door opened, admitting a trio of burly dwarfs, carrying trays of food and drink. Gotrek roared wordlessly and uprooted the section of balustrade. Hefting it over his head, he turned, red-faced, and hurled it at the rock face of the wall.

The guards dropped their trays and scrambled out, slamming the door behind them as debris rattled down from the point of impact. Gotrek stared at the door, breathing heavily. Felix, however, only had eyes for the spilled food.

'Looks like they remembered our food after all,' he said sadly.

The Worlds Edge Mountains, the Peak Pass

Ekaterina watched the Bone-Hammer's followers fight over what was left of him. After several days, only a few tattered scraps remained, but they fought over them nonetheless. The former champion's body had been rendered to rags by the Slaughter-Hound, but there was enough left that enterprising would-be warriors could find something, some token that could give luck or protection in the battles to come.

And there would be battles; not just among the dead warrior's followers, who would fall on each other to determine the new leader, but deeper in the mountains. Everywhere, men saw to their horses and chariots. Weapons were sharpened and armour repaired. On their chains and altars, the madmen foamed and wailed out prophecies to the warriors who dared to gather close enough to hear them. A hundred thousand destinies clashed among the crags, and men prepared themselves to compete for the gods' affections.

Once, she would have been among their number. She longed for Khorne's gaze to grace her just once, but it would not be found in such ways. Warriors were not made in mindless battle. She hungered for war the way others needed food or drink, but the wild death-dealing of marauders would not do. Not any more.

She needed something more. Like a gourmet, her palate had evolved. There were levels to war, battles to be fought within and without. Blood could be shed without a cut being made and a skull collected without so much as tearing the skin.

Garmr had lost fifteen of his twenty remaining lesser lieutenants in the last few days. It had been a mere matter of words to ears to set off duel after duel. Warbands consolidated and of the other four left in camp, two were loyal to her, and the other two would die quickly, if they did not join her when the time came.

She did not do it for herself, no matter what others might whisper, but for the greater glory of Khorne. The weak must be weeded out, the chaff separated so that only the strong remained, so that the horde was pure and fierce and mighty. Only then could they trample the enemies of the Blood God into the dust.

She paused before the great 'X' where the champion of Slaanesh hung, still alive, despite casual sword-strokes and spear-thrusts. It had become a popular game among the brute element for lack of any other stimulation. It hissed at her, bloody tongue jerking from a nest of shattered fangs. It seemed to gain as much pleasure from its pain as the tribesmen did, and it crooned to itself with every blow.

It offended her with its refusal to die. Its remaining eye rolled wetly in the socket, fixing on her with undimmed predatory intent. It strained against the nails that held it fixed and hissed again.

She drew her sword and put out its good eye.

She left it screaming and moved through the crowd towards Garmr's tent. She had avoided him since the Bone-Hammer's death, suspecting that the Gorewolf would view any conversation as an excuse to add a new skull to the pile. But there was no putting it off now. There was a song of murder in the air, and men whispered that they would be moving soon. Garmr's pet sorcerer had collected the teeth of a hundred dead men and cast them across the flayed hide of a horse. That which Garmr had read there had seemed to excite him, though Ekaterina couldn't see why.

Grettir was waiting for her, chained to a post outside the tent. He sat slumped, his many eyes blinking in their secret rhythm. 'The prodigal girl returns,' he said. 'Conquered our fear, have we?' He gazed lazily up at her. 'Can you feel it? Can you feel the tightening of Khorne's collar about your neck? The Master Changer encourages a profusion of fates for his followers, but Khorne prunes all but the bloodiest.'

'As it should be,' Ekaterina said.

'Then why do you buck so hard against yours?' Grettir said.

'You don't know my fate any more than I do, sorcerer,' she spat. 'Bloody and short or bloody and long, it matters not. If my skull is to decorate Khorne's throne, so be it. I will dance happily to my death.'

Grettir waggled a finger at her. 'Then why concern yourself with him?'

'What?'

'If you do not care, why do you fret so?' Grettir hissed.

She glared down at the sorcerer, wishing again that she could strike his cunning head from his neck. 'He is weak,' she said, finally. 'And his weakness takes us from the Eightfold Path and from Khorne's sight.'

'How do you know that Khorne has not asked this of him?' Grettir said.

'To deny battle is not Khorne's way. To cower in the hills is not Khorne's way,' Ekaterina said, gripping the hilt of her sword. She heard a murmur of sound from the tent. She tried to focus on Grettir, but–

'But to send others to die in your place is?' Grettir said.

Ekaterina shook herself. 'What do you mean? Speak plainly!'

'First, a riddle – what is a mutiny, when it is not open? A disagreement,' Grettir said, spreading his hands. 'It's not very funny. But I see little humour in this situation. I have seen the threads you sew, Ekaterina. The black poison you inject into fertile minds. Your hunger for glory is a bright thing, and loud to my eyes. To other eyes as well, though you recognize them not.'

'You talk nonsense,' she snarled, stepping past him. He chuckled behind her as she ripped the tent flap aside, revealing the interior of the tent. It was humid and stank of rotting meat. Braziers enclosed the squatting shape of Garmr, his head bowed, hands dangling. Blood dripped from his fingers, though whether it was his or someone else's she couldn't say. In the weird light and the dancing trails of spiced smoke, a strange shape seemed to crouch behind Garmr and hands stroked his armour. Wide wings spread the width of the tent, and carmine eyes met Ekaterina's. A talon rose and pressed its length against thin lips in a gesture for silence.

Then it was gone and Garmr looked up, his eyes glowing

within his visor. 'What?' he rasped. His voice was hoarse and inhuman.

'My outriders have seen a column of dust in the distance. They say it is Canto,' Ekaterina said.

'Hrolf?'

'No sign of him. He is likely dead,' she said, unable to resist a smirk. 'Likely so are Kung and Yan.' The last was not so pleasant a prospect, but she had known the Foul One might die. Garmr had lost his two strongest supporters, and that was all that mattered.

'Then they have fulfilled their purpose,' Garmr said, rising slowly to his feet. 'That is all any of us can ask.'

'Speaking of purposes,' Ekaterina said. 'What is ours, if not to sack that dwarf hold?'

'Do you require a reason now to spill blood?'

'No, but I want one regardless,' she said. 'Why should I not take my men and seek prey this very morning, Gorewolf?'

'Ask the Bone-Hammer,' Garmr said.

'I'm asking you,' Ekaterina said. 'I don't fear you, Garmr. I don't fear your hound or your axe.' Her hand dropped to the hilt of her blade. 'I serve you because you promised me battle.'

'You serve me because Khorne wishes it,' Garmr said.

Ekaterina frowned. Garmr cocked his head, watching her. 'Is this it, then? Have you come to it at last? You were the only one who was not forced to bend knee, Ekaterina. You are the one who came hunting the massacre wind, rather than the other way around,' Garmr said. His voice was strangely soothing, a basso hum that vibrated in her bones.

He moved so swiftly, she barely saw it. His hands settled on her shoulders and she could smell the raw, beautiful stink of him. Scenes of battles from beyond the great gates had been engraved on his armour and they seemed to move and sway with his voice. Thousands died on his cuirass as Ekaterina watched, men and daemons and worse things writhing in eternal battle. It was the loveliest thing she had ever seen. She reached out with eager fingers, stroking the scenes of bloodshed.

Garmr's head dipped. Half-remembered snatches of an old fairy-story rose to the surface and she said, 'My, what big teeth you have.'

Garmr laughed. 'The better to eat the world,' he said.

14

Karak Kadrin,
the Slayer Keep

When Felix awoke on the third day, Gotrek was standing before the broken section of the balcony, perched inches from oblivion, like a bird about to take flight. The Slayer twitched and trembled, muttering to himself. Felix's heart stuttered in his chest and he was on his feet, hand shooting out before he was even fully awake. Was this some kind of fit? Or was captivity having a more harmful effect on the Slayer than he'd first thought?

Gotrek had become morose and silent since his earlier outburst, as if sharing his secret with Felix had drained all of his vitality from him. He brooded gargoyle-like, staring north as the sun rose and fell, barely moving. Felix had never seen the Slayer so silent and still. Gotrek was normally a bundle of nervous energy, at least for a dwarf, unless he was stone drunk. But all of that energy was gone now, leaving a scowling statue in its place. Or, at least it had been.

'Gotrek? Gotrek,' Felix said, grabbing one massive shoulder. Gotrek didn't reply. His eye was closed, the lid twitching. Felix realized that he was asleep. 'Gotrek, wake up!' Gotrek shrugged, sending Felix tumbling. Adrenaline pumping, Felix was on his feet a moment later, grabbing again, though he knew he had no hope of stopping the dwarf if he decided to jump. At best, he'd go over with him. Was this how it ended, with imprisonment and suicide?

'This isn't going to make a very stirring conclusion to your saga, Gotrek!' Felix shouted, trying to snake his arms beneath Gotrek's in a move he'd seen a Tilean wrestler perform once at a country fair. He hadn't gotten to see much beyond that before Gotrek came to blows with a trained bear and its Kislevite handler.

The Slayer's eye opened, but he wasn't awake. Felix deduced the latter a moment after Gotrek slapped aside his reaching arms and grabbed his throat in a vice-like grip. The pressure on his throat set off a storm of panic in Felix's brain. He scrabbled at Gotrek's immovable fingers, trying to pry them loose. 'Gotrek,' he gurgled. 'Gotrek!'

Gotrek's only reply was to tighten his grip. He spat something in Khazalid, a burst of harsh syllables that sounded as if they hurt his throat as much as they hurt Felix's ears. Darkness began to gather at the limits of Felix's vision as a flame of frustration burned in him. It wasn't fair, that after all he'd been through, that this was the way he was going to die – strangled by a lunatic Slayer.

Lashing out, he drove a fist between the Slayer's eyes. Pain exploded in his hand, but it was worth it. Gotrek released him abruptly and staggered back, shaking his head. 'Manling, what–'

Ignoring the pain in his hand, Felix lunged, grabbing

Gotrek's beard even as the Slayer took a step too far back. His foot skidded on emptiness and then he bawled with pain and rage as Felix hauled back, falling onto his rear and pulling Gotrek atop him. Gotrek bounded up, grabbing two fistfuls of Felix's jerkin and dragging him to his feet.

'Never touch a dwarf's beard,' Gotrek snarled, shaking Felix with tooth-rattling force.

'Then don't sleepwalk!' Felix replied with equal heat, meeting Gotrek's glower with one of his own. Gotrek looked away first, which startled Felix more than the attempted throttling.

'Who was sleepwalking? Dwarfs don't sleepwalk,' Gotrek snapped, releasing Felix.

'Then what do you call it?' Felix said, trying to straighten his cloak. 'Were you trying to learn how to fly? Even dwarfs need machines for that.'

'I wasn't sleepwalking,' Gotrek insisted. He shook his head. 'I thought…' He trailed off.

Rubbing his throat, Felix looked at the Slayer. 'What?' he said.

'Nothing,' Gotrek growled.

'So you tried to strangle me for no reason then?' Felix said acidly. 'That makes me feel so much better! At least if you'd been dreaming, you'd have an excuse, but no, it was nothing.' He sneered at Gotrek and the Slayer glared at him. But Felix didn't retreat. Almost dying had a way of stiffening his spine, he'd learned. It wasn't quite an admirable trait, but it'd do.

'Daemons, manling,' Gotrek said finally, staring at his hands. 'I was drowning in a sea of daemons and lights, falling forever into the maw of an eternal battle.' He closed his fingers into fists and knocked his knuckles together.

'Sounds like a good dream for you,' Felix said, hawking a wad of spit, trying to clear his bruised throat. Gotrek shot him another glare.

'Trapped forever in an eternity without doom or death? More like a nightmare, manling,' he rumbled, scratching at his eye-patch.

Felix shivered, trying not to think about it. He'd seen enough daemons to last him several lifetimes and the idea of forever circling the drain with them took the wind right out of his sails. Gotrek rubbed his chin. 'Dreams or no, it's been long enough, I think,' he said, finally.

'What?' Felix said, taken aback by the sudden change of subject.

'You didn't think we were just going to sit here forever, did you, manling?' Gotrek said. 'Did you think I was just going to let them take my doom from me?' He snorted. 'For shame, manling, I thought you knew me better than that.' He peered at Felix. 'Maybe you're not the right choice to be my Remembrancer after all...'

'I – no – but what about the prophecy?' Felix said, stunned, his words tripping over each other.

'What about it?' Gotrek said.

'You seemed to take it seriously enough earlier!' Felix flapped his arms. 'I thought that was why you let them take you!'

Gotrek blinked. 'Why would you think that?'

'You – but I – but you–' Felix said. 'Then what are we doing in here?'

'I told you,' Gotrek said. 'There is a grudge between Ungrim and I. I did not wish to press the matter and force his hand.' Gotrek hesitated. Then, 'I am many things, manling, but a kinslayer isn't one of them.'

'So what have you been doing all of this time? I thought you were–'

'Brooding? Ha!' Gotrek's head jerked as he laughed. 'No,

manling, I was planning for our escape. It was a tricky proposition, I admit.' Gotrek tapped the side of his head with a blunt finger. 'Sometimes, with some problems, you just have to sit and think on them awhile.'

'But what of the prophecy,' Felix said again. 'Do you not believe Axeson?'

'I believe him,' Gotrek said, walking to the balcony. 'He said if I marched north, Karak Kadrin is doomed.'

'And?' Felix said, following him.

Gotrek gave a gap-toothed grin and shrugged. 'Who said anything about marching?'

The Worlds Edge Mountains, north-east of Karak Kadrin

'I prefer beer to dust,' Dorin spat. The sword-wielding Slayer stomped along beside his fellows, all of whom moved within the dust cloud of the throng's march. They had been travelling for several days, and Karak Kadrin was long behind them. They marched not within the ranks, but behind and to the side, within their own unruly mob. Despite being an honoured part of Karak Kadrin's throng, no thane worth his beard would have attempted to include the Slayers in the proper order of battle.

'Think of it as a snack before the main meal,' Biter said. He had a crude patch over his ruined eye and his new axe, etched with runes of wounding and battle, bounced on his shoulder. He hawked a gob of spittle and flashed metal teeth at the frowning Dorin. When the other Slayer turned away, Biter thrust his finger beneath his patch and scrubbed at the raw socket. It itched furiously.

'Stop that,' Koertig muttered. The Nordlander was easily

keeping pace with the Slayers, despite having only a man's stamina. 'It'll just start bleeding again.'

'See, you do like me,' Biter said, grinning. Koertig grunted and looked away. Biter kept up the grin for another moment before he let it slide off his face. In truth, he didn't feel much like smiling. He felt tired. Every muscle ached and his head felt as if the skin were burning and peeling off at the same time. He needed a drink and a sleep and not necessarily in that order.

Instead, he was marching to war.

The rumours flew like birds through the throng as it left Karak Kadrin behind, and had grown in the repeated telling over the past few days. Dwarfs gossiped as much as any other race, though they liked to claim otherwise. And what the loose lips were letting slip was dark and unpleasant.

'I should have let the Norscans take me,' Koertig muttered.

'Then you'd be dead, and not marching with the greatest army that Karak Kadrin has ever unleashed, human,' a grim voice said. Koertig stiffened as Ungrim Ironfist approached the Slayers, the jewels set into his crown-helm gleaming in the sun. 'Still, if it's death you're after, I'm sure the Chaos lovers will oblige. You, Biter, you're in charge?'

'No?' Biter said. The other Slayers had put distance between them and he cursed them all silently. He sighed. 'I suppose so.'

'Good,' Ungrim said. 'March with me. I require the voice of a Slayer to counter the other, more sensible ones I've surrounded myself with.'

'Surely you can provide that yourself, Lord King,' Biter said, grinning slightly.

Ungrim chuckled. 'Not when I'm the one tasked with the decision. Come, Biter,' he said, slapping the Slayer on the back. 'Aye, and bring your Remembrancer as well.'

The throng was making camp as they made their way back to where Ungrim's circle of thanes awaited their king. Dwarfs rarely used tents on the march, but it was the storm season and the valleys and dips of the mountains could flood quicker than a dwarf could wink. Wide pavilion tents were erected, with open sides and brass scales over the tarp to keep out arrows and reflect the sun. The tents were set up quickly and efficiently, the support poles biting the hard earth with iron anchors. It took a matter of minutes to collapse the tents and pack them for travel.

Heavy pavise shields were the next to go up, around each tent, making each of the pavilions a miniature fortress. The shields were as large as the dwarfs who planted them and as wide as three, and each had a reinforced slot that the warriors could extend spears, handguns or crossbows through. They wouldn't hold up under sustained attacks, but there wasn't a dwarf alive who didn't feel safer with a roof over his head and stout walls around him.

The king's bodyguard had set up a pavilion on the slopes of one of the low peaks that rose up around the route the throng followed. They were setting up the shields when Ungrim arrived with Biter, and a heavy, round table had been placed on a smooth disc of stone to keep it level.

Biter nodded to Thungrimsson as he entered the pavilion with Ungrim. The other thanes looked at him with distaste and Biter chuckled. Koertig stooped and slouched unobtrusively, watching but not speaking. Biter sometimes envied Gurnisson. What he wouldn't give for a more talkative companion. Talking was the only thing that kept him from hearing the screams in his head and smelling the damp of the mine as it flooded and–

'What's he doing here?' one of the thanes grunted, gesturing towards Biter.

'Tradition, Damminsson,' Ungrim said. 'A representative of the Slayers who accompany the throng must be included in every meeting of the thanes.'

'Aye, but he's no War-Mourner, nor a designated Battle-Master, like old Ogun. He has no authority,' another thane said.

'He has as much authority as any of you,' Ungrim said, his tone implying that the thanes had as much authority as the king chose to give them, when they were on the march.

The thanes grumbled into their beards, but gave no further argument. Biter gave them a cheery wave as Ungrim motioned for them all to gather around the table, where a map, drawn on the inside of what could only be a scrap of dragon-hide, had been unrolled. The map was the work of a dozen centuries' worth of information gathered by peddlers, scouts, rangers and adventuresome clansmen. Lost holds, now long vanished or otherwise rendered uninhabitable, marked it, as did those ancient routes where the savage tribes of the north travelled from the Wastes into the lands of men and dwarfs. Biter whistled softly as Ungrim traced their enemy's route with his finger.

'They struck the Peak Pass here,' Ironfist said. 'Then they split up, with one force continuing on to Karak Kadrin, and the bulk of the army retreating towards the pass.'

'The question is, why?' Thungrimsson said, leaning forwards on his knuckles.

'A better question would be, was it intentional? These barbarians can barely organize a horde half the size you're proposing. Maybe there was a rift?' another thane offered.

'If so, then why are the ones we're chasing heading back that way?' Thungrimsson said.

'Have you heard anything from the scouts?' Ungrim said abruptly. 'Are they still retreating?'

'As fast as they can,' the thane said, lighting his pipe with a long brass taper. He puffed and waved a hand. 'A few hundred or so have split off from the main bulk of the curs.'

'A rear-guard,' Thungrimsson mused.

'No,' Ungrim said, stroking his beard. 'No, they're falling apart. Just like grobi do. Infighting and losing cohesion as they move. These hills are probably swarming with detritus like that. We should–'

The eerie squall of a hunting horn echoed over the camp. Biter turned, eye narrowing. His nostrils flared as he caught a whiff of a musky animal scent. 'What's that?' he said.

'What's what?' the thane with the pipe said.

The hound was twice the size of a normal dog and shimmering scales showed through its matted and filthy fur. It crashed into the pavise shield behind the thane and thrust itself forwards, jaws closing with a snap on his head. The pipe tumbled from spasming fingers as the hound jerked and clawed, tearing the thane's head off.

Ungrim roared, snatching a hand-axe out of his belt and hurling it. It crashed against the hound's skull, splitting it. The beast slumped, its weight toppling a shield. More hounds scrambled into the gap, snapping and snarling as they each fought to be the first in. Down below in the camp, more horns sounded as men – riders – swept down the slope, howling and shrieking as if noise alone would carry the day. Biter hefted his axe and grinned. It was a worthless sort of ambush. If they had been fewer in number, or more careless, it might have done the trick. But as it stood, it was merely going to let them stretch their limbs.

The twang of crossbows and the boom of handguns

sounded as the dwarfs responded to the attack. A hound, slavering jaws spread wide, lunged for Biter. It had horns curling from its brow and a tail that was like that of a scorpion. Biter side-stepped the beast and grabbed its horn as it lunged past. He jerked hard, snapping its neck and ripping the horn from its head. He jammed the latter into the throat of another beast, killing it in mid-leap.

The thanes had reacted quickly to the attack, and soon, all of the dogs were dead. But the pavilion was still open to the enemy and a horseman galloped through the opening, sword and shield swept wide as he chanted to his Dark Gods. The horse reared and screamed, hooves slamming down on hastily upraised shields. Biter moved quickly, his axe licking out, teasing the beast's hindquarters, causing it to thrash wildly. The rider was unprepared and he fell, cursing. He just barely brought his shield up to meet Biter's axe, but the force of the blow was enough to shatter his arm. He fell back, wailing, and Biter finished him with a negligent back-handed whack of the blade. The axe was as light as a feather in his grip. 'Remind me to thank the priest for the loan of his blade, eh?' he shouted to Koertig.

Without waiting for a reply, Biter spun to face his next opponent, laughing. 'Poor Gurnisson doesn't know what he's missing,' he said, grinning savagely as he waded into the fray, his single eye blazing with berserk joy.

Karak Kadrin, the Slayer Keep

Garagrim frowned at the scroll in his hand, as if it had personally offended him. Lanterns lined the high alcoves of the library, casting a watery yellow light across the rows of stone shelves and pigeonholes, each one stuffed with books, tomes, scrolls and papyri from the four corners of the world. Like everything else in Karak Kadrin, the library had been built carefully and over centuries. Maps, both ancient and more recent, lined the walls in steel frames, and if one followed them in the right order, one could trace the expansion and eventual retraction of dwarf civilization from the Golden Age until now. Garagrim had done that very thing often as a child, seeing what had once been and what now was and wondering if there was some way to make it the way it had been again.

With a growl, he twitched the scroll aside and sat back, rubbing his eyes. He was sitting in his father's chair, in his father's library, handling his father's duties, instead of doing what he should have been doing.

'And what duties might those be, my son?' his mother's voice inquired.

Garagrim shifted in his seat. 'I didn't realize that I had spoken aloud. Forgive me, mother,' he said, rising to greet her. She waved him back to his seat. Her silent bodyguards had stayed outside. They were men of her clan, Garagrim knew, sent to ward her, even in Karak Kadrin where she was, theoretically, safe. The idea that the clans of Karak Kadrin could not protect their own queen was an insult, though not a large one, as far as Ungrim was concerned. Most of the elders of the hold had even stopped grumbling about it.

Kemma lifted a scroll, examining it. Garagrim resisted the urge to snatch it from her. In many ways, he knew that he was more conservative than either of his parents. He was more conservative than most dwarfs, in fact. He was assured of some things very strongly, and knew with iron certainty that there was a proper order to the way of things. Tradition was the shield which sheltered the dawi from the Chaos which threatened to drown the world in fire and madness. And in dwarf tradition, women did not interfere in the running of the hold, save for in the most extreme circumstances.

She saw the look on his face, despite his attempt to hide it. 'It's a bill, my son,' she said. 'It is merely a matter of accounts, nothing of import.' She dropped it on the desk.

'That's not the point,' he grunted.

'No, I suppose not,' she said, taking a seat. 'You are angry.'

'I am... frustrated,' he said.

'They look much the same, then,' she said.

'What do you want, mother?'

'Merely to inquire after your health, my son,' she said. 'Your father is doing as he thinks best.'

'What is best for the hold, or for him?' Garagrim said, laying his fists on the table.

'One and the same,' she said, looking at another scroll. 'Handle this one first. We'll need the pork the Moot provides for the victory celebration, and the little scroungers are good at "forgetting" deliveries until they're paid.'

'You think he'll win, then?' Garagrim said.

'Your father has the habit of cheating death, whether he wants to or not,' Kemma said, opening a ledger. Without asking, she snatched Garagrim's stylus and dipped it into an ink pot, and then began scratching out sums. 'These books are a mess. Your father never shows his work.'

'Why does he bear a grudge against Gurnisson?' Garagrim asked.

The scratching of the stylus slowed and then stopped. Kemma didn't look at him. 'Why ask this? Are you no longer content to hate him because your father does?'

Garagrim's jaw clenched. 'It is proper–'

'Only if one is foolish,' Kemma said. 'You overstep yourself, taking on the debts of others like some wastepenny from Barak Varr, without knowing the reason for those debts in the first place.'

'You go too far, mother. Like it or not, I am War-Mourner,' Garagrim said, rising to his feet. 'I have a right to know.'

'Ask him,' Kemma said, meeting her son's glare. 'It was Gurnisson's oath, and it is his to share or not, as it pleases him.'

Garagrim eyed his mother. Then, he nodded briskly. 'I'll do that, then. Thank you for your advice, mother.' He turned and left the library without waiting for her reply. Behind him, he heard the stylus resume scratching.

She was hiding something, he knew. Then, his mother was always hiding something. His father was relatively straight-forward, but Kemma had a mind as crooked as a skaven bur-row. Garagrim marched through the corridors, ignoring the bows and salutes of the guards. The hold was still on a war-footing, and would be until the throng returned.

He took the stairs slowly, turning the words to come over in his mind. Gurnisson had no reason to satisfy his curiosity, nor any reason to like him. Garagrim didn't like Gurnisson either and not just because of his father, no matter what others thought.

It was because Gurnisson flaunted his freedom like an ufdi. Garagrim and his father were bound by chains of duty and honour, but Gurnisson was not, and he knew it and revelled in it, disregarding custom and law and propriety with impu-nity, trusting in his status as a Slayer to protect him.

His hands clenched as he walked. Some said that was the purpose of the Slayers, to show the cracks in the foundation of dwarf society. Others said that they were a safety valve, allowing the discordant elements, the grit in the ore, to be sifted out. Regardless, though they were separate, they had to maintain a proper respect for things.

That was the War-Mourner's task, to see that the Slayers respected the few limits placed upon them. That no one had taken that office in some centuries had not caused Garagrim to hesitate at the time, though now he could see why it had remained vacant for so long. Slayers chafed at authority, even that imposed by one of their own.

Not that they truly saw him as one of their own. He had no shame of his own, no right to take the oath, as they saw it. Yet taken it he had and he would do it again in a heartbeat, to spare his clan and his father the doom that haunted them. For the good of Karak Kadrin, Garagrim had taken the Slayer's oath and though his father sought to deny him, he would garner a noble doom and free the clan from the weight of their ancient oath.

The guards snapped to attention as they caught sight of him coming up the stairs. It had been more than a day since Gurnisson had attacked them, and they were taking no chances now. The guard had been doubled, and rather than clansmen, ironbreakers were on duty. Even without his axe, it seemed that Gurnisson was deadly, at least to hear the last guards tell it.

'My prince,' one of the ironbreakers rumbled.

'Elig,' Garagrim said, nodding perfunctorily. He knew the names of most of the warriors of the hold; a feat of memory he'd put to good use since his childhood and one of the many skills his mother had taught him. 'Is there anything to report?'

'Nothing, Prince Garagrim,' Elig said. 'Some noise earlier, an argument, I think, but they've been having those since we put them out there.' He shrugged. 'Gurnisson likes to shout, and the manling isn't much quieter.'

Garagrim smiled. 'Good. Open the door,' he said, gesturing. 'I wish to speak to them.'

'Are you sure that's wise, my prince?'

'Since when have you known me to do anything wise, Elig?' Garagrim said, feigning a heartiness he didn't truly feel. The guards did as he bade without further argument. Garagrim stepped through the door, closing his eyes as the chill wind of the heights caressed him.

When he opened them, rage flooded him.

'Sound the alarm! They've escaped!'

The Worlds Edge Mountains, the Peak Pass

Canto climbed off of his exhausted horse, and knelt in the dust before the hooves of Garmr's own mount. 'I return bearing gifts, my lord,' he said. He hadn't been surprised to see the horde marching to meet him as he entered the Peak Pass. The mighty wheeled altars and war-shrines rattled at the fore of the army, and banners swayed in time to the beat of dull drums. There was something in the air as well, not simply the stench of the army, but something else…

'A fallen hold, perhaps,' Garmr said. There was a dark amusement evident in his tone.

'The remnants of a defeated army, held together and brought to you, by me,' Canto said, still staring at the ground. 'Hrolf is dead, as are Kung and Yan and the siege of Karak Kadrin with them. If I had not–'

Garmr raised a hand. 'How many warriors do you bring me, Canto?'

'A few hundred, my lord,' Canto said quickly. 'Others, cowardly curs that they were, preferred to take their chances with the army pursuing us rather than risking your magnanimity…'

'Not an auspicious number, Canto.'

'Can such a thing be said to exist, my lord, in defeat?' Canto said. His shoulders itched, waiting for the axe to fall. He couldn't stop thinking about the tortoise, on its slow, unceasing plod across the Wastes. Maybe it had reached the ocean by now. Would it stop, or would it keep walking?

'Especially then, Canto Unsworn,' Garmr said. 'Ekaterina?'

The woman urged her horse forwards, her fingers draped lazily over the pommel of her sword. She looked at Canto hungrily. Canto longed to run, but stayed where he was. His mind spun and discarded plan after plan in a space of moment, none of them better than the one he had.

'Kill one in nine and scatter their skulls before us. Let the air swim with screams and the smell of blood.' Garmr gestured. Ekaterina shrieked and jabbed her horse's flanks, causing it to leap over Canto. Chaos marauder horsemen followed, swarming their shocked fellows quickly. Garmr and Canto were in an island of tranquillity amidst the carnage. Garmr looked down at him. 'How did Hrolf die?'

'A dwarf killed him. A Slayer,' Canto said, looking up for the first time. He did not know for certain that the mad dwarf had killed Hrolf, but he suspected that it was close enough to the truth to satisfy Garmr.

'Describe him,' Garmr said. Behind them, around them, men screamed and died.

'A Slayer, my lord,' Canto said. 'Short, broad, disgusting...'

'How many eyes did it possess?'

'Two, no, one,' Canto said. 'It didn't seem to hamper him in using that axe of his.' Idly, he stroked the marks that same axe had left on his own armour.

'Ahhhhh,' Garmr said, leaning back in his saddle. 'Yes.' He looked down at Canto. 'You have done well, Canto. I have need of you now, with so many of my champions lying scattered across these hills. You will serve as my left hand even as Ekaterina has become my right. You will serve me and that service will raise you high in the esteem of the Blood God. Would that please you?'

No! Canto thought. 'Yes, my lord.'

'And what would please you, Khorreg Hell-Worker?' Garmr said, turning to look at the Chaos dwarf who had watched Canto's reception without comment. Khorreg's cracked features shifted themselves into a sneer of displeasure.

'It would please me to get back to my remaining engines and ready them for battle against the Weak Ones who dare pursue us,' he rumbled.

'So be it,' Garmr said, gesturing. 'We will drown them in fire and blade, Daemonsmith.'

Khorreg didn't reply. Instead, he stumped off through the army, armour wheezing and hissing. Canto watched him go and hoped that the Hell-Worker would hold to their bargain. A dozen heads, tied together by beards and scalplocks, fell to the ground and struck his knee, startling him. Ekaterina, covered from head to toe in blood, rode towards them. 'Shall I kill him now, my lord? Or would you prefer that pleasure yourself?'

Canto stood as Garmr said, 'Canto's skull will remain where it is, for today at least.' Ekaterina opened her mouth as if to protest, but then clamped it shut as Garmr went on. 'I wish the walls of this valley to be as red as the ground we have left behind us. Soak it in blood and meat and sanctify it to Khorne. The road must be made ready to receive its final paving stones.'

'The dwarfs,' Canto said, all of the pieces falling into place. He had been right – it had all been a ploy from the start! He and the others had been nothing but bait, designed to lure a tiger from its den. He seethed, rage warring with prudence.

Garmr looked at him, and for a moment, Canto wondered whether the warlord could see the anger boiling beneath his skin, before the monstrous helm dipped in assent. 'Yes. You were right, Canto. You have indeed brought me gifts...'

15

Karak Kadrin,
the Slayer Keep

'I've changed my mind!' Felix shouted, eyes closed, knuckles white. 'I don't want to escape! I'd prefer to stay and be executed!'

Gotrek laughed harshly. 'They wouldn't execute you, manling. We're not men, after all. They might do the Trouser Leg Ritual on you, but only if they could find a pair big enough for a human.' The Slayer whistled. 'Look at that view.'

Felix cracked open one eye and immediately wished that he hadn't. Gotrek was right, it was quite the view. The whole of the valley that contained Karak Kadrin spread out below them, obscured from moment to moment by soft clouds. Unable to stop himself, Felix twisted, looking up. It was as if the roof of the world curved above him, close enough to touch. There was light and then darkness above it, black and cold and empty save for chill pinpricks of light. He shuddered as his vision swam and he closed his eyes again as his fingers dug tightly into the rock.

When Gotrek said he planned to escape, Felix had assumed that the Slayer was planning on the direct route, or going via some hidden mechanism known only to the Engineers' Guild. Instead, they were going straight up. The Slayer had turned Felix's cloak into a connecting line, tied it around Felix and then around himself, securing them together. Humiliating as it was, Felix understood the reason for it. There was simply no way that he could have made the climb on his own, not without tools and a good deal of luck.

But Gotrek... Gotrek moved like a mountain goat, his stubby fingers and toes finding invisible cracks and crevices with unerring accuracy as he scaled the peak. He'd stood on the balustrade and led Felix to the side of the balcony, and from there, upwards. 'I used to climb these peaks in my youth,' he said as his breath bloomed in a frosty mist and wafted back over his shoulder. 'Last to the summit bought the beer.'

'Ch-ch-charming,' Felix said as the cold dug its talons into his bones. It was far colder at this height than he'd expected and he couldn't stop his limbs from shuddering. He blinked, trying to clear the frost from his eyes, and looked at the grimacing face of the ancient dwarf king opposite. He didn't look happy to see them climbing up the cheek of his neighbour, for which Felix couldn't blame him. It must be like watching a fly crawl up a dinner guest's nose. He chuckled, and then blinked. 'Gotrek, I think the altitude is getting to me,' he said.

'What, already?' Gotrek said.

'How much farther is it to the top, Gotrek?'

'Who said anything about the top, manling?'

'I thought–'

'Only a few moments more, manling,' Gotrek said. He turned back to the rock face and began to climb, much faster than before.

'Easy for you to say,' Felix muttered. The nudging pain in his shoulder was back, and growing stronger. He'd known men who'd dislocated their shoulders before, and knew that it could happen again, and easier, now that it'd done it once. He imagined the spasm of another dislocation shooting through his arm, his grip weakening. Could Gotrek catch him, if he fell? Somehow, he doubted it. 'Best not fall,' he breathed. He'd climbed mountains before, but none this high. He tried to concentrate on holding on, on willing his exhausted muscles to work.

'Ha! Right where I remembered it,' Gotrek said. Felix looked up. The bottom of another balcony, much like the one they'd left, stretched out over them. 'Hold tight,' he grunted. Then, before Felix could reply, he swung out from the peak, arm stretching. Felix's gut clenched and the world spun and then Gotrek was pulling him up onto another stone balustrade. Felix grabbed the rough stonework and hauled himself over, and collapsed in a puddle on the balcony. Gotrek dropped down beside him, grinning happily.

'That's it?' Felix gasped. 'We left one balcony for another?'

'Not a balcony, manling.' Gotrek pointed and Felix saw a number of squat machines crouched on the flat stone beyond. 'A landing strip,' Gotrek said, heaving himself to his feet. 'Karak Kadrin has a number of platforms like this at these heights. Ungrim doesn't have much time for the Engineers' Guild, but he's not so foolish as to deny the use of a few of these dragon-pluckers.'

Felix rubbed his arms, trying to regain feeling in them, as he walked around the machines. He'd seen gyrocopters before, but only from a distance. They had a flimsiness to them that seemed at odds with other dwarf war machines, despite the barrel bodies and great rotors made from canvas and metal.

Each had a bucket seat and a heavy rope ladder coiled on one side. On the other was a canvas roll containing a variety of tools, only some of which Felix could glean the purpose of. Gotrek fondly patted the cannon-like object that extended from the front of one of the machines. 'Steam-gun, manling,' he said. 'It'll wipe out a horde of charging grobi faster than I can spit.'

'Did you ever fly one of these?' Felix said.

Gotrek's smile slipped from his face. 'Aye,' he said, 'a long time ago.' His eye narrowed. 'It's forbidden to any but an Engineer to fly one.'

'You intend to steal one?'

'Steal?' Gotrek glared at him. 'I'm no thief,' he spat. 'We're simply borrowing it.'

'That implies that we intend to bring it back,' Felix said. 'Besides which, how will we both fit on this thing? It'll barely fit you!'

'We'll improvise something,' Gotrek said. He grinned unpleasantly at Felix. Felix stepped back, raising his hands, 'Oh no, no, no,' he said. 'I've had enough of being carted around like a babe in a sling.'

'It's that, or stay here,' Gotrek growled, shaking a meaty fist. 'I care not, manling.'

Felix looked at the gyrocopter, his gut sinking. Then, desperate, he said, 'What about weapons? What about your axe?'

Gotrek paused. He looked at the door to the landing strip, as if gauging the number of steps, corridors and guards between him and his axe. Then he shook himself. His hands clenched and unclenched. 'Plenty of weapons where we're going, manling,' he said finally, each word escaping his lips as if dragged by hooks. 'We'll–'

The door shifted in its frame. Hinges squealed and it swung

open. Gotrek stepped forwards, grabbing a heavy spanner from one of the canvas rolls and lifting it. Felix looked around for something to use as a weapon.

Gotrek cursed as a shape stepped out onto the balcony. 'You,' he snarled.

The Worlds Edge Mountains, the Peak Pass

Grettir Many-Eyes rode a war-altar, held tight by rusty chains themselves held tight by magics older and more fell than any he'd yet learned. Daemons had forged those chains, to bind other daemons, and they held him fast. He examined the palms of his clawed gauntlets, meeting the unblinking avian eyes which sprouted bulbously from his palms. 'Is this my fate, then?' he asked softly, knowing from experience that no answer was forthcoming. The Changer had never answered him, even as he served the god on countless battlefields, gaining more and more power, his ascent paralleling that of his cousin.

He had fought champions of the Changer, the Rot, the Lover and even the Breaker, wielding first a sword, then magics. He had broken open the Black Vaults of the dawi zharr and fended off their stone-footed sorcerer-kings in order to steal the Crystal of Crooked Ways, which he had spent a year and a day carving into the mask he now wore. He had made war on the Spellbreakers of the Shifting City and on the War-Judges of the Tahmaks, he had corrupted the monks of the White Lotus, and he had crushed the heart of Isadora Von Carstein on the steps of the Lost Cathedral in order to prevent the vampire from unravelling the Weaver's works. All of that had been done in the service of one goal... The death of his false friend, Garmr.

And then, at the Battle of the Blistered Sun, he had gotten his chance. Garmr had been there, taking advantage of Dashak Kul's distraction to stage a raid on his rival's camp. Khorne-worshippers clashed in the ruins of a city that had not existed the day before. On a screaming, pulsing disc, Grettir had skimmed low over the streets, magic crackling between his crooked talons. It had been his whispers which had driven Dashak to war with the Nine Unfulfilled, and given Garmr his opening.

So close. He had been so close. He could still taste the bitter ashes of his defeat in the back of his throat. He could still see the look of recognition in Garmr's eyes, and feel the bite of the daemon-queen's spear as it pierced his side and killed his disc. She had followed him down into the dust like a swooping hawk, with her red eyes alight with untold purpose. The ghost of that spear-thrust still haunted him, echoing through his limbs.

The Changer had seemingly abandoned him then, right in the hands of his enemies. He had been captured, bound and forced to bind another.

Momentarily, his thoughts drifted out, touching the razor-bright hunger of Ulfrgandr, the Slaughter-Hound, the Massacre-That-Walked. He had a link to it, as the one who had bound its soul to Garmr's own. It had been his hands which had plunged the eight mystical daggers into its flesh, each blade first dipped in Garmr's blood. But only after it had been beaten and captured by Garmr and his warriors. The creature had been as vicious a combatant as any army of warriors and a hundred men had been butchered on that particular altar of hubris, torn to shreds by Ulfrgandr on the Plateau of Sighs in a battle that raged from the plateau to the Crater Gates, where daemon-engines had spat fire at the combatants.

Garmr had fought Ulfrgandr to a standstill, his axe carving chunks from the monster's flesh, his armour spattered with the beast's acidic blood, his helm dented from its fangs. Then, Garmr had almost been as monstrous as the Slaughter-Hound in his berserk desire to conquer. That need to dominate had been at the heart of the binding of the beast, for Garmr had become adrift on tides of blood, his mind slipping into brute hunger like so many of his peers, less a warlord than an engine of murder.

Privately, Grettir felt some modicum of respect for his cousin in regards to that bit of self-awareness. There weren't many champions of the Blood God who could recognize the inherent limits of succumbing to the god's own madness. Most dived in quite willingly. But Garmr had forced Grettir to bind Ulfrgandr, the mystic spells allowing Garmr to force his own madness into the beast's already insane skull, thus allowing him to be fully clear-headed for the first time in a century, which, in turn, had allowed Garmr to begin his march south.

Perhaps that was his fate, he thought. Perhaps he was merely a tool, fit only to ensure that Garmr met his own destiny.

Grettir snarled. Garmr, he thought, chewing the name to shreds. Garmr Kinslayer, Garmr Childeater, Garmr Tribekiller, those were the names the great and powerful Gorewolf was known by in the north. He was not a hero there, but a monster. A devil that'd killed his own people and made a sacrifice of their guts and bones to the Blood God. And for what, Grettir wondered? He looked around, at the rolling shrines, galloping steeds and brutish riders, at the marchers with their bellicose cries. He sneered at them, though his expression was hidden behind his mask.

Garmr used them as he had used their tribe. These warriors, these proud brutes were a collection of sacrifices, waiting to be culled when the time came, all for the glory of Khorne. 'Cattle,' he shouted. 'You are all sheep trusting the wolf not to shear you!'

Through the eyes of his helmet, he saw the diverse fates of everyone he looked at. In most of those, men died. The how and the why of it were different, but still they died. Every warrior within the sound of his voice was a corpse walking, a maggot-farm as yet untilled. True, some survived. Some even prospered, rising up in the esteem of gods and men, rivalling Garmr in time, but most died.

'You're all going to die,' he said, quietly, his words chewed up beneath the creak of wheels and the thunder of marching feet and stomping hooves. 'Even me,' he continued, settling back. Like them, Grettir had a choice of deaths, ranging from the shameful to the staggering. In one future, Garmr tore his head from his shoulders once his purpose had been fulfilled. In another, Grettir died in the jaws of the Slaughter-Hound. In a third, he set his talons in his cousin's throat and they died together. That last one warmed his heart, and it was the only reason he had not yet attempted a futile and fatal escape.

'What is the first thing we were taught as children, cousin?' Garmr said. Grettir turned as the warlord brought his night-black steed in line with the creaking altar, the animal's hooves trotting in rhythm with the cloven paws of the two gorebeasts pulling the structure.

'Well?' Garmr said. Grettir looked away. 'The Changer lies, cousin. That is what we were taught. What all of us, all of them, are taught,' Garmr continued. 'Whatever his name, the Steppe-Wolf speaks with a forked tongue, the Spider-Queen spins webs from daydreams and the Raven-Kin speaks in riddles that can trap the unwary. Only in blood is there truth. They know better than to listen to you, these brave warriors.'

'Self-righteousness has always been the weapon you were most comfortable with, cousin,' Grettir said, turning. In his eyes, a kaleidoscope of swirling fates spun and duelled for Garmr. 'Blood is blood, nothing more, nothing less.'

'Do you really expect to find fertile soil for your poison?' Garmr asked.

'And what poison might that be?'

'I see it, cousin, winding its way in among the red currents of my followers,' Garmr said. 'Perhaps I should have cut out your tongue.'

'Then who would have told you your fortunes?'

Garmr grunted and chuckled. 'True, cousin,' he said.

Grettir hated that laugh. He hated Garmr. 'Ekaterina will betray you,' he said.

'And so,' Garmr said, shrugging. His armour rustled. 'We all strive for the gods, cousin, even you.'

'Canto does not,' Grettir said.

'Canto has his uses,' Garmr said.

'Even as I do,' Grettir said.

'Our path is littered with blood and bones, cousin,' Garmr said. 'I have shed the blood of daemons and men from the Wastes to here. The road trembles in eagerness. It yearns for completion.' He hesitated. Grettir knew what question was coming even before it slipped Garmr's lips. It was always the same question. 'Is he coming?'

'For such a mighty warrior, you require much in the way of reassurance,' Grettir said.

'Tell me,' Garmr said. He wasn't quite pleading, not quite. Nor was he demanding. Here, at this point, at this place on the path of fate, jailer and prisoner stood equal. They were only cousins again, boys who had grown together, becoming warriors, serving their tribe together, fighting enemies back-to-back. Grettir saw the past as clearly as all of the possible futures, and saw blood on the snow as he and Garmr, lean and sun-hardened, had roved like wolves among the enemies of their tribe, swords and axes in hand. They had served no gods save ambition, sword-brothers, blood-kin, and now... What?

'How did we come to this?' Grettir said.

Garmr stared at him silently. With a start, Grettir realized that he hadn't seen his cousin's face in more than a century. Nor had he seen his own. Both of them were trapped behind their masks, locked into their cycles of destiny. He sighed, his anger fading to a dull ache as he tried to pry one future from the web of dozens. 'He is coming. They will meet us at the Peak Pass, where we destroyed the others.'

Garmr shuddered in his armour. 'It will be complete, then. I will have my reward,' he said, like a child eager for a sweetmeat.

'Yes,' Grettir said, and bowed his head.

Karak Kadrin,
the Slayer Keep

'Yes, me,' Axeson said, gesturing to Gotrek with what Felix realized was the Slayer's axe. And that wasn't all: the priest also had Karaghul's hilt peeking over one shoulder. 'Take your axe, Slayer, there's wet work to be done.'

'What are you talking about?' Gotrek growled, not quite lowering the spanner as Axeson shoved the door closed. 'Have you come to try and talk me out of leaving, priest?'

'Where would be the sense in that, Gurnisson? Would you be swayed by words, sweet or otherwise?' Axeson said, holding out Gotrek's axe, balanced across his palms. 'Take it.'

Gotrek did, snatching the weapon and bringing it close. He

ran his thumb along the blade and then stuffed the bleeding digit in his mouth. Axeson unstrapped Felix's sword-belt and tossed Karaghul to its astonished owner.

'Why are you doing this?' Felix said, sliding Karaghul partially from its sheath. He hadn't realized how much he missed the blade until he had been separated from it. 'You were the one who convinced Ungrim not to let us go in the first place.'

'Did I?' Axeson said. 'I merely told Ungrim that if Gurnisson marched with the throng, Karak Kadrin would fall. You are not with the throng and I don't believe you intend to march...' He gestured to the gyrocopters. 'The prophecy doesn't cover flying, swimming or falling.'

'If you were a man, I might accuse you of sophistry,' Felix said.

Axeson grunted. 'If I were a man, we wouldn't be having this conversation in the first place.' He looked at Felix. 'I knew Gurnisson wouldn't be content to rest in captivity, even as I knew that he wouldn't seek to fight his way out. Not even a Slayer would shed dwarf blood so lightly or so selfishly. That left only two options.'

'That still doesn't explain how you knew,' Felix said.

'Grimnir told me,' Axeson said, shrugging.

'But why help us?' Felix said, strapping Karaghul to his waist even as he wondered what that last bit meant. When had Gotrek had to escape before? 'Why bring us our weapons?'

'Prophecies are funny things, human, especially when they are at cross-purposes,' Axeson said.

'Speak plainly,' Gotrek grunted.

'Your doom is not today, Gurnisson. Or even tomorrow or a year from hence,' Axeson said, glancing at the door. Despite the wind, Felix heard a faint noise. Horns, he thought. 'But there is a doom out there, and it is hungry for you and if it takes you, we will all die with you.'

'But if Gotrek is fated to die elsewhere–' Felix began.

'Chaos makes mockery of all prophecy and portent, even its own. What is immutable becomes mutable when the Chaos winds blow,' Axeson said. Gotrek nodded grudgingly.

'Aye, mountains become water and the truth becomes a lie,' Gotrek muttered. Then, 'You play dice with the gods, boy,' he said to Axeson.

'Then you had best see that we win, Gurnisson,' Axeson said. 'Now, take to the air. Garagrim has noticed your absence and sounded the alarm.'

'What will happen if he catches us?' Felix asked nervously.

'Best see that he doesn't, eh?' Axeson said, clapping him on the arm in a friendly manner. 'Keep him fighting, Jaeger,' he added, more softly.

'Because of the prophecy,' Felix said.

Axeson hesitated, and then nodded jerkily. The door shuddered in its frame. Someone was trying to open it. Axeson fairly flew across the distance and planted one broad shoulder against the door. 'Time's up. If you're going, go!'

'Get on, manling,' Gotrek said, climbing into the bucket seat of the gyrocopter. He grabbed a pair of goggles and strapped them over his head before tossing a pair to Felix. 'Wrap that cloak tight about yourself. It's going to get cold.'

'Concerned over my health?'

'If you freeze to death, I'll need to find a new Remembrancer,' Gotrek grunted, flipping switches and pulling levers. 'Give the rotor a push, and then get on.'

'Where, out of curiosity?' Felix said.

Gotrek pointed. While Felix had been talking to Axeson, Gotrek had stretched a heavy roll of canvas out beneath the landing struts of the gyrocopter, creating an improvised hammock. Felix stared at it, aghast. Gotrek growled impatiently. 'Manling, we use these to carry rocks three times your weight. It's secure enough! Now give the blasted rotor a shove!'

Felix did so, straining against the resistance of the rotor. Even with both hands, it took him a few tries. When he finally got it moving, it rotated slowly, in an almost desultory fashion. Gotrek pumped a lever, and the speed picked up. Felix slid beneath the gyrocopter and into the sling even as the struts left the stone, bouncing slightly and knocking the air from him. He reached out, grabbing the struts. 'Anytime, Gotrek,' he said.

Behind them, metal rang on metal. Felix twisted, looking back over his shoulder. Axeson had his back pressed against the door, and there was a look of strain on his face. He wouldn't be able to hold the door shut for much longer.

The gyrocopter bounced again and then shot upwards in a plume of dust. Felix coughed and spat and pulled the goggles awkwardly over his eyes. His whole body shook as the gyrocopter took off, and he gritted his teeth as they rattled in his head. He heard Gotrek laughing as the rotors chopped the air. Then the comforting solidity of the stones of Karak Kadrin dropped away and they were in the air.

Felix thought he might have screamed, but he wasn't sure.

'The human screams loudly,' one of the guards said, shading his eyes to watch the departing gyrocopter as it bounced through the air.

'Maybe it was a war cry. Very big on the war cry, humans,' another said.

'Quiet, both of you,' Garagrim growled, casting a glare at the two ironbreakers. 'Someone get a representative of the

Engineers' Guild up here! And pilots,' he snarled. Then he transferred the glare to the priest lying on the ground. Axeson had been knocked aside by the forcing open of the aerie door, and he sat up, rubbing his shoulder. 'Well? What have you to say, priest?'

'You're welcome?' Axeson said, heaving himself to his feet.

Garagrim raised a fist, but refrained from striking the priest. He couldn't say what stayed his hand. Maybe it was tradition or honour perhaps, or maybe fear; traitor or not Axeson was still a priest, still beloved of the gods. Or maybe he simply couldn't bring himself to strike a fellow dwarf.

Despite what he knew others said of him, Garagrim was not as hot-headed or as pig-blind as he acted. He had merely taken on the role of a Slayer, and played it to the best of his ability. But he could think when he needed to. 'You let them go. No, you *helped* them escape,' Garagrim said. It wasn't a question, though Axeson answered it as if it was one.

'Indeed I did,' Axeson said, straightening his robes. 'If Ungrim had simply listened to me, none of this would have been necessary.' He met the War-Mourner's glare. 'But he didn't. The question now is, will you?'

'What do you mean?' Garagrim said, momentarily taken aback.

'You were intending to pursue Gurnisson, weren't you?'

Garagrim hesitated. His eyes narrowed. 'Are you going to tell me why I shouldn't?'

'Actually, I was going to tell you why you should,' Axeson said. 'You must muster a second throng and–'

'It doesn't matter,' Garagrim interjected. 'I don't plan on listening to you either way. You have played us false, priest, and I–'

'Will stop bellowing,' Queen Kemma said, sweeping out onto

the balcony, flanked by her guards. The ironbreakers and the clansmen traded glares as Kemma looked around and made a 'tut-tut' sound. 'I knew he went too quietly,' she murmured.

'You expected this?' Garagrim said, looking at his mother in shock.

'Of course,' she said, 'as did you, my son.'

It was Axeson's turn to look startled. 'What?'

'The sewers,' Garagrim grunted. 'I suspected Gurnisson would try and escape, but I thought he'd go down as he did before, not up. I've had warriors stationed down there for days now.'

'Unhappy warriors, I might add,' Kemma said. She ran her fingers across the edge of a rotor.

'But how would you have–' Axeson began.

Garagrim hiked a thumb at the balustrade. 'The storm flues, priest. They lead in and out of the mountain. It is how Gurnisson escaped the last time my father tried to imprison him.' He frowned. 'Apparently he rode down them during a storm, like a log on a flume.' He shook his head. 'He was as mad then as he is now.'

'And let us pray that he is as successful this time as he was then,' Kemma said. 'Regardless, you will do nothing to the priest.' She looked at her son. 'The priest was acting under my orders.'

'He was?' Garagrim said.

'I was?' Axeson said.

'He was,' Kemma said, folding her hands into her sleeves. 'I will take full responsibility for this debacle. Let Ungrim break his fangs on my walls, if he wants, if – *when* – he returns.' She pointed at Garagrim. 'Marshal a second throng of half of those warriors who remain. You will march out at as soon as possible.'

'Me? But father said–' Garagrim began, even as a savage joy filled him.

'Do not pretend to be stupid, my son,' Kemma said harshly. 'There is more at stake than your father's honour or ours. Our people must be preserved.' She swung around, her gaze capturing the huffing representative of the Engineers' Guild as he stepped out onto the balcony, mouth open to bellow about impropriety. By long tradition, the aeries set aside for gyrocopters were forbidden to any save Guild members. 'Master Flinthand,' Kemma said. 'I need these devices of yours in the air within the hour. Scour the mountains in all directions. A storm is coming and I would know when it is drawing close.'

Garagrim watched his mother bully the engineer into shocked silence and smiled. He had hoped Gurnisson would escape and give him cause to pursue. Indeed, he had been going to see Gurnisson to propose just that. Despite their mutual dislike, he'd been certain that the other Slayer would have taken him up on his offer. This way was better. This way, there was no guilt for disobeying his father, for helping Gurnisson, for any of it. The War-Mourner's palms itched for the feel of his axes' hafts.

A Slayer would die, that had been the prophecy. And that Slayer was going to be him, even if he had to hamstring Gurnisson to do it.

16

The Worlds Edge Mountains,
high in the air

Jostled, frozen and bruised, Felix clung to the struts with numb fingers. Every limb ached and his ears throbbed with the noise of the gyrocopter's rotors. Even with the goggles, his eyes stung from the harsh caress of the wind. Too, he was having trouble breathing. Luckily, the gyrocopter wasn't meant for high altitudes, and it was descending even as it drove forwards.

'Still alive, manling?' Gotrek called out. Felix could barely hear him, over the noise and wind. Deciding to save his breath, he merely stuck a hand out from beneath the gyrocopter and waved it stiffly. Gotrek laughed. 'Good!'

Felix wanted to ask him how he knew where he was going. Actually, he wanted to ask him to land, or at least swoop low enough so that Felix could slide out. Likely Gotrek would simply ignore him. So, instead, Felix tried to enjoy the ride.

He dozed, despite the aches and the cold. There was little

else to do, hanging suspended as he was. He tried not to move too much, despite the silent pleading of his joints for even the briefest of stretches. Felix had lost track of time soon after they'd ascended, so he had no way of telling how long they'd been in the air. How fast could a gyrocopter fly, he wondered?

The sky was growing darker, but that might simply have been the shadows cast by the craggy peaks of the Worlds Edge Mountains that flashed past, intermittent monoliths of grey and brown. Scrub trees and winding paths, the latter carved by untold centuries of travellers, passed below him. From above, the mountains looked, if not beautiful, then at least breathtaking. That was a far cry from walking through them, where every bend in the trail promised some new misadventure. That was Felix's experience, at least.

At least here, high in the air, it was safe–

Felix blinked as an unpleasant sensation crept across the back of his neck. Then, casually, he glanced over his shoulder. His eyes widened. He gave a yell and jerked his legs back even as the griffon's beak snapped shut on the space his foot had only moments before occupied.

The creature had drawn close enough to stretch out its neck and scrape his boot-heel. It was a malignant mixture of bird, lion and nightmare. He had seen griffons before, in the Imperial Zoo in Altdorf – of his and Gotrek's visit to which, the less that was said the better – but this beast was no human-raised war-beast. It was feral, and infinitely more frightening for the fact that no cage separated them. More, it had the look of sickness about it. Clumps of feathers had fallen from its head and there were great scabrous patches on the once sleek flanks of its feline shape. Its claws were split and jagged and its beak cracked, as if it had been in a fight recently. In fact, its whole attitude was one of a creature driven into a berserk fury by a period of prolonged violence.

The creature's cruel beak gaped as it stretched one vulture-like forepaw towards his legs, its eyes empty of anything save a volcanic rage. From around its neck dangled a heavy collar, burdened by a trio of still stained skulls, the browning bone etched with ruinous sigils. Felix squirmed in his hammock and as he moved, the gyrocopter, thrown off by his weight, dipped. Gotrek bellowed. 'Stop moving, curse you!'

The griffon snarled and swooped, its beak snapping at Felix. He jerked to the side. He had nowhere to go, nowhere to run. He couldn't even draw his sword. His fists hammered on the bottom of the gyrocopter as he tried to draw Gotrek's attention to his plight.

The griffon fell back and rose up, eyes blazing madly as it surged towards him, like a ferret entering a rat-hole. Felix pushed himself back. If he could reach up and grab the barrel of the steam-gun, perhaps he could–

The griffon hit the sling and thrashed, its claws tearing the tough canvas. The hooked tip of its beak gashed his armoured vest, scattering rings of mail and knocking the wind out of Felix. The canvas tore and split and Felix's stomach swam upwards into his throat as he fell. Desperately, he shot a hand out, reaching for something, anything, to halt his fall. He caught hold of a strut with a flailing hand and the gyrocopter dipped and rolled to the left.

Felix felt as if his spine were a bullwhip that had just been cracked, and he gritted his teeth against the agony. In his blind panic, he had grabbed the strut with his sore arm. His shoulder burned and he grabbed it instinctively. Legs kicking, he saw the griffon swoop beneath the gyrocopter with a screech that hammered at his ears.

'What are you doing down there, manling?' Gotrek shouted,

leaning over the side of the cockpit.

'Griffon!' Felix shouted.

'You'll have to wait until we land,' Gotrek shouted back.

'No! Griffon,' Felix bellowed.

The griffon struck the tail of the gyrocopter, its claws sinking into the wood as its tail lashed. It ducked under the rotors and shrieked again. Gotrek twisted in his seat, his face splitting in a wild grin. He turned back and grabbed the control stick. 'Hang on, manling!'

Gotrek yanked back on the stick, and the nose of the gyro-copter bobbed upwards. Felix's grip slipped and he was swung back against the belly of the machine. He scrabbled at the tattered scraps of the canvas and grabbed hold, praying that it would bear his weight. The griffon, meanwhile, lost its hold and tumbled through the air, screaming. Its wings gave a snap and it was propelled upwards, passing so close to Felix that he could smell the foul, animal odour that clung to it.

It belly-flopped onto the nose of the gyrocopter, pulling it down with its weight, and Felix heard Gotrek roar. He couldn't see anything, couldn't do anything save clutch frenziedly at the scraps of canvas. The wind passed over him like soft razors, digging into his exposed flesh. The gyrocopter lurched and rolled, its rotors whining. Felix was slammed against wood and metal as the machine seemed to fall through the air. Teeth bared, lips pressed flat by the wind, Felix reached for the opposite strut. Grabbing it, he hauled himself up, every muscle howling in agony as he stretched for the base of the tail section. Boots balanced on either strut, he grabbed hold and began to pull himself along.

Of course, he had no idea what he was going to do when he got there. He looked down and immediately wished he hadn't. The ground was a spinning blur of colours, all smashed together in a rapidly approaching morass. The ground was coming up fast, too fast, and Felix knew, though he had no experience in such matters, that there was no way they could pull out of the dive in time. Where was Gotrek? What was going on?

He got his answer a moment later. The gyrocopter shook as the griffon suddenly tumbled past him in a flurry of feathers and blood. Felix nearly lost his balance as the beast writhed in the air, its talons snatching at the struts and side of the gyrocopter with predatory determination. It caught sight of him and one bird-talon swiped out, reaching for him. He hauled himself out of its path, swinging out over the void as its claws sank into the belly of the gyrocopter. Dangling out, cloak whipping in the wind of their descent, Felix snatched Karaghul from its sheath, knowing it would do him no good, but not wanting to die a messy death on its claws.

The griffon hissed, wings flapping and its muscles bunched. Then it stiffened and screamed. An orange crest rose over the crown of its head as Gotrek climbed its back. The Slayer roared out an oath and brought his axe back over his head and then down, chopping into the massive tendons of one of its wings. It spun, the bad wing nearly buffeting Felix from his slippery perch. Gotrek was smashed back against the plummeting gyrocopter. Felix was jolted loose, his fingers slipping from the wood.

He was falling, and this time Gotrek wasn't going to be able to save him.

There was no fanfare for the second throng. No rolling drums or groaning horns or cheers to send this force on their way. Instead, silent faces watched and murmured oaths. From the crumbling parapet of the outer wall, Queen Kemma and

Axeson watched as Garagrim led his throng to war from one of the blockhouses that lined the mountain face above the main doors.

'It's quite small,' Axeson said.

'So is a dagger,' Kemma said. She turned away and looked out over the plains before the hold. She shaded her eyes and peered towards the mountains. 'The gyrocopters have reported that Ungrim has nearly reached the north-eastern edge of the Peak Pass. The enemy as well,' she added, frowning. 'It will take Garagrim several days, even travelling as lightly as he is. If he is not in time...' She looked at Axeson. 'What have your stones said?'

'Nothing of note,' Axeson said, shrugging.

Kemma's frown deepened. 'That is not good enough, priest. I have sent my husband and my son into the cauldron. The least you could do is stir it.'

Axeson made a face. 'Not an entirely apt metaphor, perhaps.'

'We are not discussing poetry,' she said. 'The future of Karak Kadrin perches on the sharp end.'

'All we can do is be patient, my lady,' Axeson said, not meeting her eyes. 'All we can do is wait.'

'And we dwarfs are good at waiting,' Kemma said, with a sigh. 'Except Slayers, obviously.' She rubbed her brow. 'Will Gurnisson be in time, do you think?'

'Gurnisson will be there,' Axeson said confidently. 'He can do nothing else.'

'It is a dangerous game you are playing, you know,' Kemma said. She looked at the mountains, as if trying to pierce distance and obstacle to see her husband. 'Dicing with fate can have nasty consequences.'

'He said something similar,' Axeson said. There was no need to elaborate on who 'he' was.

'He would know,' Kemma said. 'He is a slave to fate, that one. We all are, to some degree, but him most of all.' She glanced at Axeson. 'It is the axe, isn't it?'

'I… think so, yes,' Axeson said. He trembled slightly, recalling the grim *immensity* which had seemed to squat within that blade. The stones in the temple had resonated quietly with the blade, so quietly in fact that only Axeson had heard it. Grimnir, like all of the gods of the dawi, was simultaneously an ancestor and a god. Age had lent him great wisdom and great power for all that he had been lost in the north. Something of him yet remained, in Karak Kadrin and in every temple dedicated to him, and it was perhaps that shard that resonated with the blade.

The axe was wrapped tight in chains of destiny, and its wielder with it. The priest could see them, as clear as a vein of ore shining in the dark. Dooms clustered about Gurnisson like crows, and he brushed them aside as easily. But there was one waiting for him that he would not be able to avoid. That was what Axeson had seen, in dreams and thrown stones. And he was determined to see that destiny come to fruition. If only so that he could at last discover his own.

He had been a foundling, like all priests of Grimnir must be, with neither clan nor family to comfort him. Most children were given up to the temple by clans of low status or shameful reputation, while others, like he himself, were orphans. His parents were a mystery, his origins ignored. But he knew. Dwarfs were born delvers and secrets were no harder to dig through than rock. Axeson was not his name, but it was who he was.

'The axe brought him here, in our time of need,' Kemma said, shaking him from his reverie. Then she shook her head. 'No, that's not right, is it?'

'No,' Axeson said. 'Gurnisson didn't come for us. We are incidental.' He placed bitter emphasis on the last word. He gestured to the mountains. 'Two destinies will meet in the Peak Pass, my queen. We can only pray that Gurnisson's is stronger than that of our enemy.'

The Worlds Edge Mountains, the Peak Pass

'We'll reach where old Ranulfsson's throng met their doom in a few days at this rate,' Dorin said. The Slayer sat on a dead Chaos marauder and lit his pipe. Blood covered his face and bare chest, and his sword was planted blade first in the ground. 'If this is the best that we can expect from them, I doubt any of us will find our dooms there.' Ungrim's throng had made good time, despite stopping to slaughter any groups of Chaos marauders they happened to run across.

'Except those of us who already have,' Biter said, crossing Byarnisson's limp arms over the ruins of his staved-in chest. He sighed and stood, leaving the dead Slayer staring up sightlessly at the carrion birds already beginning to circle. They'd lost four of their number so far. Not so many, all things considered.

The Chaos marauders might have been retreating, but you wouldn't know it to judge by the number of ambushes the throng had dealt with. If anything, they seemed in good cheer for the battered remnants of a defeated army. They sang as they hurled themselves onto dwarf axes, chanting the Blood God's name in all of its bestial iterations. Biter grunted. As long as they died, did it matter whether they did so happily or not?

Koertig sat nearby, gnawing on a thumbnail, his eyes on

nothing in particular. Biter joined his Remembrancer. 'Wake up, human,' he said, snapping his fingers. Koertig shuddered and looked at him. The Nordlander was tough of body, but like many men, his spirit was flimsy when compared to that of a dwarf.

'Are we on the march again?' he asked, his voice an exhausted rasp.

'Not yet,' Biter said. 'What were you looking at?'

'I thought I saw... nothing, I wasn't looking at anything,' Koertig said, leaning back and rubbing his eyes. Biter frowned and looked around. Despite what he'd told Koertig, the throng was preparing to move again. Their numbers were not much diminished, but there would still be fewer cooking fires than there had been the night before.

The sky was growing dark, but Ungrim was champing at the bit. He'd gotten a taste of blood and wouldn't be swayed now. Biter couldn't blame him. He rubbed at his patch, trying to sooth the itch in his eye-socket. He looked up. There were skulls in the hills. They'd been seeing more and more of them the further they got from Karak Kadrin. Piles of skulls, human, dwarf and otherwise, tucked into crevices and cracks or dangling from trees, like road signs or markers for the mad. Hundreds, maybe thousands, more than he'd thought possible. The ones above him had been nailed to an outcropping of rock, in a strange pattern that made his good eye water if he looked at it too closely.

Biter looked away from the skulls, blinking. Koertig jerked to his feet suddenly. 'What was that?' he barked, swinging his axe.

'Shut up, human,' another Slayer growled, collecting a tally of ears from the dead marauders. 'It was probably just carrion birds.'

'It wasn't birds,' Koertig said. Biter looked at him. 'It sounded like drums, but underground or in the mountains,' he added.

Biter listened. Then he sank to his haunches and placed one palm on the ground. He shook his head. 'Nothing,' he said.

'Your Remembrancer is going mad, Biter,' Dorin said.

'I heard something as well,' another Slayer said and he pointed a finger at the skulls. 'It's coming from them.'

'I *know* he's mad,' Dorin said, and spat.

'No more than you or I,' Biter said. 'Something's in the air.' He looked up, past the skulls. He blinked, trying to focus. He shook his head in frustration. And then Biter heard it, just at the limits of his hearing, and he wondered why he hadn't caught it before. Regardless, he recognized it.

It was the sound of marching.

'*Bugrit*,' Biter spat. 'Dorin, Koertig, with me. Dorin, grab some of those skulls. The rest of you, stay here and stay alert.'

'What is it?' another Slayer, chains running from his ear-lobes to his nostrils, growled.

'Maybe nothing,' Biter said. Dorin and Koertig followed him as he led them across the impromptu battlefield towards Ungrim's banners. The clans were already readying themselves for the march again, wounds bound and dead wrapped in the protective shrouds that would hopefully keep the birds off of them until the army could recover them en route back to Karak Kadrin. Dwarfs called out to Biter, but he ignored them, bulling his way through the press towards where King Ironfist was meeting with his surviving thanes.

A hammerer made to step into his path and Biter's head snapped out, connecting with the front of the warrior's helm. The dwarf staggered and Biter shoved him aside unceremoniously, ignoring the pain that radiated through his own head. Ungrim turned and nodded brusquely. 'Slayer,' he said.

'Something is coming,' Biter said.

'What?'

'Something is coming,' Biter repeated. 'There's something coming this way and we need to know what it is.'

'Our scouts have reported nothing,' a thane said, leaning against the iron pole of the Ironfist clan banner that he held. The honour of carrying Ungrim's standard was a great one, and the younger thanes engaged in a variety of trials, including an impromptu shouting contest, to win the right to carry it.

'Then they're wrong, because we heard it,' Biter said, gesturing to Koertig and Dorin.

'I heard nothing,' Dorin said. Biter waved him to silence.

Ungrim grunted and combed his beard with his fingers. 'Master Redbeard,' he snapped, suddenly. A heavyset dwarf, his beard not the red his name implied, but whiter than snow, pushed forwards, through the gathered thanes.

'Step aside, step aside,' he growled, his voice deep and querulous. His face was squashed between a ridge of eyebrows and a beard like an avalanche. There were discs engraved with runes dangling from the staff he carried, and yet more scored into the staff itself. The Runesmith glared at Ungrim. 'What?'

Ungrim in his turn, looked at Biter. 'Tell Hrafn, Slayer,' he said.

Biter frowned. 'We're hearing things.' He waved Dorin forwards and the latter let the skulls tumble from his arms with unseemly haste. Hrafn grunted and peered at the skulls with distaste. Nonetheless, he sank slowly to his haunches, muttering complaints the entire way. One gnarled and scarred hand plucked up a skull and then just as quickly dropped it. The Runesmith clutched his hand to his chest as if he'd burned it. He hesitated, and then ran his hand across the lot, not quite touching any of them.

He looked at Ungrim. 'The skulls tremble like stones beneath the tread of an army,' he hissed.

'How is that possible?' a thane said in a hushed voice.

'Anything is possible with Chaos,' Ungrim said, his eyes searching out the hundreds of skulls scattered around the valley. 'The road of skulls,' he muttered. 'Just like Axeson said.' He shook himself. 'The enemy is coming. We will make our stand at the Peak Pass. Thanes, muster your clansmen! We march for the centre of the pass!'

The Worlds Edge Mountains, the Peak Pass

Ekaterina could not remember when she had first heard the Blood God's voice, only that it had torn her notions of society and her place in it from her and replaced them with something far grander. Khorne's words had flayed her like the kiss of a lash, marking her body and soul. She had known, even as the pain faded into pleasure, that she would serve him forever and a day, and kill and laugh in his name until the stars were at last snuffed by his mighty hand.

When she had first met Garmr, she had thought that he was the same. That he too heard Khorne in his soul. But he didn't. Garmr heard only his own voice, reflected back at him.

Grettir's words had spun webs in her head, no matter how much she tried to ignore them. She turned in her saddle, watching the horde sweeping through the canyon like an ocean of men and animals. They had flooded these mountains, tribes coming from far and wide to partake in the grand slaughter. Many became fuel for the beast, falling to a horde that had grown impatient with Garmr's waiting game. Others had more literally fallen to the beast. Ulfrgandr stalked the slopes above, its massive form occasionally blocking the light of the sun or the moon.

A rattle of rocks heralded an avalanche caused by the noise of their travel. Men died screaming, buried under the tumbling rocks. The army did not pause.

It should have pleased her.

It should have, but it did not. It did not please her, because she knew that it would not last.

She raised her head, spying him at the head of the march. His head hung low, swaying from side to side like that of a bull. Her fingers tapped at her sword, wondering.

'I wouldn't,' Canto said, urging his horse close to hers.

She glanced at him dismissively. 'What would you know of it?'

'What, you mean treachery and betrayal? Quite a bit, actually,' Canto said. He pressed a hand to his chest. 'I'm quite the connoisseur. Always have been, actually,' he said. 'Did you know that I was there when Severus Tar betrayed Varl the Maw at the Siege of the Hot Mud Wall? True story, it was an accident, if you can believe it. You see, what happened was–'

'Silence,' Ekaterina snapped.

Canto looked at her, his features unreadable behind the curve of his helm. 'You know as well as I do that this is not going to end well,' he said.

'I know,' she said. She frowned.

'He's using us as sacrificial hogs, woman,' Canto said, more intently. 'We're nothing more than bodies to be ground up. He'll use us up and discard us when he's gotten what he wants.'

'One would think you'd want me to slay him, then,' she said.

'What, and leave you in charge? How long would I last then, Ekaterina?' Canto said acidly.

'I'd have your skull before his body stopped thrashing,' she said.

'And there we are. Impasse,' Canto said, throwing up his hands. 'I can't let you kill him, no matter how much I'd dearly love for you to.'

'*Can't* let?' Ekaterina said, arching an eyebrow. 'Can you stop me, then?'

Canto looked at her steadily. 'Who can say? I'd give it a try, I'll say that,' he said softly.

Ekaterina met his gaze, considering. She had always thought of Canto as a jester, a trained ape who capered and quipped for Garmr's amusement. But there was something... She took in the scars on his armour and the look in his eyes, and wondered whether his distaste for combat was not the sign of a coward, but rather the ennui of a gourmand. The thought of becoming glutted on bloodshed was a horrifying one, and for a moment, just a moment, she felt a stab of pity.

'What are you proposing?' she said, finally.

'Not here,' Canto said, pulling on his mount's reins. 'Follow me.'

Ekaterina hesitated long enough to issue orders to Boris and then followed, letting her mount weave through the order of battle. Men growled and cursed, but her red gaze made them fall silent quickly enough. Canto led her back towards the trundling altars and shrines. The smell of beasts and horses and human slaves washed over her, mingled with the dust thrown up by their passage. She and Canto fell into a trot beside the great altar that Grettir was chained to. The sorcerer looked at them with what Ekaterina would have sworn was amusement.

'Ah, two prodigals, come to speak of seed-pods and disagreements, eh?' the sorcerer said, his voice carrying easily over the thunder of the march. 'Whatever would your master say?'

'Silence, cur,' Ekaterina snapped.

'Yes, silence, cur; or rather, talk,' Canto said.

Grettir cocked his head. 'Ah,' he said. 'I wondered if it would be you, Canto. Your skeins are like a spider's web, going in all directions. So much possibility, it's almost intoxicating.'

'I'll take that as a compliment,' Canto said.

'And you,' Grettir said, looking at her. 'Is a daughter of the Blood God willing to betray her chosen lord?'

'He betrays the Blood God,' she said stiffly.

'Does he?' Grettir said. 'Are you certain that you do not wish to believe it is so, in order to make your treachery less stinging?'

Ekaterina hesitated, cursing herself. She did not hesitate. To hesitate was to fail to fail was to die and to die was to lose Khorne's favour. She had fought far too long and too hard to do so now. As she opened her mouth to reply, she caught sight of something crouching atop the altar. Eyes like red-hot coals met hers from within a face that was at once feminine and daemonic. She felt her heart stutter in her chest. The great spear stretched towards her, as if to tap her shoulder, and she wondered whether the blade would turn and separate her head from her shoulders.

If so, it was as it would be. *Take my skull if I have stepped from the Path*, she thought grimly, meeting the apparition's gaze. *I have ever served Khorne, and I will serve him always, even unto death.* The apparition nodded, as if satisfied. Leathery wings snapped silently, and the shape hurtled upwards, vanishing in the light of the sun.

Ekaterina met Grettir's gaze and said, 'I am certain.'

Grettir turned and gazed upwards. Ekaterina wondered

whether he could see her as well, and then discarded the notion. Of course he couldn't. Only those blessed by Khorne could see his Handmaiden. Grettir looked back at her and chuckled. 'Fine, fine, if you're *certain*.'

The sorcerer leaned back. 'He knows, by the way, if that makes a difference.'

'No,' Ekaterina said, even as Canto said, 'Yes.'

Grettir chuckled again and hunched forwards, his chains rattling. 'Garmr has planned this for centuries, before either of you were born. The road is for Khorne. It is his road to war. Eternal war, battle unending, and Garmr has spent blood and souls to see it through to completion.'

Ekaterina sucked in a breath. Grettir waved his hands. 'A thousand years ago, these mountains were soaked in the blood of daemons, blood spilled by dwarf hands and dwarf axes. Now Garmr consecrates them to Khorne by spilling the blood of men and–'

'Dwarfs,' Canto said. 'This was never about Karak Kadrin, was it?'

'What matters a fortress to one who has all of eternity to wage war?' Grettir said, shrugging. 'Garmr wants war eternal, to glut himself forever on slaughter. He's a simple soul, really.'

Ekaterina shook her head, ignoring Grettir's mockery. It was what they all aspired to, in their own way. An eternity of slaughter beneath the stars was a beautiful thing to contemplate, but only if she survived to enjoy it. Her fingers tightened on her sword-hilt.

'The one-eyed dwarf,' Canto said. Ekaterina looked sharply at him. 'I met him. Why does Garmr want him?'

Grettir spread his palms. 'Better still say, why does Khorne want him?'

* * *

The Worlds Edge Mountains,
near the Peak Pass

Felix hit the trees a few moments after he lost his grip on the gyrocopter. Branches cracked and burst beneath his weight. Karaghul went spinning from his grip and he was blind. Felix's arms acted of their own volition, grabbing for any support they could find. His breath wheezed out of his lungs as his fingers lost their hold and he was falling again. Branches connected with his rear and legs and then he was spinning, grabbing, halting and falling again. He hit a branch and held on.

They weren't very high up, for which he was thankful. Burdened as it had been by their weight, the gyrocopter had only been skimming the tree-line. He could see the ground. The branch he clung to gave a crack and he fell again. His fingers throbbed as he grabbed another branch and swung awkwardly, feet dangling. 'Sigmar, please–' he groaned.

Sigmar apparently had a sense of humour. Bark came away in his hands and he fell again, cursing all the while. This time, when he hit, it was the ground, and he fell amidst broken branches, all of the air whooping out of his lungs and all of his limbs going numb at once. He lay for a moment, vision whirling nauseatingly. Then something bright fell towards him and he cursed, rolling aside as Karaghul sank into the ground, point first, at the exact spot where his head had been only moments earlier.

Puffing, lying on his belly, Felix contemplated the sword where it quivered. Every limb felt like a lead weight and his chest hurt. He pushed himself up with a wheeze and grabbed Karaghul, jerking it out of the hard-packed soil. Then, he looked up.

A moment later, he was diving aside for a second time as the remains of the gyrocopter crashed through the branches and slammed into the ground. Felix scrambled for cover as the shattered rotor tore loose and pin-wheeled towards him, the hard wood and steel frame embedding itself in the trunk of the tree he had darted behind.

'We should have stayed in Karak Kadrin,' he grunted, stepping out from behind the tree.

The griffon crashed down atop the ruined gyrocopter, further flattening it and sending more broken pieces flying towards Felix. Felix swatted aside a chunk of the rotor mechanism and froze as the griffon rolled onto its feet with an ear-splitting screech. The beast looked the worse for wear, its wings shattered and dragging, its body and head bloody. Nonetheless, as it caught sight of him, it tore itself free of the wreckage and limped towards him, hissing.

'Fine then,' Felix said. 'Fine! Come on!' He was tired and aching and his mind was fogged with exhaustion and stress and he wanted nothing more than to hack the creature down and rest, just for a moment. He extended his sword and trembled, adrenaline pumping. 'Come on, you cursed beast. Let's finish this, shall we?'

The griffon squalled and galumphed forwards, claws digging trenches in the ground. Felix jerked aside as its beak snapped at him. Its feathered chest thumped against him with bone-jarring force, nearly taking him from his feet. He used the momentum to fall backwards and swing his sword. It crashed against the creature's neck, cutting deeply into its flesh. Talons caught him on the shoulder and then he was skidding through the dirt. He slammed against a tree, hard, and black lights burst before his eyes. The griffon staggered, head dipping, blood spurting from the wound in its neck. Why wasn't it dead? What was it going to take? It gurgled and stumbled towards him, eyes glazing even as its beak snapped blindly.

Something hissed. The griffon jerked and screamed in agony. Its back legs slid out from under it and it fell, only inches from Felix. He looked up and saw Gotrek, bloody, but unbowed, crouching on the broken gyrocopter, the steam-gun in his hands. The Slayer had apparently wrenched the weapon from its housing and he hefted it in two hands. He grinned and fired again, sending a whistling stream of steam-powered steel spheres punching into the writhing griffon.

The creature slumped with one final whimper. Gotrek hopped off the wreckage, tossing the steam-gun aside. He picked up his axe where it lay and strode towards the griffon. 'Gotrek,' Felix began.

Gotrek ignored him. He lifted his axe and brought down a bone-shattering two-handed blow on the griffon's neck, severing its head. Its feline legs kicked once and then flopped down, still. Gotrek picked up the avian head and hurled it away. 'Well, that was fun, eh, manling?' he said, looking at Felix.

'Not in the least,' Felix gasped as Gotrek grabbed his arm and hauled him to his feet. 'It... Why did it attack us? Why wouldn't it die?'

'Beasts like this need little reason to attack. We might have entered its territory, or maybe...' Gotrek extended his axe and used the curve to hook the collar that had been around the beast's neck. He pulled it up, looking at the skulls that clung to it. Felix's skin crawled at the sight of them. Something, a weak red light, seemed to issue from the eye-sockets of one of the skulls. Gotrek threw the skulls aside with an oath. They hit a tree and shattered.

'Daemon-work,' Gotrek spat.

Felix looked at the griffon in horror. 'The beast must have been in torment.'

'Aye, and now it's ended,' Gotrek said.

'Gotrek, you're bleeding,' Felix said, gesturing to the wounds that criss-crossed Gotrek's arms and chest. The Slayer grunted and dipped a finger in one of the larger cuts. He sucked on the finger and spat.

'So are you, manling,' he said, pointing at Felix with the wet finger. Felix looked down at himself, at the tears in his shirt and trousers and the bruises and cuts beneath. Suddenly he felt very tired. Nothing would please him more than settling down to sleep for a week. Sleep seemed to be the furthest thing from Gotrek's mind. 'And what of it?' he said. 'I still live.'

And I'd like to continue living, thank you, Felix thought, but said, 'Where are we, do you think?'

'Not where we need to be,' Gotrek said curtly. He licked a finger and held it up. Then he pointed. 'That way,' he growled.

'How can you–' Felix began. Then he heard them – horns, in the distance, though whether they belonged to dwarfs or men, he couldn't say. 'Oh,' he finished, lamely.

Gotrek stumped towards the shattered gyrocopter and began to rummage through it. A moment later he tossed a small pack to Felix. 'Here,' he said. 'There'll be supplies in there, dwarf bread and dried meat. Always good to have supplies, just in case you crash somewhere inhospitable.'

Felix shuddered at the mention of dwarf bread. It tasted like rock and had a similar texture. The meat was likely more edible. Gotrek stepped away from the gyrocopter with two water-skins slung over his shoulder. 'If I were Ungrim, I'd be aiming to catch them in the Peak Pass,' he said. 'Best place for a battle, and the rangers know the secret ways that'll circle around the enemy to cut them off.'

'But they're not only pursuing an enemy, Gotrek, they're marching to meet one. One that is ready for them, remember?' Felix said, hurrying after the Slayer, despite the ache in his legs. 'What happens if the enemy is already in the pass?'

Gotrek didn't slow. 'Then we'll avenge Ungrim and the rest as best we can, before I meet my doom,' he said.

17

The Worlds Edge Mountains,
above the Peak Pass

'They're dead,' Lunn said hoarsely, stepping out of the darkened outpost and sucking in a great breath of cleansing air.

'How long?' his brother, Steki, asked quietly.

'Weeks,' Lunn said, hawking and spitting, trying to clean his mouth of the taste of decay. The two Svengeln brothers were almost twins, despite the difference in their heights. The rangers they led were among the best, hardened veterans of high peak skirmishes against orcs and worse. Now they crouched in a rough semi-circle: fifteen stone-faced clansmen, armed with crossbows and short-hafted axes and shields, looking at the crude spikes planted in the ground around the outpost, each one decorated with a halo of weather-ravaged heads bound to the spikes by their beards.

'Something has been at the bodies,' Lunn continued, wiping his mouth.

'Must have hit them not long after Ranulfsson's throng was

wiped out,' another ranger said. 'That'd explain why we got no word, why no signal fires were lit.'

'Have to be thousands of the buggers swarming these hills,' another said. This was the third outpost they'd found in such condition. Those closer to Karak Kadrin had been abandoned as per the sentries' standing orders when the enemy drew too close, but only a third of the assigned sentries had returned to Karak Kadrin by the high paths. Of the others, there had been no sign, until now.

It didn't bode well. 'Ungrim could be walking into a trap,' Steki said, looking at his brother. Lunn clapped him on the arm.

'That's why we're here, brother. Let's see if we can't spring it before Ungrim gets there, eh?'

The rangers readied themselves to move out. They moved silently and steadily through the hills and gullies that spread outwards from the Peak Pass. They were all old hands at fighting the wild men who poured down out of the north every so often. The mountains were like a valve for the eastern wastes. If they didn't pour straight down into the lands of men through Troll Country, they rode down into the mountains, looking to use the crags as a ready-made fortress for campaigns into the Empire and Kislev. When they did that, it fell to the rangers of Karak Kadrin to harry them back north. Steki and Lunn had spent many a spring season doing just that, hunting battle-hungry Kul and Dolgans.

But this was different. This wasn't some petty war-chief or god-bothered shaman leading a few hundred warriors. This was something larger and more unpleasant. Even the mountains seemed different with the advent of the horde. Every shadowed crevice seemed to hold wolf-fanged ghosts and every peak shuddered with the drumbeat of unseen marchers.

Twice the rangers were forced to defend themselves against

mutant beasts, driven into the hills by the advancing horde. Big and porcine, with great maws and gouging talons and tusks, the gorebeasts flung themselves at the dwarfs, heedless of the crossbow bolts pricking their malformed skulls.

As they drew closer to the high hills around the Peak Pass, even the very air seemed tainted with the omnipresent stench of blood and rot. More skulls littered the area, placed in culverts and tree branches like macabre decorations. 'They must be killing each other on a regular basis to get this many of the blasted things,' Lunn growled.

Steki spat. 'They're no better than wild dogs, brother, you know that. If they can't find real enemies, they fall on one another.'

A slow, warm wind rippled around them, setting the ghastly bouquet of bones clattering amongst the branches of the scrub trees that clung tenaciously to the crags. Every ranger was alert as Lunn signalled for silence. On a large rock was etched the rune indicating that a blind was close by, created by some other group of rangers during some other conflict. It would allow them to survey the pass without revealing themselves.

'What do we do if they've already reached the pass, brother?' Steki said softly as they crept through the rocks.

'We warn Ungrim and hope that he'll listen,' Lunn said. 'They'll attack, sure enough, but they'll overwhelm us through sheer numbers unless we can – hsst!' The ranger stopped. The others froze, crossbows aimed and ready.

There was a sound, hot and heavy like a great bellows, squeezing air in and out. The stink hit them next, like a bear's den in the summer, with something else just below it, something sharper and alien. It wasn't a natural smell.

Claws scraped on rock. Something growled and the sound of it echoed through the bones of every dwarf, shaking them down to the soles of their boots. And then a shadow was blotting out the sun and a heavy body was landing amidst them. Claws curled out and a ranger went spinning through the air, wrapped in a shroud of blood. It moved so fast that the dwarfs could barely see what it was; scarcely so much as where it was. Crossbows twanged and the thing roared, more in anger than in pain. Lunn's crossbow was ripped from his hands and destroyed and as he reached for his axe, he brought his shield up. Fangs sank into the metal and pierced the arm beneath, eliciting a bellow of agony from the ranger. The massive head jerked and Lunn's feet left the stone as he was whipped up and over, shaken like a rat caught by a terrier. The straps on his shield broke and he went flying.

Steki roared a challenge and slammed his shield into the monster's skull. His axe swept down but became tangled with the hilt of a dagger – one of a dozen jammed into the creature's back. The creature spun, jerking him from his feet. As he flew upwards, its talons punched through his chest and out his back. Steki died, choking on his own blood. Heedless, the beast used his body as a bludgeon, crushing rangers and battering them to the ground.

Lunn, lying nearby, could only watch as his brother was reduced to a red mess. The force of his fall had broken something inside him, and his legs refused to work. So he lay, shouting curses as the creature finished off the last ranger, its grotesque jaws fastening themselves on the dwarf's head and removing it in one bite. The creature turned towards them, its eyes meeting Lunn's.

'Come on then,' he groaned, trying to lift his axe. 'Come on,' he said, more loudly.

And then it did.

* * *

The Worlds Edge Mountains,
the Peak Pass

Garmr shuddered in his saddle as the sensations of the dwarf's death ran through him. The horde was approaching the point in the twining corridors of the pass where they'd left the slain corpses of the first dwarf throng, from so many days past. He heard Ulfrgandr's howl a moment later. The beast's fury was only increased by its brief taste of combat. It wanted more and Garmr gave a sigh. 'Soon,' he murmured.

The creature ignored him, its roars increasing in fury. He closed his eyes, watching in his mind's eye as it vented its fury on the bodies, tearing at them. Then it loped into the crags, following their trail. The beast would fall on the dwarf army from the rear, savaging them even as his army did the same.

Shivering in pleasure, he snapped his fingers at a nearby chieftain of a band of marauder horsemen. 'Take your men. Follow mighty Ulfrgandr's trail above. When it strikes, so too will you.'

The chieftain blanched. No one wanted to get too close to the Slaughter-Hound, especially when it was in a killing frenzy. Garmr's hand shot out, grabbing the man by the throat. With a jerk of his wrist, he snapped the chieftain's neck. Dropping the body, he looked at one of the others. 'He was your chief?' Garmr said.

The man nodded jerkily.

'You are chief now,' Garmr said. 'Take your men. Follow the trail. Strike when it strikes.'

The newly made chief obeyed instantly, jerking wildly at his horse's reins and galloping off, followed by his companions. Garmr watched them go. The centre of the Peak Pass stood before them, a wide canyon, filled with the dead. It was the doorway to the lands beyond the Wastes, fittingly enough. And it was here that he would fulfil Khorne's wishes.

'Here, and no further,' he murmured. He could feel destiny pressing close about him, enfolding him in its wings. He made a fist and looked forwards. At his command, warriors marched up, carrying stakes and skulls. The pass would be made ready for Khorne's coming. It would stand forever blighted and stained with the blood of his sacrifices as a monument to the might of the Skull Throne. He would write his name in the very life-stuff of these mountains, farther south than any champion before him, save those who had marched forth in those first terrible, wonderful years when the gods had run riot across this fallen world. The name of the Gorewolf would echo through these rocks forever, reminding the paltry mortals of this world that he had walked and slain among them.

He lifted his axe and gazed at the runes carved into its blade. It had served him well, these thousand years. He had taken it from some chieftain or other, wresting it from his slackening grip on a battlefield of black poppies and wailing insects. It was another of Khorne's gifts to him. It hungered, even as he himself did. It lusted for blood and Khorne's mark was on it. It had been forged at the foot of the Blood God's throne, and ruinous magics had been woven into its creation. It was a thing of death, of perfect doom, and the skulls it took were dedicated to the Skull Throne. Once the Road of Skulls was complete, it would take a bounty undreamed of by the chieftain he had wrested it from.

He looked up. There were clouds in the sky. Great, angry-looking masses of bruise-coloured darkness. The rain would begin soon, as the world wept at the birth of the Road of Skulls. So Grettir had foretold. Garmr sighed. He would miss his cousin, he thought. Not enough to spare him, but he would miss him nonetheless. Like an old pain, suddenly gone. Grettir would be the first to die, when the road had been completed, and his blood would be used to baptise it. It was the least he could do for the man who had once been as close to him as a brother.

The Doom-Seeker was coming. All was right with the world. When he had first seen the one-eyed Slayer in the visions Khorne had gifted him with, he had wondered at how he might find one single dwarf in the wide world. Then, he had been led to Karak Kadrin. It had been centuries earlier, when he had served another in an earlier war, that he had first seen the Slayers of Karak Kadrin and come to know of their purpose. Where else would the dwarf he had seen in his visions have come from, save the City of Slayers?

It had all led to this moment. All of his striving, every skull taken, every rival slain, had all led to this moment, when he would match axes with his one-eyed prey. He had baited the trap with bloody meat and pulled the creature from its den, like a patient hunter. Now all that remained was to close the jaws of the trap.

'What are your commands, my lord?' Ekaterina asked, at his elbow. Garmr turned.

'Ready your marauder horsemen. You will be the point of the spear,' he said. She smiled, pleased. He had known she would be. Despite her mutinous intentions, she could not resist the call of battle. Like Grettir, he would miss her, when he collected her skull at the last. Perhaps he would carry it with him into the eternity of war to come. She would like that, he thought. 'Canto, you will see to the dregs. We will strike and you will follow,' he said, looking at the black-armoured warrior. 'Guard the hellcannon and its master. I would not lose that engine as you lost the others.'

Canto he would not miss. Despite the amusement he garnered from the warrior, Canto had ever been a living warning to Garmr. Frozen, like a bug in amber, Canto was a testament to the risks every man took when he sought the gods' favours. He was not a true devotee of Khorne, resisting the gods' call, no matter how loud. And like all false followers, he was forever trapped between life and death. But not for long, Garmr mused.

'It will be my honour,' Canto said smoothly, not even flinching at the mention of his failure. 'Shall I see to Grettir?'

'Yes. When the battle is done, bring him forth. I will require him,' Garmr said, not looking at him. He turned, casting his gaze over his horde. A thousand banners stabbed towards the sky, marking a thousand Chaos marauder chieftains, a thousand slaves of darkness. He raised his axe, and a roar swelled from the throats of the horde, shaking the walls of the Peak Pass.

'Remember, the one-eyed dwarf is mine,' he said to Canto and Ekaterina as he basked in the adulation.

All was right with the world. Today would be a good day.

The Worlds Edge Mountains, the Peak Pass

'No sign of them?' Ungrim said. Thungrimsson shook his head and Ungrim cursed. He tugged on his beard angrily. The rangers had not reported back yet. That in and of itself would not normally be worrying; rangers were independent sorts and not as respectful of the chain of command as many might otherwise wish.

But here, and now, it was worrisome. It meant something had happened. He looked ahead, where the centre of the Peak Pass waited like the jaws of some vast predator, eager to consume his throng as it had Ranulfsson's not so long ago. Thungrimsson coughed into his fist, catching Ungrim's attention. 'If we go in now, we will be marching in blind,' he said.

'If we don't, we could lose any advantage we yet retain,' Ungrim countered. Behind him and around him, the Grand Throng was arrayed for battle. The clans marched as they fought, and there would be no need to reorganize once they had reached the place of battle. Thunderers and quarrellers marched on the flanks, their front ranks occupied by clansmen carrying the sturdy camp pavises, which would be set down in irregular lines, allowing for the retreat of the front ranks as they fired. The pavises would be lifted as they retreated, protecting them until they reached the rear of the formation, where they would begin to reload.

The centre was held by Ungrim's own clansmen and those of his closest kin. With shield and axe, they would meet any charge and throw it back. At the back of their formations were the few grudge throwers which had been brought. Less than Ungrim would have liked, but he had thought speed more important than firepower. The catapults could fire over the heads of the throng, which was more than organ guns or flame cannons could do.

Ungrim glanced at Thungrimsson, who was frowning. 'What is it, old friend?'

'I wish we had more war-engines. A cannon or six,' Thungrimsson said, scratching his nose.

'We will make do without them,' Ungrim said. 'The Slayers will meet the enemy first, as is proper.' He looked at Biter, who nodded and grinned.

'And we're all about proper, us,' he said.

'Go, gather your companions,' Ungrim said. 'We will enter the pass and drive the invader back north, with their

349

tails between their legs.' He raised his axe, and signal-horns sounded, passing his wordless command to each warrior in the throng. Dust rose as the dwarfs began to march.

Thungrimsson, his hammer over his shoulder, squinted up at the sky. Ungrim followed his gaze. The clouds looked ready to burst. It was the rainy season, and it wasn't unusual for the lower reaches of the mountains to flood when melting snow and pouring rain caused flash floods that swept down into the lower valleys. More than one dwarf had been lost to a sudden surge of water cascading through the rocky gorges of the Worlds Edge Mountains. The centre of Peak Pass was high enough that it was unlikely such would happen here, however.

Rain wasn't the only thing that could fall from the sky, however. Ungrim raised his axe again, and another volley of signal-horns sounded as those formations closest to the cliffs and slopes of the pass raised their shields and pavises up over their heads. It wasn't so much arrows that he feared as rocks. The mountains were a volatile beast, and showed their displeasure with those who dared to march through them in many ways. Ungrim had been trapped in more than one avalanche in his time, and didn't intend to repeat the experience.

He saw the first of the stakes as they came around a bend in the pass, and fury bloomed in him. Around him, clansmen muttered and growled, as well they should have. Ranulfsson's throng, many days dead, had not been left to rot. It would have been preferable if they had been. Instead, each and every dwarf of that ill-fated throng had been impaled upon a spike of wood which had then been planted in the hard soil. A forest of the dead spread out before Ungrim, and an ocean of dwarf blood had long since dried on the ground. He spat an oath and gripped his axe so tightly that the haft creaked in protest.

He saw faces he recognized, here and there. Young thanes

who had petitioned him for leave to march forth, looking to add lustre to their clan's record of deeds, now hung stiff and silent, food for birds. Beards had been hacked from jowls and tied in crude melanges that hung like matted curtains, moving in a warm breeze. Skulls clattered softly, moved by the same breeze where they hung from high plinths and posts that had been hammered into the steep slopes.

The sheer dishonour of it struck him dumb for a moment. Everything stank of death, and dwarfs made cautious gestures, ancient superstitions reigniting as the throng moved into the wasteland. Several clans began to break ranks, the sounds of their dirges rising even as they sought to bring down the posts that held the bodies of their relatives. Ungrim growled in frustration and signalled again. Short, terse blasts from the signal-horns refused those clans leave to recover their dead. Voices were raised in protest and he stifled those closest to him with a savage glare. 'Now is not the time,' he barked, knowing his voice would carry. 'We will tend to the dead once our living enemies have been seen to!' He gestured with his axe. 'We hold here!' he roared out.

'I don't like having to look at that disgrace,' Thungrimsson said, jerking his chin towards the stakes and their ghastly burdens.

'It will hinder them more than us,' Ungrim said harshly. 'Let them ride through deadly ground of their own making. We will hold here, and drown them in shot and steel beneath the gazes of our dishonoured dead.'

The Worlds Edge Mountains, *above the Peak Pass*

'Hurry, manling,' Gotrek said impatiently. He clambered up the steep slope, axe in hand, Felix just behind him. 'I can hear the horns of Karak Kadrin.'

Felix could as well, but there was no reason to waste breath replying when Gotrek wasn't listening. He staggered, exhausted and aching, but forced himself to go on. They had been moving for what felt like hours without stopping, and Felix knew he was fast approaching the outer limits of his vitality. In his time with the Slayer, he had become used to pushing his body farther and further than he had at first thought possible, but he was still only human.

He didn't ask Gotrek to stop for a rest, however. The Slayer wasn't in the mood to wait for Felix and had left him behind more than once since they'd left the crash site. They were on the ridges above the Peak Pass, where outcrops of rock warred with patches of scrub trees for space on the dangerous ledges. He stumbled and fell, his foot catching on something. He went face-down, scraping his palms and chin.

He twisted, looking into the mangled features of a dead dwarf. 'Gotrek,' he called out. Felix turned. There were more dwarfs. By the look of them, their deaths had been quick, but not painless.

Felix scrambled to his feet and stepped over another body, drawing Karaghul. There was an animal smell in the air, clinging to the corpses and the rocks.

He saw Gotrek crouched near a body, his axe across his knees. The Slayer glanced at him. 'Lunn Svengeln,' Gotrek said. Felix bit back a curse. He remembered the name of one of the rangers who had accompanied them on their sortie before the walls of Karak Kadrin, though how Gotrek could tell it was him given the condition of the body, Felix couldn't say.

'What... what did that to him?' Felix said.

'I don't know,' Gotrek grunted, staring at the body. 'No

beast I know of makes marks like these.'

Felix looked around. Something moved through the rocks, catching his eye. 'Gotrek,' he said.

'I know, manling,' Gotrek said, rising from his crouch, his eye still on Lunn's corpse. 'I heard them earlier.' He turned and extended his axe. 'Come out, jackals. My axe thirsts for your blood.'

The Chaos marauders burst from concealment in a rush. A hairy warrior swung a double-bitted axe at Felix, forcing him to suck in his stomach and leap back. Gotrek cut the legs out from under two of the others, dropping them screaming to the ground.

Felix booted his opponent in the belly, bending him double. Karaghul opened his neck to the bone and then Felix was lunging past him, driving his sword into another marauder's stomach. Ripping the weapon free, he turned, catching a crude sword on his crosspiece and jerking it from its wielder's hands. He brought the sharp end of his elbow around, catching the weaponless marauder in the face. Bone crunched and Felix swept his sword out, spilling the man's guts. Panting, he looked for Gotrek and saw him driving a marauder skull-first into a rock even as he swung his axe out in a vicious arc, driving two others back.

Hooves pounded and Felix turned as a number of marauder horsemen burst up onto the crag, whipping their horses savagely. One swung a club at Felix as he galloped past, catching him a glancing blow on the head. Felix fell, his vision spinning. Through bleary eyes he watched as Gotrek shoved his axe at a horse, forcing it to rear up.

And then he saw nothing more.

* * *

The Worlds Edge Mountains, the Peak Pass

'Come on, lads,' Biter shouted. 'Do you want to live forever?'

'Quiet,' Dorin snapped. 'Don't jinx us!' Several other Slayers shouted agreement.

Biter grinned and started forwards, the other Slayers fanning out around him.

'How am I supposed to remember your deeds if I die here, is all I'm saying,' Koertig said. The Nordlander was just behind Biter with his shield held up and his axe held low. His eyes darted around nervously. 'I can see well enough from back with the catapults.'

'And what fun would that be?' Biter said. 'No, you'll thank me for this, human, you'll see.'

'Not likely,' Koertig grunted.

The Slayers ranged out far ahead of the dwarf lines, heading out to meet the foe, rather than wait for the enemy to attack. It was their right, and they had been champing at the bit since they'd come in sight of the Peak Pass. And since he was in charge, it was his right to lead them in.

Gurnisson was probably gnawing his own liver in frustration right about now. Biter smiled, thinking of the other Slayer. He admired Gurnisson, he truly did, but the Jinx-Slayer was a chore to be around, especially if you had death on your mind. There was too much destiny weighing down that one's shadow.

Biter had his own destiny, thank you very much, and he didn't need someone else's bigger, louder destiny overshadowing his. Not that he particularly wanted to die, but why test fate? Who wanted to wind up like that poor bastard Snorri Nosebiter? Gurnisson's luck had rubbed off on him, right enough. Or like that boastful drunkard Drong, who'd taken to the sea out of desperation in the days following his encounter with Gurnisson?

No, better that Gurnisson stayed where he was, safely out of the way. Biter was sympathetic, but not enough to want Gurnisson around for something like this.

The Slayers moved through the forest of stakes, heedless of the dangling bodies. The Slayers were on the hunt, and not even dead kin could shake them from it. A low mist, humid and clammy, rose from the rocks and coiled about their legs as they moved. It crawled across Biter's skin, trailing damp lines through his tattoos. Above, the clouds continued to swell and grumble.

And then something growled.

Biter looked around. The Chaos hound growled again, as it slunk from behind the post. Rags of flesh hung from its furry body and slobber dripped from its jaws. It leapt. Biter caught it in the head with his axe, caving in its skull even as he was knocked flat by its weight. Howls erupted from deeper within the forest of stakes and the monstrous forms of mutated trolls, accompanied by more Chaos hounds and marauder horsemen, exploded into view.

The woman on the lead horse was clad in half-armour and gory locks. Her sabre snicker-snacked out, taking the top of a Slayer's head off as she galloped past, before she yanked on her reins and turned her mount. She shrilled out a hawk-like scream and rode down another dwarf. Biter grinned and shoved the dead Chaos hound off. 'I like her, she's a fierce one.'

'I think she heard you,' Koertig said, driving his axe down between the shoulder-blades of a hound as its claws scratched across his shield. The woman bore down on them, a vulpine grin on her face. Biter threw himself aside as her horse reared up over them.

'No! She's mine!' Dorin screamed, his axe taking the animal's legs out from under it. It fell with a hideous scream and the woman rolled from the saddle with inhuman smoothness. She looked first at the dying animal and then at the young Slayer. A cruel smile spread across her face. Her too-wide mouth split, revealing a throat full of fangs.

Dorin faced her across the dead horse, his face strained and wild. Biter grabbed Koertig's arm. 'Leave him, human. Plenty of other foes for us,' he said. 'He's called dibs.'

The woman glanced at him lazily. Her eyes narrowed as she took in Biter's axe and his maimed face. 'You,' she said. Around them, Slayers, riders and beasts fought and died in a savage prologue to the battle to come. Horns blew and drums thumped, twin waves of sound crashing together in the centre of the pass.

'Me,' Biter said.

She turned from Dorin and gestured to Biter with her sabre. 'Garmr wants you, one-eye,' she said.

'Tell him he can't have me. Who's Garmr?' Biter said.

'A dead man, just like you,' the woman said, flinging herself towards him. Her sabre cut for his head and Biter caught the blade on his axe and shoved it aside. He punched her in the belly and she stumbled back. The ground was shaking beneath his feet and he glanced aside.

The Chaos horde was on the march, or at the charge, rather. Horsemen, Chaos knights and chariots thundered forwards in a wave of death, smashing aside the stakes like a deluge of foul water. The woman began to laugh and came for him again, her eyes wide and mad and red.

Dorin cursed and hurled himself at her, tackling her to the

ground with a wild cry even as the first rank of horsemen smashed into the struggling knots of dwarfs and marauders that occupied the centre of the pass. Biter laughed as hooves cracked against his shoulders and head and he lashed out blindly, wondering if being crushed by horseflesh was considered a worthy death.

The ground shivered beneath Ungrim's feet as the enemy made their charge. Horsemen and worse things galloped into the forest of the dead, brushing aside stakes and bodies in their mad haste to reach the throng of Karak Kadrin. The Slayer King took a breath and swept back the edges of his dragon-skin cloak.

'This is it,' he murmured. 'This is the day.'

'Let's hope not,' Thungrimsson said, his eyes hard.

Ungrim glanced at his hearth-warden and grinned. 'You will look after the boy, won't you? And my queen,' he said.

'More like she'll look after me,' Thungrimsson said. 'Besides, it's quite likely that the both of us will fall here today, my king.'

'There are quite a few of them, yes,' Ungrim said mildly. He ran his thumb across the edge of his axe and admired the bead of blood that rolled down.

'He'll make a fine king,' Thungrimsson said.

'Yes,' Ungrim said. And then there was no more time for talk. Cries of alarm rippled up and down the line. Ungrim looked and saw what might have merely been a stirring of the mist that clung to the ground. It rose up, disgorging shapes that billowed and steamed like the grotesque faces he'd fancied seeing in the forge fires as a boy. Only these weren't the childish imaginings of a beardling but nightmares made flesh coalescing before him.

The vanguard of the enemy was, to a man, clad in heavy armour, daubed in blood. They were giants, even among the Chaos marauders, who were larger than the men of the south. These were the hardened veterans of the Chaos Wastes, men who'd fought in a thousand battles across fields that burned with witch-fire and worse. No two sets of armour were the same, and each was a work of darkly intricate artifice. The axes and swords they wielded were gruesome tools, forged only to shed blood in Khorne's name. The Chaos warriors charged with a blood-curdling roar, packed with all the venom and hatred that such men could muster. Dwarfs muttered into their beards and more than one clansman shifted backwards unconsciously.

'Hold your positions!' Ungrim roared out. He turned his glare on the warriors to either side of him. 'Hold fast, clansmen of Karak Kadrin. Hold hard and lift your axes. Let them see only death here, not fear or cowardice. There is only death for the enemies of Karak Kadrin, not victory, never victory!'

As the dwarfs raised their weapons with a ragged cheer, Ungrim began to sing, letting the deep, dark words of the death-dirge of Karak Kadrin slip from between his lips. The sound met and fought with the noise emanating from the horde. Like the crashing together of rival seas, the sounds met and mingled, shaking the sides of the valley, sending sheets of rock sliding down to patter and bounce off hastily upraised shields.

The first Chaos warrior reached them a moment later, bellowing curses or prayers or both, a flail made from chains and bronzed skulls whirling in his grip. Ungrim caught the flail on his axe and yanked it from its owner's grasp. One scarred fist shot out, denting the Chaos warrior's fearsome helm. The hammers of Thungrimsson's men lashed out, killing the warrior before he could recover from Ungrim's blow. 'Death,' Ungrim roared out, 'Death to the dealers of death! Death to the forsworn! Death to the daemon-lovers! Sons of Grimnir... give them death!'

The thunderers began to fire, and smoke filled the air. Shields were lifted as the ranks changed positions, and crossbows twanged as the quarrellers covered the thunderers' reorganization. The dwarfs of Karak Kadrin had long ago learned the art of making themselves into the perfect engine of death. Every clansman was a cog in that machinery, and bullets and bolts swept the Chaos line, shattering the front ranks and breaking the charge.

Or, they would have, had the enemy been normal men. Instead, the savages charged on, through shot and smoke, trampling their dead and dying. Banners rattled and flashed as they were passed from hand to hand and the line of clansmen stepped forwards, setting their shoulders and shields. Horsemen crashed into that stolid line a moment later. Hooves lashed out, glancing from shields and helmets, crushing dwarfs; horses were falling and screaming as axes cut men and beasts down. It was wet, crimson work and the dwarfs excelled at it, but the Chaos warriors and the marauders who followed them would not retreat. They pressed ever forwards, and dwarfs fell, dragged down by numbers and mindless ferocity.

Great stones were lobbed into the sky from the dwarf grudge throwers to crash down, flattening men by the dozens. A massive grudge-stone hit the ground on its side and it bounced and rolled through the ranks of the Chaos marauders, crushing and smashing all in its path. Still they came on, shouting the praises of the Blood God.

Ungrim swept his axe out, bisecting a bare-chested warrior. Even as the man's legs fell, his front half crawled forwards, choking and snarling. The Slayer King stamped on his skull and drove the haft of his axe into another's face, denting the bestial helm and crushing the skull beneath. He roared out an oath and caught another Chaos marauder in the back as the latter darted past him.

Beside him, Thungrimsson fought in grim silence, his hammer punching out and up and down like a piston. Around them, the hammerers lived up to their name, creating a bulwark of carnage around their king and commander.

Ungrim cleft a skull in twain and took a leg off at the thigh, growling out a laugh. He longed to move forwards, to push his way into the enemy lines, to leave his guardians behind. He wanted to find his opposite number, to find the warlord or high chieftain who had dared to lay siege to Karak Kadrin and see him bleeding and gasping in the dirt.

So intent was he on the thought, he almost missed the horns of alarm sounding from the rear ranks of the throng. Snarling, Ungrim tore his mind away from the red ocean of battle madness and turned. 'What is it?' he said.

Thungrimsson turned, face pale. 'They've boxed us in,' he grated. 'We're surrounded.'

Ungrim cursed. 'Take the reserves and fall back,' he said. Thungrimsson hesitated and Ungrim grabbed him by his beard, causing the hammerer's eyes to widen in shock. 'Do it, hearth-warden! We must win this day. My life means nothing, next to that. I will hold them here.'

Thungrimsson nodded jerkily and turned, shouting commands. Before he got ten paces, something massive and foul crashed down upon him, driving him to the ground. Ungrim blinked in shock. It was large, far larger than any beast he'd encountered, save a dragon or two. Was this the doom the priest had foreseen? Was this the thing that had been fated to devour Gurnisson? It was certainly impressive enough, if a bit small. Whatever it was, it had bounded through the ranks of the throng like an eager hound, killing warriors and maiming others.

Roughly anthropoid in shape, it had a thick tail that cracked like a whip, knocking dwarfs from their feet with bone-breaking force. Vast, frog-like jaws split open, revealing a thicket of crooked fangs, and eyes like the bloated orbs of the blind fish which swam in the deep mountain rivers glared out at the dwarfs around it with more than animal malevolence. Two great simian fists pounded the ground, and then spread, revealing monstrous talons which gouged the rock. It was the colour of blood drying on slate and stank of a century of butchery. The hilts of daggers and swords protruded from its broad, scarred back, clattering with every roll of its shoulders. Scars in the shape of runes and sigils branded its flesh, leaking smoke and pus. Great chains had been threaded through its flesh at several points. One foot on Thungrimsson, it stretched and reared, pounding its chest with its fists and releasing a squealing roar, like some titanic swine.

Thungrimsson gasped and the sound broke Ungrim out of his shock. With a guttural shout he launched himself at the creature. A fist slammed down, narrowly missing him. His axe licked out and the blade shuddered in his grip as it rebounded off a patch of stone-like scales. He spun, lashing out at it again and again. It lumbered after him, deceptively quick despite its build. Claws tore the crown-helm from his head, and set his brains to wobbling in his skull.

Behind the beast, dwarfs were helping the mauled Thungrimsson to his feet. The hearth-warden snatched up his fallen hammer and made to help his king, but Ungrim bellowed, 'No! See to the rear!' He had no time to see whether or not

Thungrimsson obeyed him. The monster came for him again, herding him away from his army, jaws snapping.

Ungrim stumbled back and it caught his axe in its teeth, breaking a number of the latter even as it ripped the ancient, rune-engraved weapon from his grip. It loomed over him, its foul breath washing over him, and he drove a hard fist into one bulging eye, eliciting a shriek of rage. It caught him in its tusks and flung him into the air.

He landed hard, all of the breath escaping him all at once. Wheezing, he tried to push himself to his feet. The creature stalked towards him, thick ropes of drool dangling from its fangs as it opened its maw in promise.

'No,' Garmr said, and the Slaughter-Hound stopped.

He towered in his saddle, his axe at his side as he rode towards the greatest sacrifice ever brought before the dark gods short of Asavar Kul's sacrifice of the city of Praag. He smashed aside a stake with a swing of his axe and brained a dwarf as his Chaos knights rode through their lines. The stunted ones were fighting well, but not well enough. His warriors had momentum and numbers on their side, and that would be enough to carry the day.

Even the mightiest mountains could be worn down by the blood-dimmed tide. Garmr looked down at the fallen dwarf. Someone important, he knew. He recognized authority in another, possessing a surplus of it himself. He had commanded Ulfrgandr to seek out the leaders of the army and bring them to heel. A dwarf noble would make a fine sacrifice, once the general blood-letting was done.

'Hold him, but do not kill him,' he said. Ulfrgandr snarled and the heat of it seeped into Garmr's armour. Part of him, a small, withered bundle of ancient and long ignored humanity, prickled in primitive fear. He looked up at the Slaughter-Hound and saw in its dull eyes the same look he'd seen in those of his reflection more than once, back when he'd possessed a reflection.

The joy of destruction, of mindless violence, was addictive. The beast had long ago surrendered whatever cunning it might have once possessed to that joy, sacrificing wit for eternal war. Garmr felt a stab of contempt and the monster growled hatefully, feeling his disdain through the link they shared. Garmr's eyes were drawn to the up-thrust hilts of the mystical daggers that sprouted from its back, the tips of their blades wedged into the iron bone of its spine. He knew this because he had planted them there himself, stabbing each one in the order that Grettir had assured him would bring the beast to heel.

He could still remember the crimson tide that had threatened to engulf him during that battle, the madness that begged for release, pushing him further and farther and faster, burning him from inside out. The harder he fought, the harder it was not to fight, the madder he grew the stronger the madness was. By the end, he had been little more than a beast himself, foaming and baying at the seven moons that hung over the cerulean sea.

Garmr the Gorewolf had come by his war-name honestly. The Slaughter-Hound and the Gorewolf had each waded through seas of the dead to meet in thunderous, glorious war and at the time, in that place, Garmr had not wanted it to end, their claws and fangs and axe and dagger meeting in a rhythm as old as the world, and he had sung the praises of Khorne until in his frenzy, he had forgotten the art of language.

'That is why I bound you,' he said, reaching out. Ulfrgandr jerked back, showing its fangs. Garmr made a fist and dropped his hand. Why was he seeking to explain himself? The beast had no mind to understand him, and even if it had, it would not have forgiven him. He had taken its freedom. He had broken it and bound it, preventing it from crushing, killing and destroying as its instinct demanded. In its place, he would not have rested until he had succeeded in freeing himself.

Then, he was not in its place. He was not it, and thanks to the spell which bound them together, he would never suffer to become as it was. Garmr was a prince of murder, not a slave to fury.

The monster snarled again, glaring at him across from the dwarf. Garmr looked at the latter. 'We sit on the threshold of destiny, stunted one. How does it feel?' he said.

The dwarf's face flushed and Garmr could smell his rage. The dwarf lunged to his feet and leapt, far more quickly than Garmr had expected, but not quick enough. One of Ulfrgandr's paws snapped out and flattened the dwarf, pinning him to the bloody ground. Garmr looked down at the flushed, berserk face and then away.

The battle was not over, but that did not matter. He had accomplished what he wished. Let Ekaterina and Canto fight until they could fight no more, let them harry the dwarfs, let the dwarfs strike back, none of it mattered now. The one-eyed dwarf was here, somewhere nearby, and Garmr could smell him; he could smell the stench of fate, and he looked out over the half-shattered forest of stakes, searching.

He moved into the field of carnage, stepping across bodies, hunting his quarry. Behind him, Ulfrgandr growled low, longing to rejoin the slaughter. Only Garmr's iron will kept the beast in place. Overhead, the clouds finally burst, spilling a red rain.

It was a sign. There were signs and portents everywhere, all coalescing into meaning and method, showing him the way to the end. His heart thudded in his chest, and anticipation made his turgid blood writhe in a frenzy. He was so close now.

A trill caught his attention, a low whisper of joyful noise, like the cry of a hunting falcon. He turned and saw her, standing there, leaning upon her great spear, her eyes for him alone. One delicate talon gestured and he saw movement among the corpses. Of course! Of course he had been in the vanguard! Where else would such a creature have been?

'My queen,' Garmr said, moving towards her, his steps loud. Khorne's Consort laughed silently and stepped back, gesturing for him to approach. As he drew closer, she moved further away, her shape coming apart in the rain, like smoke. He felt a moment's disappointment that she would not be there to see him collect this last, most important skull.

It did not matter. She had shown him what he needed.

The rain started slowly at first, and then grew stronger, hammering the hard-packed soil into mud. Biter shoved the dead marauder aside and staggered to his feet, the rain washing blood off his broad frame, but leaving it stained red nonetheless. A gash marked his head, shaving a bald patch through his hair and sticking much of the rest to his scalp with blood. Biter shook his head, clearing it.

'Not quite,' he chuckled. 'Not... quite.' He turned. 'Up, Remembrancer, no lying down on this job,' he said. He reached out and grabbed Koertig's shoulder. The Nordlander rolled limply. Empty eyes and a slack mouth were the first things Biter saw and he sighed. He looked up, letting the rain wash across his face. 'Outlived another one, curse me,' he said.

'Not for long,' a deep voice said. Rock, bone and meat

crunched underfoot as the armoured giant approached, great axe dangling loosely in his grip. 'Turn, Slayer. Show me your face.'

Biter laughed and turned. 'Pretty enough for you?'

'The loveliest sight I have beheld,' Garmr said. He stopped. They stood in a bubble of calm. Biter stepped away from the bodies, his axe over his shoulder. He could see something monstrous looming nearby, a struggling form held fast to the ground.

'Good. It'll be your last.'

Garmr trembled. Biter realized that he was laughing. The sound was strange and wheezing, as if it were squeezing between the joints of his armour rather than from any human mouth. Biter felt a bit insulted. Then Garmr was moving and his axe was licking out, shearing through the soft curtain of rain. Biter threw himself to the side and bounded to his feet, his own axe snapping out and carving a crease across Garmr's thigh. 'Are we done talking then? Should have said,' Biter rasped.

Garmr turned, seemingly unconcerned by the brackish fluid leaking from the gash in his leg. 'I thought it was obvious enough,' he said. His axe chopped down, narrowly missing Biter, who stumbled aside. They traded blows for a moment, man and dwarf, their axes ringing off one another. A hard blow shoved Biter back and the Slayer crouched, breathing heavily. The wound on his head had reopened, and blood covered one side of his face and ran beneath his patch.

'I have waited for you for a thousand years,' Garmr said.

'I'm never on time,' Biter said, coughing.

'I have dreamed of you for a century, Slayer,' Garmr continued, his voice growing angry.

'I'm flattered,' Biter coughed. 'Many a lass has dreamed of me.'

'I have carved a scar in the heart of the world, just for you.' Garmr snarled and pointed at the Slayer with his axe. 'I have butchered millions and I have spilled an ocean of blood, just to ride the waves to this point, to you.'

'Walking would have been simpler,' Biter said and chuckled.

'This is not a joke!' Garmr's axe came down. Biter caught the blade with his and forced it aside. He drove his free hand into Garmr's midsection, his knuckles ringing on the baroque armour. Garmr's hand dropped like a weight on Biter's head and the Slayer was hurled backwards, against an outcropping of rock.

Biter's vision blurred and spun as he crawled to his feet. 'Woo, that was a bit of a *bok*,' he said blearily. 'My father used to hit me just the same, when I was a beardling. Of course, he only had the one hand and the two fingers. What's your excuse?' he continued, grinning through bloody teeth at Garmr.

'Stop laughing, dwarf, this is a solemn occasion, a moment of holy truth,' Garmr growled.

'Really? I thought it was just a runk, you great *wazzok*,' Biter spat. He smiled widely. 'Come on, hit me.' He barely brought his axe up in time and the weapon was wrenched from his hands by the force of Garmr's blow. Pain radiated up his wrists and forearms and with a grim laugh, Biter realized that the last blow had not only rendered him weaponless but the force of it had almost shattered his wrists as well. He rocked back, chuckling. 'Well, I did say hit me,' he gasped. 'This is right funny, this is.'

The axe looped around and caught Biter below the sternum, lifting him up off his knees and into the air. He folded over the blade and his weight tore it from Garmr's grip. Axe and Slayer fell to the ground. Biter coughed and his ruined hands flailed helplessly at the haft of the axe. 'Funny,' he wheezed. 'I knew I was fated to die. Just didn't think it'd be like this. Figured a troll would sit on me. Heh.' Glassy-eyed, he looked up at Garmr and cackled thinly.

'Stop laughing,' Garmr said again as he stooped to pluck the axe free.

'Come closer, manling, I want to tell you a joke,' Biter said and twisted like a snake, his gromril teeth snapping tight on Garmr's hand. Ancient metal buckled beneath the dwarf's spasmodic jaw-clench and Garmr bellowed and tried to jerk his hand free to no avail. Garmr grabbed his axe and he tore it free and brought it down, separating the Slayer's head from his shoulders.

Nonetheless, Biter's teeth remained clamped. Garmr resisted the urge to batter the head against the nearby rocks and the ground. Instead he dropped his axe and pried at the hideously grinning head. He finally broke the dwarf's jaw and ripped that terrible mouth from his crushed hand. The broken jaw sagged and the tongue waggled and Garmr roared in fury and triumph, raising the head to the weeping sky.

The Road of Skulls would soon be complete.

18

The Worlds Edge Mountains,
above the Peak Pass

Felix awoke with a start as rain struck his face. He touched his cheek and his fingers came away red. He gasped and sat up. They were still on the ridge among the dwarf – and now, Chaos – dead. Only a few moments must have passed.

'It's not blood, manling. Well, not yours at any rate,' Gotrek said, standing over him. 'Have a good rest?'

The Slayer's axe hand was red to the elbow and dripping and there was a grim look on his face. 'We were too late,' he said, reaching down to haul Felix to his feet. 'The battle has begun.'

'You could still join it,' Felix said, clutching his head. The bodies of a dozen marauders, perhaps slightly fewer, lay scattered about. Gotrek had been busy.

'Begun and done,' Gotrek spat. 'They were attacked from behind!' The Slayer gestured sharply with his axe, splattering Felix with blood. He sounded outraged.

'Then Ungrim–'

'I don't know,' Gotrek said. He shook his head. He looked around at the dead dwarfs and the dead Chaos marauders and grimaced. 'Too late,' he muttered.

Felix sat down on a rock. 'What are we going to do?'

'If you're smart, you'll sit very, *very* still, manling,' a rough voice snarled.

Felix froze, red rain running down his face in rivulets. Gotrek did not, but instead started forwards, both hands on the haft of his axe, his one eye gleaming. 'Come out and face my axe,' he said.

'I'll thank you to stay at a distance, Slayer,' the dwarf said, stepping out of the rocks, crossbow in his hands. More dwarfs, clad in battered travel-leathers and carrying crossbows, joined him. Rangers, Felix realised with a start. The one who'd spoken eyed them both and then took in the scene. His eyes lingered on the bodies of the dead dwarfs and he cursed softly in Khazalid and looked at Gotrek. 'Come with us, Gurnisson. The War-Mourner wants to see you.' He cocked an eye upwards and spat. 'And I want to get out of this cursed rain.'

'Should have known the whelp would pursue us,' Gotrek muttered sourly. 'There are dwarfs dying down there.' He gestured in the direction of the Peak Pass. 'And there'll be dwarfs dying up here, if you try and stop me.' He pointed his axe at the ranger. Red rain collected in the runes engraved on the blade and dripped off, forming strange patterns on the ground.

'What's left of the Grand Throng has fallen back from the pass, Gurnisson,' the ranger said, more politely than he had a moment earlier. Gotrek's axe had that effect on people, Felix reflected wryly. 'Right now, the War-Mourner is the only thing standing between Karak Kadrin and the Chaos filth that smashed Ungrim's throng,' the ranger continued, his voice growing harsh. 'And Garagrim ordered us to find you, if you could be found, and bring you to him, in chains if we had to.'

Felix groaned as he heaved himself to his feet. He fell silent as he heard strange horns wailing on the wind, piercing the veil of rain like sharp claws. The rangers tensed and Gotrek turned. He cast a glance back at the pass and then looked at the ranger. 'If the throng has retreated, they'll be coming into these hills soon enough,' he said. He looked back at the ranger. 'If you would have us go, now is the time. Take me to the whelp.'

The journey was neither a quick one, nor a comfortable one, from Felix's perspective. Climbing down into the canyons of the Peak Pass was somehow even more arduous than climbing up had been.

They saw more dwarfs as the sun began to set and the rain began to drum down hard enough to sting. Pickets had been set, for all the good it would do them. Tough-looking clan warriors, hunched behind heavy pavises or rocks piled into small barricades, hefted crossbows or axes in greeting as the rangers trotted past, Gotrek and Felix with them.

'Why hasn't the horde come charging towards us like ants?' Felix muttered. 'What are they waiting for?'

'Who knows why Chaos-lovers do anything, manling?' Gotrek said. He glanced up at Felix. 'Good question, though,' he added grudgingly.

The dwarfs had not created a camp so much as a small fortress. Heavy pavise shields created a long wall and dwarfs laboured before that wall by lantern-light, erecting wooden stakes to prevent a charge by the enemy's horsemen. Other dwarfs piled stones in square formations, creating miniature redoubts within the greater redoubt made by the free-standing shields. Heavy canvas and metal pavilion tents had been erected as well, to protect those dwarfs not working from the incessant, hissing rain. It was under one such that Garagrim met them.

Felix winced as he caught sight of Snorri Thungrimsson lying senseless on a pallet. The old hammerer was in rough shape. Blood pooled beneath him, even as dwarf physicians fussed about him. His skin had the waxy look of one halfway past dead, though Felix had seen dwarfs recover from worse wounds. Then, those dwarfs had all been Slayers, who were renowned for their inhuman vitality.

'Will he live?' he asked.

Garagrim glanced at him. 'It is up to him,' he said gruffly. He looked at Gotrek. 'I expected you to use the drains, as you did before,' he said, almost accusingly.

'That's why I used the heights,' Gotrek said, grinning mirthlessly.

Garagrim nodded. He looked at the leader of the rangers. 'What news?'

The ranger shook his head. 'If there are any survivors who didn't make it out, they're as good as dead, Prince Garagrim.'

'Prince still, is it?' Gotrek murmured, his axe resting in the crook of his arm. 'Not king, then?'

'Until we know whether my father has met his long-sought doom or not, yes,' Garagrim said. He met Gotrek's eye. 'You have something to say about it?'

Gotrek grunted and looked away. Felix felt that he might have been safer staying in the hills. Garagrim was no friend of theirs, that much had been made clear to him. How would he react to Gotrek's prodding now that he was de-facto ruler of Karak Kadrin?

On his pallet, Thungrimsson coughed. Garagrim looked at him, and then at Gotrek. 'I have a hundred clansmen, plus the remnants of my father's – of the Grand Throng. There are five times that number of Northmen in the pass, and more every hour, according to my scouts. They're growing, gathering strength like pus in a wound.'

Gotrek looked out at the encampment. 'You can't hold them,' he said bluntly.

Felix tensed, expecting Garagrim to explode. Instead, the War-Mourner merely grunted. 'No. If we had a day, or a week, yes, but there's no telling when they'll come howling down towards us.'

'You could retreat,' Felix said half-heartedly. Both Slayers looked at him dismissively and then away. Felix shrugged and shook his head. 'Never mind,' he muttered.

'The queen will have sent messengers to Zhufbar and Karaz-a-Karak,' Garagrim said, stroking his beard. 'Though I doubt reinforcement will be forthcoming.'

Gotrek laughed nastily. 'They will shore up their defences as Karak Kadrin occupies the enemy.'

'It has always been thus,' Garagrim said, somewhat proudly. 'We are the gate to the world, Gurnisson. That is no small responsibility.' He looked at Gotrek steadily. 'By rights, I should send you back to the hold under guard.'

'You can't afford to spare the number of warriors it will take to chain me, beardling,' Gotrek said. Garagrim flushed, but held his temper with what Felix considered remarkable will.

'I don't have enough warriors to do anything,' he said bitterly. 'If we defend this place, we will be overwhelmed within hours. If we retreat to a better position, they will catch us.'

'So attack,' Gotrek said.

'Our numbers are too few,' another thane protested, speaking up for the first time from among a small group of his fellows. Felix looked at them. They were young, as dwarfs judged things, he thought; save for a few, who wore bloody bandages and had a haunted look in their eyes. The survivors of Ungrim's circle of commanders, he assumed.

'What do you expect me to say?' Gotrek glared fiercely at the young thane. 'I intend to march into the pass and find this beast that supposedly did for Ungrim. Do what you wish, decide for yourselves, I care nothing for your worries or your army,' he growled.

'You never have,' Garagrim said.

Gotrek spun. His eye was wide and blazing. His mouth opened, but he closed it with a snap. Felix felt a rush of anger on the Slayer's behalf. 'If he hadn't cared, your father might not have lived this long!' Felix said before he could stop himself. Every dwarf under the tent looked at him and he shrank back instinctively.

'What was that, human?' Garagrim said. 'What do you mean?'

'It was nothing. The manling speaks out of turn,' Gotrek said, stepping between them. 'You are right that I care nothing for any dwarf, War-Mourner. I am an outlaw for good reason. Leave it at that.'

'No, tell me, Gurnisson,' Garagrim said.

Gotrek grunted. 'It doesn't matter.'

'Tell him,' Felix said, ignoring Gotrek's gesture to be silent. 'Gotrek, better to part with peace between you than anger,' he continued.

Gotrek shrugged. 'What does it matter?' he said again. 'We part just the same.'

Garagrim's hands were clenched into fists. 'Tell me what he meant, Gurnisson. As War-Mourner, as prince, I demand it!'

Gotrek shivered slightly. Then he sighed and looked at Garagrim. 'Your mother asked me to swear an oath, boy. She asked me to swear to her that I would not allow your father – or any of his line – to meet their doom, if I could prevent it. And for reasons which are my own, I did so. I saved your father from his doom, and he has borne me a grudge ever since. And because you are prince, it is your grudge as well, but my oath stands all the same.'

Garagrim stared at him. Every dwarf stared at him. Felix stared at him. Gotrek met every look with a stony glare and turned away. Looking out at the rain, he said, 'An attack is the only hope Karak Kadrin has. But to do so successfully will require time you do not have.'

'What do you suggest?' Garagrim said.

'These worshippers of the Blood God thrive on challenge,' Gotrek said lifting his axe. 'They're like wolves... Always looking for weakness, the strong preying on the weak and the weak looking to pull down the strong. When they defeat an opponent, they immediately look for another.'

'You think they'll fall on one another, as they did at Karak Kadrin,' Garagrim said.

'Aye,' Gotrek said. 'They'll rip each other apart, with a bit of help. If they've no leader to hold the reins, they'll fall to fighting, sure enough...'

Felix's heart sank. 'Oh no,' he muttered. Gotrek glanced at him, his eye twinkling.

'Aye, manling,' he said cheerfully. 'I'll kill their blasted warlord and they'll turn on each other to pick a new one. And while they're fighting, the beardling can unleash the vengeance of Karak Kadrin on them.'

'It might work,' Garagrim said, after a moment of stunned silence at the sheer audacity of the Slayer's plan had passed. His face hardened. 'But why should that honour fall to you?'

Gotrek looked at him, eyebrow arched. 'Who better,

beardling? Axeson's prophecy, if it was true, has come and gone. I am free to seek my doom.'

'I am War-Mourner, Gurnisson,' Garagrim said, as if relishing every word. 'That means it is my duty to determine who meets what doom when. *And I say thee nay.*' He clashed his axes together. 'My father has fallen, and it comes to me to do what he could not. I will meet my doom here and free my clan from our shame! And I will have no doom-thief steal absolution from me!' he bellowed, gesturing at Gotrek.

So intent on was he on elaborating on this theme, that Garagrim did not notice Gotrek stalking towards him until the older Slayer was right up on him. Felix flinched as Gotrek's forehead snapped forwards and connected with Garagrim's with a sound like stones crashing together. Every dwarf in the tent sucked in a breath as Garagrim staggered back, his eyes going cross. 'I–' he began. Then his eyes rolled up in his head and he toppled backwards to lie still.

Gotrek wiped a bead of blood from his forehead and looked around. 'Is there anyone else who wants to argue with me?' he growled. 'No? Good. When he wakes, tell him the grudge stands. Attack at dawn,' he continued, stabbing a finger at the closest thane, who pointed at himself nervously. 'The deed will be done by then, one way or another.'

'Gotrek, was that entirely wise?' Felix said as he followed Gotrek out of the tent. He glanced back and saw the thanes gathering around Garagrim's unconscious body and muttering among themselves. 'They might arrest us for assaulting the king!'

'That beardling is no king,' Gotrek spat, not slowing his pace. 'Not yet. But Kemma is queen, and she'd flay me down to my *gruntaz* if I ignored my oath now.' His voice softened. 'I couldn't save Ungrim. I'll save his son though, even if they must record my name in the Book of Grudges for it.'

Felix said nothing. It was a courageous thing Gotrek was doing. Any dwarf could die. But not many could live with the shame of having prevented another from fulfilling a sacred vow. Maybe the other Slayers had been right, he reflected with grim humour. Gotrek truly was a doom-thief, albeit not in the way they had meant.

'You do not have to follow me, manling,' Gotrek said as they headed for the line of pavise shields. 'Garagrim will not harm you, if you choose to stay.'

Felix shivered a little. Red rain ran down the collar of his shirt, sending chills down his back. 'Maybe not, but if I stay, how will I accurately record your death?'

'Are you certain this is my doom?' Gotrek said, not looking at him.

'You're walking into the heart of the largest Chaos horde to spill out of the north since the time of Magnus the Pious,' Felix said. 'I'm honestly considering just having that be the last line. The outcome is, as the playwright Detlef Sierck was fond of saying, foregone.'

'I met him once,' Gotrek said idly, 'him and his witchy woman.' He tapped his bulbous, oft-broken nose. 'She was a blood-sucker, though they seemed happy enough.'

Felix looked at Gotrek. 'He was one of the greatest playwrights the Empire ever produced.'

'Couldn't hold his liquor,' Gotrek grunted. 'He always acted like he was on a blasted stage.' He shook his head, scattering rain from his crest. 'He loved that woman though, even though she was as cold as fish dragged from a mountain river.' A muscle in his jaw jumped. 'Aye, love is a fine thing...'

'You'd know all about that, of course,' Felix said mildly.

'What was that, manling?'

'As long as I've known you, Gotrek, I've never seen you swear an oath without good reason, regardless of who was asking.' Felix glanced down at the Slayer. 'So why did you swear such an oath to the queen?'

'She wasn't queen then,' Gotrek muttered.

'What was that? I couldn't quite hear you over the rain,' Felix said, cupping a hand around his ear. Gotrek glared at him.

'None of that goes in my saga,' he snapped, shaking a finger at Felix. 'I'll not have a queen embarrassed by your loose words.'

Felix allowed himself a small smile. 'There's always a woman,' he said. He looked at Gotrek. 'That's another thing that Detlef Sierck used to say.'

Gotrek grunted. Then he cocked his eye at Felix. 'Last chance, manling.'

Felix looked around. They had arrived at the shields. Dwarfs watched them silently. Somewhere behind them, someone barked an order and two of the shields were moved aside. Felix looked back at the warm glow of the dwarf lanterns, and then at the hungry darkness of the Peak Pass. He swallowed and let his palm drop to Karaghul's hilt.

'Let's go,' he said.

Gotrek gave a flat bark of laughter and slapped him on the back. 'That's the spirit, manling. Your stories will live longer than anything from old Detlef's pen, that much I can promise you.'

'I'd settle for doing that myself,' Felix said gloomily, as the waiting darkness swallowed them up.

The centre of the Peak Pass had been filled with war-shrines and altars, arrayed in eight concentric circles, radiating outwards from a central point. The spot had been picked years before the horde had even mustered, chosen by Grettir's signs and portents. It had been the first thing Garmr had forced his cousin to do. For a hundred years or more, this spot, this wet patch of bloody stone, had been his goal. Every step Garmr had taken on Khorne's road had led him here, to this seemingly innocuous section of mountain pass.

Or not so innocuous, as Grettir assured him; in the facets of his cousin's mask, Garmr had seen the history of this place. Armies had lived and died on this spot and a hundred thousand souls were chained to these stones by death and by slaughter. It was on this spot that the dwarfs had first thrown back the forces of Chaos, so many millennia ago. Here, the one who had gone north, who had carved his skull road into the heart of the Wastes, had battled the champions of those first raw, red years – the first men to be touched by Chaos, the first to pledge skulls to Khorne and flesh to Slaanesh. Those ancient, mighty warriors had died in heaps and droves, slaughtered to a man by the dwarf. Here was where it had truly begun; it was through here that Khorne's Road of Skulls would run. And it was here that the dawi of Karak Kadrin inevitably chose to make their stand when the northern hordes swept south, though they no longer knew why.

It was nothing to him. Just stone, a little higher than some and lower than others. But Khorne's Eye was here, and that made it the most important place in the world at this moment. The Dark Gods watched and waited and Garmr was determined that they would have the entertainment that they craved.

He growled in satisfaction as the last shrine was shoved into place and the beasts and slaves were freed from their chains and traces and slaughtered, their bodies added to the heaps of flyblown meat that lay cooling in the red rain, their spilled blood gleaming in the flickering torchlight. The smell of blood was heavy on the air as Garmr climbed the eight steps of the war-shrine and looked out at what remained of his horde. It had been purged of weakness, sharpened to a killing point by all that he had done. And here, that point would be sanctified in the name of Khorne.

Visions of what was to come danced in his head. For so long, he had striven to reach this moment. Everything after was a reward. Every moment of murder, every second of the slaughter-to-come was Khorne's gift to his most faithful of servants. The world would drown in fire and blood over and over again as Khorne's legions marched on the Road of Skulls and into the lands of men, dwarfs and elves even as they had millennia past. 'Bring the prisoners forwards!' he thundered.

Ulfrgandr snarled softly, from behind the shrine. The beast lay crouched before it, its eyes sweeping hungrily over the gathered horde. For a moment, Garmr wondered if perhaps he would free it, at the end, and let it roam these mountains ever more, a living testament to his might and Khorne's will, a harbinger of what would soon stalk down the Road of Skulls. He looked as the prisoners were dragged forward.

There were a dozen prisoners, more than he'd thought, and somewhere among them, the bloody and battered king of Karak Kadrin himself, Ungrim Ironfist. Grettir had assured him of such, though all dwarfs looked the same to Garmr. Ekaterina stalked down the line, driving a boot into each dwarf's back in turn, knocking them to their knees. Garmr gazed at them in satisfaction and then roared, 'Bring me Grettir!'

Canto dragged the stumbling sorcerer through the ranks. Howls and jeers accompanied him, and stones struck him as he followed the black-armoured warrior. Canto shoved him down onto the steps of the war-shrine and stepped back. Grettir cast a glare at him and then turned it on Garmr, who crouched above him and held up a head by its matted crimson hair.

'I found him, cousin,' he said. He flipped the head of the one-eyed Slayer into Grettir's lap.

Grettir gestured to Garmr's hand. 'It looks like he found you as well.'

Garmr shrugged and rumbled, 'It is of no matter.'

'There are rites that I must perform,' Grettir said. 'Placing this last skull is a delicate business. It is not just a matter of setting up your altars and temples.'

'Then do so, cousin,' Garmr growled. He lifted his axe. Overhead, the clouds were the colour of clotted blood and a fat crimson moon rolled idiotically out from behind them, beaming its empty grin down at them. 'This ground has been sanctified twice over, and Khorne's Eye is upon us! Our time is at hand! Khorne's will be made manifest! Let these mountains echo with the screams of the dead and the soon-to-die! Here is the doom of all mankind! Here is where the world drowns in blood!' His army roared assent, the noise of it causing the night-scavengers to flee in terror. He strode up the steps of the altar and roared, 'Blood for the Blood God! Skulls for the Skull Throne!' and his army shouted with him.

'Why do we not attack the dwarf hold?' Ekaterina barked suddenly. She squatted behind Ungrim, and had jerked his head back. 'Let us tear their walls down, and let their petty king watch!' Warriors all around her broke into bays of approval, and champions as well, including Vasa and those who had replaced Bolgatz and the others who had died. 'Khorne wills it,' she shouted. 'He wills that we march, Garmr. To sit and stay is not the way of Khorne,' she snarled, and her supporters snarled with her. The canyon seemed to echo for a moment with the thunder of leather pinions beating.

Before he could reply to Ekaterina's impertinence, the squat shape of the Chaos dwarf Khorreg shoved his way through the press, his remaining assistants behind him. The Chaos dwarf's eyes lingered almost longingly over the captives, but then they turned to Garmr.

'Our bargain is fulfilled, Gorewolf,' Khorreg rasped, crossing his arms. 'We will take our engine and we will go.'

Garmr cocked his head 'I did not give you leave to go,' he said, staring down at the squat figure.

'And I did not ask it,' Khorreg said. 'We have fulfilled the terms of our bargain, Gorewolf. Our engines have brought you victory. We return now to Zharr Naggrund.'

'I said that I did not give you leave to go,' Garmr snarled, incensed by this second challenge, and from an unexpected quarter. 'I will require your engines–'

'We have done all that we agreed and we have lost valuable resources in the doing,' Khorreg grated, meeting Garmr's fury with haughty disdain. 'The Daemonsmiths of Zharr Naggrund always honour their bargains, chieftain. No more, no less.' He swiped the air in an imperious gesture. 'We take our remaining cannon and go.'

Men began to mutter and murmur. The hellcannon, even by itself, had done the work of a hundred men, battering down walls and enemy phalanxes alike. But even worse was the challenge. If Garmr could not keep the dawi zharr from leaving, perhaps there was a reason? Garmr hesitated again, and cursed himself for doing so even as he did it. 'You will not leave,' he said, striding down the stairs of the altar, axe in hand.

Khorreg cocked his head, his piggy eyes glowing balefully.

'Will I not, Northman?'

Garmr paused, considering. He was confident that he could kill the Chaos dwarf, but what purpose would that serve? No, better to save his chastisement for later, when he could bring the full might of a strong horde upon the black walls of Zharr Naggrund. He looked around, realizing that every eye was upon him now. Vasa the Lion and Ekaterina watched him, their faces eager and expectant, though he couldn't see Canto anywhere. His men watched him, Chaos champions and warriors and marauders alike, and every expression was the same, like that of animals sniffing for weakness.

Ulfrgandr growled warningly and Garmr chuckled. In another time, he would not have noticed the trap closing about him. He would have simply attacked the Chaos dwarf for defying him and likely died in the attempt, one way or another. 'Is that Khorne's will, then?' he said, spreading his arms. He looked at Khorreg. 'Go then, Khorreg Hell-Worker, Daemonsmith of Zharr Naggrund, your services have been rendered and our bargain is done.'

Khorreg's eyes narrowed, and the murmur grew. The Chaos dwarf had not been expecting that. Nonetheless, he nodded and turned, his armour hissing and wheezing as he strode away, his assistant following. Garmr looked around.

'You should not have let them go,' Ekaterina said, and her supporters growled with her.

'We do not need them any longer,' Garmr said loudly. 'Khorne's fist will crack the holds of our enemies! We walk the Road of Skulls, warriors, and our victory is certain!'

'What hold, Garmr? We see no hold, no enemy! Only bloody stones! If you will not lead, you are not fit to command this horde,' Ekaterina said.

'Who else will lead it, if not me?' Garmr said, turning his

back on her. 'I am the strongest, and so I lead. When you think to change that, challenge me.'

Ekaterina raised her sabre and said, 'Garmr!'

Garmr stopped.

'You do not deserve Khorne's blessings,' she said. The horde fell silent. 'You do not deserve to lead. You are a false servant of the Skull Throne,' she continued, stepping closer.

'And you are more worthy?' Garmr said. He still hadn't turned around.

Incensed, she stepped closer. She said, 'Than you? Yes. Khorne led me to you to take from you your undeserved title, Gorewolf. Valkia herself watches over me, and I will shed oceans of blood and take mountains of skulls for the Blood God, not for myself. Not for some road, but for the glory of the god!' She raised her sabre and extended it towards him. 'Face me, Gorewolf!'

19

The Worlds Edge Mountains,
the Peak Pass

Felix followed Gotrek through the forest of stakes as they picked their way towards the small city of shrines and wheeled altars that had been set up in the centre of the pass. 'There must be hundreds of those things,' he muttered. It had taken several hours to reach this place, and he wondered what could maintain the attentions of the horde for so long. What had prevented them from simply plunging through the pass and sweeping aside Garagrim's throng as they had Ungrim's? He put the question to Gotrek as they crept through the abattoir leavings of the earlier battle.

'What of it?' Gotrek said, far more loudly than Felix would have liked. The Slayer's shoulders bunched as he took a two-handed swing, shattering a jutting stake and causing it to topple with a crash. 'Let them come!'

Snarls echoed through the night as monstrous shapes scrambled towards them, alerted by the Slayer's bellow.

Gotrek met their snarls with one of his own. Felix drew his blade, but before the scrambling shapes reached them, a heavily armoured form, black and imposing, stepped between them, sword in hand.

'Hold,' the Chaos warrior rumbled in rusty, archaically accented Reikspiel.

'You,' Gotrek growled. 'Going to run away again?' he continued nastily. As they drew closer, Felix recognized the armoured warrior as the one they'd fought upon first coming to Karak Kadrin, in the Engineers' Entrance and later, during the final battle of the siege. He even still had the marks of Gotrek's axe on his cuirass.

'Not quite, no,' the warrior said, a hint of dark amusement in his words. He leaned closer. 'You are... expected, dwarf.'

'Of course I am,' Gotrek snapped.

'Who's expecting us?' Felix said, keeping a wary eye on the crouching shapes. Men moved among the beasts, their features obscured by the rain.

'Not who you're thinking of,' the warrior said. He snapped an order at one of his followers, and a curling ram's horn was lifted to alert the horde. 'Best hurry up, dwarf. The eye of the storm is over us, and destiny is gnashing its yellowed fangs.'

'Very poetic,' Felix muttered, trying to find courage in sarcasm. Both Slayer and Chaos warrior ignored him.

The latter led them deeper into the belly of the beast. Several times, the warrior leading them was forced to strike out at over-eager Chaos marauders or worse things. He seemingly had no problem killing his own troops, which turned Felix's stomach. There were no bonds of loyalty here, or even shared purpose. The enemy was held together by the slenderest of threads – a shared love of slaughter. This, he knew with a sickening sense of realization, was what the gods of

Chaos wanted for mankind, regardless of whether they were gods of murder or pleasure. Each man sunk into personal depravity and madness, caring nothing for his fellow man or even something greater than the next kill, the next massacre. The Chaos marauders weren't even beasts, but puppets, acting out the sickening fantasies of an impersonal and alien intelligence.

Felix shuddered and pulled his cloak tight, wishing he had taken Gotrek's advice and stayed in the dubious safety of Garagrim's camp. Even if this scheme worked, even if this army ripped itself apart as Gotrek predicted, there was no reason to doubt he'd be ripped apart along with it. He cast a quick look at the sky. Less than an hour until dawn, he wagered, and plenty of time to die a horrible death.

The light of the torches grew eye-achingly bright as they were led into an open circle within the rings of shrines and altars and stakes. He grabbed Gotrek's shoulder and said, 'Gotrek!' as he saw the prisoners. Ungrim was among them, Felix was glad to see.

'I see them, manling,' Gotrek said, but his eye wasn't on Ungrim and the others, but on the scene playing out before them. Felix saw a woman – no, not a woman, something that might have once been a woman – challenge the armoured giant he took to be the warlord. She cried out a challenge and her voice was like the scratch of razors across his ears.

'Just in time,' the black-armoured Chaos warrior murmured.

The giant turned and he rumbled something in reply, his voice echoing oddly from within his helm. The sound of his voice threatened to turn Felix's legs to jelly. This creature – he wasn't a man – was caught between one world and the next, Felix thought, as was the creature in robes and battered armour chained to the altar near him. Thunder rumbled in the ugly clouds overhead and the rain began to pound down once more as Gotrek shoved past their escort and stumped forwards, heedless of the army that surrounded them.

'Aye, why would you do that when you could face me instead?' he bellowed, apparently understanding their dark tongue well enough to interrupt. 'Gorewolf, are you? Well, Gorewolf, turn and face Gotrek!'

All eyes found Gotrek in the silence that followed. Every Chaos follower, from marauder to warrior to champion, stared at the Slayer as he stalked forwards. 'Do you hear me, you butcher's leavings?' Gotrek continued. 'Face me!' He gestured with his axe, and Felix thought the warlord watched the blade as if it were a snake about to strike.

He knew, with an instinct born of experience, that they had walked into the middle of something. They hadn't been waiting for Gotrek, no matter how much it might look that way. He looked for their escort, but the Chaos warrior was gone.

'Face me!' Gotrek bellowed again, loud enough to bring a groan of sympathy from the slopes above. 'Give me a doom the gods will boast of! Come and take my skull, if you dare!'

As if Gotrek's words had snapped him out of whatever reverie he had been lost in, the Gorewolf gestured with his axe. 'I will face you,' he rasped in broken Reikspiel as he stepped down from the altar. 'I will take your skull. And the road will be complete, no matter who stands in my way.'

'No!' the woman snapped, lifting her sabre. 'One challenge at a time, Gorewolf,' she went on, gesturing with the curved blade. Like the Gorewolf, she spoke in Reikspiel, and Felix wondered if it were for their benefit. 'I have waited too long for this. Khorne demands your head, and it will be my blade that takes it, aye, and the dwarf's as well, come to that.' She gave a hideous, too-wide grin. 'The road will be complete, but it will be your skull that completes it, Garmr.'

Warlord and champion glared at one another for a hard moment. There was lightning in the air and Felix felt as if he were back in the Underway, with the spark hissing towards the explosives.

'Is that the way it is to be then? Fine,' the Gorewolf snarled, brandishing his axe. 'Have your challenge, Ekaterina and for you, dwarf, a doom!' As the Gorewolf's words echoed, a massive shape, heretofore hidden behind the altar, rose and snarled eagerly as it scrambled to its feet and flung itself through the crowd, killing tribesmen as it thrashed towards the Slayer.

'Gotrek–' Felix began as the monster charged towards them.

'He's mine, manling!' Gotrek said, shoving him aside. 'I'll take care of this overgrown salamander.' He raised his axe and let loose a tooth-rattling roar as he charged to meet the monster.

Gotrek was moving quicker than Felix had ever seen him move before, tumbling, running, twisting to avoid the creature's berserk, ground-shaking initial attack. As he watched, Gotrek leapt over a stabbing tail and spun, swinging a two-handed blow that drew a spray of ichor from the creature's back. It screamed and launched a backhanded swipe at Gotrek, catching the Slayer a glancing blow on the skull and sending him sprawling.

Blood pouring down his scalp, Gotrek rolled aside as the creature pounced like a cat, landing with all four feet where the Slayer had been lying only moments earlier. Gotrek was on his feet in an instant, his axe chopping into the creature's shoulder like a woodman's into a tree. It surged up, jerking Gotrek off his feet, and rolled, as if seeking to crush him beneath its weight. Gotrek released his axe and instead grabbed for one of the dagger hilts that rose from the thing's back.

As his hands seized the hilt, the creature arched its back and bellowed in agony. Gotrek jerked on the hilt, trying to drag whatever it was attached to free. The creature reared up and reached blindly for Gotrek, trying to pluck him from its back. Gotrek hung on, cursing.

Felix hesitated, caught by indecision. If he aided Gotrek, the Slayer would never forgive him. But if he didn't, and the Slayer died here, Felix knew he wouldn't last much longer. Felix cursed as well as he charged towards the combatants. Gotrek might want the beast all to himself, but whatever Felix could do to keep him fighting and on his feet, he would, even if it meant incurring the Slayer's displeasure. Karaghul was light in his hand as he swept it across the thing's exposed belly.

The monster screamed and staggered. It reached for Felix with one paw, shredding the edge of his cloak as he whirled aside. Karaghul slid across its arm and it snarled. Felix avoided another blow and saw that Gotrek was using the daggers as handholds. The Slayer was steadily pulling himself towards his axe. But every time he touched a hilt, the beast thrashed as if in agony.

Could it be–? Could those blades be connected to something vital in the creature's grotesque body? Who knew what sorcery the warlord had worked to gain control of such a monster?

Felix ducked another blow and spun about, seeking a way clear of the monster. His eyes locked with those of the strange robed figure he'd seen standing near the warlord when he and Gotrek arrived. Time seemed to slow around him and the world went vague and soft. A thousand eyes blinked at him from the thousand facets of the crystalline helm it wore, and in them, he saw glimpses of things – dreams of past moments, perhaps, or memories not yet formed. He saw Gotrek battling the undead beneath Wurtbad; he saw the war-engines of the skaven rupture the streets of Nuln and saw a vast, impossible airship duel with a monstrous serpentine shape in the skies above the mountains. All of this he saw and more, hundreds of memories and yet-to-be and never-were moments cascading across his consciousness like water.

And then the images were gone. Felix was left blinking, but not for long. Snapping from his reverie, he only just managed to avoid a flailing claw and he threw himself forwards as the beast whirled about. Rolling to his feet, he shouted, 'The daggers, Gotrek! Pull out one of the daggers!'

As Ulfrgandr loped towards its prey, Garmr's axe purred in his hands and he swept it out in a loose, looping blow, driving Ekaterina back. 'I have already fought this fight in my head, woman. You lost,' he said.

'Dreams are treacherous things,' Ekaterina said, lunging. The tip of her blade scored his armour. His axe twisted in his hands, fully awake now, for the first time in a long time. It sensed that the road was almost complete, that Khorne's time was almost come, and its hunger grew in proportion. Ekaterina's skull would make a fine gift to put at the Blood God's feet. Garmr bulled into her, forcing her back, putting his greater mass to use.

'So are many things, it seems,' Garmr said. His axe was light in his hands as he hewed at her. It chewed flinders from her blade, knocking her back. He had always been stronger than her. He was stronger than all of them. He was Khorne's will made manifest.

Ekaterina leapt aside and bounded to her feet, her blade slashing out across his back, drawing sparks from his cuirass. He whipped around, grabbing her matted hair before she could jerk back, and yanked her from her feet, hurling her to the ground. 'Did you think it would frighten me, Ekaterina? Did you think I would be paralyzed, frozen by indecision when the Doom-Seeker appeared, alive and whole and demanding my attentions, just when I thought victory had been gained?'

She barely scrambled aside as his foot slammed down, nearly crushing her head. 'Do you think so little of me?' he roared, his cry echoing the Slaughter-Hound's as it battled the Slayer. 'I have slaughtered nations, woman. I have butchered races undreamed of, and gouged my name into a billion skulls!' His axe sank into the ground, narrowly missing her leg as she rolled aside, trying to gain her feet. Garmr could tell that his speed shocked her.

'But I am not angry,' he said, stepping back, letting her get to her feet. 'Without challenge, how can I prove worthy?' He glanced at the others, at Vasa and Canto. 'When will you challenge me? When will you prove your worth in Khorne's eyes?' He gestured. 'Come to me, Lion. Come, Unsworn. Join us in our dance. Come join us on the road. Let us baptise Khorne's path with the blood of heroes...'

Vasa twitched and bared his fangs. His eyes were alight with battle-lust and with a snarl he ripped his heavy sword from its sheath and lunged to the attack. He had been waiting for this moment, Garmr knew. All of them had, except for Canto, who stepped back. They had joined him only to challenge him, only to take what was his in glorious combat. And what better moment than this, what better time than now to do it, as the gods themselves watched? Vasa's blade emitted a growl, like a beast hungry for flesh, as it chopped towards Garmr. He stepped back, easily avoiding the blow. His axe scraped Vasa's side, drawing blood and staggering the champion. Ekaterina shrieked and used the crouching champion as a springboard, diving towards Garmr. He swatted her from the air easily, and then Vasa was driving him back, his great rending blade hacking wildly.

As he fought them both, Garmr felt the old red joy rising in him, the thunderous longing for the Eternal Battle. It had all come down to this moment. Here, in this place, in this moment, he was victorious. Surrounded by enemies, locked in combat, he was victorious.

'Prepare, cousin,' he howled, catching Vasa by the throat and hurling him into Ekaterina and knocking them both sprawling. 'Ready yourself for War Unending!'

'I have been ready for a long, long time, cousin,' Grettir said. Garmr turned as the sorcerer stood and shrugged off his chains.

'What–?' Garmr said.

'War, cousin,' Grettir said. 'War and death.' He extended his golden talons and spat baleful words, and the world directly in front of Garmr was ripped apart by a whirlpool of coruscating destruction.

The monster roared and shuddered as it reared up, clawing for Gotrek. He crouched on the monster's back, heaving at the hilt of one of the larger daggers. As Felix watched, Gotrek sank to his haunches and his muscles swelled like those of a dockworker preparing to heave a barrel over his shoulder.

The dagger tore loose from the creature's spine with a wet cracking noise. The monster's subsequent scream seemed to hold as much triumph as it did torment. It thrashed and

Gotrek stood up on its back, still holding the blade, and grabbed his axe. It shrieked and grabbed him, plucking him free and smashing him against the ground. Felix leapt over its lashing tail and hacked at its legs, forcing it to turn and spin away from the Slayer. Its long arms tore into the onlookers, gutting Chaos marauders and flinging an armoured Chaos warrior into the air. Felix ducked beneath another sweeping blow, leading the creature to vent its fury on the crowd, which began to pull back at last, the awesomeness of the spectacle giving way to the very real danger of becoming an unwilling part of the proceedings.

The tree-trunk-like tail snapped out, carving a red arc through a close-packed group of Chaos marauders, pulping their bodies and the altars and war-shrines behind them. Spears and swords bounced off its hide as it bellowed and tore at the sea of enemies that surrounded it. Overhead, the dark clouds were retreating from a glow on the horizon.

Then, as if the capricious gods had decided to add to the confusion, a sorcerous inferno suddenly sprang to life, sweeping over the ranks of Chaos marauders. 'Down, manling,' Gotrek growled, grabbing his cloak and jerking him back as the flames, all colours and none, washed across the warriors nearest Felix. The men screamed as their bodies were wracked by sickening and uncontrollable mutations. Felix scrambled back, his gut churning as the flames faded, leaving ruin in their wake. 'What was that?'

'Whatever it is, we'll sort it out later,' Gotrek rumbled through bloody lips. His face was swollen and bruised, and blood dripped from dozens of wounds on his frame, but his savage vitality was undimmed. Like his monstrous opponent, agony only seemed to spur him on. He lifted his axe and gestured towards the captive dwarfs, who were doing their best to take advantage of the chaos around them. Between the beast's rampage and the strange, terrible fire, the Chaos army was in upheaval. As Felix watched, Ungrim snagged a Chaos warrior's throat with his chains and dragged the man down. The King of Karak Kadrin planted his knee in the Chaos warrior's back and hauled on the chains, snapping his captive's spine with an audible crack.

The other dwarfs followed suit, lashing out with their chains, to trip, strangle or batter their enemies. Given the situation, Felix couldn't blame the enemy for simply giving the captives a wide berth, rather than striking them down out of hand. Even as he thought it, however, a few moved to do just that. A Chaos marauder lunged out of the pressing, heaving, confused crush of the horde as if to stop the dwarfs and Gotrek cracked the man's skull like an egg.

Felix gutted another as Gotrek turned his attentions to the prisoners. His axe dropped, shattering a dwarf's chains. It was dawn, Felix realized. The sound of distant dwarf horns shook the pass. Garagrim must have recovered from Gotrek's headbutt. 'Gotrek, did you hear the horns?' Felix said. 'Garagrim is coming! We've done it!'

'Garagrim,' Ungrim said, confused. 'My son–'

'We've done nothing, manling,' Gotrek said, as he freed the other dwarfs. 'Not yet.' As the last chain broke, he turned towards Ungrim, but did not move to cut the king's chains. 'The War-Mourner does you proud, King of Karak Kadrin,' Gotrek said. 'Were I you, I would make your way towards him. Let him know what he marches into.' He gestured towards the path through the canyon that had brought him and Felix to the enemy. The stones echoed with the sounds of Garagrim's throng at the march. The dwarfs of Karak Kadrin were bringing the fight to the enemy once more, even as the War-Mourner had promised.

'And you, Gurnisson?' Ungrim said, still holding out his chains to be cut.

'Someone must see that you have time to reach him,' Gotrek said and looked at Ungrim. 'If this day be my doom, tell the queen I have fulfilled my oath yet again.'

'Not your doom alone, Gurnisson,' Ungrim growled, shaking his chains. 'Free me! We shall wade through them and take the Gorewolf's head, or meet our doom together!'

'Like we would have, at Karak Ungor, against old Bashrak?' Gotrek said.

Ungrim's eyes widened. 'Gurnisson–' he began.

'I made an oath,' Gotrek said, grinning.

'Let me loose! I command you – free me!' Ungrim roared.

'I made an oath,' Gotrek said again. 'Our grudge is not settled, Ungrim Ironfist. It will never be settled, not while there is still strength in my arm. Go, King of Karak Kadrin! Go, Ungrim! Let me find my doom unhindered!' He looked past the red-faced and cursing king to the other dwarfs. 'Take him to his son. You swore an oath to defend Karak Kadrin and its king, and you will take him from this place, even if you have to knock him over the head to do it!'

'Gurnisson, no,' Ungrim snarled. 'Let me have my doom! This is not right! This is not the way!'

'I have never done things the proper way,' Gotrek said. 'Take him!' He thrust the ends of Ungrim's chains into the chests of the other dwarfs. 'Take him and return and put the enemy to flight!'

The dwarfs looked as if they might argue, but Gotrek's glare put paid to any resistance. The set off quickly, dragging their frothing, struggling king behind them. Ungrim cursed virulently, hurling oaths at Gotrek as if they were stones. Gotrek remained unmoved, finally turning away. 'Now, where did that beast get to? And its master. My axe is thirsty,' he said.

20

The Worlds Edge Mountains,
the Peak Pass

Garmr planted his feet as the coruscating magics of the Changer washed over him. He held his axe up, blade outthrust against the multi-coloured flames. Khorne had protected him from worse, and did so now. Vasa was not so lucky.

The lion-headed champion howled as Grettir's mutating magics bowled him over and his brawny, bestial form became even more so. Armoured plates and snake scales and diseased feathers burst from his flesh as his shape became something other than humanoid. His screams degenerated into squalls of mindless pain as he was twisted from Chaos champion to gibbering Chaos spawn. Ekaterina, shielded from the flames by Vasa's bulk, took the opportunity to ram her blade into Garmr's back, even as Grettir's flame faded.

However, it wasn't her sword which caused him the pain that suddenly shot through him. Instead, he felt as if something vital had been torn from his spine and he sagged, the weight of his axe pulling him down as a howl of pain erupted from his throat. Ekaterina stepped back in surprise, and Garmr turned and rose in one berserk motion, his axe striking out with brutal speed. Ekaterina stared in shock at the weapon as it sank into her chest. She fell back, and Garmr ripped it loose, turning towards Grettir, who faced him with open hands.

'What has been done can be undone oh so easily, cousin; this road of yours, for instance, or the spells which bound Ulfrgandr to you. Does it hurt?' Grettir sneered.

Garmr, mind filled with red, uttered an inarticulate snarl and lunged. Grettir avoided the blow with malign ease. 'Would it be more palatable, if I told you that this was not, in the end, about you, or us? It is about the gods, cousin. It always has been. They move in opposition, like heavenly bodies caught in the cosmic tide, and this was never going to succeed. We are pawns, cousin. Even in our hatred, we are but the playthings of the Dark Gods.'

Garmr barely heard his cousin's taunts. In truth, he could hear nothing, see nothing, but the carnage that Ulfrgandr wreaked. It overwhelmed him, blinding him with the raw frenzy of a murder-lust too long bound by mystic chains. Now the Slaughter-Hound was venting its centuries of frustrations on his horde as it made its way towards him, eager to resume their former contest. He could feel it drawing nearer, killing its way towards him.

And in his own way, he welcomed it. He welcomed that battle, and hungered for it. As the calming effects of Grettir's binding faded and the Slaughter-Hound was unleashed once more, so too was Garmr; he was free. Free of plans, free of waiting and striving. Free at last to kill and burn and maim with nothing more asked of him. All thoughts of the road were washed aside and beneath his helm, he smiled.

'If we are playthings, cousin, then let us play,' Garmr rasped. He charged, ploughing through the magics that Grettir unleashed against him. Multi-hued flames caressed him, and shrieking winds plucked at him, and ethereal talons gouged him. Grettir's magics shattered war-altars and shrines, and flung marauders and nearby Chaos warriors into the air, broken and splay-limbed. But Garmr barely hesitated. Khorne had made him strong, and not even the Winds of Chaos could stagger him.

Grettir backed away, cursing. Garmr followed him doggedly. But before he could crush his cousin once and for all, a wave of bloodlust reverberated through him and a crawling shadow swept over him. He paused and then turned.

Ulfrgandr glared down at him, jaws sagging in what might have been an expression of joyousness. Its claws tore the ground as it rose to its full height. Images of torn bodies filled his head and the tang of blood blossomed on Garmr's tongue. It was everything he could have wished.

The Gorewolf roared and leapt to meet the Slaughter-Hound.

'Gotrek, Ungrim didn't look happy.' Felix shouted to be heard over the cacophony erupting in the pass. Garagrim's throng was drawing close and those Chaos forces that were closest to the approaching dwarfs were already streaming to the attack. Whatever ceremony or undertaking they had been preparing for in the centre of the pass was forgotten as the prospect of battle loomed. Screams and battle-cries filled the air. Those who weren't on the march were dead or, amazingly, fighting amongst themselves. Gotrek had been right: the Chaos army had come unglued.

Felix danced back to avoid two brawling Chaos champions, both clad in heavy armour, much battered. They struck out at one another with heavy blades as around them, their followers did the same. A dozen such minor skirmishes were taking place around them, as if the horde had been a pot too long on the fire that had at last boiled over.

Gotrek hacked his way through them regardless of who they seemed intent on fighting. If they got in his way, they died. Felix did his best to guard the Slayer's blind spot, but it was like following in the wake of a typhoon. Every time he stopped to fight off an attacker, Gotrek outpaced him, leaving screaming wreckage in his wake.

'He'll get loose soon enough and be back here, aye and Garagrim behind him. But not quickly enough to take what's rightfully mine,' Gotrek growled, shaking blood off his axe.

'For a moment, I thought you were doing it for the queen,' Felix said.

Gotrek glared at him. 'And what if I am?'

'Maybe there's some poetry in you yet, Gotrek,' Felix said.

'Keep your poetry, manling, all I want is that beast,' Gotrek said and picked up his pace.

'And if you die here, in the middle of this horde, what happens to me? Have you thought about that?' Felix snapped, hurrying after him.

'You'll be fine. If you haven't died yet, you aren't likely to do so,' Gotrek said without stopping.

'Your confidence is heart-warming,' Felix said.

Something with too many limbs and mouths suddenly rose up before them. A hairy tendril struck Felix and sent him sprawling. The Chaos spawn screeched and clawed at Gotrek, who barely slowed as he grabbed a jutting tusk, hauled himself up onto one undulating shoulder and brought his axe crashing down on the centre of its bloated skull. It fell heavily and Gotrek jerked his axe free with a disdainful grunt. 'Not the right monster,' he grunted. His eye widened in glee as he stepped off the creature's twitching carcass. 'There it is!'

Felix climbed to his feet and saw the monster. It had risen up over the Gorewolf and as he watched, it brought its fists down on the armoured shape of the warlord. The Gorewolf staggered and chopped at the creature. Felix looked at Gotrek. 'I think it's going to do our job for us,' he said.

'No beast is taking my doom from me,' Gotrek growled. After knocking the warlord down again, the monster reared back on its hind legs and drove its great fists into its chest, issuing a thunderous bellow of challenge. Before Felix could stop him, Gotrek's axe flashed out, catching it in one bulbous eye, and the orb burst in a rush of foul liquid. Half-blind, the monster turned as Gotrek charged towards it and it caught him up and slammed him down again and again, as if trying to reduce the Slayer to dust.

Felix raced forwards and leapt for the monster's back before he fully realized what he was doing. His skin burned as he grasped the hilts of the many blades sunk into the beast's back. What had worked once, might work again, or so he hoped. He found a likely looking hilt, covered in sharp edges and rust and worse substances than blood, and, choking down a wave of bile, grabbed it in both hands. Feet planted, he hauled on the blade with every ounce of strength he possessed.

He ripped it free with a sickening pop and tumbled to the ground in a heap. The monster stiffened and screamed, clawing at its back. Felix flung the blade aside with a cry. His gloves were torn through by the hilt's sharp edges and his palms were blistered and weeping from gripping it. He staggered to his feet, his hands clutched to his chest.

Even as it had before, the removal of one of the blades had

caused the monster intense pain and distracted it as it writhed and screamed. Gotrek, dazed, shook his head and shoved himself up out of the miniature crater his repeated impact had created. As the monster staggered above him, he looked up and his good eye gleamed. He lunged upwards and caught the handle of his axe where it jutted from the beast's skull, and ripped it loose in one gory gesture. The monster reeled back and Gotrek bounced to his feet and drove the blade upwards, into its belly.

It roared and clutched the Slayer with its hooked talons, tearing open his back as it pressed his face to the scales on its chest. Felix drew Karaghul, despite the pain in his hands, but even as he made to aid Gotrek, the monster spasmed and then toppled over, carrying Gotrek with it, remaining eye closed, jaws sagging as it slumped atop the Slayer, burying him beneath its bulk.

'Gotrek,' Felix shouted, rushing towards the monster. If he could hack an opening, free him–

An armoured fist shot out, catching him on the jaw. Felix tumbled to the ground, head ringing. The Gorewolf loomed over him, bloody axe in hand. The sheer malevolence that radiated from the warrior struck Felix like a blow. This was no man, no mere general, but was, in his own way, as much an engine of destruction as the monster Gotrek had just dispatched. This thing – not a man – could wade through an ocean of blood and not drown; it could level cities and not tire. 'The Doom-Seeker has gotten his wish,' the warlord growled. 'Will you join him?' he said, lifting his axe.

Felix could only stare upwards as his doom raced towards him. Then, at the last moment, the axe missed his head, embedding itself in the ground mere inches from his cheek. The Gorewolf staggered, clawing at his back where the spiked blade Felix had extracted from the monster's back had suddenly sprouted.

The robed figure, crystalline helm cracked and flickering, stepped back with an air of satisfaction. The Gorewolf sank to one knee and painful shudders wracked his frame. Felix could tell that whatever fell magics were contained in that blade were causing the warlord pain.

'What about you, cousin?' the latter said in a cracked and hissing voice. 'Will you join them in death? Do you recall that blade, cousin? It was the one I gave you, to plant in the Slaughter-Hound's back. The blade that bound its life to yours, and ensured that while it lived so too would you. Now I give you your life back. Have you no words of thanks?'

The Gorewolf ripped the blade from his back and wheeled about awkwardly. 'My thanks, cousin,' the Gorewolf snarled as he leapt forwards clumsily and drove the blade into his cousin's gut hard enough to lift the sorcerer from his feet. 'You have done all I asked,' the Gorewolf went on as the robed body fell backwards. 'I release you from your shackles.' The crystalline mask shattered as it fell, and Felix scooted back as several of the fragments slid towards him.

The Gorewolf turned back towards Felix and strode in his direction. Felix scrambled to his feet as the warlord jerked his axe free and raised it again. He could tell that the warlord was in pain. Though, in the end, he didn't think it would alter the outcome of any fight. 'Now it's your turn,' the warlord said. Felix swallowed and lifted Karaghul, wondering how he'd be remembered.

'Not quite.' At the words, both Felix and the Gorewolf turned.

Gotrek shoved his way out from under the monster's body, and snarled, 'Is that it?' The Slayer staggered away from the still-thrashing body of the monster, his broad frame streaked with cuts and bruises. Nonetheless his eye blazed with a single-minded intensity. 'Gorewolf – your beast is dead and I am not. If you can't do better, I'll be very disappointed.' He glanced at Felix. 'Stand back, manling. He's mine and mine alone. Not you, nor Ungrim, nor Garagrim, nor Grimnir himself will take this battle from me!'

'You,' the Gorewolf croaked, hefting his axe. The weapon was as formidable looking as Gotrek's own, though it dripped with brutal malice rather than grim ferocity.

'I heard you were waiting for me, Gorewolf,' Gotrek said nastily. 'You are my doom, I'm told.'

'And you are mine,' the Gorewolf rasped. 'The Blood God promised you to me, and here, at the last, despite everything, he has sent you to me.' He extended his axe and raised it. 'The others were weak... false. They do not understand. They sought to bar my path, to trick me. No matter who stands in my way, I will have my victory. Let the legions of Khorne himself bar my path and I will cut them down! Do you hear me?'

'I hear you,' Gotrek rumbled. 'If you're finished, my axe waits.'

The Gorewolf laughed. 'Then let it drink deep, Doom-Seeker!' Then he roared and charged. Gotrek came in with a roar of his own. They traded blows that sparked and snapped like sparks in a forge. The two weapons chewed into one another and sawed wide, the edges crashing against one another with tooth-shivering intensity. Again, time seemed to slow even as it had when they'd arrived, and Felix thought that the world was holding its breath. It was as if they were in an arena and the Dark Gods crouched high on the ridges above, looking down and waiting for the outcome of this conflict between two competing fates.

The two axes had become twin blurs. One weapon, forged by dwarf hands in a time of woe and filled with the stubborn ferocity of a dwindling elder race, met another, forged by daemons and hungry for the doom of all things. Every time the blades connected, the world seemed to shudder. Gotrek moved as if he weighed no more than a feather, as if he were fresh to the fight. He fought in silence, determined to meet his end, but not alone.

The Gorewolf fought silently as well, and with equal enthusiasm. Felix had never witnessed such terrible lust for combat before this moment. The axe spun in Gotrek's hands, spinning lightly between his fingers as he deflected a blow and countered with dizzying speed even as Garmr attacked again with a forceful chop, shaving bristles from Gotrek's beard.

Blood welled as the warlord's axe took the Slayer on the chest and then on the thigh. Gotrek staggered but didn't slow, ramming a shoulder into the Gorewolf's midriff and knocking him back. He brought his axe up and the Gorewolf's drove down and the two weapons met with a hateful screech. The two warriors strained against one another. Gotrek's muscles bulged and swelled with reserves of strength that Felix had not even suspected to exist. Nonetheless, the Gorewolf pressed his weapon inexorably down, less a man than a murderous device, intent on its function.

The rain pounded down and for a moment, Felix wanted to drop to his face, to grovel and hide from the malign weight of it all. Instead, he swept the red rain from his face and prayed that now was not the time that the Slayer's luck – ill or otherwise – chose to desert him. More than just Gotrek's honour rested on the outcome of this battle. Gotrek fought quietly, trading bone-rattling blows with the Gorewolf as the rain swept down and turned his flesh as red as his crest. All around them, thousands of skulls chattered and clattered in an infernal wind.

Then, abruptly, they stopped. The red rain slackened. The axes sheared apart with tooth-shivering speed. Gotrek's axe took his enemy in the chest, sinking deep into the baroque cuirass. The warlord's own snapped down and gashed the Slayer's shoulder, but Gotrek didn't break away. Instead he bit down on the pain and grabbed his opponent's helm and jerked his axe free, staggering the Gorewolf.

With a guttural cry, Gotrek hacked the warlord's hand off at the wrist, sending both hand and axe twirling away. Then he chopped into the giant's knee, dropping him down. Armoured fingers fastened tight about Gotrek's windpipe and the Slayer's face began to go purple as he shoved the warlord's head back, trying to snap the man's spine.

There was a sound like logs being split and then the fingers digging into Gotrek's throat released their hold and the warlord flopped back, dead. Gotrek stepped back awkwardly, rubbing his throat, staring at the corpse. The body twitched and thrashed, like a broken-backed snake, and he saw that there was still fire in the eyes within the helm.

'Gotrek, he's still alive,' Felix whispered.

'Not for long,' Gotrek rasped, lifting his axe. 'Join your beast, Gorewolf.' The axe fell with cruel finality and Garmr's head rolled free. Gotrek hefted it by the mane of hair attached to the helm and stared into the flickering eyes, holding the head's gaze as the fire in its eyes dimmed and at last went out. Gotrek hawked and spat into the snarling muzzle and then tossed the head aside.

The rain stopped. The last skull fell silent. Felix turned, letting out a breath. Then, with a sickening realization, he saw that they were surrounded. The Gorewolf's demise had not passed unnoticed. Though most of the vastly reduced and dis-organized Chaos force was already engaged with Garagrim's throng in what would likely be the former's last battle, some had remained behind – cagey champions and chieftains, wait-ing for their warlord to fall in order to swoop in and claim the spoils. Now, they urged their warriors on and Chaos maraud-ers surrounded the Slayer and Felix.

'Well,' Gotrek said, noticing them. 'Who's next?'

They approached slowly, confident in their ability to over-come their prey despite all evidence to the contrary. Given the sheer number of them, Felix thought that their confidence wasn't entirely misplaced. He glanced down and saw one of the fragments from the sorcerer's shattered helm. In it, a ghostly image of he and Gotrek, lying dead, swam to the sur-face and he felt a chill.

The first marauder lunged, driving a crude sword towards Gotrek's head. The Slayer grunted and his axe chopped through blade and the belly behind. 'Is that it? I kill your warlord and his pet and this is what you send me?' He looked up and shook his axe at the sky. 'Is that it?' he howled. There might have been laughter hidden in the distant rumble of thunder that answered, but Felix didn't want to think about it.

Felix blocked a spear thrust and opened the man's throat with Karaghul's tip. As the Chaos marauder fell, legs kicking, Felix looked around at the marauders that now surrounded them on all sides. Weapons pressed close to them as Gotrek and Felix came back-to-back, facing their enemies. The Slayer looked tired. The days of constant fighting had begun to sap even his inhuman constitution.

'I guess we're both meeting your doom here,' he said shakily.

'Aye,' Gotrek said, hefting his axe. 'It's time to finish this.'

'You don't sound happy about that,' Felix said.

'The moment has passed,' Gotrek spat. 'The Gorewolf or his beast... Those would have been dooms. But this... This is just death.'

'Seems fairly similar to me,' Felix muttered. Spears and swords ringed them on all sides. Preferences or not, they were likely to die here. He felt a moment of bitterness, but before he could vocalize it, a man screamed. Then another and another, as a great, foul shape rose with a choking scream from amidst the gathered marauders.

The monster lurched suddenly to its feet, burst eye weeping, jaws sagging, the cleft in its skull oozing. It gurgled and lunged and men went down in a red rush, broken and dying. A champion, too slow, tried to avoid a titanic backhand and was sent hurtling through a war-shrine, scattering brass sigils and bloody skulls.

The monster lunged, driving into the middle of the gathered marauders, scattering them with its bestial momentum. Men flew in all directions and bodies thudded to the stone as the beast drove north-east, its agonized roars trailing behind it. As it ran, it carved a path of carnage through the forces that remained in the pass.

'It's not dead,' Gotrek said wonderingly. A smile spread across his craggy face and he turned to look at Felix, beaming as happily as a child. 'It's not dead!' Gotrek shook his axe and called out, 'Come, manling! It's getting away!'

'It's heading north,' Felix said. Behind him, he could hear the sound of the throng of Karak Kadrin drawing closer. Felix did not look back, but he could hear the thunder of handguns and the war-dirges of the dwarf clansmen as they approached the now confused ranks of the Gorewolf's leaderless and unprepared horde. If he stayed, they would welcome him. There was safety there.

'So?' Gotrek roared back. 'I'll track it all the way to the Chaos Wastes if I have to! Now come on, it's getting away!'

'But… but–' Felix began, watching the Slayer stump swiftly north, in pursuit of the beast, heedless of the crippled Chaos army that reeled around him. Gotrek knew as well as he that the Gorewolf's horde was done, and the Slayer didn't concern himself with beaten foes. Ungrim and Garagrim would smash what was left and send them running north on the heels of the beast. Gotrek had bigger prey.

Felix looked down and saw more shards of the shattered sorcerer's helm. They were growing dull, the images they held fading at last. He saw death in them, and other things, moments of joy and renown; victories and happiness.

But always, Gotrek was there. For good or ill, he and the Slayer were bound together by bonds stronger than simply friendship or obligation. Something that might have been the laughter of dark, distant gods whispered at the back of his head.

'Come, manling!' Gotrek shouted, whooping happily. 'We go north!'

'Of course we do,' Felix said with a heavy sigh, as he followed the Slayer into the heart of the Chaos horde, in pursuit of an unkillable monster. 'Of course we do…'

ABOUT THE AUTHOR

Author of the novels *Knight of the Blazing Sun, Time of Legends: Neferata* and *Gotrek and Felix: Road of Skulls*, **Josh Reynolds** used to be a roadie for the Hong Kong Cavaliers, but now writes full time. His work has appeared in various anthologies, including *Age of Legend* and several issues of the electronic magazine *Hammer and Bolter*.

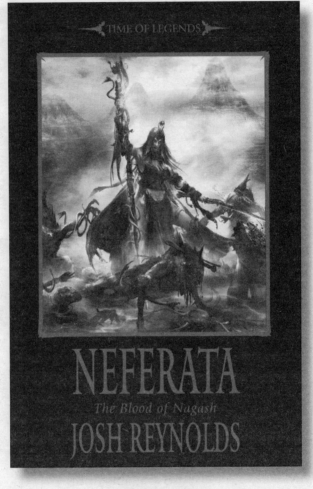